THE
WISPRIAN
WORLD

THE WISPRIAN WORLD

BOOK I
TEARS OF ALPHEGA

W.N. CLECKLER

WhisperedPress

CHEYENNE·LOS ANGELES·NEW YORK

Published in the United States
by Whispered Press
www.thewisprianworld.com

This is a work of fiction. Names, characters, businesses, places, events and incidents are either the products of the author's imagination or used in a fictitious manner. Any resemblance to actual persons, living or dead, or actual events is purely coincidental.

Printed in the United States of America

ISBN Paperback: 978-1-7325673-0-6
ISBN Special Edition: 978-1-7325673-1-3
ISBN Hardcover: 978-1-7325673-2-0
ISBN ebook: 978-1-7325673-3-7

Cover design by Jenna Elise
Interior Design by Ghislain Viau
Illustrations by Hector Nazario, Louis Eliopoulos, and Kate Moody.

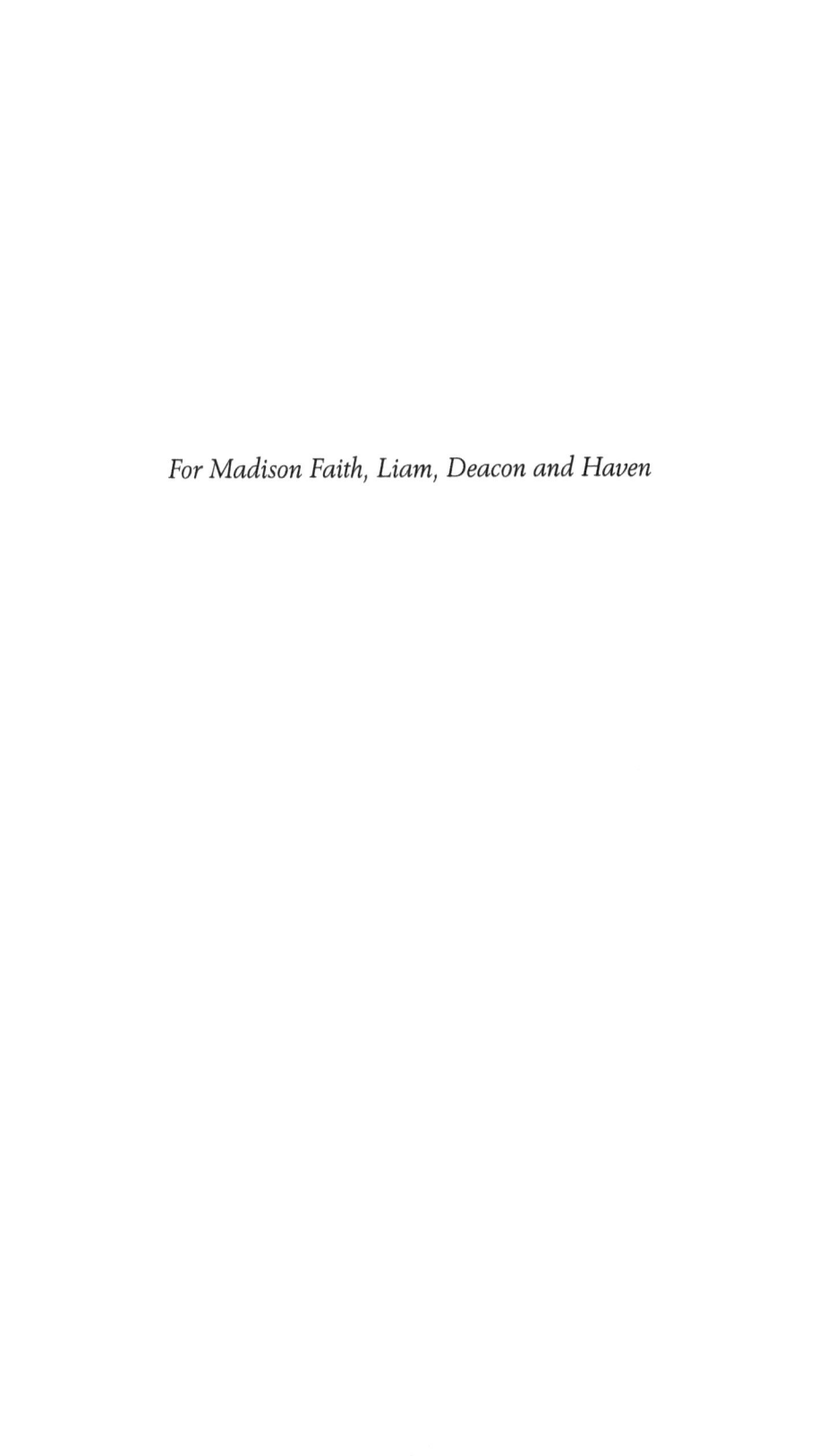

For Madison Faith, Liam, Deacon and Haven

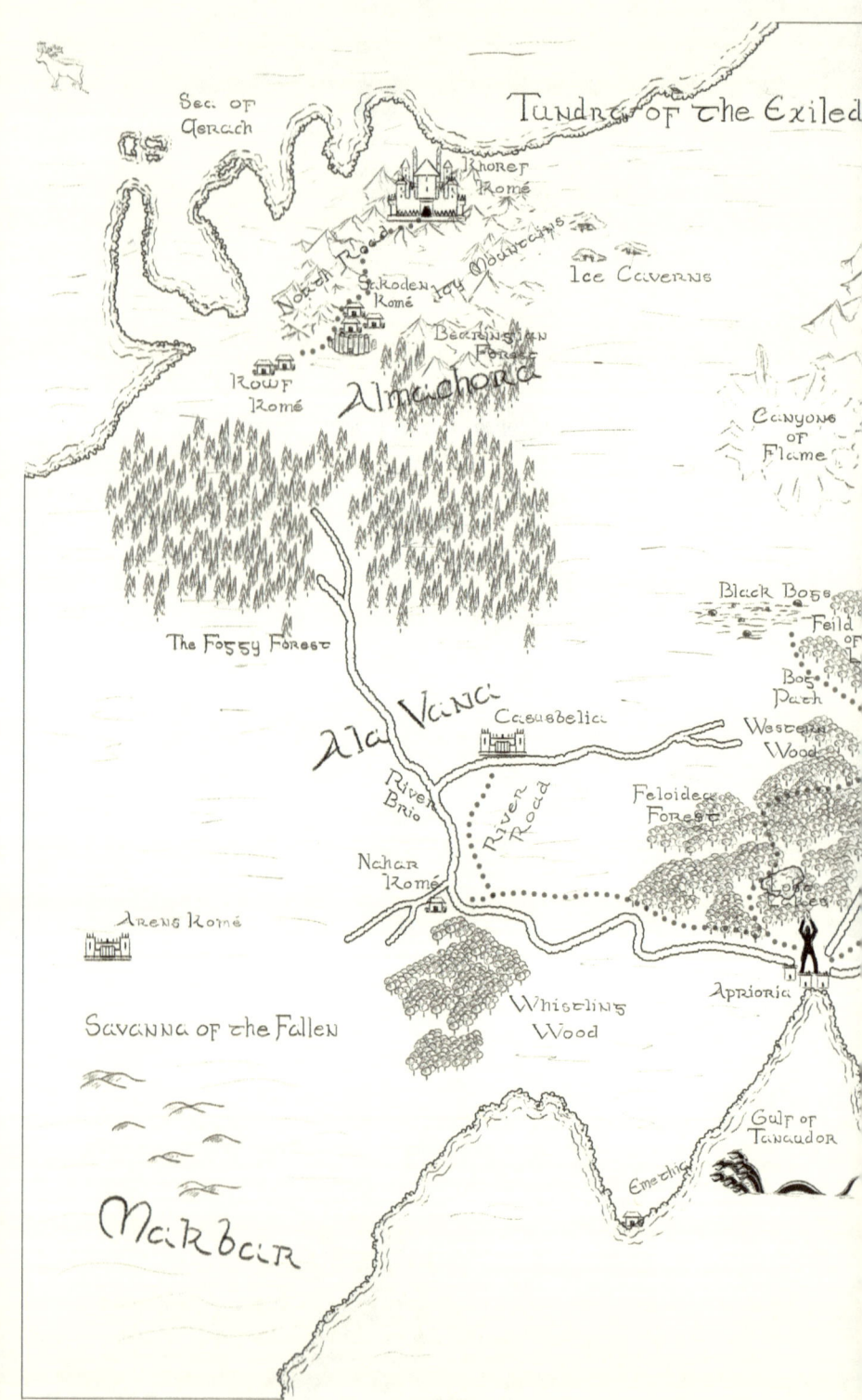

ARCHIVE OF SCROLLS

BEFORE

If this book of scrolls has made its way into your hands, beware, for the reader of these scrolls will gain insight and understanding. With knowledge comes pain. With wisdom comes sorrow. Preceding victory, there was defeat. The reader of this book must realize that secrets will be unlocked—secrets which have remained secrets for all recorded time, secrets from an erased past, a past which only exists in this collection of scrolls. These scrolls were pliable at one time, then they were turned to stone. After that, those same stones were frozen during the age of ice—the destruction of Wispria. All life was destroyed. Yet the cold, stone scrolls survived, and were found and compiled into a series of manuscripts by a most intriguing individual—the Maven. The Maven's story is for another day, for he was not an inhabitant of this old world. Be that as it may,

to the perceptive reader a cryptic message from the Maven may still be found in these very scrolls.

The beings and places mentioned here have been removed from the course of time. This book tells of before the Beginning and of before Adam. It tells of the old Earth, a world that was whispered—The Wisprian World.

The inhabitants of the Wisprian World included gigantic reptiles, drakons, fierce mammals, and races of human-like creatures. The Leviathan, Thanatoph, Sprinters, Sarxans, Reflections, and countless others were part of My creation then. Creatures that today, one can only imagine. Yet, in the following pages their tragic story will be told for the first time. The mysterious lands and perilous geography that these beings traversed has, to this point, remained an enigma. The ancient language these creatures spoke, Wisprian, is perhaps the only residue of their existence, echoed still in the souls of some of you today when you don't know what to say. Nevertheless, sadly, still lost, for these scrolls have been translated, and that language, forgotten at Babel, will remain a mystery.

In those days, I chose to prevent Myself from looking into the future. In My power, I shut My eyes. A world was crafted, a world above and a world below. In the world above, My most beautiful dreams and purest imaginations were realized. The Sun, Moon, and planets, as they have become known as in this age, did not exist then. Nor had I created the stars. The upper realm was so bright that it shed its light onto the lower world. Day and night in Wispria, as well as the changing of seasons, and the calendar as a whole, were not based on solar or lunar cycles. The light-source for the lower world was the upper world. However, there came a time, out of necessity, that the light from the upper world had to be hidden, leaving the lower world in constant darkness. Therefore, the term *day* will be used to refer to the time when most creatures are awake. The term *night* will refer to the time when most are at rest.

The upper world, Agapia, was made from pure agapate, a substance, which holds many untapped, mysterious powers. Earth, the world below, called Wispria, was made from a desire to have something else on which to shower My unconditional love. Millennia passed and, unfortunately, in time, I was not the only one who desired something more.

An Archeon, the most glorious, bright and pure one, Lure, became discontented with the upper realm, and embittered toward Me. To him alone I gave the privilege of traveling between the upper and lower realms. At first it brought Me joy to see how much he appreciated the lesser world. Sadly, this innocent fascination would not last. He gazed below at the world underneath the clouds and was filled with envy, lust, and hate. He hated Me for placing value on creatures that weren't nearly as brilliant as he was. With every glance and smile I gave at these imperfect ones, Lure's jealousy increased to the point of malevolence. It wasn't enough that I loved him, he wanted to be the only one I loved, he wanted all of My affection. Ironically, Lure despised the creatures below for their flaws, even while he set out to purposefully exploit and increase their faults in an effort to show Me how corrupt they could be. Whereas I loved My creation regardless, Lure saw the lower world as a prize and a threat; something he wanted and something to be destroyed. For, he thought that by conquering

the Wisprian World, he would have the power and resources to conquer the heavens and Agapia—and ultimately supplant Me. Unfortunately, there were other Archeon who, through sour words spoken in misguided encounters, galvanized Lure's perilous perspective.

Prideful, Lure tragically believed he could rise above his Creator. Lure was a persuasive, cunning, charismatic leader, and many of these other Archeon joined his cause. I saw, for nothing is beyond my sight, Lure as he made several preparatory trips to Wispria. I saw his harshness as he wavered not in laying his snares. Still, even as he arranged to carry out his plans, I hoped that he wouldn't. Until the last possible moment, I hoped he would stay with Me, abandon his dark ambition, and love Me as I loved him.

The most beautiful and dangerous thing that I ever created was free will, the ability to desire and in turn make decisions to acquire what one desires. Lure's will consumed him to the point that he no longer could see what was noble and true. On more than one occasion I tried to dissuade his malevolent intentions. Yet, his will was resolute and determined. Furthermore, he was immortal. The Archeon were given immortality, while all of the inhabitants on Wispria were mortal. Lure made an everlasting, irreversible choice. Together with his mutinous followers, he set in motion his plans to conquer Earth; becoming the first to disobey Me. Due to this, I was forced to banish him and his legions from Agapia and all of the heavens.

Thus, the Battle of Agapia began. The loyal Archeon drove Lure and the rebellious Archeon out of the heavens. They had driven them all the way to the Gate when, in an act of desperation, Lure destroyed the Gate to Agapia. This was the one window between the two worlds. Until that point, the light from Agapia was filtered through the thick agapate gate, making the light bearable to lesser creatures. Once destroyed, I was forced to cover the window with dark clouds in order to protect the Earth, for no earthen creature can withstand the full brilliance of Agapia's direct light. Lure also used this diversion to capture many of the Archeon that remained loyal to Me; taking them against their will when he fell. In addition, immediately upon falling to Earth, Lure and his minions imprisoned the loyal Archeon. Then, after taking on the shape of Reflections, for Lure and his followers, like all Archeon, could change their appearance to that of anything in creation, they began violating my creation, Reflection and beast alike, in order to create a new race loyal only to Lure. The Dephilim, a race of large, adulterated, deformed creatures, were the product of this profanation. The Dephilim were both swift and relentless in carrying out their leader's wishes.

The fate of the worlds that I had created, both Agapia and Wispria, would depend on creatures that, until that point, I viewed as unworthy to enter Agapia. Creatures that were unperfected, unproven, blemished. The nature of the inhabitants of the old Earth was rebellious; in many cases faithless. For every faithful act was followed by an unfaithful one. As a whole they were, at best, tepid. It is true that Adam was the first to bring death to mankind, for he was the first human. However, because of their prior transgression, the incomplete, human-like beings before Adam, those of the Wisprian World, had already experienced death for many millennia—without

the hope of Agapia. There was no eternal torment or eternal paradise. These creatures just ceased to be. Mankind was still a dream not yet realized; a dream that would not be brought into such evil times.

So for those born from the earth, I had not yet given a chance of life after death. This would prove to be a disadvantage. For, as I have said the rebel Archeon, or Archeskotos as they were now called, could not be killed—only contained. The Dephilim could be killed. Yet, as they were seeds of Archeon, their spirits would live, wandering the Wisprian World, looking for something to torment.

I could do nothing. For, in my power, I tied My own hands, so that I would not interfere when bidden to by My compassion. I had to find out if, when given freedom to make choices, the goodness of My creation would overcome the wickedness.

THE FIRST
OF THE TEARS

long the River Brio, there was a popular spot where Reflection women liked to spend the day washing clothes, daydreaming, or fishing; Reflection women, especially those of the river villages, loved to fish. This particular spot was along one of the river's flood banks where most of the time the waterline would come up into the grass and fish would swim among the blades of grass, making them easy to spot. The usual spirited flow of the River Brio was smoother and calmer in this particular section, as it wasn't rolling over many rocks, and wasn't moving downhill.

Melony Cantiq and Harmody Cantiq, twin sisters, came to this place nearly every day. The twins were sixteen and both

had long blonde hair with large curls and bright blue eyes. They were of an average size and build for Reflection. The only noticeable difference was Melony's face was slightly more round and Harmody had a small, light brown mole under the right side of her bottom lip. Though physically the girls were difficult to tell apart their personalities were very unique from one another. Melony loved pretty things and prided herself on being beautiful and maintaining that beauty. She would take her favorite blanket to the edge of the river and spread it out over the soft, bright green grass, so she could lie on her back and watch the clouds. Harmody, in contrast, craved adventure. She rarely wore dresses. In fact she usually borrowed one of her father's shirts and, though it was too large for her, wore it with her favorite dark brown fishing trousers that came down to just below her knees.

This day started out no different from the previous ones. The twins finished their chores and headed out from their town of Nahar Kome', through the Whistling Wood, down to the river in the late afternoon, when most of the other Reflections had already left for the day. Both girls carried with them, over their shoulders, skins for collecting water. Harmody also brought with her a fishing spear, one of the many she had hand-carved from the long reeds that grew along parts of the river bank. The reeds were called lilweed, but not because they were small.

Newly sprouted lilweed was thin, pliable, and bent in the wind. Once full grown the stalks could reach twenty feet in height and three inches in diameter. Mature lilweed also contained a hidden hazard. After the outer hard layer of skin was removed, or in Harmody's case, whittled away from the stalk, a paralyzing ooze would secrete from the inner stalk, making them impossible to eat, but great for paralyzing fish or any other hunted animal. Lilweed was used in weaponry as well. On larger targets, such as Reflections, the paralyzing effect was only temporary and only affected the portion of the body struck by the weapon, once it broke the skin. This paralyzing ooze would permeate the reed, lasting for many months, and one reed could paralyze many fish over time.

Upon reaching the river, Harmody's excitement grew as she saw the shallow water at the bottom of the hill, close to the bank, bubbling with fish near the surface. She launched her spear at a bubble from several meters away, before she was in the water. She then pulled her spear from the water to reveal a rainbow shimmering fish the size of her hand. Melony laughed, amazed at her sister's skill and tickled at how different they were. The sisters loved each other deeply. They realized and appreciated the blood-bond they shared, taking not for granted the fact that they shared more in common with each other than they did with any other Reflection.

As she prepared to spread out on her blanket, Melony was suddenly distracted by the burst of brilliant light in the sky. Harmody had not removed the fish from the end of her spear when she also saw the light.

"I've never seen anything like it," Melony said.

"It's so bright and beautiful," Harmody agreed.

Melony's eyes were fixed on the sky, specifically northward towards the beams of light.

"How can you look at it so long, the light is so bright it hurts my eyes," Harmody continued, her eyes shut.

"It does hurt to look at, but I can't explain it. I'm captivated by it. It is more beautiful than the prettiest dress I've ever seen—more beautiful than *anything* I've ever seen! What do you think it is?" said Melony.

With her hand on her forehead and through squinting eyes Harmody answered, "I'm not sure, but don't look at it for long, you may damage your eyes."

But, as Harmody was finishing her statement, as fast as the brightness came, it left. The sky was black. Thick grey clouds quickly rolled in where the light had been shining the brightest.

"What happened?" said Harmody.

"What do you mean?" replied Melony.

"I mean the blackness, what is happening?" Harmody said with concern.

"What blackness? It is only bright and glorious. The beams are so pretty", Melony said, oblivious to the fact that the light was no longer there. She was unaware of the change because the brightness of the light had blinded her.

Harmody grabbed Melony's face with both hands and looked into her open eyes. But Melony couldn't see her. Unbeknownst to Melony all she could see was the brilliant glimpse of Agapia, forever branded in her cornea.

Frantic, with concern for her twin, Harmody shouted, "Mel, look at me!"

Placing Melony's hands on her own face Harmody continued, "Can you feel my nose, my lips? I am in front of you, but you can't see me, can you?"

Beginning to realize the gravity of what Harmody was saying, Melony answered in a stricken tone, "No, I can't see you."

Just then several drops of a shiny, shimmering, substance fell from the sky like rain, but Harmody knew it wasn't rain, she had never seen such a substance before. The drops made several splashes in the river, then stopped falling.

"We need to go home now!" Harmody asserted.

Melony still in a state of shock answered, "I can't see, 'Mody, I can't see! How will I find my way home?"

"I know. I know you can't see. I'll guide you. Just let me fill our water skins for Mother, and I'll lead you. I won't leave your side."

Dipping her own skin into the river first, Harmody then put her fish in the skin with the water, as she commonly did, to keep the fish fresh. She then filled her sister's water skin as well. Afterwards, Harmody tossed the skins over her shoulder and grabbed her sister by the arm, as the last residual light from above faded into darkness. The wind and rain began to fall steadily as they started their trek.

Harmody ran through the stormy darkness in the direction of her home. For the time being, it seemed she was as blind as her twin given the totality of the darkness. The blackness was tantamount to blindness. The stumbling twins grasped at one another for reassurance that they were not alone; Melony because she realized she was blind, and Harmody because she was terrified at what she could see, nothing. The girls crawled with panic up the hill they had come down to reach the river.

Melony's fear was heightened by Harmody's fear. Harmody was usually daring. If she was scared, then Melony knew something significant was happening. The girls reached the top of the hill and started down towards the more challenging section of their journey, the Whistling Wood.

The Whistling Wood was aptly named for the phantom chirps and howls that one would hear. Yet no one ever saw from whence they came. Melony remembered that, as children, Harmody would talk her into playing games that involved chasing the sounds to find out what made them. And, in her current state, as much as the games of the past made her uncomfortable, she would gladly play them again instead of tripping blindly through the brush. The path from the girl's village to the river only went through a small portion of the wood, however, this portion of the wood was more expansive than the part in which they usually wandered. Currently the girls were in danger of groping their way into the heart of the wood. Briars cut their hands and faces. Their knees banged against unforeseen rocks and branches scattered on the ground. Several minutes passed, which to the girls felt like hours. Eventually Harmody accepted reality—they were lost.

The whistles the girls heard were accompanied by thumps and crunching that was becoming louder and more frequent. Harmody rested her back against a tree and held her sister tight in her arms.

"Harmody where are we, I still can't see anything," Melony whispered.

"We're still in the wood."

"I know, but why aren't we home yet?" asked Melony.

"I haven't found the way," replied Harmody.

"Why can't you find it? You know the way."

"I can't see. It's so dark," said Harmody.

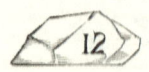

"'Mody, I'm scared," Melony said, a little louder.

"I am too, but we'll get back, don't worry, I just want to wait and see if the light returns. Try to rest," Harmody answered, squeezing her sister even tighter.

The twins sat huddled against the tree for many hours. They were weary, hungry and thirsty, but they couldn't rest with the cracks and thumping happening in the trees around them. With every sound they heard they thought for certain their doom was approaching. Insects crawled over them and buzzed around their ears. The twins were miserable and had no sense of how long they had been lost.

"Harmody, I'm so thirsty. Where are the water skins?" Melony asked.

"Here they are, but don't drink a lot, because I don't know how long it will be before we get home," Harmody said, handing the skins to Melony.

The girls were unaware that the silvery drops from the sky were agapate and that the agapate had mixed with the water.

Melony took a blind sip from the skin containing the fish. She was so thirsty that she drank many sips before tasting the fish and spitting her last sip out.

"You put your fish in your water skin again didn't you?" Melony accused.

"Oh, yes I did. I'm sorry. Hand it to me and I'll keep it separate from the other skin."

Melony handed the skin containing the fish to Harmody. Reminded of her own thirst, Harmody then took a drink from the fish-less skin, and as she let out a sigh of satisfaction, her attention was drawn to Melony. Her twin was grasping for her.

Melony's mouth was opening as if to scream, but no sound was coming out. Harmody could see that she was breathing heavily, her chest was rising up and down rapidly, but no sound came from her mouth. Melony then clenched her teeth together and squinted her blind eyes in pain. Harmody could feel her twin's grip tightening and she felt Melony's finger nails sink into her forearms. Harmody also felt a sudden soreness in her throat, but she was too preoccupied with caring for Melony to give it much thought.

"Melony, what's wrong? What can I do? Talk to me! Let me—," said Harmody, but as she was finishing the last word of her sentence, something extraordinary happened. She said, "help", but it sounded like, "*heeeeeeelp*". The sound that came forth had pitch and a vibrating quality about it. The dissolved agapate she drank caused the one speaking chord that she had in her throat to split in two, a phenomenon that would eventually be called vocal chords. However, neither Reflections, nor any other creature of those days had two chords. Not only did she have two chords, but the sound, today it is called singing, she produced with her agapate-coated chords was as holy and pure as the agapate itself. Until then, only the Archeon and those from Agapia had ever sung before. And though singing is still a very powerful force in modern times, no singing in the history of time could match what Harmody was now capable of, though little did she know or understand it. When she was moved, whether by love or hate, joy or sorrow, the sound she made could captivate, literally paralyze, like the lilweed spear, those with evil intentions. If the hearer's intentions were not malevolent, they would be unharmed by the Agapian sound, but to those who meant the girls harm, the sound would make them as still as stone. However, the sound was so powerful, as she would come to find out, that whenever she unleashed her voice, the force was so supernatural, she would be left speechless for some time after, every time she used it.

Melony also drank the agapate-adulterated water, but her change was much more involved. Harmody held on to her sister and, while she was still trying to understand the sound she just made, Melony produced a similar one.

"*Harmodyyyy* it *huuuurrts*," Melony sang out in pain.

She could feel a burning sensation under her skin on her neck, forearms and chest. The fiery feeling continued down the tops of her thighs and to small patches of her feet. Her body began to bleed in all of these places. Not profusely, but a light covering, like a layer of sweat, was over her body. Finally, a knifing pain burst from behind her ears down the back of her jaw-line, under her hair on the upper portion of her neck. Melony placed her hands on the spots on either side of her face and she noticed that it seemed her skin was detached. She ran her hand down her arms and chest and it felt smooth to the touch going one direction, but if she ran her hand on the same part of her body the opposite direction, it was rough.

The agapate water Melony drank was mingled with the fish, and her body took on some of the qualities of the fish in sporadic locations. She had patches of scales on her arms, chest, thighs and feet and inconspicuous flaps on her neck that served as gills. In between her fingers and toes there was a new found subtle webbing. In addition, her speaking chord also split in two which gave her the ability to sing like her sister.

Melony sat shaking in the wet soil, her body still in pain from the transformation. During the life-altering ordeal, Melony had broken away from her sister and writhed in a mixture of dead leaves, twigs, moss and mud that covered the ground. The blind, bloody, dirty, scaly girl was in shock. Her sister was also quite rattled, but was focused on making sure that Melony was going to survive.

Lightning moved in where the clouds were and though the thunder heightened their stress, Harmody was grateful for any amount of light. And the occasional flashes in the sky at least allowed her to see, though erratically, what was around them.

Harmody helped her sister up from the ground. She could not yet see how extensive Melony's change was. Harmody was taken aback by the scaly arms of her sister when she touched them, but she kept her thoughts to herself, not wishing to upset her twin more than she already was. Harmody did not at all recognize where they were. But she led her silent sister by the shoulders through the wood. They would walk when the lightning flashed and stand still in the darkness.

Harmody craved excitement and challenges, but her present state was unnerving. She had long passed the point of fear. She had grown used to the feeling to the point that she was no longer scared. Her fear had turned to a temporary, hallucinogenic, near borderline dementia—it was all she could do to trudge step by step through the dense forest. She daren't hope they would find the way out. After all that had transpired, she only hoped she could achieve numbness and escape the present reality that was all too real to her.

It was because of her mental state that Harmody wasn't sure if she was seeing a mirage when the two flickering lights appeared off in the distance to her right. Two orange lights were moving parallel maintaining a constant distance from each other through the bushes and trees.

"'Mel, quickly, I may see help up ahead," Harmody said, pulling her sister along.

The two tore through the wood with desperate abandon, making noise as they cracked branches under their feet and snapped small limbs that blocked their way.

"Hello, can you help us please!" Harmody shouted, as loud as she could with a voice still hoarse from her singing.

The lights were still moving away from the girls but Harmody kept shouting, "Wait, don't leave, help!"

This time the orange lights stopped and shortly after were coming toward them. As they came closer, Harmody could see they were torches and two figures were carrying them.

"Harmody, Melony, is that you?" the figures called out simultaneously.

"Mother, Father, help us!" Harmody shouted with hysteria that had been waiting for a chance to come forth.

Dal Cantiq and his wife, Hebel, were hustling through the bushes to reach their daughters. When they finally did, Harmody fell into her father's arms sobbing incessantly. Her uncontrollable weeping caught her parent's off guard. The parents were indeed worried, but, like Melony, to see Harmody in such a state, told them the girls had been through something perilous.

"Oh, Alphega, thank You, thank You, You've brought our daughters to us!" Dal said.

Hebel followed with, "Oh my little darlings, let your mother hold you. Come, let us get you home and take care of you. Your father and I were terribly worried."

Hebel put her arms around Melony, who was silently standing still. Holding the torch where she could see, Hebel began to speak but stopped. The torchlight and shadows accentuated the gruesome change Melony had undergone. Instead of speaking she began to scream out of control. She would scream and take a deep breath and scream some more. All the while, Melony stared ahead.

Dal grabbed his wife, "Sweetheart, calm down, get a hold of yourself. We need to get the children home."

"That is not my child," Hebel said. "What happened to my beautiful Melony?"

"Mother I cannot begin to tell you now, just take us home," said Harmody.

With one hand, the girl's father held out the torch that was struggling to stay lit in the rain, and with the other reached into the quiver hanging across his back and pulled out a spear while gathering his daughters to him. With a protective look, he let his wife know to stop questioning the girls. He himself was upset by their condition, but knew he had to suppress his concern for the girls' sakes. In the wind and the rain, and with many of the eyes in Whistling Wood watching them, the family started back toward Nahar Kome´.

Melony was silent the entire trip and slipped and fell in the mud countless times, much to her mother's dismay. Before long the family, all except Melony, could see the glow of the fire in the fireplace through the window of their home. Their cottage was the furthest on the edge of town and was the first coming out of the wood.

The two-room cottage was made of large, smooth, round, stones. It was a humble residence, yet, compared with much of the other cultures of that time, quite nice. One large window was in the front of the cottage and another smaller window was on the side of the house and looked into the parent's bedroom. The doorway was square and had a thick, wooden door. A table with benches on either side was in the middle of the larger, front room and was the first thing a visitor to the cottage would see. Directly behind the table was the fireplace, which sat about knee high above the floor. A large black cauldron-looking pot was directly to the left of the fire. Also in this room were two flat wooden surfaces that served as beds to the left of the table, these were for Melony and Harmody. Across the stone floor to the right of the table was the door that led to the parent's room.

The parents brought the girls inside and had them sit beside the fire. Dal warmed some water over the fire then, dipping a clean rag in the water, began to wash Melony. Blood and mud were wiping off in clumps. However, once she began to come clean, Dal was surprised at the beauty of his daughter. True, her look was quite eccentric, but the rainbow scales only enhanced the beauty already present.

"As beautiful as ever, sweetheart," he said sincerely as he finished washing her.

Melony didn't give a response.

Hebel brought the girls dry clothes from the shelves beside their beds. While the girls changed clothes entirely, Dal went back into the second room. He shifted the bed from where it was in the room and got down on his knees. He then, with his fingers, began slowly lifting some of the stones from the floor underneath his bed. After a few minutes he had uncovered a piece of wood that covered a tiny pit under the floor. Originally when he built the house, Dal made this secret den to hide his girls in the event that raiders ever attacked the village, as had happened at several other towns up and down the River Brio. He was thankful that he never had to use it, but now he uncovered it, unsure of what to expect now that the world was dark. Unfortunately, the hole was made when the twins were much younger and now it would only accommodate one of them. Harmody, he thought, could at least somewhat defend herself, but Melony, especially in her current state, would need the protection.

After uncovering the hiding place, he returned to the front room to be with his girls. An awkward hush was present as Melony still wasn't speaking, Harmody didn't know what to say, and their mother was silently becoming angrier at what had happened. Sitting next to her sister, Harmody put her arm around Melony and held her, as she had done for the past few hours.

"Are you ready to tell me what happened?" the mother asked.

"There is so much, need I explain it all right now?" Harmody answered.

"Yes, I think you should, I want to know how one of my daughters became blind and covered in those, those nasty scales," her mother pressed.

The father made an uncomfortable clearing of his throat, unsure which side to take.

"One minute she was looking at the light and the next she was blind. I don't know how she got the scales; all she did was drink from the water skin with the fish, but I've accidentally done that before, and that never happened to me," said Harmody.

Her mother replied, "No, of course it didn't, because if it did, you wouldn't care, you'd probably get great joy out of looking like one of those squirmy fish! But instead it is my beautiful Mel, my pride. Why her? You deserve it. Not Melony, you're the one running around in clothes too big for you, disheveled, dirty—"

"Hebel! You don't mean that, what happened is not Harmody's fault. Do not blame her. Harmody, your mother is just upset," Dal said sitting beside the girl.

But in her mind Harmody knew her mother blamed her. She made it clear in subtle but meaningful ways that Melony was her favorite daughter. Harmody didn't feel unloved, but less loved. Yet, in many ways Harmody was glad. Many times the way her mother chose to show her love to Melony was by putting her down, telling her she needed to be prettier, better mannered, or other shallow criticisms aimed at making the girl all that her mother wanted her to be. Most of the time Melony took the berating mildly, but ever so often, it would become too much for the girl and she would break down sobbing, in private, to Harmody. Dal also noticed the blatant favoritism, and though he loved both girls equally, he went out of his way to make Harmody feel special, with fishing trips, hikes, and other small adventures. In addition, this favoritism toward one daughter, and ill-treatment of the other from Hebel, was one of the primary factors in strengthening the bond between the sisters. Both sisters could see how wrong such behavior was from a parent, and both sisters felt compassion for each other because of it. For some sisters, there is a rivalry, a competition for affection, not so with Mel and 'Mody. The girls loved each other with a rare purity.

Dal saw the pain that Hebel inflicted on both girls, but most of the time he felt powerless to intervene. The most dangerous kind of woman is the emasculating kind, and that is what Hebel was. For years she had ordered Dal about, telling him to clean, hunt, or pay her more attention. In the beginning Dal resisted, fought back. He had been a fierce warrior and hunter in his younger days and refused to be mastered by a woman. But whenever Dal did hold his ground, Hebel would throw a temper tantrum or weep and wail accusing him of not loving her. She was a guiltsmith. So eventually Dal learned to live with her, but he still harbored a manly, fighting passion that was waiting for a chance to show itself again.

That chance would come sooner than Dal was ready for. But for now, he and the rest of the family were tired.

"Why don't we try to get some sleep, we can talk about everything after we have rested," Dal suggested.

Continuing, Dal said, "Mother, why don't you let the girls sleep with you while I stay here and keep watch in the event any other unusual things happen."

Hebel started to protest, wishing to discuss the strange events, but a stern look from Dal let her know the idea wasn't up for discussion.

"Come along girls," Hebel said, "I don't know which is worse, sleeping beside my odd-looking daughter or sleeping beside my daughter that let her get that way."

"Hebel!" Dal said impatiently, as he helped the girls to the other room.

Shortly afterwards, the girls and their mother lay in the bed while Dal sat by the brightly blazing fire—though none could sleep. Cries and screams in the darkness that seemed to be coming from the nearby cottages through the woods, in various parts of Nahar Kome´, made all of them uneasy— especially Melony, who could only hear them.

The distant sounds of anguish were suddenly interrupted by a frantic rapping on the door. Dal sprang to his feet. He was instantly conflicted, countless thoughts flooded his mind all at once. Was the knock someone in need or was the knock an attempt to enter for some malicious purpose? Dal couldn't be sure.

Bosheth Barnsrot burst through the door before Dal had a chance to make up his mind. A heavy set, unattractive woman, Bosheth had many times taken care of the girls when they were younger, much to the girls' dislike. Although Dal could never figure out precisely what it was about Bosheth the girls didn't like, she seemed nice enough. Living alone, not far from the Cantiq's, Bosheth seemed to love children. In the distant past, Dal thought it mutually beneficial to occasionally let her watch after the girls, it gave him time with Hebel, back when he enjoyed time with her, and it gave Bosheth a chance to be around children. Now that the girls were older, it had been years since they had really spent much time around Bosheth. Still, whenever her name was mentioned, neither girl smiled and both would try to change the subject.

"Please, Dal, you must help, there are wild beasts running amuck throughout the village! I swear there was something outside my cottage. Hearing it near the front door, I jumped out of my bedroom window and ran here as quickly as I could," Bosheth said, out of breath.

Dal was about to respond when Harmody came into the room wide awake.

"If you are going, father, then I'm coming too," Harmody said.

After a few minutes of father to daughter arguing about the safety of such endeavors, Dal and Harmody left to go investigate the disruption. Harmody made sure to grab her quiver of lilweed spears before leaving. Dal slung his quiver across his back and also took with him a torch. Hebel stayed behind to look after Melony, though the term "look" wasn't necessarily accurate, for she would barely glance at her daughter. The shaken up Bosheth sat by the fire to await what Dal and Harmody discovered.

Several moments passed and in that time Hebel reluctantly answered questions about Melony's condition the best that she could. Had Hebel been paying attention to Bosheth, she might have been disturbed to see that Melony's former, sometime-caretaker was almost pleased to learn of the girl's blindness and inability to speak. A demented hunger shone in Bosheth's eyes, replacing the look of panic she had when she burst into the cottage.

Bosheth remembered how long it had been since she had been alone with Melony. And without thinking, but giving herself over to the lust that was seizing her, the fat, dirty woman looked around the cottage. The closest thing to her was the large cauldron by the fire. Lacking any sense of guilt, Bosheth bent down and with both hands lifted the pot over her head and brought it down violently on Hebel's head, splitting her skull. Hebel dropped to the floor with a thud and never moved again.

Although Melony had been in a state of shock since her transformation, she was not completely oblivious to the world around her. She couldn't see her mother's murder, but she heard the cracking sound followed by a thud, and the sounds made her quite uneasy. Still, silent she remained.

Assuming Melony was both blind and dumb, Bosheth moved over to her. She ran her hands through Melony's hair like she used to. She stroked her now scaled arms like she used to.

Continuing to run her hands over Melony's body, Bosheth said with a voice like quicksand, "Remember this? Remember how I used to love you? I guess you don't now, you dumb old thing. But we had some good times you and me."

A feeling welled up inside of Melony that she recognized from her childhood. Back then she had been too bewildered and afraid to scream, but in her present state she had no inhibitions; though she still couldn't make a noise at first. She was so overwhelmed that nothing came out the first couple of tries—it was hard for her to breathe, much less make a sound. Then finally a sound came forth; yet scream she did not. The sound she made came from deep inside her, it was a song. She sang, but not words. Vowel sounds seemed to be the only sounds Melony could find to express how she felt. With a shiver of fear and despondency, Melony sang out, her new voice trembling. The sound was only beautiful in how powerful it was, for it was not a delicate sound.

Bosheth became like a statue of flesh, unable to move. Her hand stiffened on Melony's chest. Her heart quit beating. Melony quickly jerked away from her, anticipating a struggle that never came. Little did she know what she had done. The little cottage was quiet and still. Melony sunk to her knees and crawled on the cold floor to where her mother lay. Placing her hand in a pool of blood, Melony followed it all the way to her murdered mother's face. She then cried silently and dryly, her crimson hands dripping in her lap. As if Melony wasn't reeling enough from the recent events, she was now all the more disturbed.

I wept. I wept for the abuse of My creation. I allowed one of My tears, with a trace of one of My qualities, to fall to the Earth. The tear landed on one of Melony's blood soaked hands, creating a wet circle on her palm where it eradicated the red away. She mistook the tear for one of her own, though none flowed from her burnt eyes. Still, for a moment, Melony was at peace. Yet little did she know the power she now possessed.

"She rarely wore dresses."

SAGE

Oppressing darkness covered the land. Rain, once a welcome visitor, had now settled down to stay. It wasn't from lack of rain that the vegetation in the forests and plains struggled to exist, but from lack of light. The rain had been falling and the lightning flashing incessantly since the very time the great light from above vanished. Earth, the Wisprian World, still rotated, as it had done since it was whispered into existence, and it still revolved beneath the source of the now hidden light of Agapia. This had allowed for seasons of sowing and reaping of the earth. Yet, now that the light was gone, a premature winter season would set in and soon grip all of Wispria. The temperature was steadily dropping; especially in the higher elevations of the mountains.

At the foot of one of those mountains, specifically the Moaning Mountains in the land of Eremos, Sage Swiftsoul

tightened the straps that kept his crude backsack in place. Looking down at his toe-less boots, he thought it best to tie them one more time, for he would not have a free hand to tie them once he was on the mountain. Sage was a Sprinter. And it was a common quality among the race of Sprinters to be mildly obsessive compulsive. Sage had already retied his boots three times. However, in his mind he had a valid reason.

Today was the first day of the harvest and every Sprinter knows that, on the first day of the harvest, all of the Sprinters come together to cheer on their clan's two climbers in the race. This was not just an ordinary race up the side of a mountain. It was a race to determine which tribe would be victorious that year. The winner of the race would have his name carved on the rock of champions, and for Sprinters, winning was the goal that outweighed all others. There were twelve tribes of Sprinters scattered throughout the valleys of the Moaning Mountains, and Sage's tribe had not won in seventeen years. Though, in past decades they had won more than any other.

Tribal banners waved for each of the twelve clans of Sprinters. Each banner contained the tribe's colorful and symbolic emblem of heritage. Some banners were made from skins of animals; tacked between two tree trunks. Smaller patches were sewn onto clothes by mothers and daughters. Sage had the emblem of his tribe, Kuma, sewn onto his backsack, as did many of the other racers. Kuma's emblem was a wooly mammoth and a wave. This was a symbol indicative of the myth passed down by Sprinters of how they came to be in the land of Eremos. Looking out into the crowd, Sage caught a glimpse of his tribe's banners glowing in the light of torches

kept out of the rain. He saw younger, littler Sprinters chanting, "Kuma, Kuma!" This thrilled him and gave him a palpable feeling of pride that stuck in his throat—he was bursting with excitement to let it out and race for his tribe.

The object of the race was not as simple as it may seem. First, the climber had to climb near the summit of the mountain. Once near the top, the Sprinter would find the only brightberry tree in the land. Some would argue that the next part of the race was also the most difficult part, selecting the right fruit. For those who may not know, brightberries were larger than a Sprinter's head and could weigh up to thirty pounds. In addition, the reason the race was on the first day of harvest was because none of the brightberries would have been picked yet, leaving a large selection from which to choose. Now brightberries were many different shades of opal and had varying degrees of flavor, depending on the size of the fruit. Once the berry was selected, the competitor then had to be the first to make it back down the mountain with the fruit intact. Part of the legacy of winning was picking the perfect brightberry for the Elixir of the Champion. Every year the race winner was rewarded by having his name used as the title for that year's vintage. So, not only did the competitors have to carry a thirty-pound fruit back down the mountain, but they had to find the best tasting berry, to be certain the elixir would taste better than that of the previous years, for Sprinters are competitive creatures.

This elixir, called pearl port, was the Sprinters' favorite brew, and the primary reason for their obsession with brightberries. The fermentation process of pearl port involved many different fruits and berries, but the overwhelming taste was that of brightberries. One thirty-pound fruit could make about four bottles of extremely potent and expensive elixir.

Racing with Sage was the Sprinter who taught him all that he knew about racing, his father, Odem Swiftsoul. Odem's name as a champion, Odem the Wild, appeared on the rock of champions many times. However, he was older now, one hundred and thirty-eight in fact, and hadn't won in quite some time. Odem knew, though, that Sage was just reaching his prime. Sprinters, Reflection and other humanoid races of the Wisprian World matured at a rate similar to that of humans, and Sage was twenty-two. Said another way, from birth to adulthood took roughly the same number of years as a human, but the length of years that these creatures of Wispria walked in their prime was many, many years longer than an inhabitant of the new Earth. An eighty-year-old Sprinter or Reflection could be just as physically capable as a twenty-year-old human of the new Earth. The reason for this was simple, there was no sun to promote the aging process, and instead of sunlight they had the eternal life-giving light of Agapia as a light source. Sage and his father had spent many memorable days climbing the mountains. From the time Sage could run, he and Odem had raced up the steep sides. Yet, Sage frequently pointed out that Odem hadn't actually beaten him in years.

The very fact that Sage raced and represented his clan was inspiring; that Odem was able to train him to get to the point where he was one of the best racers, was extraordinary. For Sage was a runt. Sprinters, like other humanoid mammals gave live birth. Unlike humans, though, they had litters. At

one time, a mother Sprinter on average would give birth to five little ones. Sage was one of seven and he was always the smallest, weakest one. But Sage had a good heart. Odem had already decided that when Sage won, he would surprise him and give him the title, Sage the Determined.

As a runt, Sage's earlier years were challenging. Physically he wasn't as big or strong as others, but his primary difficulty was socially. In a culture that was so physically active, Sage was looked down upon and harassed and intimidated by many of his peers because of his smaller size. As a young Sprinter, he was tricked into following some of his friends deep into the mountains, at which point they proceeded to sneak back to the village without him, leaving him to fend for himself in the darkness, and find his own way back to his family. Many other events transpired when he was younger that, when coupled with the inner fortitude Sage possessed, only served to strengthen him. This inner strength betrayed him at times, however. For when Sage was faced with external forces that came against him, he had a warriors grit, refined by years of having to defend himself. Yet internally, so many hurtful words and events had taken their toll, and when it came to these inner battles he had within himself, Sage's strength waned. He often took to blaming himself for events quite beyond his control and not at all his fault—the chief of these being the sudden disappearance of his mother, his greatest encourager, a few years back. Nevertheless, up to this point Sage had managed to overcome the dark thoughts, and press on, becoming one of the most accomplished Sprinters in the village.

Though Odem was up in years, he was still nimble, as many Sprinters were. The Sprinters physique was a slender, flexible, and coordinated one. They weren't very tall, but, then again, they weren't short. A Sprinter's face usually displayed a gentle, kind disposition. Their skin was not only pale, but also smooth. The only hair a Sprinter had was on the top of his head, plus eyelashes and eyebrows. Rarely would one find an obese Sprinter. Sprinters had metabolisms that were extremely high. This came from years of running and climbing. Their bodies were not weighted down with bulky muscle, (although what flesh they had on their bodies was all muscle). Of particular note, were their forearms and calves, which were disproportionately large from all of the grasping and jumping. Due to a healthy lifestyle, many Sprinters lived to be quite old before they died of natural causes. Of course, many had fallen to early deaths from the rocky ledges on which they spent so much time.

Another distinguishing physical feature of the Sprinters was their toes. Since they had spent generations climbing and running, the Sprinters developed toes that were nearly as long as a human's fingers. Sprinters used their toes when hanging onto the treacherous rock walls they encountered in many of their climbs.

Due to the newly oppressive darkness, this climb would be more treacherous than the climbs of the past. Odem still remembered the races when the mountains were bright and brilliant.

"The race was easier when I could see what was in front of me," Odem said, gazing up at the mountain.

Many days had passed since the light above was blotted out and, Sprinters, who were native to only the Moaning Mountains, were rather removed from the rest of the world. Seldom did an outsider make the journey to the villages of the Sprinters. It was even more uncommon for a Sprinter to explore the world beyond the Moaning Mountains. Entire wars were fought, kings were dethroned, marvelous discoveries were made, and all the while the Sprinters were oblivious to the outside world. They would have been unaware of the events transpiring now beyond Eremos, were it not for the darkness which affected even their secluded land.

"These days, the only thing I have to light my path is your pale skin," Odem teased Sage. Though, it was not uncommon for a Sprinter to have pale skin. In fact, nearly all Sprinters had pale skin.

"Well then, it is fortunate for you that I'm faster than you. Otherwise you would have nothing to light your way," Sage replied. "And besides, if I had done this race as many times as you have, I would have my path memorized by now," Sage joked, though he knew full well that the rocks of the Moaning Mountains were constantly shifting. This shifting of the rocks was to blame for many of the deaths that had occurred. A shift would occur without warning, sometimes displacing the rocks on an entire mountain face. Therefore, it was impossible to memorize a route. Plus, in recent days this particular mountain's moaning had intensified, though few Sprinters noticed.

"I will just never understand why Alphega took the light away," Odem questioned.

Oh, Odem, if you only knew. I did not take it away.

"Father, why must you cling to those fables? Stories passed down by our ancestors of an all-powerful being, Alphega, who created and has control over everything. There is no Alphega," Sage argued.

"Sage, He does exist. He must," replied Odem.

"I am not going to talk about this now," Sage said, agitated.

"Son, do you remember when we could look up the side of this mountain and see the green shades of the trees changing with the light and wind? I remember how your mother loved to gaze at the beauty of the mountains. The colors of the rocks would change depending on the angle you looked at them, and now, darkness. And the only light we have comes from the flashes in the sky that accompany the roar of the clouds. It is nearly impossible to…"

"Father, I know. We've been through this before. I do not have the answers. Right now we have to focus on this race, but yes, how mother did love the mountains," Sage interrupted.

"And we loved her. And she loved you," reminded Odem.

The clouds above the Sprinters were moving rapidly. These were angry storms that came in from the north. Odem's shoulder-length gray hair swirled about his smooth face as he looked at his focused son with pride and hope. The wind was blowing hard and the air was quite chilly, even for Sprinters, who normally love cold and did not easily take a chill. Sage loved the cold more than the average Sprinter. While many of the climbers were in their long-sleeved tunics and pants, Sage wore only his knee-length, frayed pants, toe-less boots, and leather backsack.

That moment Angust Sproutwell, an arrogant racer from a neighboring tribe, quickly walked past the Swiftsouls. Smirking at them, he said, "They want all of us climbers at the starting rock."

After nodding at Angust with gratitude, and brushing off the provocation with ease, Odem and Sage looked at each other with a glance of camaraderie and began walking toward the starting rock. On the way, they passed groups of Sprinters scurrying to find a spot to watch the event. Some claimed a spot of grass in the rain-soaked valley. Others who preferred to stay a little drier and, perhaps have a better view, slid up the trees and leapt from limb to limb until they found an adequate spot.

Sage and Odem were some of the last climbers to get to the rock. The judge, an elderly and stately Sprinter with a long pointy nose and the palest skin of any Sprinter there, stood on the rock of champions with his walking staff in one hand and starting horn in the other. Scaler, as he was called, because he had won more climbing races than any other Sprinter, gave Odem and Sage a stern look to let them know that they were late.

"Now that we have all gathered," Scaler said, "let me remind you of the rules of the race. You will all start from behind this rock and at the sound of this horn make your way to the tree near the top of the mountain. You may get to the top by any natural means necessary. This means no tools and you may not touch another competitor. Once you have a brightberry, one at least the size of your head, bring it back to me at this rock. The first one back will have his name used as the title of this year's batch of pearl port, and his tribe will receive one bottle of the Elixir of the Champion made today. Oh, yes, and there will be Sprinters on either side of the mountain all the way up, in position as I speak, to aid you if you are in trouble, and to make sure no one breaks the rules. If there are no questions, then take your positions behind the rock."

Sage jumped up in down in place to get himself ready for the competition. Other competitors stretched their lanky limbs. Odem seemed lost in the clouds above, his gaze fixed on them in a thoughtful expression. At the same time Scaler was practicing, over and over, softly, blowing the horn. For like other Sprinters, he was obsessive compulsive.

"Be fast but careful, son," Odem said to Sage.

"We are going to win this," Sage replied.

"You represent the Kuma clan well," Odem added.

"Climbers ready," Scaler shouted.

"Be fast but careful," Odem reiterated.

Sage squatted slightly to make sure that he got an explosive burst from his legs at the blow of the horn. Odem, standing behind his son, looked at Sage's back and a surge of pride flooded his body. Just then Scaler pressed the horn, made from a hollowed-out tooth of a fanged tiger, to his lips and blew out a high-pitched whistle. The race was under way.

Sage dashed out in front of the other competitors. One of his strengths and faults was that he was impassioned at the start of the race. The sides of the mountain became steep quickly, and although Sage could not see them behind him, many other racers were on all fours. This close to the bottom of the mountain large, jagged boulders scattered the path. Most of the Sprinters quickly, but carefully, used their hands and feet to move from boulder to boulder. Sage was not concerned as much with safety as he was with winning, though. He was still upright and leaping from one boulder to the next. Looking a good distance ahead of himself and planning his route while he ran, he hoped to get to a particular rock chute before the other Sprinters. You see, there were two primary routes to reach the top. Some Sprinters chose to take the longer, less steep way, which was safer, but slower. This took them up the jagged boulders to a plateau, which they would cross before climbing another steep wall of boulders. The problem was that crossing the plateau took them the opposite direction that they needed to go.

The chute Sage was looking for was at the top of the bolder section he was almost through now. Completely vertical, the chute required extremely adept climbing ability. Even then, it was only by chance that one did not slip on the way up, especially with the rain beginning to fall faster and when hurrying as much as Sage. At the top of the chute there was just a short boulder field before the tree. The reason Sage had to get to the chute first was because it was particularly narrow. Only one Sprinter could go up at a time.

Odem meanwhile, was leading the other Sprinters. They were at least forty yards behind Sage at this point, and Odem knew that he had to get to the chute before the rest of the Sprinters, if any were headed that direction. Otherwise, he would not be able to help Sage get the berry.

The walls of the chute were slick and cool. Rain fell into Sage's eyes as he looked up at the sides above him. All of a sudden the fatigue of bursting up the mountain so quickly hit him. He struggled for breath to fuel oxygen to his limbs while he pulled and pushed his way up the chute. On more than one occasion his boot slipped on one of the smooth, wet rock sides. Unfazed by the danger below him, Sage climbed farther. He arrived at an opening in the top of the chute where it widened. He could no longer wedge himself in between the two sides to keep from falling. Sage chose a side to scale. He could barely hang on, with not more than a centimeter of his toes on the rock wall, but he continued up the surface. Almost to the top, Sage came to a point when his arms and legs were spread as wide as they could reach in order to find enough rock on which to hold. His long toes curled outside of his boots in an effort to somehow hold on better. At that moment Sage regretted wearing his boots. They had protected his feet over the jagged boulders, but now they compromised his natural advantage. The rain was loosening up the dry gravel that wedged together many of the larger pieces of the rock wall. While looking for the next rock to grab, the rock Sage was holding onto with his left hand pulled out and tumbled below. Luckily Odem wasn't beneath the chute yet. Sage however, pressed his chin and face into the rock wall and somehow willed himself to stay in place. He now had both his left and right hands on the same rock and pushed himself against the rock wall with his toes. After he regained his balance, Sage reached back to the hole created when the rock pulled loose. He grabbed hold of the soil and stuck his fingers in as far as they could go, and then continued up the chute.

Once Sage reached the top of the chute, he let out a deep sigh. For a split second he realized how close he had come to

falling. He felt warmth in his stomach from the adrenaline. Still, his overwhelming desire to win caused him to continue running across the boulders. Looking up, Sage could see the tree about one hundred yards uphill from him. Seeing the tree caused Sage to run even faster; the excitement of winning taking hold of all of his fear and exhaustion. Just then, as Sage glanced up at the tree once again, with sweat and rain rolling down his cheeks, his foot slipped on one of the slick boulders. His right leg slid underneath his body and he landed on his right ankle with the side of his foot parallel to the ground.

An audible "crack" was heard and the pain shot through Sage's leg.

"Aarrgghh!" cried Sage with his eyes winced in pain.

He knew he had weak ankles because he had broken both of them before, but he never imagined that today, of all days, he would break one again. The rain was pouring harder now and Sage couldn't see far in front of him. Yet, he could see that the tree was near. Frustrated and sitting in the mixture of rock and mud, Sage reached for the nearest rock he could find, his eyes still closed with pain. Grabbing one that seemed heavy for its size, he lifted it high above his head and, with all his might, struck the boulder on which he had slipped. Sage wasn't prepared for what happened next.

When the stone in his hand made contact with the boulder, the entire mountain shook. Everywhere Sage looked, rocks were falling and rolling. A crack in the mountain went up from the boulder all the way to the brightberry tree. The crack split the ground underneath the tree and caused it to collapse on the ground in Sage's direction. Sage could hear screams from the other Sprinters below him on the mountain as they were dodging the falling rocks. He looked down at the rock in his hand and, to his amazement, the rock was glowing. The rock looked like all of the others around it, however, it was heavier than it should have been and it seemed as though a dim light was coming from inside it. Sage was so fascinated by the rock that he no longer felt the pain in his leg and he completely forgot about the race. Wanting to stand up, Sage lifted the rock in an effort to gain balance on his healthy foot, while using his other hand to help steady him. Before he knew it, he was up—but not standing. He was taller; but he didn't grow. He continued to get higher and higher until he was frightened and wished to stop going any higher. He looked below and realized he was still sitting, but the mountain had actually built up underneath him, and a tower of rock was taking him as high as he wanted to go. Sage was extremely frightened. He could hardly breathe once he realized what was happening.

Looking down below, for the tower of rock had taken him high enough to see everything below him, Sage's eyes were drawn to the chute. It was completely blocked off by some of the falling rocks. However, in one of the flashes of lightning, something else caught Sage's attention. From one of the spaces between the rocks Sage could see long gray hair swirling in the breeze. His heart sank at the thought that it may be his father.

Still clutching the rock in his hand, Sage tried to maneuver down the tower of rock, but as soon as he began to try to get down, the rocks shifted and the tower crumbled back to the original height of the mountain. Back on solid ground, Sage

ran down the side of the mountain toward the silver hair. He was unaware that his leg was broken; his pain was denied by his intense need to find out the truth about which Sprinter was under the rock.

Before he arrived at the chute, Sage cried, "No, Dad!" as his fear was confirmed.

Odem was crushed by the falling rock. Frantically, Sage tore at the rocks, flinging them in every direction. Tears of rage mixed with sorrow, despair, and helplessness flew off of his cheeks. He finally uncovered Odem's bruised, cut and shattered body. With a balance of care and desperation, Sage lifted Odem from the chute and placed him on level ground.

"Dad, hang on. Listen to me, you're going to get through this," Sage pleaded.

Odem's body was limp and motionless.

"You're strong, Dad. I know it. I didn't mean to cause that rockslide. I didn't know...Dad..." Sage wept while holding his father's head in his lap.

Blood was covering much of Odem's body. Sage's body was covered in his father's blood as well. The rain was beginning to fall harder. Rainwater mixed with Odem's blood was trickling down the rocks. Looking below, Sage could see that the other Sprinters had run for cover from the rockslide, and those left were in the process of fleeing. There was no one to help Sage with his father. Even the Sprinters placed on the mountain to help in situations like this had fled when the rocks started falling. Though Sage didn't even know if he wanted anyone's help. What would he tell them? Especially after the disappearance of his mother. His family would surely blame him, and rightly so he thought, for he knew he caused the rockslide. Could he look into someone's face without revealing his guilt? Sage was never effective at hiding his true feelings. Anyone who knew Sage could tell what he was feeling by looking into his eyes.

So Sage sat paralyzed. He was consumed with shock and fear and sorrow. He knew that his father was dead. Not only because Odem had no pulse, but also because Sage could sense the loss.

In a trancelike state, Sage lifted his father's body onto his shoulders and started back up the mountain. He took a step and then saw the peculiar rock with which he had struck the boulder. Sage had set it down when he reached Odem. Kneeling down, Sage picked up the stone and put it in his pocket, although he didn't know why he was concerning himself with such trivial matters. Sage couldn't explain any of his actions. He didn't know why he was walking up the mountain carrying his broken father. He had no purpose. It was as if he was climbing the mountain in an attempt to do something—anything at all. For inside Sage felt that the moment he stopped he would have to face the reality of all that had happened; how his life had changed instantly. Sage didn't think he could survive it. His ankle was broken, but that hardly made a difference. He had completely forgotten that fact. Sage had forgotten the incredible event that caused his father's death and the small stone that seemed to unleash extraordinary power. The only thought going through his mind was, "I killed my father."

All his life Sage had wanted to impress Odem and to be like him. For years Sage had tried to gain strength, speed, skill,

and wisdom in order to be a worthy son for his father. Instead of honoring his father, Sage felt he had killed him.

"I deserve to die," Sage moaned through more tears and pain. "Please, somebody, kill me…I want to die," he lamented as he continued to climb.

Sage passed the fallen brightberry tree and didn't give it a second thought. He just kept climbing to the summit. Even his soaked, long and light-blonde hair looked defeated, as if it was clinging to his head only because it had to. After several minutes and many more audible pleas that he wanted to die, Sage reached the top and sat holding his dad.

Looking out from the top of the mountain, Sage was reminded of the countless times he had gazed from this spot with his dad beside him. His dad was beside him now, but he could not look with Sage this time. The darkness was thick and Sage couldn't see as far as he could in the previous years. That thought reminded him of the last conversation he had with his dad; a conversation of what the mountainside looked like before the light was taken away. This caused Sage to remember what his father had said about Me.

Gently caressing his father's forehead, Sage whispered through more tears, "What about Alphega, Dad? You said he was in control. He wouldn't let this happen, especially not to you."

Though My hands were tied, My eyes were not. Again I wept. I wept for the anguish of My creation. I allowed another one of My tears, with a trace of another one of My qualities, to fall to the Wisprian World and land ever so lightly on Sage's forehead. To him it felt like a warm drop of rain amid the countless other cooler drops falling on him, and for a brief moment Sage was at peace.

Then, with a burst of rage, Sage stood and looked up at the dark sky as he shouted with all of his might, "You don't exist! There is no Alphega!!"

He collapsed back onto the rocks in a pile of defeat and self-hate. He hated himself for all he had done. He hated himself for causing his father's death. Now he hated himself because he wanted to die, but somehow couldn't bring himself to jump off of the mountain.

While he was still trying to work up the ability to kill himself, Sage glanced over to a shimmer on the ground nearby. Curious, and relieved to have anything occupy his thoughts, Sage stumbled over to it. It was a message written in the rocky ground. The shimmering was intriguing, but what was more staggering was what it said. Sage fell to the ground in sheer awe and amazement at the words he saw. The glistening message read:

SAGE CONQUER YOUR PLIGHT
QUICKLY SEEK THE LIGHT

"Carrying his broken father."

THE NOBLEST COMMITMENT

"Alphega, thank you for my family. Thank You for my loving wife Alaise, she is far more than I ever deserved. Thank you for her loyal and caring nature. Thank you for Palat, my obedient and loyal son. Thank You for my sweet adorable daughter, Penielle. Thank you also for Oze, you surely have placed that creature in my life for our joy and protection. I am humbled by Your goodness, Your greatness. My days here are more than tolerable; they are joy-filled and showered with simple blessings," the Reflection male, Animus Asaleutos, moved from kneeling on the ground to laying face down in the snow and gravel.

"We have had all we needed always. You fill our stomachs with food, our chest with air, and our hearts with love for You

and each other. Thank You for giving me the wisdom to realize the mistakes of my youth. I've realized the importance of my role as father and husband—it is the most sacred duty You have bestowed upon me. There is no worthier undertaking. I realize how imperfect I am at fulfilling this responsibility, but then You have given me grace and mercy and have helped me. Where I fall short, You are there."

"Yet lately, since this darkness, it seems that You don't hear my petitions. I recognize that my pleas never deserved to fall on a hearing and listening ear, but, Alphega, this present silence and darkness is more than I can bear. As You know, evil times have befallen this world, all Your creation is currently being destroyed by these merciless invaders. Every attempt by a Reflection to stand their ground against these diabolus has been futile. I don't know whether to run or fight. You have placed my family in my hands for protection and I will protect them with all of my being; there must be a way to save them from this evil. But if I leave Sakoden Kome´ to fight, who will keep them safe?"

Animus lay face down in the snow silent for several minutes, having spoken what he needed to. He had never heard an audible answer from Me in the past, and he did not expect one now. However, Animus did believe that I spoke to his mind and would give him answers there. Usually the answers came in the form of circumstances that would arise in Animus' life; a door that would open or close. Animus was usually patient in waiting, but lately he hadn't been able to sleep because he knew that this matter was ever so urgent and that his loved ones' lives were at stake.

Animus lived in one of the three northernmost cities in the Wisprian World, Sakoden Komeˊ. Close by was Kowf Komeˊ on the coast of the Sea of Qerach. Further to the north was Khoref Komeˊ and the Castle of Ice. Almachora was the name given to the northern region where they were located. Almachorans were known to be larger than most other Reflections.

As such, Animus was a man of great stature; he was more than half as tall as Oze the cave bear that he raised from a cub, and when standing on two legs, Oze was taller than Animus' cabin. Animus felt personally responsible for Oze. There once was a great blizzard, when Wispria was still lit. Though there was light, the snow was blinding. It had been snowing for several weeks and Animus' family was running low on food, so Animus went on a hunt in the blizzard. Animus purposely never hunted mother bears—not because they were the fiercest, but because, without a mother, young cubs would die. On this particular hunt, Animus made an error whilst the dense snow hid from view the cub that was Oze. Animus fought his mother and, with his axe, slew her. It was only after the fierce fighting Animus saw the baby cave bear. Animus had a noble heart. He was saddened by what he had done and felt the only way to pardon himself was to raise Oze as his own. He took the skins from Oze's mother and made garments from them that he would always wear, this was one of the reasons Oze took so kindly to Animus. When he was a cub, Oze would curl up in Animus' arms and if he closed his eyes he could imagine his mother was holding him. Oze didn't see Animus kill his mother and was too young to remember the event.

The furry bearskin that was made from Oze's mother went across Animus' shoulders and behind his neck. He had cut holes in the skin for his arms but the outer garment was sleeveless. It was as long as his knees and covered the entirety of his back. His boots were also made from thick layers of the bearskin. His other garments were a series of sturdy leather skins and assorted firs layered for warmth and protection.

Across his back he carried his heavy marbled diamond axe he rightly named Azarmuth meaning, "sure helper of death", which he wielded with his strapping, scarred arms, felling trees and enemies alike. Made from the hardest substance on Earth, Animus couldn't carve the blade. Marbled diamonds were far stronger and superior to the diamonds of the new Earth. The marbled look was caused by a brilliant, metallic, mineral that adulterated but also reinforced the stones. He happened upon the piece on a journey through the steep and jagged Icy Mountains, an area known for marbled diamonds. The piece he found, while not aesthetically perfect for a blade, was very sharp and the perfect size and weight. One end of the blade was broad with an extremely sharp edge. This end was larger than the size of Animus' hands when held out beside each other. The other end was smaller in diameter, about the size of his fist, with a rounded edge, more club-like. Animus wedged the stone into a piece of bearingian wood, found only around the region where he lived.

What Almachorans called bearingian trees, were evergreen and often had trunks wider than ten men. Strong and durable, the wood was exceptionally difficult to burn, but even harder to crack or split. For added support and stability, Animus lashed the blade to the handle with scarlet vine. When cold, the chord was as hard as a rock and was helpful in binding, but scarlet vine actually was not a vine at all. Almachorans used this term to describe chord that was made from the sinews of snow snakes.

The snow snakes were unusual creatures to say the least. In the coldest of times when the temperature was freezing, the snakes would freeze. Their scarlet and black bodies would become solid like a twisted cylindrical piece of ice, making them easy to hunt. But the creature would stay alive indefinitely in this state of hibernation. Then, when the temperature warmed, the snakes would thaw out and behave like any other serpent.

"Animus," a voice called out in the darkness.

Animus looked up to see large torches and a group of Almachoran Reflection males walking toward him. The warriors were clothed as if going on a long hunt or conquest. Large furs and leather pieces were draped across them. Clubs, axes, bows, spears, and shields they carried.

The largest of the men, larger even than Animus, was a Reflection called Har. The tan-skinned, long and full, gray-bearded leader of the group was wearing a hooded woolly mammoth fur that covered his head and extended the length of his body down to his boots fashioned from the same animal's fur. Grasping his thick leather belt with one hand and his marbled diamond battle hammer with the other, Har said, "Animus, the villages in the south of us have sent riders to us to ask for help. As far as we know all of the villages south of them, those in Alavana, have been destroyed already. We go to fight the invaders away from our homes, in an effort to defeat them before they reach Almachora."

"I am a man of faith, but I doubt you can defeat them, Har," Animus said.

"We must try, die trying we may, but the alternative is waiting for the inevitable destruction of Sakoden Kome´ and then the Ice Castle. You are strong, a great hunter, many beasts have you single-handedly slain. With you and your animal friend, you add much to our small band."

"My prayers go with you, and I am committed to your cause, yet, there is a greater commitment—that of protecting and caring for my family," said Animus.

"Yes, but Animus protecting your family is what I am getting at. We must defeat this evil before it reaches us and our families. Many of us are in your very situation. You have but one wife, many of them have multiple wives and children. Would you claim that you are more needed by your family than we are by ours? Your family needs you to fight for them by lending your strength to our cause," Har argued.

Animus was silent, reflecting on this point of view. At present his countenance looked deeply troubled. The short beard on his chin and above his lip failed to cover his anxiety. His shoulder length brown hair blew erratically in the blustery darkness.

"Please consider our request my friend. We go to muster more men. When you hear the drumming at the city gate, we will be gathering there to march out. Our plan is to reach the northern edge of the Foggy Forest by week's end. You haven't much time to decide, but my hope is that you come to the same conclusion as the rest of the men," Har said.

Har stared at Animus with expectation, then said, "Let us go, men."

With that, Har and his men disappeared into the snowy darkness and left Animus to ponder his choice.

"Oze, come on down, we're going home," Animus called out to his bear friend, who had managed to climb into one of the large, nearby bearingian trees.

The sound of branches cracking was heard as Oze quickly made his way down. Oze was deceptively quick, his size was massive, but it didn't hinder his speed. Animus had already begun walking towards his cabin, while Oze followed behind at a distance, pausing to smell this or that, or twitching his ears at a distant sound.

As he walked, Animus wrestled with the choice he had to make. Both causes were noble, but was Har right? Would going to battle more effectively protect his family than staying behind?

Suddenly, Animus was hurled to the ground by a hairy paw. Oze had sensed his master's anxiety and, in his way, tried to lighten the mood. Animus' hair was stuck to his face by the large tongue that was covering him in slobber. Oze had him pinned to the ground.

"Thank you, sir," Animus said, "But we are in a hurry."

Realizing his tactic wasn't working, Oze let Animus out from under him and the two continued on home. Animus could feel a chill in the air and was aware of the temperature dropping as he spotted the glow from the fire inside his cabin. There were also two tall torches stuck in the ground outside of the front door giving off light in the falling snow.

The cabin was made of whole, young bearingian trunks. For the older, larger trees were quite too large to be easily moved.

The fire made the cabin warm enough to melt the snow on top of the roof. There were leather troughs hanging from the roof down the sides of the cabin to catch the water as the snow on the roof melted. The water followed the leather troughs into the cabin through a space between the logs, and landed in buckets inside the cabin. That was how most of the people of the northern lands collected fresh water.

Just across from the cabin, Oze noticed fresh meat had been placed at his dinner tree, and he hurried to devour it. As he approached, Animus could hear the voices of his wife and children. He was unsure how to tell them what he was considering. Yet, before he had a chance to think any further, Alaise met him at the door with a warm hug.

"There is my loving husband," she said, greeting him.

Little Penielle ran and wrapped her arms around her daddy's leg. "Daddy!" she shouted as Animus removed the leather gloves made by his wife in order to pat his little girl.

Palat smiled from across the room, "Dad look at the stone I found," he said, holding out a small orange glowing rock.

"He was out behind the cabin playing in the ashes of the fire pits again," Alaise added.

"Palat, you know to obey your mother. The ashes from the fire pits get all over everything. And I told you, you never know when a hot coal will still be simmering in them," Animus said as Palat bowed his head.

"That said," Animus continued, "That truly is a unique stone. I've never seen anything like it. You will want to hold on to that."

"Look how it glows!" exclaimed Palat.

"That it does son, after supper I'll have to examine it more closely. Oh, my family, I've missed you all," Animus said, his heart full.

"How was your walk in the wood?" Alaise asked.

"I thought about you all and how much I love you," Animus warmly responded, walking across the cabin to sit in his chair.

Palat sat on a bench next to the water bucket ready for supper; he had to wait to eat until his father came home. He had just sat on the bench when something wet began tickling the back of his elbow and forearm. Looking behind him, he saw Oze's long tongue slipping through the cracks in between the cabin logs.

Letting out a giggle he muttered, "Oze, what are you doing, boy?"

Alaise interjected, "Palat, did you take Oze's water out to his tree like I asked you?"

"No," Palat answered, rising to carry out his mother's previous request and carefully placing his small stone on the shelf next to the table for safe keeping.

Noticing that Penielle was busy with her wooden toys by the fire, Animus reasoned this was an opportunity to tell his wife what was troubling his mind.

"Har is gathering warriors to fight the invaders," he said bluntly.

"Then I am glad that you are a husband and a father and not a warrior," Alaise answered in an effort to end the discussion.

"Alaise, you know he needs as many bodies as he can get," Animus argued, regretting his choice of words.

"Bodies! Exactly. I am not sending my husband off to come back as a body on a sled, or worse," Alaise said with growing impatience.

"Of course not, but hopefully I wouldn't come back like that. Hopefully I would be gone for a little while and come back victorious," said Animus.

"Listen to yourself. You don't even believe that statement. I know you. You are a man of great faith. And it is obvious when you make a statement you don't believe in your own heart. Please don't think of this anymore. Let Har fight his battles. There is plenty for you to do here," Alaise said as she placed the food on the table.

"Yes, there is plenty for me here. My duty is to make sure you are all taken care of. And Alaise, if these so called diabolus and Dephilim destroy the southern lands, they will come here next. It is said they are allied with the Sarxans as well. If I am the only hunter left in Sakoden Kome´, I will not be able to fight them off. They will kill every one of us. Yet, if I go with Har and his warriors we can fight the battle away from Almachora. True, we may all die. But we might win. The alternative is to wait here for seemingly certain death," Animus said more sternly.

Though she was only three, little Penielle looked up at this statement, as if fully comprehending the weight of the situation.

"Or you could let Har fight the battle, and live to take care of us if he drives off the invaders," Alaise said, realizing she wasn't gaining ground in the argument.

"That is a cowardly statement. I would hope you would think me better than a coward," Animus answered.

"Dad's not a coward," Palat said, when he returned from outside.

Animus glanced at his son and smiled then looked at his wife, realizing the discussion had to end.

"He sure isn't. Mmm, the food smells delicious. Are you hungry son?" Animus said, changing the subject.

A large fish was placed in the center of the table, from which the family would cut portions. The fish was accompanied by a grain and berry mixture. Usually the family drank water, although occasionally they drank milk or fermented beverage if they were available. Before every meal, Animus would give thanks to Me for providing it, however, this night evoked a weightier prayer than usual.

After glancing around the family's small dinner table at each of his loved ones, Animus took a deep sigh and prayed, "Alphega, we are humbled by your goodness to us. Thank you for this meal. Thank you for blessing us with food and shelter and meeting our needs. Thank you for Penielle, Palat, and Alaise. We are thankful that you have allowed us to be in each other's lives."

While Animus was still praying Alaise looked up slightly to make eye contact with him, but his eyes were closed and he was concentrating.

Animus continued, "Please, we know you hear us, we ask that you give us many long years together—,"

"And my whis'le," interjected little Penielle, who often asked for the whistle she lost a while back.

Animus smiled as usual, then proceeded, "Continue to bless us with each other's company for longer than we can hope for. Protect us. Let us eat."

After the prayer that was more desperate sounding than a blessing for food, the family ate their dinner. After dinner the children and their mother went to bed and Animus sat staring into the fire searching for answers. He knew that at any moment the drums would sound at the gate to the city, and he still didn't know if he would follow them. While he was still pondering, and while Oze slept outside in his normal warm spot against the fire side of the cabin, the war drums sounded.

Animus sat up straight, he knew the time for thinking was over. He ran outside to see what Oze was doing. He thought perhaps the cave bear would give him a sign. Oze stirred slightly but was still asleep. He went back inside and found his wife sitting in his chair.

"Don't tell me you came back in here to tell me goodbye," she said with fear in her voice.

"I—" Animus was cut off.

"Not like this, Animus. The children, they are asleep. How can you tell them goodbye when they will barely remember it," Alaise pleaded with disbelief in her tone as a tear began to form.

Without premeditation, Animus discovered what he was going to do—at least for the immediate present. From the shelf where Palat had placed the stone, he grabbed several blocks of dried meat preserved in cloth, and a few other dried food items—as much as he could spare.

"I'm just going to take them some supplies, and go ask them what direction they are heading next, so that if I wish to follow behind them soon, I can. I will be back in a little while," Animus reasoned.

"Promise. Promise me you will be back tonight," Alaise pleaded.

"I promise," said Animus.

Animus gave his wife a long kiss. She then went about tending to the children who, because of the talking, were beginning to wake. Animus then grabbed his axe, not because he was going to fight, but because he never went anywhere without it. In the untamed land that was Almachora, danger could show itself anywhere, anytime. He tossed the supplies in a sack and running outside, he woke Oze. Oze was groggy, but he understood there was no time for wallowing in his warm bed. Animus grabbed hold of Oze's thick fur and hopped onto his back. Usually Animus walked or ran, but when in a hurry, nothing got him where he was going quicker than a fast cave bear.

"Let's go to the gate, the gate, Oze!" Animus said.

The gate to Sakoden Kome´, where the two were heading, was part of a wall crafted from bearingian wood. The wall was more than triple the height of Oze when he stood on two legs. The trunks were placed, side by side, vertically, deep in the snow and ice, and were made into sharp points. At two places across the wall there were lookout platforms. The gate, also made from bearingian wood, used to remain open except for when the town was threatened. However, since the darkness, it remained closed until someone needed to pass through it. The wall did not stretch around the entire city. Sakoden Kome´ was situated at the foothills of the Icy Mountains which surrounded over half of the city. The remaining side of the city, the side facing the valley, was where the wall was placed. The wall stretched from the western icy glacial slope to the steep hill on the eastern side of the town. On the hill was a dense group of bearingian trees that created a natural bottleneck path. In theory, an invading army could ransack the village without going through the wall. Yet, when considering an icy climb as easy targets for archers and spear throwers or trying to move with agility through unyielding, thick trees up a steep slope through a narrow passage, most would take their chances against the wall head on.

Animus lived in the northern part of Sakoden Kome´, the area of town furthest from the wall. There were no roads for him to travel. Roads seemed pointless in an area that frequently received heavy snow. There were, however, paths through the most traveled areas of town, though Animus and Oze did not take them. They chose the most direct route up and over a moderately sized hill that was in the center of Sakoden Kome´. A few cabins sat on top of the hill, but it was mostly trees. On the other side of the hill the Sapphire Stream cut across town. During the warmer times it flowed, and was flowing now, but ice was beginning to form over it due to the new darkness and cold. Soon all the water in Almachora would be frozen over, like it was during the coldest times.

The snow was falling heavily as Oze made it over the hill, his paws sinking down into the snowy slope. Animus held on tight as the cave bear splashed through the Sapphire Stream. Most of the inhabitants of Sakoden Kome´ were already asleep and most of the torches were out. Therefore, it was fortunate the bear was guiding the way, for the snow and darkness made it nearly impossible to see, but Oze could smell his way to the gate.

As they were making their way to the gate, Animus felt a stinging cold coming from the northeast, penetrating his back. He could notice a difference as if there was a fire in the direction they were heading and no fire behind them. The fact was, there was no fire in any direction, so Animus wondered what was causing the intense cold.

Ahead of him he could see the torches of the gate. The gate was closed; he had missed Har. But Animus knew the guards quite well and hoped they could tell him which direction Har went.

"Hello friends," Animus said from the back of Oze. "Would you open the gate and tell us which direction Har the Khorefian went?"

One of the guards answered, "He asked if we had seen you, Animus Asaleutos. No doubt you and Oze will be a welcome addition to their band."

The other guard added, "We watched them head Southwest, said they were marching toward Kowf Kome´, but it wasn't long before we lost the light from their torches in the blizzard," as he opened the gate.

"If you hurry I'm sure you can catch them," said the other guard.

"Thank you," shouted Animus, waving his arm behind him as Oze rushed through the gate.

Even with the heavy snow, Animus could see the remains of tracks heading in the direction of Kowf Kome´. Animus followed them for several minutes. He and his bear were well on their way when a noise from back at Sakoden Kome´ startled him. There was a loud whistling like the angriest of winds that lasted for at least a few minutes, followed by several piercing cracking sounds. A blast of cold wind coming from Sakoden Kome´ hit his face and he instantly felt the temperature drop several degrees. Animus was used to extreme cold. However, never had he felt such a sudden and palpable change. Concerned, he turned Oze back in the direction of home.

His uneasiness grew when from a distance he could see that the torches at the city gate were no longer lit. As he came closer he kept expecting the guards to relight them, but that never happened. When he reached the gate he saw the guards standing at their post, but they didn't acknowledge him.

"Permission to enter Sakoden Kome´ requested by Animus Asaleutos," Animus shouted.

The guards were more stoic than before.

"Hello. Can you hear me? I was just wondering what that noise was," Animus continued with a shiver running up his back caused by cold and dread.

Upon receiving no answer yet again, Animus climbed off of Oze to see if the gate would open, perhaps it wasn't locked. When he touched the gate he realized how slick and hard it was; much harder than bearingian wood, and few substances were. Animus felt all over the gate and then the walls, they were all cold and slick. Noticing that the guards hadn't even shifted their weight or moved the slightest amount, Animus was beginning to understand what had happened—everything was frozen solid, ice.

Desperately Animus pounded against the gate. Sensing his master's urgency, Oze too, threw himself into the gate trying to break in, but Animus knew that it was folly to even try.

The gate didn't budge. Hoisting his axe, Azarmuth, Animus used every fiber of muscle in his body to bring the axe down into the gate; only to have bone-splitting pain shoot through his hands and arms upon contact. He felt as if every tooth in his head would rattle out with the blow. But the only damage to the gate was a chip in the ice the size of the axe's blade.

Oze snarled and made a motion with his head towards the right. Realizing the bear was correct, Animus said, "You're right Oze, take us through the trees."

Animus jumped onto Oze and held on as the bear sprinted toward the great bearingian thicket. The two were just beginning to get into the thick of the trees when they saw what must have made the cracking sound. Entire trees were snapped off in the middle of their trunks. Oze hopped onto the downed trunks and it actually made his climb a little easier as he dug into the icy trunks with his claws. Occasionally his claw wouldn't penetrate the ice and he would slip and land hard onto one of the trunks. But nevertheless, he quickly continued up the steep, tree-littered slope. Along the way, Animus thought he noticed enormous tracks in the snow, yet he didn't wish to risk the time to stop and investigate them; he was worried about his family.

When the two came out of the frozen trees, and started their descent from the slope, Animus was alarmed to see every single torch and fire in the village was out. There was no source of heat, or for that matter light, to be seen.

"Faster Oze, take us straight home," Animus shouted.

Tired though he was, the bear continued bounding down the slope with great speed. They passed several cabins that all had a glossy look to them like the frozen gate and trees. The water in the troughs on the side of the cabins had frozen mid-trickle. The Sapphire Stream was solid.

Finally coming to his dark, fireless cabin, Animus leapt off of Oze and ran to the front door. The door was frozen shut. However, his front door wasn't near as thick as the gate to the city and it had no lock, so after a few times of throwing his body against it, the door cracked open. The floor was slick when he entered, and Animus fell onto his backside looking up into the empty frozen room. Standing to his feet, Animus didn't need to go any further to find answers. He could see in the next room Alaise was sitting up in the bed with Palat under one arm and Penielle under the other. They were all smiling as if Alaise had told the children one of her cheerful bedtime stories. They were smiling, but smiling eternally. Their peaceful expressions didn't change, and their eyes never blinked, as their skin was as shiny as the icy tomb of a cabin where they lay.

Animus stood shocked and speechless. Gingerly he touched the ice statues that were his family. He was afraid to hold them for fear he would break off their fragile, icy fingers. Quickly, he stemmed his utter hopelessness with decisive action. Animus took in his hands the fire stones that sat by the fireplace. After hitting them together violently, many times, all of the ice was knocked off of them. Then striking them in the fireplace, he realized the wood was also frozen. He frantically moved about the cabin, searching for anything that would burn; everything was solid ice.

He felt utterly helpless. He was frustrated by his strength, for even his strength couldn't produce flame from ice. He knew his family was beyond hope, but in the back of his mind he could delay the pain of loss by trying to still save them—but how?

"Alphega help me! I need you," he cried out.

"Save them! Melt the ice from around them! Create fire from snow! I know you can, Alphega, please!" he continued.

With his axe he began smashing into the logs of the cabin, but he had much the same result with the gate to the city. Growing more frantic, he smashed into the dinner table and benches, all of which were frozen solid. Then he brought his axe down onto the shelf by the table which then burst into flames. The fire was so sudden and so instantly mature that Animus knew he could not have made the flames.

"Thank you Alphega, thank you! Thank you for this miracle!" Animus said full of joy.

Little did Animus realize that the small stone his son had placed on the shelf earlier was a piece of agapate. Animus put all of his will and desire into his swing when he swung Azarmuth. Unknowingly, he brought the axe down directly onto the agapate with such force, that the agapate, with the ability to produce fire, was instantly melded to the blade of Azarmuth, and his desire to create fire was unleashed through the stone that was now part of his axe. After chopping the burning shelf into a few pieces with his axe, Animus moved the burning pieces beside the bed and his frozen family. Already the floor and other parts of the cabin were beginning to thaw from the fire. Animus brought the benches and firewood to be thawed out in order to keep the blaze going; all the while making sure that the water from the melting ice didn't put out the fire he had at present.

It wasn't long before his wife and children were dripping wet and their skin was soft to the touch again. Animus kept touching each one of them, hoping for a sign of life. No sign ever came. Once they were fully thawed out, Animus closed their eyes and spread them gently onto the bed. He was more painfully bewildered than ever. He could see his family was dead, but if they were dead why would I start the fire? Had he done something wrong while trying to save them? His entire purpose had been to protect them, yet still they were dead. What creature could have done this? He was full of questions, but finally he succumbed to the overwhelming feeling of loss that had been gnawing at him, and Animus then sobbed loudly and openly. Given the icy silence of Sakoden Kome´, his weeping could be heard from far off, only there were no red-blooded ears to hear it.

But I heard his weeping. I wept with him. Then the third one of My tears fell to Earth. It landed on Animus' head, but he did not feel it. At that point, he wouldn't have noticed if the entire roof of his cabin fell on his head.

"Animus was a man of great stature."

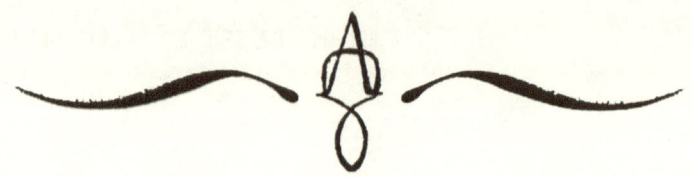

THE EXPLANATION

Standing and glancing erratically around the mountainside, Sage looked for who could have written the message.

"Hello? Who is up here? Do I know you? Did you see what happened to my dad? Come out so I can see you," Sage shouted frantically.

Just then another glimmer of light caught his eye coming from across the top of the mountain. It was about twenty-five yards away, so he couldn't make it out from where he was standing. Carrying his father's body, Sage went towards the light. Once there he saw what it said:

YES

Sage's curiosity was growing, but so was his agitation. He wanted to sit and grieve in a pool of guilt mingled with

self-pity over his father's death, but whoever was writing this was keeping him from it. It was also keeping him alive though.

Becoming familiar with what to look for, Sage spotted the next flicker. It was farther down the opposite side of the mountain. However, if he were to continue in that direction, the path would take him deeper into the Moaning Mountains. This message read:

TRUST

Sage was impatient and flusterd as he was now beginning to feel fatigued from the events of the last hour. He continued to carry Odem and his upper body was becoming tired. He spotted the next light quite a distance away. It was farther downhill and on the edge of the tree line. Sage's motivation for following the light was quickly switching from curiosity to aggression towards whatever was taking him deeper into the mountains with a broken ankle and the body of his dad. The ground was becoming less rocky and the message was in more dirt now than rock. It said:

THE RACE GOES NOT TO THE SWIFT
BUT TO HIM THAT ENDURES TO THE END

"What are you talking about? I don't care about the race!" Sage shouted through the trees. "My father is dead! Can you help me or not? I'm tired of following you."

The next light he saw was on the side of a tree farther in the dense woods.

It said:

A LITTLE FARTHER

Sage paused, breathing heavily from exhaustion and exasperation. He debated in his mind whether or not to go on. Looking around he couldn't even see a light. The bushes and trees were thick and the darkness was oppressing, but Sage wanted to know who was writing these messages.

And besides, Sage thought, *what do I have to lose? If there is danger ahead, perhaps I'll die, and this thing will do me a favor.*

Still, he couldn't see a light. Assuming that he should continue heading downhill and deeper into the woods, he went in that direction. He still carried Odem, although not as gracefully as when he began. Both of them were cut and scratched by the thick thorns and bushes. Sage had to throw his father's body across his shoulders. He continued through the woods for a lengthy period of time. Sage was about to collapse and give up when he saw the next light. Picking up his pace he quickly got to the next message, which was also written on a large tree:

WELL DONE NEW FRIEND
THIS TREE ASCEND

"This tree ascend...what does that mean? New friend... hello?" Sage questioned.

Remembering the stone he still had in his pocket, Sage set Odem down under a nearby bush and grasped the rock. Sage wanted to rise above the tree. The combination of Sage having this thought and holding the stone caused the earth to tremble. Again, a tower of soil and earth shot up underneath

Sage's feet and carried him higher than the tree. This time he didn't even lift the rock above his head. He was holding it, but before he could try to use the rock, he was already above the tree. It was as if the rock knew Sage's will.

Once above the tree, Sage didn't have to question where he was supposed to look. He saw a clearing that appeared to be ablaze with white flames. The strange communication Sage had been following culminated in one vast message written in the ground below him. At first, Sage was too tall to see the writing clearly. So, by just thinking of his dilemma, the tower of earth beneath him lowered. Now he was close enough that he could decipher what was written. It read:

A PROPHET OF ALPHEGA, TELLE IS MY NAME,
I KNOW YOU ARE SADDENED, CONFUSED, I WILL EXPLAIN,
BEFORE DARKNESS CAME, WAS WAR STARTED BY LURE,
HE AND HIS FALLEN ARCHEON NO LONGER PURE,
ARCHESKOTOS TO DEPHILIM GAVE FOUL BIRTH,
DESTROYED THE GATE BETWEEN AGAPIA AND EARTH,
ALPHEGA REPLACED THE GATE WITH DARK CLOUD'S VEIL,
AGAPIA'S DIRECT LIGHT EARTH CAN'T AVAIL,
FROM THE MOST POWERFUL SUBSTANCE, AGAPATE,
WAS MADE THE STONE YOU NOW HOLD AND ALSO THE GATE,
WHEN THE GATE WAS DESTROYED MANY PIECES FELL,
LURE SEEKS THESE PIECES, FOR THEY ARE MOST POWERFUL,
WITH EACH NEW PIECE HE FINDS, MORE POWER HAS HE,
ACROSS THE EARTH, CONCEALED, FIND THEM FIRST MUST WE,
LURE AND HIS MINIONS EARTH WILL USE FOR ILL,
YOUR HEART IS NEEDED SAGE, IN THIS STAND AGAINST EVIL,
ALL YOUR LIFE LED TO THIS MOMENT, I CAN SEE,
YET OTHERS MUST WE FIND TO ACHIEVE VICTORY,
ALPHEGA IS REAL, YOUR FATHER LOVED HIM DEAR,
YOU KNOW THIS IN YOUR HEART AND BEAR ALPHEGA'S TEAR.

After reading the message, Sage stood motionless and filled with amazement. He had a sense that all of this must be a dream. *Surely I must be dreaming*, Sage thought. *Maybe Dad didn't die. Maybe the race hasn't even occurred yet. Surely I can't cause the earth to move under my feet. Surely all that I read couldn't be happening to me.* He was paralyzed with disbelief.

Just then, a large horse ran into the middle of the field. His hoof prints distorted the words in the ground. It was the most magnificent horse Sage had ever seen, and the largest. His coat was as gray as the dark clouds that blanketed the sky; his tail, mane and the bottom of his legs were shiny black. However, Sage was most fascinated by the beast's eyes and head. The horse's eyes were a blinding bright silver. In the middle of his head was a single horn that was also silver. After smoothing out a section of the ground containing the message, the creature bent its legs and lowered its head to place the tip of the horn into the soil. The horse was writing. He wrote:

YOU ARE NOT DREAMING

Sage was frightened and fascinated by what he witnessed.

"You wrote the message! You are Telle? Did I say that correctly? It rhymes will bell, yes?" Sage asked, hollering down from atop the tower, not wanting to offend such an extraordinary creature.

The gray unicorn nodded his head forcefully up and down and let out a loud sound of affirmation. The creature then ran to the base of the tower where Sage was standing. Sage only had to think, and he was back down on level ground with Telle.

"You're a horse," exclaimed Sage. "Well, I mean, not just any horse, I can clearly see that. Telle. You are fascinating."

With quick and erratic flips of his head, Telle began to write again:

A HORSE I WAS BUT WISDOM CHANGED ME
FOLLOW ME AND CHANGED WILL YOU BE

The feelings of shock and amazement were not wearing off, but the weight of Odem's death and the burden of utter exhaustion had caught up with Sage. "What is happening? I can't—where is my father?" Sage ran to Odem's body. Again he fell on the ground and wept. Sage was quite delirious. With grace and gentleness, Telle walked softly over to Sage and, bending his front legs first, knelt beside him. Telle's large jaw lay on the ground against Sage's bent legs. The two sat in silence for several minutes.

At that moment, Sage was filled with a feeling of comfort that seemed to come from his newfound friend. He felt that this one being (albeit an animal) would not condemn his recent actions. A flicker of hope remained in Sage Swiftsoul's heart.

In almost a whisper Sage asked, "Will you help me bury him?"

With an exhale through his big horse lips, Telle stood above Sage and Odem. Telle felt empathy for Sage since he had also lost a father. Then, Telle began to write again.

USE THE STONE

Sage's family had a tomb in the sacred caves of the mountain where they buried their ancestors. Sage never imagined that he would bury his father anywhere else. However, he did not want to turn back. So, he picked up Odem one last time and hobbled to the center of the clearing where Telle had written the long message. Lovingly, he lay down Odem's body. Then, while he was reaching in his pocket for the stone, a perfectly-sized hole immediately opened in the center of the clearing. Just like earlier, earth altered before Sage could even grasp the stone. It took all of the energy Sage had left to place his father in the ground with his ankle swollen and throbbing. Then, lifting up Odem's shirt, Sage saw Odem's slingshot fastened to his belt, like always. The use of slingshots was one of the many skills Odem passed on to his son. This slingshot in particular was Odem's favorite weapon, and he had promised it to Sage. As a last remembrance of happier days with his father, Sage took the slingshot, "I love you Dad. I love you so much. Thank you...I'm sorry."

With that, he took one last look at Odem and then stood. When he looked back down, the earth had covered the hole. Telle let out another long exhale and nodded his head. Sage gathered some nearby rocks and arranged them into an "O" over the grave.

The storms to the north were flaring again and the wind and lightning were becoming more frequent. The trees around the two new friends were swaying in all directions. Telle knelt down slightly to cue Sage that he should climb on his back, although there was no saddle.

Most Sprinters had never ridden a horse. With Sprinters' speed, agility, and the fact that they rarely left the Moaning Mountains and the rugged terrain that surrounded them, they found little need for riding.

Sage grabbed hold of the thick, dark mane on the back of Telle's neck and pulled himself onto the wise animal. Whether from pain, exhaustion or the rhythmic and hypnotic, smooth plodding of the horse as it found paths through the dark forest, Sage fell into a deep sleep. His head was resting gently with his cheek against the middle of Telle's back. His four limbs were dangling symmetrically—one arm and one leg hanging off each side of the large unicorn.

Unbeknownst to Sage, the two avoided many dangers that night. Telle's experience with the surrounding landscape and his profound knowledge of the many evils that had only recently started lurking in the world, gave him a keen ability to avoid confrontation.

Sage awoke in what appeared to be a cave. An orange light reflected off of the jagged walls that came not only from the nearby fire, but also from the rock of which the walls were composed. Sage felt dizzy and realized that he was sweating profusely. He failed to notice that on the wall behind him was a smooth section of rock with numerous carvings. Glancing around him he called out, "Telle! Telle, are you here?"

Nothing answered. Sage tried to stand but a sharp pain radiated through his leg. He looked down and noticed a group of sticks were lashed together around his ankle for protection and support. He wondered who had done such a thing, for he assumed that even the wisest of unicorns did not have the dexterity to lash a splint.

The corridor in which Sage sat was fairly narrow. The other side of the cave was only twelve feet in front of him. He seemed to be in the center of a curve in the passageway. He looked one way and saw that about six feet from him the tunnel went around a corner and vanished into darkness. Looking the opposite direction, he saw the fire and a well-lit corridor that also vanished around a corner about twenty feet from him.

While Sage was curious to know where he was and what would happen next, his thoughts quickly turned to the loss of his father and the sudden course of events that had surely changed his life forever. Sage thought to himself about his mother. She had disappeared a few years earlier and Odem had helped him cope with his grief. Cope was all he did, though. He had not fully conquered it, and now that Odem was gone it was compounded exponentially. Sage thought of the six brothers and sisters he had left behind. He loved them dearly. He needed to be there with them, helping them. But how could he tell them what had happened without lying? His sense of duty brought guilt, but the guilt of his father's death outweighed the responsibility. At this point, it had not even occurred to Sage that he might never see his siblings again. And, as it appeared he wasn't going to kill himself, and he would go on living, he began to deal with the new agony of missing his loved ones.

These thoughts continued to overwhelm Sage. He would drift in and out of hot, sweaty sleep. The fire was dying, becoming less luminous little by little. Every time he awoke, he was less sure of how long he had been sleeping. As he sorted through the many thoughts in his mind and dealt with them, he began to focus on more primal needs, such as the rumbling in his stomach. He realized that, for all that he had been through, he had yet to eat.

Awake for the fifth time since he had been there, Sage saw that his foot was greatly swollen—so swollen that he thought it best to remove the splint that was becoming tighter.

He had not yet begun to remove the splint when another thought entered his mind. Sage's deepest desire was to do some great thing. To most of the other Sprinters, winning the great race, producing a large family, or discovering a new peak to scale, were accomplishments worthy of a lifetime. The rest of his friends were content to live a normal life filled with kindness to one another. Sage respected them and saw the value in such a lifestyle. However, he had long desired to use the life he had to be the greatest Sprinter of all time. He wanted to do more than just win a race or be loved while he lived. He wanted to change the world for the better. He wanted to leave a lasting impression of an unknown goodness to all of the inhabitants of the world (those seen and unseen) in his land and in distant lands. But, to his dismay, he felt that goal was completely out of his reach.

He decided not to reach for the splint. Instead, he lay back against the wall of the cave to drift off into sleep. Depression overwhelmed him. He felt as if a force was actually pulling and pushing him to the ground, preventing him from rising. His thoughts were so self-indulgent that he overlooked the fact that Telle had saved him and that he was still in possession of the most powerful object he knew.

Again Sage slept. As before, his sleep was troubled and unfulfilled. Sage constantly felt the pain of his nagging injuries; those of his ankle and of his heart.

A murmuring voice awoke Sage this final time. Around the corner where the fire used to burn, Sage saw another light, though he could not make out its source.

"We must hurry," a voice said followed by a huff that Sage recognized as Telle.

Immediately thereafter the light became increasingly bright until a large figure stood above Sage. The being was quite luminous as if light was radiating from somewhere inside its flesh. The light was not blinding but was a gentle glow that at least dispelled some of the vast darkness that had so completely filled the world at present. It was difficult for Sage to determine the gender of the creature, but it seemed to be male.

"Hello Sage, I am Gad," said the kind yet stern figure with a voice that was more warm and comforting than any Sage had ever heard.

"Telle has told me much about you, and I am sorry to have left you alone, but Telle and I were attacked while gathering provisions for the journey."

"What journey?" Sage asked.

"There isn't time to explain anything now. You must trust me as you have trusted Telle. I will fill you in on as much as I can when we are on the way," said Gad.

"Telle mentioned someone called Lure, and a-guh-pah-tay— "

"A-GAH-pate, it rhymes with gate," corrected Gad lightly.

Sage continued without immediately noticing the correction, "—and Alphega, but I don't see how that concerns me since I don't even believe in Alphega or the rest of it. Besides, I don't understand why you would need me. See! I can't even pronounce agah-PATE correctly! This is the first I've heard about it all. I can't even be trusted to run up the side of a mountain without getting my dad killed. I've got a broken ankle and would rather lie here to face whatever end there may be for me."

Sage looked directly into Gad's enchanting lavender eyes. He then noticed that Gad was much larger than himself. Gad was easily nine feet tall and his build was more muscular than Sage had seen in any previous race, although Sage's exposure to others was limited. Gad's upper body, though muscular, seemed to be covered in a down-like hair. It was not feathers nor fur, and not hair, but a creamy-white, soft outer covering. The only sort of garment the creature wore was an armored skirt that was most resplendent, and made from a substance Sage had never seen before. Sage counted five toes on each of Gad's two bare feet. Sage also noticed many deep cuts and gashes on Gad's chest and arms. Furthermore, the wounds were obviously fresh. Blood did not seep from these wounds though. Instead it was in these places where the light seemed to be streaming in narrow beams from within Gad.

"I know very little about you, Tear Bearer. But the war was and is real. Many of my brethren were taken captive, or worse, by Lure. The world is larger than your eyes can behold."

"Why do you call me Tear Bearer? Telle mentioned something about a tear before. I'll have you know I don't normally cry as much as I have in these past few hours. Is that why? Again, I just buried my best friend, my dad, knowing that my temper and that AGAPATE killed him," Sage interrupted.

Gad continued, "You are already pronouncing it correctly. You are an intelligent creature indeed, Sage Swiftsoul. The rest will all be revealed to you in time. There are dangers and evils you cannot envision. But there is also a world—light, brilliance unequalled in your heart and thought. Agapia, my home. The only safe place left for any of Alphega's creation. I am an Archeon. I come from the upper realm, Agapia. Telle found me as he found you. There are others like us, others that Telle has seen in his prophetic visions. And we must find them before Lure does."

Sage bowed his head in an effort to understand all that he was feeling. Telle looked peacefully at Sage, his round silver eyes staring as if to speak volumes to Sage.

"With regard to your belief in all of this, as if your very being here wasn't enough, look at Telle. Have you ever seen a creature so unique? Look at his silver horn and eyes. Telle wasn't always like that. Journeying from his homeland of Makbar, a piece of agapate, the same material your stone is made of, fell and landed, hardening in a cone shape directly on his head. Penetrating his equestrian brain, the agapate gave him prophetic wisdom and foresight. He has wisdom far beyond any unicorn or other creature for that matter. These are miraculous, supernatural events. Before long, no creature will need proof of Alphega's existence, because they will come face to face with Alphega's enemy, Lure."

Softly, Gad continued, "There are those that need you Sage. At present, I don't know why, but I do know if Telle has seen it, it is true. If you yourself don't want to live, then that will actually be a source of power for you. For life, as all of this world has known it, will change and change quickly. You cannot hope to salvage the life you, even now, try to hold onto so desperately. But by putting your own, old desires to rest, and by being unafraid of death, you can perhaps help save all of creation. It is a selfless road, a selfless road for all of us that would fight to save the upper and lower realms."

"You need me?" Sage questioned with a glimmer of hope.

"Yes, I need you, as does Telle, as you need us and we need each other."

Gad walked toward the passage he had come through, then turned back to look at Sage.

With a sigh, and pressing against the walls of the cave for balance, Sage hesitantly stood up.

"Thank you Sage," said Gad as he helped him up.

When he was standing, Sage glanced around, noticing the carvings on the walls.

"What are those? And what is this place?"

Gad replied, "Telle and I carved the drawings as we shared the knowledge each of us had attained on our journeys. We also strategized how to most effectively move forward. And this is where we have been hiding out the past couple of weeks, here in the Canyons of Flame—"

"Canyons of Flame! That's where I am? How did I get here? How long was I out?" Sage inquired. He tried to take a step, but was thwarted by a knifing pain in his ankle. He stumbled off balance and Gad put his hand under Sage's shoulder for support.

"A few days. Telle brought you through a portion of the Cracked Plain of Desolation to get here, which was the fastest path to take. I was away during that time attending to another matter in the Treetop City. Now follow me, as I said I'll tell you all about it on the way."

As Gad was leading Sage to the exit of the cave, a few of the images on the walls were imprinted on his mind. One in particular was a hideous creature, the likes of which he had never seen before; it seemed to be bursting forth from a woman's stomach, though the creature was far too large, and mutilated the woman as it came forth from her. Another drawing was a circle of what looked like splinters of wood or thorns radiating from the sky with figures tumbling down among the shards. He told himself he would ask Gad about them as soon as he had a chance.

Once Sage was outside, he noticed Telle was carrying bags on his back with what looked to be enough provisions to last several days. The wind was swirling through the canyons whistling all about the three of them. The sky was as black as before, but the orange rock of the jagged Canyons of Flame gave off a warm, orange glow. This gleam and the ever-present lightning that didn't cease regardless of how far they traveled, were the only sources of light available, other than the light that radiated from Gad.

Sage had only seen the Canyons once before, however it was from a distance, from the tops of the trees in the forest that was to the northwest of their current position, while on one of the many treks Odem had taken him on. They were called the Canyons of Flame, not because they produced any kind of fire, but rather because their pointy silhouette on the horizon, coupled with the rust colored rock, gave the appearance of large flames leaping towards the sky.

Hastily, Gad lifted Sage up onto Telle's back.

"There are no reigns, but Telle is careful about keeping his rider from falling, if you start to slip grab hold of the bags that hang across him. I will run ahead and scout out our path—oh yes, and do not mislay the agapate. That stone is one of many we will need if we are to have any chance at overcoming the rolling tide of cold darkness that is so imminently upon us", Gad explained.

Before Sage could argue or inquire, Gad was running up the side of the canyon. Sage always prided himself on being one of the fastest of the fastest race of creatures he had known on Earth. However, Gad quickly humbled Sage. His tall, thick, muscular body, though it looked slow and cumbersome, moved with a grace, ease and speed Sage had never seen.

With a quick jerk of his head, Telle also was dashing up the mountainside. Sage quickly discovered he would need both hands to stay atop Telle. Needing a safe place to place the stone, he held on tight with one hand and with the other he wedged the agapate down in between the lashing around his ankle.

The slopes of the canyon were so steep that if Sage lay flat against Telle's back, he was nearly vertical. Sage was amazed that Telle could ascend such a rocky, perilous, wall. The sound of the loose rocks and gravel that were falling behind the unicorn made it difficult for Sage to hear, yet off in the distance up ahead he could hear a sharp shrieking noise. The two continued to follow in the direction of Gad as the shrieks grew louder.

"What's that noise?" Sage asked Gad.

"We'll know at the top of this ridge, but it sounds to me like a thricorn," Gad yelled back.

"You mean one of the giant lizards?" Sage was both worried and excited.

"Yes, Sprinter," Gad calmly answered.

"Scouts from my tribe have reported seeing such monsters from a distance, but none have ever brought back proof. They say some of them are taller than the trees," Sage exclaimed.

"Yes, they exist and can be quite large, but the giant lizards come in many different forms. Some with horns, some with claws, others that are extraordinarily large but harmless. In truth the thricorn is a docile creature under usual circumstances, but since the light was removed from the Earth, nothing can be certain," said Gad, as he reached the top of the canyon.

Staring down into the canyon that lay before them, the trio could barely make out a large blur of a shadow. This shadow seemed to be congruous with the source of the shrieking. A flash of lightning revealed a figure.

"What do you make of it?" Gad asked Telle.

Lowering his head Telle quickly wrote in the ground with his horn:

THE ANSWER IS NOT IN THE THRICORN'S WAIL
'TIS AGAPATE THE CANYON MAY UNVEIL

"What does that mean?" Sage questioned impatiently.

"It means we are going down there—care to help?" Gad replied, eyeing Sage's ankle brace.

"Uh...I..I'll try," said Sage as he realized inside that he really didn't care to get to the bottom, in fact he was petrified about what could be lurking in the darkness. Nevertheless, Sage proceeded to use the agapate. He thought to himself how he needed to get the three of them to the bottom of the canyon. A few moments passed.

"It isn't working," Sage said, confused.

Telle began slightly bucking and huffing.

"Whoah, what is it, I'm sorry—," Sage began.

"Maybe Telle thinks you should try it while on the ground," Gad calmly stated.

Telle made a short confirming puff.

Gingerly, Sage climbed down from the unicorn aided by Gad. Sage stepped to the edge of the canyon and stared down at the figure. Before the trio had time to prepare themselves, the ground beneath them was rumbling. Suddenly a wall of rock was shooting up on every side of them. It looked as if the canyon was growing up around them, consuming them. But in actuality they were steadily sinking to the floor of the canyon, with the displaced rock shooting into the air above them, instead of falling down to the creature below.

The three reached the bottom of the damp canyon. Sage coughed on the dust of the rocks as they settled into place. Before he had a chance to look around, Gad picked him up from behind and set him on the back of the unicorn.

"Well done, Sprinter," Gad said encouragingly.

Sage didn't reply as he was focused on the noises coming from behind the boulders in front of them. Gad leapt onto the largest of the boulders to get a vantage point. Sage noticed that Gad was instantly surprised and concerned with what he saw.

"What is it? Is it a thricorn?"

"More than that, it has a woman pinned down between two boulders. I believe she is a Reflection," Gad answered, as he disappeared over the top of the boulder.

"A Reflection?" Sage asked, for he hadn't seen a Reflection in years.

Reflections were a group of beings that were created to resemble Me in appearance. They were a Reflection of My image. They were in essence like those inhabitants of the world to come, Humans—except they didn't have the Breath, the Breath that gives Humans an immortal soul. If a Reflection or any other creature of the Wisprian World were to die, that was their end. Unlike Humans, who do have the Breath and do exist after death, whether in bliss or despair—according to the choices of their free will.

Sage remembered that the last time he saw a Reflection he was with Odem. A traveling band of Reflection storytellers, from the Forest of Fools, wearing masks and costumes, travelled to the hills near the Moaning Mountains to tell tales of Me. Reflections were the most faithful of My creation, though in recent decades their faithfulness had faltered. It was also Reflections that, long ago, inspired Sprinters to have banners and emblems for their tribes. For Reflections long had Emblems of Heritage for their villages and various factions; a custom that spread not only to Sprinters, but to many creatures of the Earth. Odem had taken Sage to see the troupe to educate the boy about My ways. With every second that passed, Sage realized how correct his deceased father was.

Telle continued to maneuver his way through the rocks, making his way to Gad. As the three came closer to the lizard, the ground was shaking with every step the creature took.

The Reflection woman noticed Gad first of the three. She was weary and banged up from fleeing from the thricorn. She felt the warm, damp blast of a snort from the lizard's nostrils as it inched closer, wedging and ramming its way in between the cluster of boulders where she hid.

"Help me, please, it's getting closer, I can't move any further!" she shouted. She screamed as one of the lizard's horns lunged in between the two boulders where she was crouched. The trio of rescuers feared the worst.

The light in Gad brightened as he grabbed a huge boulder about thirty times the size of the largest brightberry Sage had ever seen, and hurled it at the reptile. The rock found its mark right in between the bony plate that held the reptile's three horns and the back of its neck. For the first time the creature noticed Gad and his companions and turned its focus from the Reflection woman to them. Letting out another loud, bellowing shriek, the thricorn charged Gad. The ground shook even more as the creature bounded with speed across the rocky canyon bottom. Sage thought Gad wouldn't be able to withstand a charge of this magnitude, yet Gad was ready. He jumped into the air and landed atop the thricorn, standing in between the beast's shoulders. Enthralled with watching this action unfold before his eyes, Sage failed to realize Telle was charging the reptile as well. Telle lowered his head and buried at least a foot of his horn into the lizard's left side. Telle quickly removed his horn to parry the thricorn's counterattack, as Sage tried hard to not fall off Telle's back.

At the same time, Gad leapt from the beast to grab another boulder. This time the lizard caught him off guard. Instead of attacking Telle, the thricorn broadsided Gad with the side of its front horn, knocking Gad to the ground. The thricorn quickly turned its attention back to Telle and Sage. The intensity of the battle caused Sage to forget his fears. He jumped high in the air off of the back of the unicorn and came crashing down on the ground in front of the thricorn. His landing was more than anyone present had anticipated. The sound that it made was louder than all the thunder claps around them. A crack shot through the floor of the canyon from Sage's foot straight under the creature and continued past it. Both the front and back right legs of the thricorn fell into the newly created crevasse, trapping it. Thinking ahead, Sage was already grasping Odem's slingshot with a rock in-hand, preparing to hurl it.

"Wait!" cried Gad. "This lizard is no longer a threat to us. See to the woman."

The odd thing was that at that precise moment the woman stood and was casually walking towards them. This sudden change was most peculiar. Sage hurried over to meet her, now greatly favoring his right ankle, as he had come down directly on it. Gad struggled to his feet and approached the lizard.

"I've never seen a thricorn so aggressive. Even in such dark times, I don't understand why it would so relentlessly attack a Reflection. The air is so cold I am surprised it can move, much less attack anything." Gad placed his hand on the creature's side as it lay motionless.

"Its skin is ice cold," he said as the thricorn slowly opened its eyes.

Gad looked into the open eyes of the thricorn and noticed a peaceful tranquility that had not been present moments before. There was no evidence of the raging beast that sent him to the ground. This sudden change disturbed Gad to the point that he said nothing of it.

Through the cuts and the clay smudges, Sage noticed that this woman was stunning. Her beauty captivated him like he had never before experienced. She had chestnut hair and piercing blue eyes and her lips glistened in the wet darkness like dew-laden red rose petals. For a moment, Sage forgot all of the recent evils and focused on her face.

"Thank you for saving me," she said with a large gaping hole in her torso where the thricorn had stabbed her. The wound should have killed her almost instantly, yet she seemed to be unfazed.

"You're welcome," Sage muttered after a few seconds had passed.

"Although really my companions did more than—" Sage was cut off.

"I'm not talking to your companions, I'm looking at you, do you see me?" she said.

"Yes. I do," Sage replied. He then noticed for the first time the deep wound from the horn. "We should get you help. I'm sorry, I didn't see that. How can you bear that wound? You should sit down and rest. Gad, Telle!"

She giggled as if she hadn't noticed the gash before, "Nevermind the wound. I meant me. Do you see me? My name is Reverie. Would you like to come with me?"

"Where are you going?" Sage was both excited and reminded of his companions and the quest on which they had just set out. It felt a little silly to tell Reverie that he and his new-found friends were on a journey to collect a powerful substance called agapate in order to defeat an evil enemy called Lure and save Wispria. "Oh, I mean, my name is Sage, but also, I don't know where you are going—but you can come with us, once we get you taken care of."

"Unfortunately, I don't think I can," she was saying as Gad and Telle came near.

Turning to Gad and Telle, Sage said excitedly, "This is Reverie. She has a really deep wound, but it doesn't seem to bother her. Still, I think you should look at it. She is from... well actually we didn't get that far yet...but we saved her and I think she should join us."

Ignoring Sage's sophomoric banter, Gad inquired of Reverie, "Are you alright? You seemed to be badly hurt and exhausted."

Gad reached to examine her wound.

"No! Stay away from me. I'm fine. Really, it looks worse than it feels," said Reverie as she made an effort to hide the injury with her garments.

Reverie smiled peacefully.

Gad was flabbergasted at Reverie's response. He couldn't understand why she didn't want her wound attended to.

"Please, if you would let me at least dress your wound—," said Gad.

Reverie was firm, "I've seen your kind before. You will do no such thing!"

"Alright then, if you insist," Gad reached into the supplies and took out a piece of clean cloth to use as a bandage. He handed it to Reverie as he continued, "Here, I trust you will take care of it yourself. So, where did you come from? How did you get out here? And what caused a thricorn to be so intent on killing you?" Gad continued.

"Shouldn't I be the one asking you who you are? A silvery horse with a horn, a Sprinter, and you, you must be one of those celestials from above that destroyed my village. Why did you now help me? After what was done to my loved ones by those like you!" said Reverie in an attempt to deflect the focus from her.

"I'm sorry. My name is Gad. But I am not one of the fallen from above, rather I was forced from Agapia, my home, with the rest of the virtuous Archeon, by Lure the prideful one. It is his underlings that I'm sure are responsible for your town. And for that I am truly sorry. Yet, do not yet lose all hope, for my companions and I are determined to set things right again, I guess that starts with making sure you are safe. Would you like us to see you to safety?"

"Thank you, but no. Though I am grateful for how you saved my life. As Sage told you, my name is Reverie. I am a Reflection," she answered.

"She is a Reflection," Sage said enthusiastically.

"Yes, Sprinter," Gad said with patience.

"Reverie, let us help you," said Sage as he took a wobbly step on his hurt ankle towards her.

Reverie looked down to see Sage's ankle and noticed the odd stone wedged in between his bracing. Her eyes widened as she recognized what it was.

"Is that a piece of agapate?" she asked quickly with an urgency none in the group had seen in their brief encounter with her.

"Yes!" Sage quickly replied.

"Well, actually we're not sure yet," Gad said cutting Sage off. Gad looked back at Sage so Reverie couldn't see his expression.

Gad's face seemed to tell Sage not to give away such precious information, in case the wrong person were to find out.

"You're not sure?" Reverie suspiciously questioned.

"No, have you seen agapate before? How have you even heard of agapate? It is not a substance found in Wispria," Gad responded.

"I told you my village was attacked by those creatures."

"Yes, but that doesn't necessarily mean that you've seen agapate," Gad continued.

"Stop interrogating me!" Reverie said increasingly emotional.

"Gad, why are you being so secretive? I think we can trust her," Sage chimed in.

"And you wanted me to join you? I knew I couldn't go with you," Reverie said to Gad. Continuing, she looked at Sage, "But my offer still stands for you, do you want to join me?"

"Have you not heard me? We are together. I am glad we could rescue you, but we cannot be separated. If you won't come with all of us I can't let Sage wander off with you," Gad said sternly.

"Gad, I still make my own decisions," Sage said defiantly. "I agreed to go with you, and I do want to help, but I can still make my own choices."

"I realize that Sage, and I am not trying to mislead you. But you must realize there are forces in this world that Sprinters can't see. She still hasn't answered my questions, we don't know how a Reflection ended up deep in the Canyons of Flame running from a thricorn, and we don't know if she is who she says she is. How has she heard of agapate?" Gad argued.

Sage stared again into Reverie's enchanting face. He felt himself completely defenseless. He wanted to do whatever it took to stay with her. Gad put his hand on Sage's shoulder and he was reminded of the last time he received a pat on the shoulder, it was from his father. This served to bring Sage back to reality, if just briefly.

"I can't leave my friends without knowing how you got out here or where we are going" Sage said hesitantly, fearing he would push Reverie away, which was the last thing he wanted.

Reverie stood staring at the floor of the canyon for a moment, before her eyes became teary and she slowly sank to the ground. "Everyone from my town, Casusbelia, is dead. The light grew blindingly bright briefly, then, the darkness overcame it. It was then that the creatures came out of the sky with no warning. They were merciless, barbaric murderers. They didn't just kill. They mangled, ripped, crushed and ate the bodies of our men. Then they took the form of our men as the women were overpowered and violated. Within minutes the women's stomachs grew, and shortly thereafter they were killed instantly when hideous creatures, the likes of which I have never seen, burst forth from them."

Sage's mouth dropped and he was speechless at the sudden telling of such a horrific story.

Gad interrupted her saying, "Telle, this sounds like the drawing you made in the cave."

Telle nodded and Sage remembered seeing the drawing as Reverie continued, "I watched from my dying flower garden as this happened to my mother and my sisters. Not long after the beasts came from the sky, the giant lizards came running into Casusbelia from the nearby plains destroying walls and buildings. I knew I would join the dead if I stayed, so I ran.

I was almost over the hill near my garden and out of sight when a shiny fleck of light slowly floated down from the sky, blown by the wind. It looked like nothing I had ever seen, so I snatched it from the air while running. Yet one of the reptiles caught sight of me. The creature was bounding towards me and I wasn't prepared for what happened next. I kept running, but I was much faster than I had ever been before. My feet barely touched the ground. It felt more like they were running on a thin layer of air slightly above the ground. Even with this new speed I barely stayed ahead of the thricorn, who also seemed to be running with a supernatural speed. I ran for days, even weeks, but I knew that if I stopped the lizard would kill me. I drank water from streams and ate what I could find, I don't know what force drove me to survive, I don't know why I didn't just lie down and wait for the inevitable. I finally grew weary shortly after reaching these canyons and that is when the beast caught up with me. Shortly after that, you appeared. You asked if I had seen agapate. Perhaps you can tell me if I have."

Reverie reached in her ragged garments and produced a tiny fleck of a stone that looked very similar to Sage's stone and Telle's horn. Though it was light blue in color whereas Sage's was a dark grey and Telle's horn was silver, they each glowed with the same inner light.

"To travel that distance, for that long, at that speed, is nothing short of miraculous. It would be impossible even for Telle. And by impossible, I mean he wouldn't come close to travelling that far in that amount of time," said Gad astonished and in great disbelief.

"It is the truth!" argued Reverie.

"Regardless of whether the story is true, what is true is that she holds a piece of the gate," stated Gad to Telle.

Telle had been silently observant for some time.

"Oh, so all of a sudden you know for sure what it looks like?" challenged Reverie.

"I said the gate, not agapate," said Gad "Or did you already know the gate was made of agapate?"

"No, I didn't, I don't even know what gate you are referring to," said Reverie defensively, "I thought you said, 'agapate'."

"Either way, no Reflection would have heard the word before," said Gad.

"Gad, weren't you listening to her, her entire town, everyone she loves is destroyed, show some compassion," said Sage with empathy.

"I overheard the creatures mention agapate when they arrived—that is how I heard it!" Reverie angrily snapped.

Gad stopped the interrogation, aware that he had been harsh on Reverie. In an attempt to make amends and after a long sigh, Gad said, "I'm sorry. Perhaps I have been too hard on you. I am only trying to be cautious. It saddens me to hear that Casusbelia is destroyed. I too, was in Casusbelia the day the gate was destroyed. I battled Lure, and in that battle I was thrown down to this world. I fled Casusbelia immediately as my Archeon brothers had been captured before the fall. The few of us Archeon that fell to this world in the battle, those Lure didn't find, have been working in this world ever since to regroup and establish a resistance to Lure. I met up with Telle shortly thereafter near the Lost Lakes."

Gad continued, "Very well, since you have that piece of agapate, I suppose I should explain what it does. While the full extent of agapate's power is still shrouded in mystery, it would seem that agapate takes on the power of whatever it first touched here on Earth after leaving Agapia. Agapate becomes an extension of the already created; as it was used by Alphega to create all. Sage's piece must have touched rock first, so it has the power of rock and earth, Telle's entered his equestrian brain and made it more knowledgeable, while giving him a useful weapon at the same time, yours it would seem met the air first, though, I'm not sure how. I would think it would have to touch something more than just air, perhaps your running had something to do with it, but as I said, agapate, and how it reacts with the things of this world, is still an enigma. Therefore, it would be wise for us to stick together. Powerful forces will try to take your piece from you, and take our piece from us. Our chance of success will be greater if we stick together."

"I may acquiesce, on one condition. You must go with me to see if my uncle is still alive in Aprioria," said Reverie.

"Aprioria, I'm not sure about that. That is one of the most faithless places in all the Wisprian World. I doubt we would find sympathy for our cause there. Telle, what says your wisdom?" asked Gad.

Once again Telle wrote in the clay with his horn.

FROM ABOVE THE PIECES FELL
NORTH AND SOUTH AND EAST AND WEST
ON EACH PATH WE WILL FIND THEM
NORTH AND SOUTH AND EAST AND WEST

SO WILL OUR FOE SEARCH AS WELL
NORTH AND SOUTH AND EAST AND WEST
TO BRING THE PIECES TO HIM

"I suppose that means we can go with you. Hmm…perhaps Aprioria may be exactly where we are supposed to search next," reasoned Gad. "I'll lead the way out of the Canyons. You and Sage can follow on Telle's back. Once we are on the other side, I'll need both of your input to help me discern the safest way to Aprioria."

Sage was happy that Reverie was coming along as she helped him onto Telle's back. Yet he was disturbed by her story and frightened for his own people.

"Gad you don't think the tribes of my people are in danger from Lure, do you? I mean, I don't want what happened at Casusbelia to happen at the foot of the Moaning Mountains. If you think they are in danger I think we should go back to help defend them."

Gad understood Sage's concern and as gentle as he could he said, "Sage, I would be lying to you if I told you your people weren't in danger. However, we are no match for Lure's forces at this point. We would only join them in defeat if we went back. We do not yet know the full extent of our enemy's power. But I do know we are not ready to challenge him."

The forces against them in their quest were indeed powerful, cunning, overwhelming, and undefeatable—as they would soon begin to fathom.

Sage hung his head in sorrow and disappointment at Gad's words. Once again he felt helpless and depressed. Reverie placed her hand on him for comfort. But Sage was not comforted. Furthermore, his ankle was quite swollen and sore from using it so heavily.

As the group was leaving, the thricorn let out a low bellow and died. Gad stopped and ran over to the dead reptile. Touching it again he said, "Freezing cold, this creature died of exposure to the cold." But to himself Gad was thinking over and over again about the fact that the creature had as much energy as it did. He thought about Reverie's story. Agapate gave her the power to run quickly for a long period of time. But what power allowed the thricorn to run for days in weather that should have killed it? Sage and Reverie weren't alarmed at Gad's explanation and were oblivious to his doubts, as he said nothing more to them, but continued leading the way. Gad however, now regretted revealing his knowledge of agapate to Reverie. And he was curious as to why she was so obstinate about hiding her wound. Yet, he wasn't the only suspicious one. Telle continued trotting along behind Gad, keeping one eye on the ground and one eye on Reverie.

"A prophet of Alphega, Telle is my name."

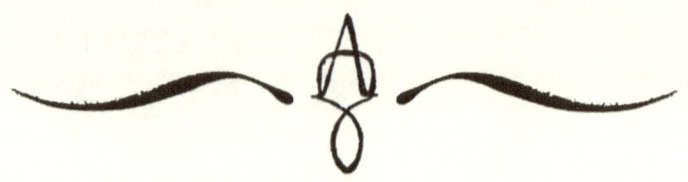

SCROLL 41

ORPHANED

al and Harmody were not in the woods long before they discovered the answers they were looking for. From atop one of the cottages, they saw a huge pale Archeskotos looking down on them. Before the pair could react, the creature leapt down upon them, Dal suffering most of the blow. Dal was picked up by his forearms and whirled around the creature's head before being slammed into the root-filled soil.

Harmody launched her spear in the direction of the shiny beast that was grappling with her father. It found its mark in the creature's neck, but without the result Harmody wanted. The empty eyes of the pale, gray beast glared at her and, with one motion, the creature slid the spear from its neck and split it in two across a nearby tree trunk. The paralyzing effects that a lilweed spear would normally have did not materialize. Furthermore, where any animal she had previously seen would have been greatly bleeding from such a neck wound, this extraordinary thing released a deep shade, more dense than the thickest black smoke, in place of blood. Even in the darkness, the shade that came from its neck was even darker. It was a palpable blackness that, were she in arms reach, she could hold in her hand.

Not slowed by this apparent wound, the creature spoke. With a voice that shifted back and forth from sounding like the clanging of swords to sounding like a soothing breeze on a warm day, the creature said, "You Reflection are so inferior. How fitting that those who are a reflection of His image should be so weak. Serve us, the Archeskotos, or be eliminated with the rest of your inferior kind. "

Both Harmody and Dal were stunned that the creature could speak. And there were times when the very sound that it made so soothed them that they wished it would continue speaking. But it did not. Unsatisfied with her lack of response, the Archeskotos charged at Harmody. With a spear in each hand she stuck the beast in either side of its torso, with the same effect as the previous spear. By now the creature had her on the ground grabbing her by the throat with both hands. Normally her throat would have been crushed instantly, but the Archeskotos paused when he saw the girl up close.

"You are a pretty weakling, aren't you?" said the Archeskotos debating what to do with his prey, his appearance was beginning to morph into that of a Reflection.

Harmody didn't respond before Dal had driven two more spears through the neck of the Archeskotos. The sulfurous, black shadow that seeped from the Archeskotos' neck briefly hovered around Harmody's face. But quickly the beast, having lost all resemblance to Reflection, turned on Dal and swung its huge arm, connecting squarely with Dal's chest stopping his heart and crushing his lungs simultaneously. Dal crumpled to the ground. Upon witnessing her father's murder, Harmody wailed at the top of her lungs, unleashing the unknown power of her lyric-less song.

Harmody anticipated a similar attack from the Archeskotos and she was fully prepared to join her father. But the attack never came. The beast never turned back around. He was standing completely still staring down at Dal's crumpled body. Perplexed, Harmody was as unmoving as her enemy. Several moments passed before she rushed to her father. She wrapped her arms around him and kissed his face in an effort to somehow revive him. It was clear that her father was dead. Immediately, Harmody buried her grief inside. There would be time for mourning, but that time was not now. She delicately, but laboriously slid her father underneath a nearby patch of bushes—she would come back for him after she had retribution.

Distant shrieks and screams were sounding from within the cottages scattered all around Nahar Kome'. The sound of splitting and crashing wood was heard as the marauding Archeskotos were tearing through doors ransacking the village. Harmody would not hide in the darkness; she was prepared to fight every one of them if that is what it took. Still unaware of the power in her voice, she was planning to foolishly rush into the fray throwing her spears, hoping to have more success than before. Then suddenly she heard a familiar voice among the screams.

"Dad! 'Mody!" Melony yelled in the distance.

Harmody stopped immediately and turned toward the direction of home. "Mel!" she tried to yell back, but only a hoarse whisper came forth; her voice was too much in shock from the might it had unleashed.

She was bounding through the bushes and trees, frequently leaving the path to shortcut through the brush. She wasn't the only one running toward Melony's voice. Three Archeskotos also heard the girl scream and were all converging on the Cantiq's cottage. One of the beasts tore through the window and the other two shattered the front door; a piece of it hitting Melony who was still crumpled on the floor, but was now startled and alert, fearing the new presence of the Archeskotos. Even the Archeskotos were shocked at the scene inside the cottage and the bizarre creature on the floor. They briefly thought perhaps Melony was part of their raiding party.

"What are you? Do you serve the light-giver, Lure and his Archeskotos?" asked one Archeskotos in a voice that was like metal mingled with honey.

Melony didn't answer as the three evil bodies towered over her.

"Answer slave!" demanded one of the three, striking Melony on the back of her head, his own head bent over, for the ceiling to the cabin was too low for the Archeskotos.

Another Archeskotos bent down to examine Hebel's body.

"Don't touch her!" shouted Melony, her voice having returned since she stilled Bosheth.

But the Archeskotos didn't stop. By this time, Harmody was making her way up to the doorway and, by the dim light of the dying fire, could see Melony on the floor with her mother and the three towering Archeskotos. Harmody was hoarsely yelling for Bosheth to do something, unaware she was unresponsive. As the Archeskotos reached his hand across Melony's body to touch her mother, she grasped hold of it and once again let out a sound that made them all like statues, unable to move.

"*That is my mother!*" Melony said with an unmatched vocal power.

Harmody had arrived to witness the sound and the effect it had on those present. She also realized what she had done with her own voice moments before. She was astonished at the occurrence, but all the more shocked to see her mother lying dead on the floor. The image would certainly be with her the rest of her life. Still, she ran to Melony and embraced her deeply.

"Mel, I'm here. Are you hurt, they didn't hurt you did they?" Harmody asked, her voice nearly back.

"Bosheth killed mother! Where did she go and what about the creatures? Look out for them, don't let them take mother!" said Melony in a soft, scratchy voice.

"I'm so glad to hear you speak again, Mel. I didn't know how I was going to help you, when you weren't speaking to anyone. Bosheth and the creatures are still here. But they are paralyzed," Harmody answered.

"Did you get them with your spear?" whispered Melony.

"No, it would seem you paralyzed them with your voice and the strange sound that came out of it. I can make the sound too and I also stilled one of the Archeskotos," explained Harmody.

"You mean when I cried out? How can a sound paralyze someone?" Melony wondered.

"I can't explain it. But I can't explain many of the things that have happened as of late. I can only tell you what I saw, and for some reason the sound does not affect us, except to make speaking difficult for a short time following," Harmody explained.

" ...Mel I have something else to tell you," said Harmody, her throat tightening as she fought back the tears.

"...Father...," said Harmody as Melony, sensing the truth, hugged Harmody tighter.

"Father is dead," Harmody eeked out before bursting into tears.

"One of those horrible creatures," Harmody continued groping for breath.

Melony was stunned.

And the two sisters sat weeping and holding each other on the floor of their cabin. Meanwhile, the terror continued all around them. Several minutes passed and the girls didn't speak or move, they just sobbed.

"We have to take them to Lithosis. We have to give them a proper burial," said Melony with a strength she didn't know she had. "Where is father?" she asked.

"Back out there. Yes, I will bring him here," Harmody said.

"Or should we take mother to him? We have to get to Lithosis, which means taking the Great Road. Is Father nearer to the Great Road? How are we going to carry them? We need a cart and horse," reasoned Melony.

"There are more of those things out there. I don't see how we'll ever make it to the road," said Harmody.

"But our voices; can't we just continue to use them to fight them off? If what you said is true, then no matter how many of them there are, we can paralyze them and go on our way," said Melony.

"That is an idea. Still how can we move them? I don't know if there is an animal still alive out there," said Harmody.

Nevertheless, the girls, and their resourcefulness, were determined to find a way. Suddenly, Harmody had an idea, "If we can get them to the river, we can take the river to Aprioria. Maybe everything is still fine there. At least hopefully someone there will be able to help us."

This seemed like the best option to Melony as well. In the opposite direction of the Whistling Wood was the main branch of the River Brio. There were many small, crude docks lining the bank in and around Nahar Kome´. Harmody trusted she would be able to lead Melony, with both of them carrying their mother through the woods, directly to the river, hoping they would find some kind of boat when they arrived.

First, Harmody took a sharp cutting stone from beside the fire and went to her parent's bed. Taking a blanket from the bed, she cut a long narrow piece, the length of the blanket. Then she grabbed some provisions from around the cabin and placed them in a satchel, draping the satchel, as well as the water skins that held the agapate water, over Melony. Harmody took every remaining spear from the house and placed them in her quiver. She also put the cutting stone in her waistband. She tied the long strand of cloth she had cut around one of her wrists and the other end around Melony's wrist, to help guide her. With the remainder of the blanket, she wrapped her mother's head with care.

"Are you ready, Mel? I have gathered as many supplies as we can carry. Are you sure you are up to this?" Harmody questioned.

"Do I have another choice? Today started out so wonderfully, resting by the gentle waters. How quickly our lives were altered. We are forever changed. Our parents murdered, our home abandoned. What will become of us?" wondered Melony, as her throat tightened in an effort to fight back tears.

"We will survive as long as we can. We will seek out justice for their deaths. Beyond that, I cannot say," Harmody said. "But we must go. I need you to help carry mother."

Harmody and Melony each reached underneath one of their mother's shoulders. It took all of their might to lift the lifeless woman from the floor of the cabin, but they succeeded. Each of the girls held one of Hebel's arms across their upper backs. They walked with Hebel's feet and legs dragging the ground. The long strand of cloth connecting the girl's wrists, though not made for the purpose, served to help support and distribute the weight of the body. Harmody led the way through the destroyed doorway of the cabin, turning sideways to accommodate Melony and Hebel.

Once outside and away from the fires of the village, the darkness was again, blinding. Harmody slowly found a path through the roots, trees and shrubs, giving verbal guidance to Melony all the while. Fortunately, they did not see any more Archeskotos on the clumsy trek down to the river. The bank was a few feet above the water and the girls had to find a way down to the water level. They were unfamiliar with this area as they usually went to their tranquil spot that was more accessible. If there was any good to come out of the situation, it was that, because there were only a few places on the bank that were down level with the water, they were sure to find transportation. And they did.

The small, modest raft wasn't the transportation the sisters would have initially hoped for, but, as it was their only choice, they were glad to have it. Getting Hebel's body onto the raft would prove a most difficult task. The water became deep close to the shore, so Melony had to hold onto Hebel while Harmody pulled the raft onshore entirely. From there, they placed their mother's body onto the raft. It was a difficult decision, but in order to retrieve their father's body, the girls had to leave their mother on the raft.

Harmody then led the way back to Dal's body. The girls were almost to him when, in the darkness, Harmody saw a small, squatty creature run across the path they were traveling. Harmody didn't want to frighten Melony so she said nothing, but quickened the pace. They came to their father's body and it was all Harmody could do to not abandon everything and fall on the ground sobbing over her father. Her love for her sister kept her focused. She and Melony bent down to pick him up, but when Harmody looked up there was the creature she had seen moments before. Its face was grotesque and its eyes were blacker than the darkness surrounding them. It was hissing and laughing at the girls, mocking their loss. Harmody didn't give it another thought. She opened her mouth and blared her voice at the baby Dephilim. Melony was startled. The baby Dephilim didn't move, its face stilled in a hideous expression.

Quickly, using the same technique as before, the girls carried their father's body back to the raft. All the while, they heard a variety of screams and other strange sounds. Harmody kept seeing the face of the baby Dephilim in her mind. She thought how she had never seen anything so wretched, and she decided that her sister's blindness was a blessing in certain instances.

Once the second body was placed on the raft, Harmody untied the band of cloth from her wrist and had Melony sit on the raft. She then noticed that there were no poles or paddles . for the raft, probably to dissuade thieves from stealing it. Furthermore, the raft had but one rope, this used to affix it to a dock or tree. Harmody found herself wishing she had brought rope from home, but that wasn't one of the necessities she had thought of. The rope would have helped secure Dal and Hebel's bodies to the raft, for the currents in the River Brio were violent and it would be treacherous enough for Melony and Harmody to stay atop the raft without worrying about their parent's bodies.

Harmody ran back up the steep bank to search for a fallen limb that would make a suitable pole. She found a large knotty limb quickly enough, but had wandered a little distance from the raft in the search. Then she heard rustling in the leaves that came from several different directions. The scurrying was as if a plague of small woodland animals was quickly moving in her direction; yet, Harmody knew better than to suspect animals. Her voice hadn't returned since the baby Dephilim she halted, so with her limb in hand she swiftly made her way back to the raft.

She grabbed the end of the raft and tried to push it into the river. However, the weight on the raft was bogging it down into the mud of the bank. Unwilling to let Melony off of the raft to help, Harmody continued to lift and push, all the while her feet were slipping in the slick mud. She hadn't budged the raft, when, from behind, one of the young, rapidly-developing Dephilim jumped on her shoulders yanking out fistfuls of her hair as it gnashed its teeth at her. Harmody reached behind her and grabbed the miniature Dephilim by the head and hurled it into the rushing river. She had no sooner done this when three others leaped onto her from the edge above. Hearing the commotion and the struggle of her sister, Melony sang out, *"Leave my sister alone!"*

Several small Dephilim, including the ones latched onto Harmody, fell to the ground as if someone had hurled tiny statues at the girls. Little did they know that these were the newly birthed offspring of many of their now deceased friends and neighbors in Nahar Kome´. Had they not escaped the Archeskotos, they too, would have ended up mothers of such abominations.

Harmody realized that Melony's voice had at least afforded them a little time, "Melony give me your wrist again." Harmody tied the band around her wrist then asked Melony to help her shove the raft into the river. The raft moved into the water and the girls hopped on. Harmody had not forgotten to grab the limb she would use as a pole.

The current was swift, but for the time being, the water was flat and the course straight. Harmody peered ahead into the darkness as she undertook the daunting task of steering the raft in blackness. She couldn't see more than a few meters in front of her, so the best she hoped for was to keep the raft in the center of the river and avoid hitting anything.

After a while Harmody adjusted to the intensity of the situation and began to reflect over the tragic recent events. Everything seemed surreal: her sister's condition, the invading creatures, witnessing her father's death, and now floating down a dark river on a small raft with the bodies of her parents.

"'Mody, who is Lure, the so-called light-giver?" Melony asked, breaking the silence.

"I've never heard of such a name," Harmody answered, intrigued.

"The creatures that were in the cabin with me mentioned the name," Melony continued.

"If this Lure is the light-giver, then where is the light? And if Lure is associated with the, what did they say? Archeskotos? Or those other strange little creatures, then Lure better hope our paths don't cross. For the vengeance and hate that are welling up in me will eventually be loosed on someone," said Harmody.

Though the girls had not mentioned it, both were wondering how long the trip was to Aprioria, knowing they didn't have long before the bodies of their parents would become rather unpleasant. Melony was pondering these questions and others when she finally, for the first time since her transformation, fell asleep. Harmody was not afforded the luxury of sleep as she was the only one who could keep watch and steer the raft.

More than two days passed as they floated down the River Brio. Harmody was exhausted and fought to keep her eyelids from closing. "Mel," she said, "We are going to have to pull ashore for a little while so I can rest. I'll need you to listen closely and keep watch with your ears, alright?"

"How far do you think we have come?" asked Melony.

"I'm not sure, but I know I've never been this far down river. The Whistling Wood is no longer to our right. The banks are more steep and becoming rockier," answered Harmody.

Soon Harmody saw a flat bank of small stones jutting out from the bank above. Here she brought the raft ashore and rested. There were a few trees on the bank overhead, and their leaves rustling in the breeze and the sound of the river was all that Melony could hear. After positioning herself onto the rocks in such a way that she had a place for both arms and her head, and so that none of the stones were jabbing her in the side or back, Harmody fell into a deep sleep.

It wasn't a sound that caught Melony's attention first, rather it was a smell.

"'Mody, wake up, I think someone is coming. I smell something burning."

Groggily, yet still quickly, Harmody wrestled to her feet. She could see with her eyes what Melony could only smell. Coming down the river towards them were what looked like several small boats with passengers, lit with many torches. Harmody's instinct was to call up river to them for help. But once she thought it through, she realized they may be hostile, so she decided to wait until they were closer. For lack of a better plan, she scattered some of the provisions among the rocks and had Melony cover her unique features and lie down as if she was as dead as their parents. Harmody also spread out on the ground but kept her gaze on the approaching boats.

As they came closer, Harmody could see that it was three canoes, pulling a large raft, at least five times the size of the sisters' raft. On the large raft was a huge, jagged block of a clear stone. Harmody had never seen anything like it before. The silhouettes of the passengers also revealed to Harmody they weren't Reflection, yet they weren't Archeskotos either. They were hunched over and their foreheads were big and jutted out nearly as far as their noses. In the firelight, she saw their bodies were covered from head to toe with coarse hair. Though she had never seen a Sarxan before, from all that she had heard of them, she knew these were Sarxans rowing the canoes.

Harmody couldn't decide whether or not to trust them and she was running out of time as they were almost upon the beached raft. She was about to stand when, from behind the stone, an Archeskotos stood. He was clearly the one in charge and the Sarxans seemed to be loyal to him.

"Row faster you lazy Sarxans! Aprioria is a long way yet," he ordered. "Lure has never been one to be patient. He will be missing his marbled diamond! If you row fast enough, Lure may give you a position on one of his great warships. He has plans to—"

"Hood, my master, there seems to be a wreckage up ahead," one of the Sarxans yelled back.

"Wreckage? Slow the row. What can you see? Wait, I sense agapate nearby. Stop rowing!" commanded Hood.

The canoes pulled up alongside Harmody's raft. The parent's bodies were still on the raft, and Harmody was on the ground, in between the raft and Melony's position further ashore.

"I'll handle this, mind the boat. Bring me alongside that raft," Hood said in a razor-sharp voice.

The Sarxans did as they were told and the large platform carrying the piece of marbled diamond dwarfed Harmody's raft as it bumped into it. Even in her fear, Harmody couldn't help but notice the beauty of the large marbled gem. She knew she could use her voice, but she wasn't sure she could reach all of them with the sound and she feared others were nearby. So she decided to hide instead.

Hood was at least as large as the Archeskotos she faced with her father. Unlike the other Archeskotos, Hood had shiny black armor that covered his torso and a skirt of armor down to the middle of his thighs. His forearms and shins were also protected. The armor was not organic. Harmody thought Hood must have had it assembled in Aprioria, for she was unaware of any other people who were as adept at such craft. Also, appropriate for his name, the Archeskotos had a black hood that was attached to the back of the neck opening of his armor and covered a majority of his head. When Hood turned, Harmody caught glimpse of a large sickle slung across his back.

Harmody almost abandoned her plan when Hood tossed and slung the bodies of her parents all over the raft. She wanted so much to save what dignity they had left in death, yet she knew that making herself known could endanger Melony and herself. Hood was feverishly looking for the agapate, though Harmody didn't even know what agapate was; she had never heard the word until Hood uttered it. From her current position, she was well out of the torchlight, as was Melony.

Hood recklessly looked around the raft for a few more moments before giving up and returning to the task at hand. "Nothing but rotting corpses; get back to rowing!" he ordered.

Harmody watched breathlessly as they drifted out of sight. Once they were gone she moved to her parents bodies and began gently positioning them on the raft, "Mel, I don't know how much longer we can keep Mother and Father with us. The river is unsafe and you heard that creature say Aprioria is a long way yet; and then from there even further to Lithosis."

Harmody thought for a moment then said, "There are rocky cliffs all around us. We could maybe make them a private tomb somewhere along this river. I know it isn't what they deserve—"

"You're right, it isn't," said Melony.

"What other choice do we have?"

"We continue down the river until we reach Aprioria."

"And what if there are more creatures? And I didn't want to say it, but their bodies are beginning to smell. Is that how you think they want to be remembered?"

"No!" and realizing the situation Melony began to sob again.

Harmody moved to comfort her sister, "They are gone. Holding on to them for a proper burial was a worthy cause, but we can't make it to Lithosis. So now we need to let them be at peace."

Agreeing with her twin, Melony asked, "I can't see, are you sure the cliffs around us are secure? How can we make a tomb or get them up there?"

"I'll help you," said a soothing voice from the dark bank above them.

Warily, Harmody sprang to her feet. She had heard a similar sounding voice from the Archeskotos. "Show yourself," she said sternly, in an effort to hide her fear.

While she was still awaiting a response, what looked to be an Archeskotos leapt from the bank above and landed in front of her. Its eyes were like amber torches as they were all that pierced the surrounding darkness. As best she could tell, the outer covering of this one was a different shade than the others she had seen, it looked to be blonde colored; like the color of honey or perfectly toasted bread. When she got over the initial shock of how quickly it had confronted her, and freed herself from the momentary trance that the brilliant eyes had put her in, she did the only thing she knew to do—she sang out in terror.

"You can sing?" he said in response.

Harmody was speechless, not only from the normal exhaustion that accompanied her power, but also out of disbelief. She wondered if she no longer had her unique power.

"I thought only those from Agapia could sing," the Agapian creature continued, his tone sincere, but the sound of his voice was deep, and intimidating. "Please don't look so frightened. I will not harm you. I saw you hiding from Hood and how he treated your parents. I'm sorry. I truly only wanted to help you."

"Harmody, what is happening? Are you there?" Melony asked, her voice quivering.

"Yes, I am still here," came a raspy reply from Harmody.

The towering figure moved in to aid Harmody, but she quickly withdrew to hold her sister. "Do not touch us, if you come one step closer I will fight you to the death," warned a still hoarse Harmody as she drew a spear.

"Please put away your weapon. I am Zimrawth. I also can sing. If you do not want my help, I will come no closer."

"Leave us," said Harmody coldly, noticing several patches of what looked to be singed places on the limbs of Zimrawth.

"I will go back to my position on the bank. But be warned, there will be many more boats going to and from Aprioria. Lure is using the city as his central fortress. I would not recommend venturing there."

With that, Zimrawth leapt back onto the upper bank and sat looking down upon the river and the twins. His eyes were like two fireflies hovering in the dark air above them. Harmody continued to hold Melony as she debated what to do next. *This creature surely could not be trusted, he is one of the enemy,* she thought to herself. *Yet, if we leave he could follow us without us knowing and kill us in our sleep. Why does he offer his help?* For many moments she contemplated. She noticed his ears were small in relation to the rest of his head, and his nose did not protrude forth from his face to the degree that a Reflection's nose did. Inconspicuously she would cut her eyes in the direction of Zimrawth to see if he was still there, trying not to let him catch her looking. He was still there.

"Why did you offer your help?" she said finally in a loud voice.

"May I come down and tell you?"

"Yes."

Zimrawth again leapt down to the twin's level and said, "I know not how much you know of what is happening in this world. But undoubtedly you have some idea of the evil that has besieged it. I was part of that evil—a coward. I feared Lure. He is the leader of this devastating attack. His aggressiveness and intimidation bid me join him instead of fight him. But little did I realize how dark and terrible his plans were. I would rather have remained captured, a noble Archeon, than to roam free allied with one so vile. So I deserted the Archeskotos; for that is what they are now, those who were once Archeon but rebelled. I doubt I can ever undo the evil I have assisted in carrying out. But I must try. Alphega, the all-seeing, and full of grace and mercy, may yet find a way to forgive me for my faltering if I can now aid the cause of good. You happened to be the first I have come across that survived the initial annihilation. If I can begin by helping you in whatever way I can, then I will be taking a step in the right direction—and the path to redemption, like all journeys, begins with a single step."

"'If you do not want my help, I will come no closer.'"

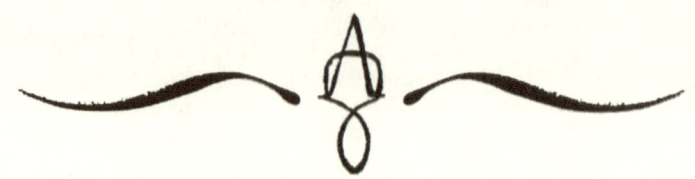

THE ICAEMOTH

nimus Asaleutos had never before experienced loss on such a level as in recent dark days. The three dearest loves of his life were dead before him. Guided by trying to do My will, he never envisioned My will would be so devastating—and he was right.

My perfect will was for none of My creation in Agapia or Wispria to ever perish. But My perfect will was also for liberty. I gave My creation freedom to choose their path. Unfortunately, most were not like Animus. From the beginning, Reflection and all of the other creatures of the Wisprian World sought a selfish path—this led to destruction. Likewise, in Agapia, this selfishness was fully exemplified in Lure's rebellion. Witnessing Animus in such pain made Me wish that I had not tied my hands, and I vowed that when this first war was over, I would never tie them again.

What Animus didn't realize, and rightly so for it was little consolation at the time, was that his seeking of My will, his unselfishness, would help to fight the war against Lure and the forces that killed his family. For, had he gone with Har, he would not have been there in this moment with his family, he would not have found out about their death for some time, he would not have found the agapate and he would have met the end that Har and the rest of the men did. And had he not gone after them to learn where they were going, had he stayed at home completely, he would have perished with his family. You see, as it turns out, though it brought much pain, Animus left at precisely the time he had to; though he would never understand that, as such omniscience was beyond him.

Yet for now, Animus had to lay his family to rest. The peoples of the northern lands did not bury their loved ones, for food was often scarce and beasts would dig up their graves, the cold ground preserving the bodies. They also lived too great a distance from Lithosis and the Sheol Caverns to take their bodies there. Therefore, Almachorans cremated their dead.

Lithosis was the most glorious and grand Reflection city; its grandeur paid for by the deaths of many of the inhabitants of the lands and towns that surrounded the well-fortified city. Lithosians had turned death into a lucrative business. The Sheol Caverns, used as burial tombs, were located to the east of Lithosis. To the east and north of the Caverns were the Muerte Mountains, full of lodestone deposits, but with nearly impassible cliffs. Therefore, all those who wished to bury their dead in the safety of the Caverns had to pass through Lithosis. As it happened, because of the long life-spans of those who dwelled in the Wisprian World, death was a most significant event, and the final resting place of an individual was of great importance. The Sheol Caverns were considered the preeminent location to be interred.

The people of Lithosis were not evil, but their kings were greedy, and the ever increasing prices for passage to the Sheol Caverns had been the cause of many battles between Lithosis and the other realms of Wispria over the years. Yet, Lithosis was the most naturally fortified city on the Earth. It sat atop an enormous plateau of granite stone that stretched for miles and was nearly impossible to scale, except for the Great Road that was cut out of the stone and the only feasible entrance to the walled city. The Great Road, later named the Highway of the King, originally went from Lithosis to Aprioria (the primary exporter to Lithosis), but eventually it was expanded to stretch all the way to Kowf Kome´. The large granite outcropping was surrounded on nearly all sides by Lake Lithos, formed from rain running off the smooth granite slopes. A vast land bridge was made across a narrow portion of the Lake from the stone that was chiseled out of the granite to make the Highway of the King. If the natural defenses weren't enough, in time a wall was built around Lithosis, and another town lay at the entrance of the land bridge. Mizpah, as it was called, was a small city of several tall towers inhabited by former Lithosians in order to watch for potential invaders.

Animus had never seen Lithosis or its surroundings, but how he wished he could safely bury his family there. As it was, he knew what he must do. He gently laid his wife on their bed. Right beside her, on either side, he placed his son and daughter. Through tears, he kissed his daughter. He kissed his son. Coming to his wife, beautiful even in death, he beheld her in his eyes, then held her in his arms one last time—a final kiss.

His pain unbearable, he cried out, "Alphega, please! Bring them back to me. Stop me from carrying this out. Let them live!"

His only answer came from outside the cabin. A painful, coarse, wail came from his cave bear. The animal sensed the overwhelming burden his master was bearing, and had been leaning against the wall, as close to his master as he could be.

After a long quiet silence Animus underwent the greatest test of his strength he had ever experienced; he walked out of the room and out of the cabin. Taking with him only a few provisions and his axe, Animus shut the door of his cabin. The fire smoldered beside the bed, and Animus went behind his cabin to chop more wood. He chopped two pieces with the same result as he always had. However, when he went to wield his axe a third time, he noticed the blade's orange midsection. Having only seen the color once before, recently, when Palat had shown him his stone, Animus stood perplexed. His only assumption was the correct one; that somehow in his frenzy he had smashed it with his axe. He even wondered if the stone had caused the fire in the first place. The third log lay before him. Lifting his axe above his head, with all of his strength he lay into the log with the purpose of setting it ablaze. Ablaze it went—and Animus was in awe of his newfound power.

He took the burning log and the other two and set them at the foot of the front door to his cabin. In a display of anguish, torment and release, Animus proceeded to strike the door and

exterior walls of the cabin with the axe. Everywhere he struck flame followed. Within minutes the cabin was fully engulfed.

With Oze at his side, Animus stood back and watched, with tears streaming down his face, the funeral pyre of his family. Unblinking, he stood. Smoke swirling about his nostrils and eyes, he stood, his gaze focused. Staring into the flames he resolved he would not rest until he had justice on whatever had done this to his dear ones. He watched as the roof collapsed. Until there was naught but smoldering embers and ash, he watched.

And I watched. I watched with My beloved Animus. I watched as his loved ones were reduced to ash and dust. And I remembered that dust. That very dust, that was so precious to Animus, would one day be remembered by Me. I vowed to use the dust of this faithful family, in another age, to begin anew.

Solemnly, Animus walked into the center of the embers; his thick wet boots allowed him a few moments of time to stand on the hot coals. He was standing beside where the bed would have been when he bent down and grasped one of the coals. Through his damp gloves the heat from the ember still penetrated. Animus pulled back the fur and leather armor from his chest and directly over his heart—where his greatest pain was originating—he pressed the burning ember. His countenance did not change. No sound came from him. The mental and emotional anguish of this night would forever stay with him and Animus wanted to have a physical symbol of the inner pain he would carry with him from that moment.

He then hurried out of the cinders and onto Oze's back, determined to follow the tracks they had seen. He knew Har needed him and feared he and his men would not live to tell Animus of their trials. Yet, at the moment, there was a danger tantamount to the Dephilim and Archeskotos and Animus was off to face it, though he knew not what he would face. More than an hour had passed since Animus first left the gate to Sakoden Kome´ and he hoped the tracks still remained.

Arriving back at the series of broken bearingian trees, Animus did not see any footprints. Therefore, he and his bear followed the broken trees, realizing that something had to have broken them. They hadn't followed them long when they came to a clearing and there were no more trees, just a sea of white slopes. There was no trace of his quarry. The now heavy snowfall would erase Oze's tracks in a few minutes, and Animus knew whichever direction his enemy had gone would certainly be hidden from them now.

"Alphega, guide me. Lead me in the direction I need to go," Animus prayed.

He then chose a direction and started downhill towards a group of snow-covered hills. In the distance, directly in front of him, he saw a herd of northern caribou. Animus knew it wouldn't be long before Oze's presence would send them running. And Animus was partly right, Oze did frighten them, but they didn't run. To Animus' amazement, they took a few running leaps and gently lifted off the ground into the air, but they never landed. They floated dozens of feet off the ground. Animus stood in amazement. He thought he must be mentally fatigued by the recent tragedy, and imagining things; but Oze was gazing up in the air as well, equally confused. The two had hunted caribou many times, but never had they flown away.

Animus and Oze watched as they began to disappear into the darkness. Yet, Animus was still fascinated by the sight, so he motioned for Oze to follow after them. The large bear fur that covered Animus' shoulders flapped in the cold air as the bear sprinted. The snow froze to the tips of Animus's beard and eyelashes, making it even more difficult to see. The caribou had almost entirely vanished when a stream of ice shot up at one of them from somewhere below. Frozen solid, the poor animal fell rapidly to the snowy slope, the impact driving the caribou deep into the snow. Again, Animus was astonished at what he witnessed. But before he could analyze what had caused the icy blast, another caribou was hit, then another. Those that were left in the dark sky began flying back in the direction of Animus.

Animus tried to watch them, but at the same time wanted to find what they were fleeing from. He didn't have to search for long. There before him, towering in the black distance was a giant of ice. Not nearly the height of a bearingian tree, though taller than most of the lesser trees, the giant was not like any living thing Animus had seen. It only resembled a living creature in that it obviously had legs and arms and a head, but there was no hair, skin, flesh, muscle or other fiber that would suggest a living being, rather, the entire body seemed to be solid, jagged, pointy, ice. The ice giant spoke not. Instead when it opened its mouth a wide flow of slushy ice shot out in Animus' direction. Oze lurched out of the way of the blast which followed closely behind the bear's dodge.

Animus did not even question, but knew in his heart that this was the thing that murdered his family. Still, Animus wisely understood that his desire for justice, though it could inspire his natural abilities to another level, did not make him omnipotent, and this behemoth may be more than he and Oze could handle. However, this fact would not keep him from trying.

Oze circled behind their icy foe before it had time to move, for if it had a weakness it was that it was not nimble. Animus then jumped onto the creature from behind, landing just midway up its left leg. From there he climbed the pointy shards of ice that stuck out all over the creature. He made it all the way to the top of its back and from there he could see Oze was a great distance below him. Oze meanwhile was on two legs swiping madly at the legs of the ice giant, with little avail. A few of the cave bear's claws broke off in the rough icy beast. Animus' presence did not go unnoticed. However, there was little the ill-dexterous creature could do to swat him off, for the creature's fingers, hands, and arms, if they could be called that, were large and stiff and did not have the ability to grasp.

Standing upon the icy shoulder of his adversary, Animus lifted high Azarmuth, remembering the fiery power it now possessed. He put all of his will into his stroke and came down mightily in between the neck and shoulder of the behemoth. Flame leaped out of the wound, melting the portion of the creature that was struck, only to be snuffed out by the water created by the melting. The cold giant's wound was frozen back together within seconds as if Animus had never harmed it. Disheartened by the lack of effect the blow had on the giant, Animus paused just long enough to be jostled from atop his enemy. He fell to the ground, but the snow kept him from injury. Oze rushed to his aid and Animus climbed onto the bear's back.

The Icaemoth, as Animus would come to call it, had him bewildered. Animus did not know how he was going to defeat this enemy. Little did he know that a large piece of agapate was responsible for creating the Icaemoth, and furthermore bestowing it with the power to wield ice. Ignoring his better judgment, Animus decided to continue to battle. He turned Oze back in the direction of the Icaemoth and charged at it. The long, hard arm of the Icaemoth swiped at the bear and rider knocking them several meters back across the snow. While Animus could see that even his hardy companion Oze was shaken up from the blow, he suddenly had hope and a plan. He spotted a thicket of trees, not bearingian, much smaller, but evergreen, a few meters from them. Though the Icaemoth wouldn't burn, the trees would, and he thought maybe a forest fire would be enough to overwhelm the Icaemoth's power.

Instinctively, Animus leapt back on top of Oze and guided him toward the trees. The Icaemoth followed closely behind, determined to catch them in his frosty breath. Once in the center of the thicket, Animus dismounted and began cutting down trees with all of his might and speed, aided by the flame from Azarmuth. Animus set three trees ablaze then proceeded to cut them down. By the time the first tree fell, the Icaemoth was among the trees headed toward them. Animus realized he hadn't the time to continue felling trees, instead he went about the business of setting them all on fire. He would strike one and immediately it was burning, then he would continue on deeper in the wood and strike another. He moved in a crooked path to keep the Icaemoth guessing as to his whereabouts; the darkness and the trees aiding his cause of concealment.

"He put all of his will into his stroke."

The forest was heating up, as a good number of trees were fully involved. The one felled tree had already set a few others on fire. Realizing that the Icaemoth was too easily avoiding the burning trees, Animus knew he needed to bring one of the fiery ones down on top of his adversary. He circled back around behind the Icaemoth, unnoticed. Then he put all his efforts into one tree situated at the back of the Icaemoth.

"Alphega, give me strength! Help me bring Your justice to this wicked creature for the deaths of my family!" roared Animus as he tenaciously buried his axe deep into the closest tree trunk, with a burst of flame.

With the help of the flames and a final push from his cave bear friend, the tree fell directly on the Icaemoth; striking him directly between where his two shoulder blades would be. The creature stumbled forward catching itself on another blazing tree. This however, did not bring pause to Animus' attack. Instead of watching victoriously as the Icaemoth melted, he continued deeper in the woods setting more trees on fire in an effort to fully trap his enemy.

Yet, in the darkness, he didn't realize that he was also trapping himself. The wood was engulfed so he could no longer travel back through it, and in a moment he would come to the other side of the forest and a steep, snowy slope. Through the fire, Animus could no longer see the Icaemoth, but he did see his predicament. He continued to set fire to the trees until he came to the steep edge.

"This way, Oze, follow me," said Animus, knowing that the slope was too steep for him to ride down on top of his bear.

The bear crept to the edge. For all his adventures in the wild,

Oze had never attempted anything so treacherous. Gingerly, he put one foot in front of the other, waiting to see what his master would do. Animus glanced back at the forest for a sign of his ultimate victory. The flames and smoke were within arms reach, and he waited until the last possible second. Burning branches were falling all around and the thick smoke was making the darkness even blacker, and breathing even harder. Finally, with Oze at the edge hesitantly feigning taking his first step, Animus came to the edge holding Azarmuth with the axehead pointed toward the ground. He sat on the cold ground, dug the axe into the snow and shoved off down the mountainside.

The snowy, rocky slope bruised the backs of his legs as he slid down, nearly uncontrollably. He would slow the speed of his slide by pulling back on the axe handle and digging Azarmuth deeper in the snow. Meanwhile, Oze had willingly, though cautiously, followed his master, but with less control. On all fours, Oze spun in circles all the way down. He nearly clobbered Animus when he sped past him on the slope. More than one exposed rock nicked Oze and he roared out in aggravation.

The top of the ledge and the fire were entirely out of sight when Animus heard the loud whistling sound he had heard outside the bearingian gate of Sakoden Kome´. What he did not see was the dripping wet, sloppy, piecemeal Icaemoth as it stretched out his arms as if casting an icy spell. A blast of cold wind originating from the Icaemoth and blowing out in all directions from it, instantly puffed out the forest fire and at the same time froze the trees. The wind returned to the Icaemoth, healing the melting wounds the behemoth had received from the lethal flames.

Animus reached the bottom in one piece, but he was not fully relieved to be at the bottom. He deduced that the sound he heard was the Icaemoth and feared that he had not vanquished his adversary. He found Oze nearby, licking his wounds and in a particularly grumpy mood. Animus would have returned to best his opponent, but fortunately for him, the slope would be far too difficult for him and his bear to climb. He knew he had to continue on, but he was hesitant to leave behind the colossal ice-beast that killed his family. Animus had no idea what to do or which direction to head. So he and his bear continued in the easiest direction the mountains would provide, south. All the while the uncertainty of justice being done on the Icaemoth would nip at the back of his mind. He told himself he would return when he was better prepared; this thought at least justified his heading away from the Icaemoth for the time being.

The two trudged silently ahead. Animus walked beside his tired, injured friend and thought of his family. The falling snow swirled all around them in the biting wind. Shelter would have been an imminent necessity for anyone else, but the fire in Animus' heart warmed him and bid him keep hiking. The valley they walked in was narrow and white mountains hemmed them in on either side; that much Animus could see through the dark. The land was silent, bleak, as if the life had been taken out of it. A nearly frozen stream barely trickled a few meters away from them. Animus determined they would follow its path for the time being.

Several hours had passed when Oze walked up alongside his master and nudged him in the side with his head. This was the signal to Animus that the bear was hungry. Animus hadn't thought about food, but now that he did, he also needed nourishment.

"Do you smell something?" he asked Oze. "Run get us some dinner if you want, then. Just don't go off too far."

Having heard the best words spoken from Animus in some time, Oze bounded off with newfound energy. Animus found some branches scattered on the ground and gathered them into a pile near the stream. He found a short, fat branch he used as a seat. Meanwhile, he used his axe to start a fire; a task which he had never found easier.

Animus had just kneeled to pray when one of the flying caribou landed and bowed down beside Animus. With a rack of antlers with twenty-four points, this was the patriarch of the herd. The great caribou was carrying an object on one of its antlers which he placed on the snow beside Animus' bowed head. Opening his eyes, Animus was surprised to see, not only the caribou with its hoofs that sparkled with flecks of light, but also, his daughter's whistle that was dangling from its leather chord on the antler.

"My daughter lost this some time ago, and was greatly upset," Animus said.

Given to Penielle by Alaise on her last birthday, the whistle was made from a hollowed-out vine of the Almachora Rose. The thorns were removed, and the holes they left were used to play the instrument that was also hand painted by Alaise. Animus gently placed the whistle in his mouth and blew with nostalgia. When he blew, the most unique, delicate and high pitched sound came from the whistle. Animus remembered the sound well. To his further amazement, when the sound was made, the entire herd of flying caribou assembled above him, as if awaiting his command. Animus realized the noble animals were making a treaty with him. Though in the past Animus had hunted their kind, they watched from afar as Animus fought the beast that killed several of their herd, and realized they now had a common enemy. From that moment on, whenever Animus was in danger in the land of Almachora, if he blew the whistle the flying caribou would come to his aid.

"Thank you Alphega! And thank you my friends! Many far and near will hear of the flying caribou that come bearing gifts, though few, I'm sure, will believe me," Animus shouted. "May we fight this evil in our land together. If ever you need me I will also help you as much as is in my power."

Then turning to the great caribou that bore the whistle Animus said, "Your name will be Doronorth, which means 'Gift of the North'—I hope in time I will give you as dear a gift as you have given me."

Doronorth bent both of his front legs and bowed his antlers toward the snow before Animus. Then in one burst of movement, Doronorth was once again in the air above, leading the herd through the chilly air.

The pine branches in the fire popped and crackled and gave off thick smoke while Animus waited on Oze to arrive with dinner. He gazed at the whistle and rolled it back and forth between his fingers before placing it around his neck and tucking it against his thick chest. He was reminded of the simple, consistent prayer of a child who never lost hope that I would find her whistle; were she only there to see it. A single tear nearly made it past Animus' jaw before it froze to his cheek in the cold wind.

He hadn't been reflecting long when from the Foggy Forest to the south he heard the unmistakable sound of Oze growling and roaring. This specific roar was only reserved for fierce fighting, never for hunting, so Animus was concerned. He sprang up from his position around the fire and headed toward his friend trudging through the thick snow. Soon he made it to the edge of the trees and proceeded ahead with cautious haste. Again Oze was making ferocious noises, yet occasionally he would cry out in pain as well. The darkness wasn't helping Animus find his friend any faster, so he paused long enough to use Azarmuth on a downed limb, making a torch. The only disadvantage to this was that whatever had Oze in trouble would see the torch and Animus coming and he would lose the element of surprise.

Before long he was out of the trees and in a small clearing. Across the way he saw Oze being attacked by a large band of Sarxans. Unfortunately, they saw him as well. Six of them had Oze surrounded and were jabbing long spears at him; he was bleeding in many places. The cave bear was taking a toll on the Sarxans as well though. Scattered along the ground around the bear were four mangled Sarxan bodies. That left ten Sarxans to take care of Animus. When they saw Animus, one of the Sarxans played a particular rhythm on a drum that hung around his neck; a call for help, which let Animus know the Sarxans he saw would be joined by others very shortly. At first, Animus thought Oze had accidentally stumbled upon a hunting party, but if there were many others nearby, it was far too large to be merely a hunt.

Animus and Oze had been outnumbered before, and the way it stood at present he felt confident he and his bear could

dispatch the remaining sixteen Sarxans; that is, unless their reinforcements arrived. Wasting no time Animus dropped the torch and charged the barbarians. Azarmuth took off the arm and then the head of the first Sarxan he came to. A rock launched from a slingshot ricocheted off of Animus' stout bearskin armor at the shoulder. He dodged a spear thrust, then brought Azarmuth down on the weapon, cutting the shaft cleanly in two.

Meanwhile, Oze had also broken a spear, by snapping the shaft in his powerful jaws. In doing so, he jerked one of his attackers towards him and gutted him with a swipe from one of his mighty paws. Again, the drums thundered out into the wilderness. Animus thought he heard sounds coming from the trees, but couldn't afford the time to look. Neither could he take the time to blow on his daughter's whistle, a simple gesture that in hindsight he wished he had already done. He fumbled and reached for it around his neck, but every time he had to abandon his tries in order to parry an oncoming attacker. Animus decided to try a distraction. The next Sarxan he bested by not only cutting into his collarbone with Azarmuth, but also setting the Sarxan ablaze. Indeed, the others were momentarily stunned as they saw their comrade burst into flame.

A piercing sharp pain then shot through Animus' left bicep. He had taken an arrow in his arm, but none of the Sarxans he was fighting were archers. In his mind he reasoned that others must be in the trees. Knowing the general direction from which the arrow originated, Animus shifted as he fought his enemies, putting them in between himself and whoever shot the arrow. He needed the free use of his arm so he quickly yanked the crude arrow from his arm, slinging blood from his arm as he did. Across from him, Oze continued to gain ground, breaking a neck with another swing of his paw.

The other Sarxans began to reveal themselves as they quickly moved out from the cover of the trees. There was at least fifty that had heard the drum and arrived. Conventional fighting would no longer bring Animus a victory. With every swing of Azarmuth he tried to set whatever he made contact with on fire. Wooden weapons, clothing, and Sarxan flesh were all catching fire from Animus' axe. Seeing that Oze was going to be outmanned imminently, he yelled to his bear, "Oze get out of here! Run! Go home. I'll meet you at home!"

Though Oze didn't understand all that Animus said, he did understand "home" and that Animus was telling him to go there. So Oze charged past the two Sarxans directly in front of him, taking the sharp point of a spear for his efforts. Still, with great speed he was into the forest and away from the fighting. He continued to run until he realized he was no longer in any danger.

Animus however, was in danger. His powerful axe that was bringing fire to whatever it touched had caught the full attention of more than fifty Sarxans. Animus continued to hack away, refusing to surrender. The Sarxans were known for being a brutal, uncivilized race and Animus wasn't going to trust them to treat him with integrity; especially since a short mound of Sarxan bodies was accumulating around him. It was in the midst of this valiant stand that suddenly everything went black for Animus. A stone from a slingshot had nicked him in the head and knocked him unconscious. Fortunately, the rock did not kill him.

The Sarxans moved in like fleas deprived of flesh. They quickly bound Animus with crude ropes and their leader picked up Azarmuth.

"Do we have time to torture him?" a hairy Sarxan snapped.

The large Sarxan sunk the axe deep into a few of his fallen warriors but no fire came forth. This angered the Sarxan, and he determined to interrogate Animus when he awoke as to how to bring fire forth from the axe. "We take him to Krue. We need proof of why we late and the gift of axe of power will gain me favor," he growled.

The other Sarxans did not attempt to track down Oze because they were so far behind schedule after the battle. They had been moving across the wilderness on their way to meet up with an Archeskotos by the stream to the southwest when they accidentally came upon Oze; an opportunistic hunt turned into much more than they had anticipated.

Not tracking the bear would eventually catch up with them as Oze, instead of going all the way home, waited patiently on the other side of the trees for his master. When Animus didn't arrive, Oze stalked back through the trees in search of him. When he arrived back at the sight of the brawl, all of the Sarxans were gone. Mangled Sarxan bodies lay stripped of every worthwhile weapon and article among the snow, but there was no sign of Animus. Oze was not deterred. The bear used his keen sense of smell to pick out the scent of Reflection blood among the scent of Sarxan blood. He would use the bloody scent from Animus' bleeding arm to pursue them from a safe distance, biding his time.

"The cave bear was taking a toll on the Sarxans."

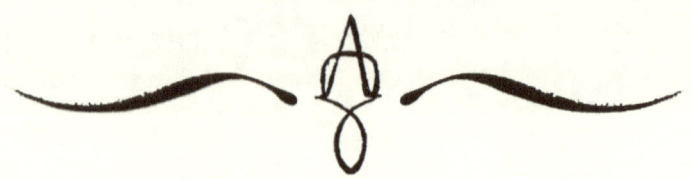

OF CHAYKAF AND
THANATOPH

he four travelers had hiked for several days and were
nearly out of the Canyons of Flame when they decided to stop
and sleep. This wasn't the first time they had slept together
and they were developing a routine; Sage and Reverie would
talk, Gad would make sure the necessities were taken care of,
and Telle would have visions.

That night, Gad produced a substance from his pack that
caught Sage's attention. It was a creamy white, bread-looking,
substance that gave off light in the darkness. Though it looked
like bread, Gad didn't eat it. Rather, he pulled it apart and
poured it into his mouth, every last bit of it. Gad seemingly
drank a solid substance. Or was it that the substance was liquid

but appeared solid? Sage wasn't sure, however, he was sure that it was one of the most bizarre sights he had ever seen—and lately he had seen a myriad of marvels.

"What was that?" Sage asked, amazed.

"It is called chaykaf; though you might think of it as heaven's bread. It comes from Agapia. Yet, we Archeon do not need food in the sense that the inhabitants of Earth need food. For us, chaykaf is a kind of spiritual nourishment that renews our senses of hope, peace, and purpose. It is only ever needed when one of us ventures outside of Agapia," Gad explained.

He then continued, "Whatever you may be thinking, let me warn you, do not attempt to consume this. Chaykaf is not for any creature of Wispria. Alphega originally created it for an Archeon of Agapia. I cannot tell you what effect it would have on a lesser creature such as a Sprinter or Reflection."

Of course hearing this made Sage want nothing more than to taste it. And from that moment on he looked for an opportunity to do so.

After consuming the chaykaf, Gad proceeded to make a fire from some of the supplies Telle carried, and Sage and Reverie enjoyed the warmth and light the flame gave off. The rain had nearly ceased for the time being, but off in the distance angry lightning could still be seen.

"Can I see your piece of agapate?" Sage asked Reverie as they were seated by the fire.

Reverie held out her hand with the small piece of agapate resting in her palm.

Sage went to take it from her hand and she closed it quickly and withdrew her arm away from him.

"You can see it, not hold it. No offense, but I still don't know who I can and can't trust," Reverie snapped.

Sage reached over to his nearly empty leather backsack and yanked out a strand of leather chord used for cinching up one of the pockets.

"I promise, you can trust me," Sage said looking into her eyes as if to show her his inner integrity.

Withholding her initial response, which was to tell him "no" again, Reverie slowly opened her hand and gave the agapate to Sage.

Smiling, Sage said, "Call me overly worrisome, which I have been called before, but I think something as important as this agapate should be well fastened to your body. Affixing my piece in between my brace has been most comforting."

So Sage tied the leather strand in many angles around the piece of agapate that was no larger than half the size of his smallest finger, and much thinner. After he was satisfied that the stone wasn't capable of slipping out, he motioned for Reverie to turn her back to him.

"There, I think you will find that to be a better way to keep up with it," said Sage as he tied the leather strand holding the agapate around her neck.

"Thank you," Reverie replied. "And I'm sorry for what I said. I do trust you, Sage. In the little time I have known you, I have grown to have a deep affection for you."

Sage was astonished at such an intimate statement from one he had just met, especially after so many years of people teasing him in his youth. He wasn't quite sure how to respond, but he liked it.

Reverie moved over closer to Sage and cuddled up next to him. She appreciated the warmth from Sage's body, though Sage was surprised at how cold Reverie's body felt. Nevertheless, he was glad for the touch of another, and they slept holding each other. The rocky ground was hardly comfortable, but in each other's arms they didn't mind a little discomfort.

"We have to decide which path to take to Aprioria," said a voice, waking them up.

They opened their eyes to see Gad towering over them, ready to continue on the journey. "Though you and the rest of the creatures of the Wisprian World need sleep, Lure and the other Archeon, including myself, do not. We never sleep. Lure is never ceasing in carrying out his plans. Therefore, we must only rest as long as is absolutely necessary."

"Well then, I guess we should take the quickest, most direct route," said Reverie, trying to hide the fact that she did not know what the best route to Aprioria was.

"The quickest, most direct route I believe to be south, which will take us straight through the Black Bogs. I went scouting while you slept and saw them over that rim," said Gad as he pointed to the south at what appeared to be the last rim of the canyons of flame.

"I've never heard of Black Bogs, but just the way you mention them lets me know I don't want to see them," said Sage.

"They were always perilous, but Telle has shown me a new evil, the Nwarbet, that dwell there, and I dare not try to pass through," Gad said sternly. "If we go around them to the west it will be a long journey and will take us close to Casusbelia. Reverie has already informed us of what happened there.

To the east should be a shorter detour, but I know not what geography awaits us in that direction; for all I know, at this point something even worse than the Black Bogs could await. But then again, it could be an amicable path. I was hoping your new... little friend... would help us decide," said Gad indicating his disapproval of the growing connection Sage had with Reverie.

Reverie answered with a lie, "Yes, of course, I never intended we should go through the Bogs," she said coolly, "east is the quickest and safest path to Aprioria."

"It is settled then, we will cross that ridge to the left and then head east around the bogs," stated Gad warily.

Then the three of them made preparations to journey on. But they stopped when they realized Telle was not with them. It didn't take much looking to find him, and when they did, they noticed he had written another prophecy in the rocky ground.

IN BITTER COLD
IN CAVERNS OLD
ON STORMY SEA
AGAPATE BE
ICAEMOTH FREEZES
MURSA DISEASES
LEVIATHAN WAVE
A LAMB WILL SAVE

"What does it mean?" Sage asked Gad.

"I'm not exactly sure. I've heard of the Leviathan that dwells in the depths of the Gulf of Tanaudor. But I've never heard of the Icaemoth or Mursa. Either way we should remember this prophecy for I'm sure that in the future it will be very insightful. Now we must move on," Gad replied.

So, the four of them started the steep climb out of the Canyons of Flame. Off in the distant sky they could hear shrieks that sounded like the thricorn. But these sounds came from several thanatoph; winged creatures that were not birds. In fact, they didn't have feathers at all, they had wings made of skin that was similar to that of the thricorn. Their heads were long and narrow with hundreds of long pointy teeth. They had tails that were like whips lined with razor sharp barbs. A single thanatoph could carry two or three Reflections on its back; though very few Reflections had managed to tame the beasts well enough to ride them. Those that were tame were usually raised from eggs by Reflections.

"Be on your guard. There are thanatoph circling nearby," Gad stated.

Gad debated in his mind whether he should put out the torch he was carrying, in case the thanatoph were drawn to it. But for the time being he kept it lit so he could see the tricky jagged terrain beneath his feet.

The climb was slow going and the four were nearly on top of each other most of the way up, so Sage thought this would be a convenient time for conversation.

"Gad, remember when you referred to me as Tear Bearer? Can you now tell me what you meant by that remark?" Sage asked from the rear, as his injury greatly hampered his climbing ability.

Telle let out a fierce neigh in response to Sage's question and Gad looked back at the Sprinter with an unmistakable stare that let him know not to mention such things now.

Reverie had never heard the term Tear Bearer and was quite intrigued by it. "Tear Bearer? What an odd thing to call someone, unless for good reason," she said.

The only reason that Gad was unwilling to talk at present was because he still did not trust Reverie, but he covered up his true reason by saying, "When we met Sage he was most despondent over the death of his father, the injury to his ankle and the circumstances he had been unwillingly thrust into. He cried, a lot. I'm sorry Sage, I didn't mean any harm by it, Telle and I knew you were hurting, but we just wished you could have handled it with more maturity."

Sage had no idea what Gad was talking about, and he was about to protest, until he caught a glance from Gad that was more serious than any look Sage had ever received from him. Sage was puzzled, and more than a little offended, but the dire look in Gad's eyes outweighed his need to proceed with the conversation at present, and he muttered an annoyed, non-verbal response.

At this, Sage and Reverie ceased their questioning and the group continued the careful trudge up the final rim of the Canyons of Flame. When they came to the spot from where Gad scouted, they were able to see faint outlines of the geography that spread out before them in all directions. Straight out from where they stood they could see the flat lowlands dotted with darker splotches of black through the shadowy gloom that were the Black Bogs. They saw tiny flecks of light that looked like distant fires burning in the west. The least discernable path was in the direction they had decided to head; in the East it looked like thick woods awaited them.

"Ooowawwkk!" came a sudden screech right above them.

Before they could react, a thanatoph perched on the cliff right in front of them. This thanatoph had a single rider, though it was not a Reflection. As added protection for the creature in the ever dropping temperatures, the thanatoph had several animal furs draped across its torso and neck that had been clumsily sewn together. The rider was recognizable only to Reverie, for none of the other three had actually beheld a Dephilim. What a grotesque sight it was. The rider was nearly equal in size to Gad, but lacked all the aesthetic qualities that Gad possessed. The Dephilim's face was deformed and the muscular arms and legs that protruded from its torso, while more muscular than Gad's, seemed to be alive and rotting off at the same time and lacked the downy texture of Gad's. No light shone from the Dephilim as it did from the Archeon. In one hand the Dephilim grasped a makeshift reign that had been fastened around the thanatoph, and in the other it wielded a large bone from a creature that, from the looks of it, had been alive just hours earlier.

Immediately, Reverie leapt hands first, down the side of the canyon they had just climbed. The thanatoph lurched at her with its long head, but Sage jumped in the way. The creature's teeth sank deep into the pack on Sage's back and ripped it from him, his provisions scattering among the rocks.

Gad went directly for the Dephilim, more than anything he wanted to remove the perverse looking creature from the face of the Earth. The very sight of the Dephilim dimmed Gad's natural glow. He wasn't as quick as he needed to be, and from the back of the winged beast the Dephilim swung the bone that was easily half the length of Gad's height and hit him on the side of his torso. This didn't deter Gad, it only served to knock him into the side of the thanatoph, and Gad grabbed the Dephilim by the throat and hurled him off of his winged transportation.

Meanwhile, the thanatoph had been snapping at Sage trying to catch him in his powerful jaws. Sage thought of using the agapate, but he didn't know how he could harm the adversary without harming his companions. Sage was on the ground rolling out of the way of one of the creature's bites when Telle sunk his horn deep into the long neck of the winged beast. The thanatoph jerked his head up and down and Telle was slightly lifted off of the cliff several times, unable to dislodge his horn once it found its mark. Seeing that Telle had afforded him a few seconds of time, Sage took hold of Odem's slingshot and put a jagged palm-sized rock in it. Sage then let the rock fly straight into the eye of the thanatoph, who had shaken himself free of Telle's horn and was bleeding all over the cliff.

Gad, who was outmatched in strength by the Dephilim, was now pinned underneath the foul-smelling abomination. The bone of the Dephilim was pressing into Gad's neck under his chin. Sage saw this as an opportunity. He lightly dabbed his foot on the ground and a short hump of rock shot up from underneath Gad, throwing the Dephilim off of him. Sage was pleased with how adept he was becoming at using his powerful stone.

Telle had been nicked many times by the lashing tail of the thanatoph, but had managed to pierce it several times as well. Again, Sage hurled his slingshot at the creature, blinding its other eye. The small, short legs of the thanatoph were its weakness and Sage chose this opportunity to exploit it. Again he struck the ground, harder this time, and the ground shot up from under the thanatoph's legs. Blinded, off balance, and bleeding profusely, the thanatoph tumbled down the side of the canyon, never to return.

The Dephilim had been dumbstruck when the ground moved beneath Gad, affording the Archeon the upper hand. Gad wrestled the huge bone from the Dephilim and bludgeoned his head with it. For a few moments all was silent. Then came the sound of other thanatoph screaming through the darkness. Reverie, who had been hiding down in the canyon, made her way back to the top and to the other three, with only minor cuts and bruises from her leap.

"Rather hide than help?" Gad said sternly.

Reverie answered, "I—"

"We don't have time for explanations. We have to make it to those trees in the southeast. Place your necklace on Telle's horn," commanded Gad.

Reverie was going to protest, but Gad already had the necklace off her before she had a chance. Gad then hung the necklace on Telle's horn.

Then Gad said, "Everyone get on. Telle, I hope Reverie's agapate works for you the way it worked for her. Take us to the trees as fast as your hoofs can carry us."

The Archeon and the supplies would have been enough to weigh Telle down, but Sage and Reverie also climbed on. Telle could barely walk, much less run with all of the weight, and he let out a frustrated puff of air. Then what they hoped for happened. The agapate made Telle's four legs lighter and faster than they had ever been. The unicorn raced with ease down the slope. Though their lives were in danger, Telle was enjoying his new power. Within minutes they were under the canopy of the trees and out of sight of the thanatoph above.

The forest was thick and many bushes and vines littered the ground they had to walk through. Gad lost the torch in the fight and his inner light was again the only light the company had. Once they made it far enough into the trees Telle stopped. Reverie swiftly snatched back her agapate and hopped off of the unicorn.

"Who do you think you are, cloudrider, that you can take what doesn't belong to you," she said pointedly at Gad.

"Impossible. How do you know that word? Who or what are you?!" Gad said, quite seriously.

"What is a cloudrider? I don't understand why that is a bad thing?" questioned Sage, innocently.

"It is not only what it is, but my concern is how she could possibly have heard the term before?" Gad suspiciously questioned.

In an effort to explain her offense, Reverie said, "It was just what I heard one of those things that attacked my village call one of you. I'm sorry."

"I doubt that," Gad said firmly to Reverie. "You see, Sage, only Lure was given wings to travel between Agapia and Wispria. None of the other Archeon were given such a gift, and he coined the term cloudrider to refer to all the rest of the Archeon, as a means of disparagement. But again, no inhabitant of Wispria would have ever heard the term". Towering over Reverie, Gad continued, "Don't ever call me that again.

Furthermore, I just saved us, and you are worried about me taking your things? I didn't take it; you have it back in your possession. But our survival depended on Telle using the agapate. As I have said before, if we are to have any chance at all, we must work together—and not only us, we need others. I don't know what would have happened if we didn't have your piece of agapate back there. Maybe we would have still escaped, but maybe not. Next time our success may depend on something or someone we haven't even come across yet," Gad argued.

The discussion was interrupted by Sage, "Telle looks hurt. He's bleeding in many different places and he's breathing heavy as if he's thirsty."

"Give him water from one of the skins draped across him. He's probably tired from the fight." Taking a close look at Telle's wounds, Gad continued, "his wounds are substantial, but not threatening. He'll be fine."

Indeed, Telle was tired from the fight, but the run from the canyons to the trees, though long and fast, was nearly effortless. Nevertheless, the water was quite refreshing to Telle, and Sage drank some also.

"I lost the supplies you gave me in the fight; my sack is strewn across the rocks back there," Sage told Gad.

"We will have to find provisions soon. I knew we would need more, but with the loss of what you carried, they will not last much longer," Gad warned as Sage gave a sip of water to Reverie.

After resting briefly, they continued to walk through bushes and briars. Every few minutes a new sound would come from the woods around them. The forest they were in was unnamed and untraveled. With the Canyons of Flame on one side, the

Black Bogs on another side, and the Cracked Plain of Desolation on yet another side, very few travelers would have ever desired to adventure where they were walking.

The rain began to pick up again and the breeze through the branches of the trees was chilly. Sage wished he had thought to take one of the furs from the back of the thanatoph, for now even he was beginning to shiver. Reverie noticed this, and frequently the two of them would walk arm in arm through the dense brush.

Eventually, they came to a clearing in the wood. There was a thin, trickling stream running through the tall grasses of the open area. In the darkness, none of them could see how far the clearing stretched, but they all assumed that they would eventually come to trees again on the other side. Their primary concern was that they would not have any cover to hide them if another thanatoph flew overhead.

When they were in the trees, they didn't realize how strong the wind was blowing. Yet, now that they were out in the open, the wind was actually causing them to correct their steps to the left or right when it knocked them off balance. Sage was no longer mildly shivering; with the strong wind, rain, and falling temperature, he was shaking uncontrollably. Reverie's ability to withstand the cold, especially in her lightweight clothing, was odd. What clothes they had were soaked. Everything around them was wet and cold. The elements quickly became their primary adversary.

Sage stopped abruptly and squatted beside the stream, hugging his knees to his chest. Reverie followed and got as close to Sage as she could to keep him warm. Gad and Telle were not affected by the worsening conditions, but saw how serious the situation was becoming for Sage.

"Sage, why don't you and Reverie ride on Telle's back for a while and save your energy?" Gad asked.

Barely able to grind out words through his shaking, Sage answered, "It is too cold on his back. The lower to the ground we are the less the wind affects us. I just want to stay here for a while. I can't go any further right now."

The combination of the weather, the lack of adequate food and the exhaustion from the journey were all working together to weaken Sage and his ability to continue. Reverie's status didn't seem to be as critical as Sage's, but she also wasn't in a hurry to carry on.

For several minutes, the two stayed squatting with their knees to their chest, paying no attention to what was going on around them. Sage could have fallen asleep in the very position he was in. Hypothermia was trying to completely take hold of him. Mentally, he didn't care what happened to him, the only thing his mind could focus on was creating warmth for the rest of his body, and right now that meant conserving all his energy. For the moment, he had forgotten all about agapate, Aprioria, and the purpose of his journey. His entire life became simple in an instant. Find a way to stay warm. Soon, with his chin resting in between his knees, he did fall asleep. Were it not for Gad and Telle, Sage's journey might have ended there. If unattended, the hypothermia would have caused all of his faculties to shut down. Reverie also seemed to be colder than usual, but she hadn't yet progressed to the point of hypothermia.

Gad lifted both of them onto Telle's back, and since he wasn't sure how far off the trees and shelter were, they went back the way they came to where they had last been underneath the trees. Gad was hesitant to start a fire, not only because of the difficulty of lighting the wet branches, but also because a fire would be easy to spot in the darkness.

Instead, Telle lay on the ground and Gad placed Sage and Reverie up against the large belly of the unicorn. Reverie placed her arms around Sage because that is what one Reflection did to another who was cold. Telle nuzzled up close to the two of them to add warmth. Meanwhile, Gad set out to find the dead thanatoph they had fought in order to gather the furs off of its back for Sage and Reverie, and try to recover the lost supplies.

In the time that Gad was away, Telle had managed to warm Sage and Reverie to the point that they were awake. Noticing they had awoken, Telle jostled the makeshift bags at his side in hopes Sage would drink some water to refresh himself. Sage did just that and gave some to Reverie as well. When reaching for the water skin, Sage noticed the pocket where Gad had gotten the chaykaf. Suppressing the urge to take a piece took much self-control; in fact, were it not for Telle and the risk of being caught, Sage would have.

"Where do you think Gad is?" Sage asked Reverie.

"I'm not sure, but he must be alright because the horse is not alarmed at his absence. And besides, the supplies were quite a distance back there. I'm sure it is just taking him a while to go all the way there and back," Reverie replied. "How are you?"

Distracted, Sage answered, "Exhausted and hungry, I wish I knew where he went."

The temptation of the chaykaf continued to dominate Sage's thoughts. He stood to his feet and began taking the load off of Telle.

"I don't think we'll be pressing on anytime soon Telle, so let me take these packs off of you so you can truly rest," he said.

Sensing Sage's motives weren't necessarily what he made them out to be, Telle gave an agitated swoosh of his tail, and made much huffing and puffing. However, in the end he didn't prevent Sage from removing the supplies from off of his back.

Moving about with a newfound energy that came from the possibility of sneaking a piece of the chaykaf, Sage set the packs against a nearby tree. He gave a quick glance back at Reverie and Telle and then quickly rummaged through the pocket from which he saw Gad take the chaykaf. Finding several pieces, he palmed one in his long fingers and closed the pack. He then, with his back to Reverie and Telle walked a few steps further until he was hidden by the tree. There, Sage broke the spongy bread and poured it into his mouth as he had witnessed Gad do previously. By the time he walked back around the tree to where his companions were, the chaykaf was affecting him.

Sage sat with his back against a tree trunk and a feeling of complete euphoria overtook him. His head nodded with his chin resting on his chest as all pain, tension, and care left his body. Drool fell from his lips as every muscle, including his facial muscles, relaxed and refused to function properly. Every care left him. Odem's death, his own destiny, and the fate of Wispria mattered not to him. He wasn't out of his mind, Sage was aware of what was happening to him, but that was all he was aware of. The chaykaf made him feel so good, he couldn't focus or even think about another thing. He was no longer cold. In fact, he was quite warm now. With eyes closed, he saw visions of gold and light and heard a sweet sound unlike any he had ever heard. Sage lost track of time, though he was in this state for quite a while. Sage fell asleep as the effects of the chaykaf began to wear off.

Sage woke up when he was covered with many large furry objects. He opened his eyes and flailed his hands about until he saw Gad standing over him.

"I thought the furs would help you stay warm," Gad said. "I'm glad to see you are feeling well enough to move about and attempt to make camp—I assume that's what you were doing when you removed the equipment from Telle's back." Groggily, Sage answered, "Thank you, Gad, yes I'm feeling better. I just thought we probably wouldn't be moving along since you were gone."

Immediately, in his mind, Sage could think of nothing else but creating another opportunity to take a piece of chaykaf. Now that he was reminded of the rain, the cold and the darkness as well as all of the death and peril that had been so much a part of his world as of late, Sage realized what an escape the heaven's bread had been for him and how it hadn't caused him harm as Gad had warned. He suspected Gad just wanted to keep it all for himself.

What Sage didn't realize was that, for Gad, chaykaf didn't cause the same reaction in his body. When Gad consumed chaykaf it gave him a feeling of renewed purpose and life and it was originally created only for those who would leave Agapia, meaning Lure. When Lure would travel between the two worlds he would use it because he would venture so far from My presence. But the rest of the Archeon had no need for chaykaf. When the gate was destroyed by Lure and everything changed, Gad fought against him. As Gad was being forced from Agapia in the fight, he had the foresight and brief opportunity to grab some of Lure's chaykaf and take it for his own nourishment in his time away from Me.

Gad noticed that Sage was greatly preoccupied with thought and asked him to walk with him for awhile. Once they were a generous distance away from Reverie, Gad spoke:

"I suppose you would like to know what a Tear Bearer is. I should apologize for the earlier explanation. I of course, realize that wasn't an accurate description, but I gave an answer to satisfy Reverie."

Sage nodded in appreciation as Gad continued, "Shortly after Telle found me, he had one of his visions. From what I have seen, this vision was more specific and more involved than any other vision he has had. In it, he saw the Throne. He couldn't see the One on the throne, for none can look upon Alphega, even in a vision. But from the One seated on the throne, seven tears fell, one by one. In his vision, Telle could see inside each teardrop and saw the different powers each possessed. Each one of them contained a quality of Alphega. He didn't show me if he knew where each tear fell, but he did write that he had seen visions of each of the seven on whom the tears fell. These seven I, in turn, referred to as the Tear Bearers; for they each bear a tear from the One. I say 'bear' because, though they each contain a quality of Alphega, choosing the appropriate time to use the power they possess can cause great pain; for the quality that the tear carries can be used only once. In fact, in your case, as may very well be the case of the others, you don't even realize you possess this hidden quality. And I cannot tell you which quality you have been given. Telle's horn only showed me the overall vision through cave drawings, not specifics. I trust that when the time comes, you will know what to do, even if you do not know now."

After he listened to all of this, Sage sat still for a moment. Then said, "You're telling me Alphega Himself cried, and one of his tears fell from Agapia and landed on me, granting me one of His qualities that I can only use one time, even though I don't even know I possess the ability?"

"Yes," Gad answered.

"But I never felt a tear of any kind land on me," reasoned Sage.

"In many cases, if we are too focused on ourselves at the time, we will be unaware of Alphega's touch," counseled Gad.

"Well what quality do I have? Or what quality could I potentially have?" said Sage with wonder.

"That I can't answer. Who can quantify Alphega's qualities? He is all-knowing, He is present everywhere, His power is boundless, the original source of light and life, among countless others, any one of which alone would be exceedingly powerful," said Gad realizing again for himself what unknown, marvelous ability this small Sprinter carried.

Sage didn't know what to think. His lack of faith in Me was certainly being challenged by his hope that what Gad had said was true. In fact, he believed Gad's words. He believed partly because of how special it made him feel, but also because he truly believed. And for the present, at least, his mind was taken off the allure of the chaykaf.

I was glad. I was glad that Sage was growing to believe in things he previously did not. Though, it is a true statement to say that a large part of his belief was based on evidence such as Gad, chaykaf, and Telle. Faith is another matter altogether. Faith is a unique privilege given to those mortal inhabitants of Earth, whether Wispria or the world that followed. It should be understood that it is impossible for an inhabitant of Agapia to have faith. All the Archeon could see Me, knew of My existence, and so therefore by definition, they simply could not have faith in Me. One cannot have faith in something seen with the eye. This is why faith is such a gift for those who haven't seen Agapia or seen Me. It follows then that Sage was indeed growing in faith, for he hadn't seen Agapia or Me, yet a portion of his belief was from a place of knowledge and proof. This is all to say nothing of trust. Trust is different than faith. All those in both Agapia and Wispria have the ability to trust. Ultimately, it was this lack of trust in Me that caused Lure to rebel. So then, faith and trust are each important, and it brought Me great joy to see that Sage was increasing in both.

"Reverie answered with a lie."

REUNION

apone and Kelly Kome´denyd were brothers. They grew up together in the Treetop City of the Forest of Fools. Capone was born five years before Kelly, but from the moment Kelly entered the world, he and Capone spent every day together for twenty-six years until Capone left to pursue his dream of storytelling. Capone traveled from town to town to the ends of the Wisprian World. Coincidentally, it was Capone's band of storytellers that traveled through the Moaning Mountains; Sage had seen Capone perform. The shows were commonly referred to as *Fools Tales*, though even the most skeptical listener could not deny the truths the stories told.

On this day, however, after several years abroad, Capone was returning home. The dark events that had recently trans- pired worried Capone, and he was inclined to come back to

the Forest of Fools to find Kelly and his other loved ones; for Capone carried a burden. The wisdom that comes from, among other things, time and reflection, had revealed to Capone the mistakes and regrets of his past that he had previously been oblivious to. Time had also weathered his face with a few lines, though his light blonde hair didn't have one stand of gray, unusual for a Reflection male in his early 40s.

His dark green traveler's cloak was blowing about him as Capone made it to the outskirts of Treetop city, in the Forest of Fools. Immediately, Capone could sense there was a lack of mirth in the woods where he grew up; not only because of the constant darkness, but also because he saw no one else. The Treetop City was a well-kept secret to outsiders, but the Forest of Fools was normally bustling with inhabitants from the city. Capone saw none of his kinsmen lounging or talking in the Forest below as he came to the large tree that served as the front entrance to Treetop City. On the ground beside the tree, visible only from a pathetically small fire, huddled under what appeared to be a blanket, was a lonely vagabond, the eyes of whom were downcast and hopeless. The Treetop City was a city of outcasts, so this individual was an outcast of outcasts. Shivering under the blanket, whoever it was, was not appropriately outfitted for the dropping temperatures. There was a pile of belongings on the ground and resting on top of the pile was a most peculiar pair of shoes. Capone felt certain he had never seen shoes like these before. Capone had a yearning to see if this poor creature needed any assistance, but his need to find his brother was too urgent to allow him to stop.

The Treetop city was not visible to those who did not know what to look for. Jesters, poets, storytellers, musicians, magicians and artists, exiles from Lithosis, were the founders of Treetop City. They were ostracized not because of their chosen professions or the talents they possessed, but because most of them upheld a belief in Me and spoke out openly against the greed and corruption of Lithosis. A full generation had passed since the first settlers arrived in the Fool's Forest. The name was given to the forest by Lithosians who knew the origin of its inhabitants. Still, though the Forest of Fools was widely known in Wispria, few knew of Treetop City, the actual home of the exiled Lithosians.

These artisans that settled the forest were so adept at their craft, that they fashioned a faux canopy in the top of the thick forest. The trees in the Forest of Fools were the tallest in Wisprian World, and so over time an interconnecting tree-city was constructed in the tops of the trees. While some were building the wooden walls and floors of the city, other artisans were painting and sewing together the largest canvas ever made. The canvas was hung underneath Treetop City, between it and the Forest floor below. This thin canvas moved with the wind like tree branches and was painted to resemble the forest ceiling when looking from the ground. It was a most affective concealing device. Aided by the simple fact that most travelers that ventured through the Forest were preoccupied with looking in front and behind, the veil had never been discovered; allowing Treetop City to be a well hidden haven.

Living among the trees had also given these particular Reflection a keener understanding of the natural world. They

were more like Sprinters or Sarxans in regard to their knowledge of flora and fauna.

Capone knocked on the hollowed out tree in a series of long and short knocks. The sound reverberated up the inside of the tree to the Treetop City guards far up the trunk. Shortly thereafter, a platform was lowered down to the floor of the forest. Capone boarded the platform and rode it to the surreptitious city above.

The entrance was just as Capone remembered it, except that now there were torches and candles stationed about the wooden platform that circled the large tree. Large pieces of canvas were draped over the limbs above to create a fairly tall ceiling to the entryway. The candles and torches that were not under canvas were in decorative boxes to shield them from the incessant rains.

"State your business," said the first guard, gripping a bow in his hand.

The Fools were all skilled with bows and arrows, as a life among trees demanded.

"I am Capone Kome´denyd. I have returned to check on the well-being of my brother Kelly," replied Capone.

"He's cleared. Well this is a pleasant surprise. Capone Kome´denyd, I must say I didn't know if I would ever see you again," said Rowand, the leader of the Fools, as he embraced Capone.

Rowand was a short, slender Reflection that appeared to have already lived around at least seventy years. His full head of straight, grey hair was cut short, a common practice among the Fools to keep their hair from getting caught in the branches that hovered all around them. His face was angular, with very little facial hair. His eyes were unique, not just in shape—but also in the prudence with which they took in another. His build was moderate, but he was certainly firm for a man of his age. Rowand wore a long, hooded brown robe that opened in the front to reveal a light shirt and knee length pants the color of tree trunks, on top of the robe was a woven belt that fastened about his waist. On his feet were lightweight leather shoes that came up to just above his ankles.

"I saw your brother just a little while ago; he still lives on the same landing. You remember the way I'm sure. I know you must be anxious to see him, so I won't keep you, but do come find me soon. I have much to tell you," said Rowand as he sipped shawthak brew from a wooden straw that was decorated with detailed carvings.

Shawthak brew was similar to tea, only it was made from the leaves of the shawthak tree. Shawthak trees were plentiful only in the Forest of Fools, and the brew was the most common form of libation in Treetop City, it provided its drinkers with an overwhelming sense of calm and warmth. The brew had a simple preparation; leaves were dried and crushed up and hot water was poured upon them. However, they had developed a unique method of drinking the brew. Gourds were also plentiful in the forest, and so most Fools had a hollowed-out gourd for the specific purpose of holding shawthak. In addition, hollow segments of reeds were used as straws. One end of the reed segment was open, this was the end that touched the lips; the other end was closed, as it occurred in nature. Yet, at the closed end small holes were poked into the reed allowing the

shawthak to be sucked up through it while keeping the leaves from being sucked up as well. Since it was an artistic culture, both the straw and gourds were often elaborately decorated with carvings or dyes.

Capone could smell the hot shawthak coming from many landings as he gazed out over the maze of wooden platforms and bridges, canvas roofs of varying heights, rope bridges and ladders dimly lit by candles that hung from branches all around the wood. This was his home and he had missed it. Each family and each shop in the Treetop City had its own landing; which was basically a series of wooden platforms that were built around a tree. They were all unique. Some landings had many different levels and others were built out horizontally, depending on the base tree.

Crossing the main wooden bridge from the entry tree, Capone continued through the light rainfall over several rope bridges and up a ladder. All the while he heard the familiar sounds of insects, bats, other flying creatures that also called Treetop City home, as well as the familiar sound of the breeze through the branches. The sounds were nostalgic for Capone and brought a smile to his face.

When he reached the top of the final ladder, Capone knocked on the door which was directly above his head, in the floor of the landing. Soon the door opened, and Kelly stood wide-eyed and speechless at the sight of his brother. Kelly had mid-length wavy hair that was falling over the top of a piece of dark brown cloth tied around his head as a headband. He wore a long-sleeve cream colored shirt and a simple green and gold vest. Around his waist he had two belts...one to hold up his tan pants, and the other that was most unique. This second belt was one-of-a-kind. It was hand crafted, and had little leather pouches all the way around, each just big enough to hold an inkwell, the corked tops of which were sticking out of the top of each pouch. Kelly's brown boots laced up over his pants all the way up to just below his knee. On his wrists were two thick leather bands, and he wore a dark brown cloak.

"So I suspect you are surprised to see me, brother?" said Capone with a grin.

"More surprised than ever before! Let me help you up here. I have never been happier to see you!" said Kelly, stepping back so Capone could enter.

The brothers embraced for a long moment.

Several pats on the back later, Kelly said, "Are you hungry? Thirsty? Come sit down. You are at least going to have a drink, or many, with your brother."

Capone obliged, and the two sat at the small wooden table looking out over much of the city; the Kome'denyd's landing was above most of the others, which made for a beautiful view, especially with the glow from the flickering candles and torches. Hours passed, and so did the hot shawthak brew between the two brothers. They spoke of everything from the darkness and where each of them was when it happened, to Capone's travels and Kelly's writing.

Eventually Kelly said, "I have something unbelievable to show you. I promise you won't believe it if I tell you, so just let me get it and show you."

Kelly was already halfway up the small stairs that led to his sleeping platform by the time he finished speaking, and before Capone could respond Kelly was headed back down with a quill and inkwell in hand.

"Is it some of your writing you want to show me?" asked Capone.

"Interesting question. Not in the sense you think. Again, just let me show you," responded Kelly.

"What would you like to have in your possession that you do not have currently?" asked Kelly.

Capone looked puzzled by the question. Kelly made a look to suggest Capone name anything at all.

"Hmmm, that is an odd question. I guess one of grandmother's pies. She would always have a fresh one ready for the eating. I notice you aren't quite as hospitable," Capone joked.

"A worthy request indeed," answered Kelly as he dipped his quill into the ink.

He then began to draw one of their grandmother's pies directly onto the wooden table.

"Isn't that ink going to make a mess?" questioned Capone, ever the overly responsible one.

"Just watch," answered Kelly as he continued to draw. "Blueberry or pumpkin?"

"Pumpkin," said Capone skeptically.

"Pumpkin, of course. If I remember, you liked the crust barely cooked, yes?" asked Kelly.

"Good memory," said Capone.

"I thought so. I, however, like a rather browned crust, so I'll draw one half of the pie darker than the other," Kelly said.

As much as Capone was happy to spend time with his brother, this charade, he thought, better have a decent payoff.

Within moments Kelly finished drawing the pie, and to Capone's utter dumbfounding, an actual pie rose out of the table exactly how Kelly had drawn it, with brown crust on half of it.

"Dessert is served," said Kelly as if nothing out of the ordinary had transpired.

Capone stared at the pie, then at Kelly, then at the quill. He poked at the pie. Then he lifted the pie up to inspect the table. The table was unchanged.

"It's getting cold. At least let me cut my piece before you continue your inspection," laughed Kelly, reaching for a wooden knife.

"Impossible. Is this some new magic trick? Where did you learn to do this? What is the secret?" questioned Capone.

"There is no secret. It isn't a trick. Whatever I draw with this quill becomes palpable. My thoughts become reality when I draw them with this quill. Don't you notice? It even smells just like grandmother's pie," explained Kelly.

Still in disbelief Capone asked, "Where did you get it?"

"It is the same quill I have used since I can remember. I have always had it. The thing is, on the day the light went out I was on the ledge writing. Shortly after the sky went black, a drop of what appeared to be a melted substance fell directly onto my quill and hardened onto it. I stopped writing and examined the quill, but really thought nothing of it. Shortly thereafter, after the initial chaos of the darkness was over, I went back to writing. Nothing was different. Then one day I was having trouble focusing on my writing and I started to draw in the margin of the scroll," Kelly continued, but reached into his pocket to reveal a mountain. Quite literally, a mountain

the size of the melted remains of the candle they had been using for light on the table. It fit easily in the palm of Kelly's hand; complete with miniature trees and a flowing waterfall.

"I had been wondering where you must be; what adventures you were having. And so, I drew this mountain. Moments later, like the pie, it became reality in the exact scale that I drew it. Smell it. It even smells like mountain air," exclaimed Kelly.

"This is incredible, and beautiful! What else have you drawn?" asked Capone.

"Many things, I have no idea what the quill's limitations are. As far as I know, it is only limited by my imagination, amount of ink and size of my drawing surface. Come upstairs and I'll show you many other creations—you have no idea," said Kelly.

"You drew the mountain because you were thinking of me," Capone said, primarily to himself.

"Uh-huh. Come on, let me show you," Kelly said with an excitement that turned to concern when he saw Capone's face.

"What is it? What's the matter, Capone?" asked Kelly.

"Let's not go up quite yet," said Capone, surprised that the moment had arrived.

Capone was caught off guard by his own candor. But he realized the time was now. Capone walked to the edge of the landing, away from Kelly. He was nervous, but also relieved that he would now have the chance to tell his brother all that was inside him.

"I remember when we used to run and climb all over these trees," said Capone with a nostalgic chuckle.

"We did move through Treetop City like we owned everything, didn't we?" replied Kelly happily.

Kelly continued, "Brother, those were the best days. We had no worries. What is this about?"

Capone fought back a tear with a smile, then turned and looked at Kelly as he spoke, for he couldn't hold in his feelings any longer. Slowly, as if tending a wound, choosing every word in such a way as to get his point across, Capone said, "Listen, Kelly." Then Capone paused before speaking again, "Now that it comes down to it, I can't find the words. That's ironic. I am supposed to be a teller of tales and yet when it comes to my own life, I can't find the appropriate words."

"What is it? Just tell me, brother," said Kelly.

Continuing Capone said, "Something has been weighing on my heart for years. I'm sorry. I haven't been there for you when you needed me. I wasn't the older brother I should have been, and I realize that, I've known it for some time. When I think about you when you were younger, I think how pure and genuine you were. And then I quickly remember how everything was a competition between us; and I was older, so I always won. I should have looked out for you more. I don't know why I never saw then what I see now, that we were the same, and that what was mine was yours. And that if you were sad, I should be sad, instead of victorious that I had won whatever that day's petty rivalry was. We are the same, you know. On the exterior, we manifest who we are differently, but on the inside at our core, you are more like me than any other, and I like you. When I left you, do you know why I wept? It wasn't because we would be apart. It was because I realized in that moment, in that one moment, that those years we spent together, just the two of us, were over. I realized they were over, and I realized I couldn't

go back; that my self-centeredness had robbed us both of something—each other. And I'm sorry for that, for both our sakes. So I've been waiting ever since for the moment to tell you, and I realized that every day that passed was another day I couldn't get back. I decided that I couldn't lose any more days, I would tell you today. So here I am. I don't want another day to go by without you knowing the love I have for you, brother. I'm so horrible with relationships, so inept at showing people that I love them. It has never been a question of having love for people, but a question of loving them in a way that shows them. I long to be selfless, and maybe one day I can achieve that aim. Until then, please bear with me."

Kelly was touched by his brother's words, and he was uncertain of the proper response. Nevertheless, he said the words that came to him, "I would say thank you, except for fear you would take it as a confirmation that I agreed with all that you said. But thank you for your willingness to address our relationship. That alone shows me what I already knew, that you love me, brother. And I love you. I would die for you. You are not the only one at fault, so don't carry that burden alone. We have both hurt one another through the years. Though there is one thing I disagree with you about. The years aren't over for us. Yes, we can't go back, but here we are together, brothers. We can move forward together. And also, let's not write off the past to failure. As we just finished recalling, we moved through this city like kings. We made the most of our time together, I have no regrets. So I will accept your apology on the condition that we can let it go now. I can. Will you? Will you release yourself of such a heavy burden?" said Kelly,

knowing that what he just said did not accurately communicate how grateful he was for Capone's words or the depth of healing they brought him.

Tears were welling up in Capone's eyes at the graciousness of his brother, "Yes, brother, I can do that. Thank you."

"Thank you. Now, will you follow me upstairs? You cannot prepare yourself for what you are going to see!" said Kelly with enthusiasm that came from a newfound affirmation of his brotherly bond.

"Lead the way!" said Capone.

They rounded the spiral steps to the next level and immediately Capone was stunned. Kelly's bed was as elaborately decorated as the King of Lithosis' would have been with golden, jeweled bedposts and colorful silky sheets and cushions. A mountain stream with live fish cut through the floor platform, but didn't leak or drip to the lower levels. Also, two large candelabras lit the room, with ever burning candles. On the table was the largest gourd for drinking shawthak brew Capone had ever seen, and there was piping hot brew in it that was perpetually warm.

"All the hot shawthak you could ever want, and I never have to brew it," said Kelly, beaming.

"Did you draw all of this?" asked a shocked Capone.

"Well I certainly couldn't have afforded it or crafted it myself. Like I said, the possibilities with this quill are limitless. However, I do have a very limited supply of ink," said Kelly with a wink, as he opened a cupboard with shelves full of ink. Kelly then with both hands patted the many ink bottles in the belt around his waist.

"Let me guess, you drew your own ink?" asked Capone, as he raised an eyebrow.

"You are beginning to understand," said a chuckling Kelly as he reached for a wooden box on a shelf.

"Has anyone else seen your landing? Have you shown anyone else what your quill can do?" questioned Capone.

"No. And it has been most difficult to keep the secret; especially with what is in this box. This could be the most incredible of all," said Kelly motioning for Capone to step closer to the box.

Kelly removed the top of the box to reveal a creature the size of a baby bird. Yet, this was no bird. It was a creature of Kelly's own concoction. Through the quill, Kelly's imagination had birthed this winged creature that resembled a miniature drakon.

"Kelly! You can actually create life! This is a most powerful object. There is no telling what you could do with this," Capone said.

Kelly motioned for his brother to keep his voice down, "I know. I always wanted to see a drakon. I just drew what I thought one would look like, but I made sure to make it really small. And of course I feel I should use the quill for a greater good, but I'm not sure how or what to do. I know I shouldn't keep it for myself alone," said Kelly unselfishly.

"Yes, you should use it to help others, but you should also use caution. Up to this point you have been able to control your creations. Make sure you don't draw anything that could be beyond your control," warned Capone.

Just then a bright red arrow stuck hard into a wooden box inside the Kome´denyd's landing, striking a small bell that hung inside the box. This meant there was danger in the forest below. There were certain families throughout Treetop City that were charged with the responsibility of alerting the city when there was trouble approaching. The Kome'denyds had always been a part of the chain. Already Kelly was reaching for his bow and aiming for the box at the rope-maker's shop. After letting the red arrow fly, Kelly put out the candles around his landing. Looking out over the city, Capone could see that lights were going out all over, the warning was working. The Fools constantly had scouts posted in the trees at the four major entrances to the Forest of Fools. If they saw a threat, they would send an arrow to another guard's post, and that guard would send one to the guards at the front entrance to the Treetop City. The entrance guards would then each send an arrow in a different direction in Treetop City. It only took a few brief moments for the entire city to be warned of imminent danger.

"Have you had many red arrow warnings of late?" questioned Capone.

"Yes, the darkness has brought with it many ill-intentioned creatures through the forest. Usually they pass by underneath us without a confrontation," explained Kelly, as he pocketed his quill and inkwell into his vest, for he never went anywhere without them.

The two bothers made their way to the ledge and looked out over Treetop City. Whereas a little while before they gazed out over a host of glowing lights, now there wasn't a single source of light to be found. Earlier they could hear boisterous conversations coming from the surrounding landings, but now only the sound of the forest's original inhabitants.

Quietly the brothers waited for several moments, their senses heightened to discern any apparent threat. Before long the indiscernible sound of distant voices broke the silence. Shortly thereafter, the brothers noticed a faint glow coming from the west. Both of the brothers simultaneously experienced a sinking sensation, realizing, more clearly with each passing shallow breath, that one of the greatest threats to the Treetop City had materialized.

"Fire!" shouted Kelly, realizing as he spoke that this was probably the word the voices in the distance were shouting.

Fire was a most dangerous visitor to the Treetop City, though the inhabitants had long prepared for such an unwelcome guest. Near the top of each tree that contained a landing in the treetop city, there was fashioned a large bladder that wrapped around the trunk of the tree, and from the time the city was constructed, these bladders remained full of water. There were four stoppers in each of the circular bladders that touched each trunk in four different places. Attached to these stoppers was a long cord that ran down the trunk of the tree to the platform level. All one needed to do was to pull these cords and a great gush of water would flow down the length of each tree trunk. While this would help deter fire from consuming the foundational structures of the Treetop City, the outer branches were still susceptible to flames. The inhabitants knew this, but they also knew that the recent constant rain certainly aided their cause.

"Now I'm certainly thankful for these relentless rains we've had. Remember to wait to pull the water cords until the fire is right at our doorstep," reasoned Capone.

"Ever the older brother, eh?" joked Kelly.

True, the rains did help keep the fire in the upper portion of the Treetop City at bay, however, the canopy that hid the city from the lower portion of the Forest of Fools also served to keep the lower forest much drier than the upper part. This would eventually cause the forest to burn right out from underneath the Treetop City, and its structures would crash with their foundations destroyed.

"What caused such a fire while we have had these constant rains? That is what I want to know," said Kelly. "I do not think this threat, whatever it is, is going to pass by without a fight. The red arrow, followed so quickly by a fire, this seems like a direct assault on the city. I'll swing up to the upper heights and see what I can find out."

"I agree, lead the way," replied Capone.

The upper heights were a series of platforms and landings that were higher than the rest of the Treetop City. They were also in the western part of the city, so naturally the brothers thought they could better assess the threat from there.

The brothers had left the Kome´denyd landing and were about to take hold of one of the ropes to swing to the next platform along their way, when strangely Capone had a thought of the vagabond down below on the forest floor.

Kelly handed the rope to Capone. Capone didn't take it. "What's wrong brother? What are you thinking?" asked Kelly.

"Actually, I'm not going to follow you just yet. There is someone, a poor, desperate outcast down below. I felt compelled to help him on my way to see you, but didn't. If the forest is on fire he will not know how to escape," said Capone.

"Outcast? I know of no such outcast. But if you feel you must go, then go. If things become perilous, meet me at the eastern ropes, otherwise look for me at the upper heights," said Kelly, more than a little concerned.

"Yes, brother," answered Capone.

Capone then quickly made his way through Treetop City and back to the entrance tree. There he found that Rowand and the other guards were nowhere to be found. Capone assumed they had gone to attend to the red arrow situation, as no one would be permitted into Treetop City under such circumstances anyway. All the more reason to go help this vagrant thought Capone. The only problem was that, with no one to operate the platform, Capone would have to climb down below to the Forest of Fools, and then returning to Treetop City with the feeble stranger would be even more difficult. Nevertheless, he spotted a rope ladder on the guard platform for just such purposes. He lowered the rope and descended. Capone was surprised to see, despite the urgency in the trees above, the peculiar traveler with the odd shoes was exactly where Capone last saw him.

Approaching the hooded character, Capone said, "Are you well friend?"

No response.

He continued, "There seems to be more danger than usual in the woods at present."

No response.

"You are welcome to come above and refresh yourself with warm food and drink if you like," said Capone, becoming more dumbfounded.

No response.

"My name is Capone," he said warmly.

"Capone," the stranger said.

"Yes."

"Tell your brother that Telle said to wear these," said the stranger as he handed the peculiar shoes to Capone.

"Kelly? But what are they for? Who is Telle?" asked Capone.

"There is no time to explain. Long have I waited for you to come. I fear it is almost too late, for the destruction of the Treetop City has already begun. Quickly now, find your brother. I must keep the enemy at bay as long as possible," the stranger then stood and, before bounding through the forest, changed shape from a feeble Reflection man into a glorious Archeon, a creature that Capone had never seen the likes of before. The Archeon's lavender eyes seemed to see straight to the core of Capone's being.

In a moment, the Archeon was too deep into the forest for Capone to see him. Carrying the shoes, Capone made his way back up the rope and into the Treetop City. With haste he crossed from platform to landing, making his way to the upper heights and to Kelly. The situation was rapidly deteriorating however, and many inhabitants of the city were running, swinging and jumping in the opposite direction of Capone with shouts of, "fire", "danger" and "flee the trees". The fire was visible now in all of its blazing terror. It had not yet reached the upper heights, for Capone could now see them.

After ascending one of several tall ladders, Capone found Kelly. But Kelly did not see Capone, for he was engaged in a battle for his life with a host of Sarxan warriors. With no

weapon, Capone instinctually charged into the fray, shoving two Sarxans over the edge of the platform, through the faux canopy to their deaths on the forest floor many feet below. This advance freed Kelly from their clutches for a moment. What guards were still alive and holding their positions in the Treetop City came to the brothers' aid with arrows fired from nearby landings.

"Fall back to the eastern tree," voices shouted, "the city is overrun!"

Capone and Kelly, barely armed that they were, needed no more prodding. The brothers tore through the Treetop City in a manner that they hadn't done since they were young. Amid such peril, the brothers were enjoying this moment together.

They were all the way back to Kelly's landing, when they noticed they had, for the moment, outrun their pursuers.

"We are a good distance ahead of the destruction, and there are a couple of items I want to save from inside, since I doubt we will ever see this place again," said Kelly.

"Kelly, are you sure that is necessary? We don't have much time. I will be glad if we both escape with just each other's company," said Capone.

"I will hurry, brother," Kelly answered.

"Well first, take these. I don't know what they are for, but the vagabond that I went to help turned out to be some other creature, the likes of which I've never seen. But he told me to tell you that Telle said to wear these shoes," said Capone hastily.

"I don't know of anyone named Telle."

"Trust me, Kelly. If you saw this creature...I don't have time to explain now, just wear them."

Kelly took the shoes from Capone and put them on. They were a perfect fit.

"Wait right here," he said to Capone, as he rushed inside.

While Kelly was inside, Capone was approached by a most enigmatic figure.

"Excuse me, can you help me?" the stranger said in an ethereal voice.

"I've only got a moment, but what do you need," Capone answered.

Unfortunately for Capone, the stranger was a Guiler. And the brief response that Capone gave was all the attention that he had to give to the Guiler in order to completely fall under the spell of one of these weavers of words.

Guilers were servants of Lure that went about their task in a most crafty manner. Their sole purpose was to distract, cause diversions for, and captivate with entrancing tales, the enemies of Lure. Guilers came into being when the first Dephilim were killed. The dark spirits of the deceased Dephilim would possess other hosts, usually Reflection, and with their new physical forms they would set about serving their master in this deceitful way.

Kelly returned in a few moments and saw Capone listening to the bizarre figure on the landing.

"Capone, we can go now," said Kelly, as he pulled the chords to unleash the water from the bladder around the tree that supported the Kome´denyd landing.

"Not quite yet, I was just listening to this tragic story that—I'm sorry I missed your name—this traveler was telling me. You'll never believe it, come here and listen. Would you mind starting over? Tell my brother what you just told me," said Capone.

"Very well," said the mysterious figure.

"We don't have long before the enemy will be upon us, so tell me quick," said Kelly as he moved over to join his brother.

And that was all it took. Tragically, both Kome´denyd brothers were now fully hypnotized by the Guiler's words. As the Guiler continued to tell her false tale, she began leading the brothers slowly through the Treetop City. If the brothers had looked away from the Guiler's eyes, they would have seen other Guilers leading other inhabitants of the City in the same manner and direction.

The Guilers brought their followers to the eastern side of the Treetop City and led them down to the floor of the Forest of Fools. There, in the exact place that those who weren't under the Guiler's spell, had fled, was the Archeskotos named Aven and his army. Aven had sent part of his forces to burn the forest from the west, and then he and the rest of his legion circled around to the east to apprehend the survivors as they fled the City.

Once in the clutches of Aven, the Guilers released the spell over their prey. Stricken, the Fools cried out as they were given the option of either rejecting their belief in Me and enlisting their talents in their many crafts into the service of Aven, and so Lure, or else being chained and beaten, and forced to march the long road to Aprioria. Many of the artisans of the Treetop City would not forsake their beliefs to join forces with their conqueror, and so the numbers of prisoners was greater than those who denied Me.

There was one long chain that connected all of the prisoners and, with each new captive, a new length of chain was added that branched off from the main one. At the end of each of these individual chains was fastened a large hook which would be inserted through the lip of the prisoner. This would serve to keep the captives from trying to flee, as well as prevent them from trying to sit down and rest on the long journey to Aprioria.

Those who did join Lure were forced to carry out their first command; that of inserting the hook through the lip of each of their enslaved kin.

Aven made his way to Kelly, who refused to join the side of his captors. Next, Aven gave Capone the option. With a plan devised, Capone agreed to join Aven. Kelly was about to protest, but Capone gave him a wink to let his brother know that he had a plan. His hope was that he would be assigned to Kelly, and as such, he would spare Kelly from torture on the journey.

"Welcome, servant of Lure. Prove your devotion" said Aven as he handed Kelly's hook to Capone to insert into his brother's lip.

Aven then continued on to the next Fools in line, offering them the same choice.

Capone saw that Aven was distracted and, instead of putting the hook through Kelly's lip, Capone whispered to his brother, "Bite down on the hook with your teeth to hold it in your mouth, brother. I will watch over you, until we see an opportunity to make our escape."

Kelly did as his brother asked.

Eventually all of the Fools had made their choice and Aven commanded them to begin the march to Aprioria.

The Fools marched south, their nostrils and eyes burning from the smoke given off by their blazing homes.

The chained Fools had only gone a little distance, when Capone's plan went terribly wrong. One of the chained Fools that was badly wounded fell to the ground, pulling the entire chain of prisoners down to the ground with him, the hooks working as they were designed to. All of the prisoners were on the ground, except Kelly, whose hook had been pulled from his teeth in the fall.

Aven noticed Kelly immediately, though Kelly quickly tried to cover for himself by falling to the ground as well. Yanking Kelly off of the ground by grabbing a fistful of his hair, Aven said, "No hook was stuck through this one. Who is responsible for this?"

Scanning the few Fools that agreed to serve him, Aven's eyes found Capone, and he spoke, "You were responsible for hooking him, come stand by me, wretch."

Capone cautiously moved over to stand by Aven, as Aven spoke, "In Lure's army there can be no traitors. There is no room for those who are not willing to fully comply with their master's commands. The price of treason is death."

In one swift move, Aven hoisted Capone in the air above his head, and brought the Reflection male, back first, down onto the knee of the Archeskotos. An audible crack was heard by all who were nearby as Capone's back was broken. Carelessly Capone's broken body was tossed to the ground by the pitiless Archeskotos.

Utter horror gripped Kelly after watching his beloved brother's life so suddenly and cheaply destroyed in front of him. "Brother!" Kelly cried out as he ran toward Capone, but he was intercepted by Aven's strong hands.

"Your brother didn't want to hurt you by putting a hook through your mouth. Very well. You will carry this wounded comrade all the way to Aprioria, and every time you fall or have to drop him from fatigue, you will cause all of your fellow Fools great pain by pulling them all to the ground by their hooks. Now, onward to Aprioria!"

The wounded Fool was none other than Rowand, and Kelly picked him up in his arms and marched, with tears pouring down his face, barely able to keep from hyperventilating with grief. All the while his mind was racing, trying to figure out a way to escape and run to his brother's body.

Rowand whispered in his ear, "I'm sorry, Kelly. I'm so very sorry."

I wept at the sight of true brotherly love. I wept for Kelly when faced with losing his brother, taken from him so brutally. I wept that their relationship so recently mended and healed, and blossoming like never before, was prematurely and abruptly severed. Again, one of my tears possessing one of my qualities fell to the Wisprian World and landed on Kelly. Like Kelly, how I longed to see the brothers live and laugh and take on new challenges together. Sadly, the time for such things had passed.

"'The possibilities with this quill are limitless.'"

THE SHEPHERDESS

umbled by the thought that maybe I did care for him, Sage's mind conjured up images of Odem and his mother. He recollected all of the perfect times they had spent together with all of his brothers and sisters. He remembered the joy that times with his family brought. His heart was finally realizing that such joy had to be a gift. A gift from someone, somewhere or something—and to whatever the source was that had given him such times and such joy, he wanted to show his gratitude. He just didn't yet know how.

"Are you ready to keep moving?" said Gad from beside a fully-provisioned Telle, as he handed Sage his backsack, ripped as it was from the thanatoph.

Sage nodded and the refreshed travelers continued across the dark clearing. Eventually they came to the other side. The

types of trees they were walking through began to gradually change from the coniferous, evergreen trees that lined the Canyons of Flame to squatty, knotted bark trees with long drooping branches that hindered their hike. The soil was also becoming more damp as they went along, signaling they were closer to water than before. Mud was flung from Telle's hooves as he trudged along. Large insects pestered Sage and Reverie. Those he could reach, Telle swatted with his tail, but occasionally one would sink its pinchers into Sage's neck or other exposed skin. The beetle-like insects were easily the size of Gad's thumb and their bite left a large red welt.

Few words were spoken between the companions as the wind steadily increased and made listening arduous. Though the rain had stopped for now, they were still getting wet, as the low, water- soaked branches smeared water on them every time they made their way through them. Reverie rode behind Sage on Telle's back; her arms wrapped around his waist and her head usually resting on Sage's upper back.

Their journey was long and tiring for several days, as they hiked through the forest. Provisions were running short and already they were all eating the plants and berries of the forest that they knew to be safe for food—all except Gad, who still had plenty of chaykaf. Then, without any warning, they came to what looked like a tiny, abandoned farm and another clearing like the one they had seen days earlier. A flimsy, wooden shack could be seen in front of them in the distance as well as the remains of a few wooden animal pens.

"I sense there is something here. We should proceed with caution," said Gad.

Sage and Reverie then dismounted Telle and the four of them walked slowly up to the side of the shack. Cautiously, they circled around it to the front door, listening as they went, for any sound of inhabitants. Once at the door, Gad knocked lightly then opened it. Telle and Reverie waited outside as Sage and Gad walked slowly inside, Gad's body giving off a dim glow. The interior of the shack was peculiar. Although much of the shack was what they expected, barren except for a few essentials, by the bed in one corner was a small table littered with some of the finest objects Sage had ever seen. Any one of these items would be worth more than every possession of Sage's family members combined. But there before his eyes were at least ten priceless artifacts. Everything from a precious necklace made from marbled diamonds, to a jeweled comb with artwork that looked to be Lithosian. There was also a colorful headdress made from the finest silks and fabrics ever beheld in Wispria. Additionally, there was a dagger, a weapon Sage had rarely caught sight of, for metal objects were scarce outside of the major cities. Yet, this dagger looked as though it had never been used; the filigreed hilt and pommel carved in the shape of a great palace were without the slightest scratch or blemish.

None of these items seemed to impress Gad in the least. He was drawn to the most inconspicuous looking object on the table; a palm sized stone with a yellowish brown reflection that seemed to have an inner glow—a piece of agapate. When Sage saw Gad reach for it, he was disappointed that he hadn't noticed it first.

"Another piece of agapate?" Sage inquired.

"I believe it to be," responded Gad, his upper body hunched over as he was too tall for the small shack. "Though it will be difficult to discover what power it has."

"Will Telle be able to discern it?" asked Sage.

"Perhaps," Gad replied as he turned to walk out the door with the stone.

As Sage was following Gad out of the small doorway, suddenly he felt a hard object grapple around his throat and a thud in his back. He tried to speak, but his airway was cut off. He banged his hand against the door to get Gad's attention.

"Why have you come here? What do you want?" said a voice from behind Sage.

Gad whirled around, but couldn't make out the figure that was hidden in the dark shack.

"Your people killed all of my babies, my entire flock! Why!? I saw what was done to them, the atrocious way they were killed! Were I in my homeland my father's entire army would have already destroyed you for that. Why do you return?" the voice continued.

Gad quickly interjected, "We have never been here before. We didn't attack your flock—"

"Do not try and deceive me. They all looked just like you! They came out of the Western Wood. What are you? And what do you want from me? Tell me quickly before I strangle your friend," said the now obviously feminine voice.

Sage's throat was burning and bruised from what appeared to be a shepherd's crook. He was struggling to free himself, but the shepherdess had him in a precarious position. The pressure his current body position was placing on his right ankle was excruciating. He thought of using the agapate, but he sensed his adversary wasn't evil, and though he wanted to free himself, he didn't want to harm her.

Meanwhile Reverie and Telle were outside with Gad, unsure how to proceed. While the three were standing outside the entrance to the shack, a lamb wandered up from the woods. Its white coat was pink and brown with bloodstains and its movement was labored as if it was tired or injured. When the shepherdess caught glimpse of the lamb she immediately released Sage and ran past him out of the door. Behaving as if the others didn't even exist, the shepherdess fell to the ground and wrapped her arms around her lamb, kissing his soiled, smelly face.

"Lum, my baby, Lum. I thought I'd lost you, come let me take care of you," she said as she began to cry.

Dumbfounded, the others stood and watched as the Reflection shepherdess ran inside to find food and water for her lamb. She had a pastoral look, but that wasn't to say she wasn't beautiful. Curly red hair the length of her shoulders bounced as she ran. Her face was dotted with a myriad of light orange freckles. Even the eyelids that closed over her tea-green eyes were dotted with small freckles. She was tiny and thin and pink-skinned. The way she carried herself suggested a lifestyle other than one of tending animals, and her clothing was flowy and luxurious. She moved with a gracefulness that complemented the loveliness of her countenance.

Wisely, in an effort to gain her trust, Gad said, "Let us help you. What do you need?"

The twenty-year-old shepherdess didn't respond but returned with a water skin and a dish of grain. "Here Lum, drink and eat your dinner. I'm so glad you're home."

Lum was breathing heavily and was clearly traumatized by something. His legs were shaking involuntarily and great streams of foam were dripping from the lamb's mouth. Fortunately, it seemed that most of the bloodstains weren't from Lum; for, except for a few minor scratches, no deep wounds could be noticed.

"Ssshh. It is alright. I'm here now. You've just got to rest," said the shepherdess with a calm, soothing voice—much different from the tone she had used with Gad.

But the lamb's condition was worsening. Even as the shepherdess poured water into its mouth, the lamb's breathing was becoming heavier and more frequent.

"It seems like the animal is in shock. Do you have something to calm it down and help it relax?" Sage asked.

"No," conceded the shepherdess.

"Unfortunately, we don't either," added Reverie.

Then Sage remembered that they did have something that made him forget his cares and that forced him to be at peace. The very thought of the chaykaf made him nearly indifferent to the lamb's needs. The thought of something else eating it other than himself or Gad didn't excite him at all. Still, he spoke up, "actually we do have something that will help."

"What are you talking about?" asked Gad.

"Just wait, you will see," replied Sage as he moved over to Gad's provisions.

Taking out the chaykaf he made his way over to the lamb.

"What are you doing with that? I told you never to touch that. I don't know what it will do to you or a helpless lamb," said an angered Gad.

Sage was making his way over to the lamb when Gad grabbed him by the arm, "Give me the chaykaf."

"I already ate some! I know you told me not to, but I couldn't resist. It made me forget all of my cares and gave me a feeling of peace, so much so, that it made me want nothing else. But a small dose, could be just what this lamb needs," said Sage impulsively.

Gad was silent. He purposely was holding his speech until his intense anger and distrust subsided.

"Please, if you think the chaykaf will help Lum, give him a little," said the shepherdess.

Gad remained silent. Sage glanced at him, hoping for a confirmation, but none came. "Just a little, ever so little," said Sage.

The girl's eyes were wide as she saw the solid, yet liquid food, being consumed by her lamb. After a few moments the creature closed its eyes and its breathing became smoother. Lum's legs were limp and any tension in his body vanished.

"Thank you," said the shepherdess.

Gad finally spoke, "That was not yours to give, Sage. Perhaps no harm will come of this, but nevertheless, you were wrong to take the chaykaf."

"I'm sorry," said Sage.

"Very well, I will not hold it against you, but see that you learn some self-control and refrain from taking it next time," Gad responded.

"That is a most peculiar name, and quite the amazing substance. What is chaykaf anyway?" asked the shepherdess.

Gad and Sage looked at each other to see if either of them was going to tell her.

The shepherdess continued, "I'm sorry, I guess I should introduce myself. My name is Duolos Dayroar. I apologize for the lack of hospitality I showed you, I can see by your actions that you are not who I thought you were. But you must realize, there were several large creatures that looked similar to you that attacked my flock of sheep. I am thankful, for I didn't even realize Lum survived; and now you have helped him—he is all I have left."

"I understand Duolos, I don't hold our first encounter against you, these are troubled times we are living in, and evil, it seems, is always lurking. My name is Sage Swiftsoul, I'm a Sprinter. The large white one is Gad, an Archeon. Yes, he is not unlike the other creatures you saw, but Gad is different, which I'm sure he will explain to you. The horse's, or rather, unicorn's name is Telle, and this is Reverie," said Sage.

"Hello," said Reverie in a tone that suggested she wasn't ready for another Reflection female in their company.

Gad spoke, "Chaykaf is heaven's bread. Yes, I am an Archeon, servant of Alphega and I come from Agapia—the celestial realm. Those who attacked you were rebellious Archeon—"

"Yes I remember them using the word Archeon, but they said they no longer called themselves that. Now they were Archeskotos. They wanted me to serve their leader, Lure. But why? Why would they come down from Agapia, if that is indeed what they did?" asked a skeptical Duolos.

"Archeskotos, 'the first darkness', an appropriate name for them to call themselves. One of the Archeon's original purposes was to worship the Day Star. Among other rebellious acts the Archeon, or Archeskotos, turned from the Day Star and fought against Alphega and the loyal Archeon. Unfortunately, this war has exceeded the boundaries of the upper realm and the front lines are now here in your world, in Wispria. But tell me, how did you escape the Archeskotos?" asked Gad.

"I am still not sure. I was trying to hide from them in the fields, and they acted as if I disappeared, it was very odd. I know I wasn't that well hidden among the tall grasses. True it was very dark, but still, unless they have trouble seeing, I thought for sure I would be found. Of course I did have my lucky stone—except wait, you took it from me, I remember now. I saw you take it from my table. May I please have it back?" answered Duolos.

"Lucky stone, eh? I will give it back under one condition, you must join us, help us in our quest. Oh, and never again refer to it as 'lucky stone'. It is a piece of agapate. It comes from Agapia and is very powerful," corrected Gad.

"That certainly is a big condition. I am grateful for your help, but I don't know that I can join you on your quest. I was never a follower of Alphega. I always wondered why one would believe in something that existed before them and would exist after they were gone. Those who believe in Alphega, what do they get out of their faith? In the end, they can't change their fate. Even believers die. They still exist in just a blink of an eye, and then are gone, nothing, forgotten forever. So why would I believe in a creator that made me, only to watch me die and forget about me?" argued Duolos.

"I assure you, Alphega forgets no one and no thing. And what the believers understand is that they can experience the blessings of Alphega in this world. Why do Reflection marry? Is it for some reason after death? No, it is for love and fullness in this life. An even greater fullness can be found with faith in Alphega in this life. Alphega wants immortality for the creatures of the Wisprian World, but thus far, it is the rebellious nature of His creation that is keeping them from His eternal presence. He longs to breathe His Spirit of eternal life into His beloved creation, and I believe one day He will. It is said He will even raise the dead back to life," stated Gad.

Then Gad continued, "And furthermore, take your sheep for example. Your sheep were created for a purpose, perhaps mainly to provide you with wool. However, is it not better for the sheep when they completely fulfill their purpose in this world? What if one was to leave your flock and forsake its ultimate purpose, would it not have to search for food? Would it not be more vulnerable to predators? Likewise, by completely fulfilling its purpose to you, its shepherdess, it is in turn, also living the best possible life for itself. If a simple animal such as a sheep knows this principle and benefits from it, I am at a loss to understand why more of Alphega's more intelligent creatures do not recognize this and benefit from it—benefit from living out their true purpose. Perhaps intelligence is the reason, or rather putting faith in their intelligence, instead of trusting the wisdom of the Almighty. But do not misunderstand me. Alphega does not need any one of us. That is true. He doesn't need us to fight against Lure. Ultimately, Alphega has already won. We fight because we love Him who created us, and we want to please Him. Though Alphega does not need us, He wants us desperately, for He loves us deeply, and only desires our love in return."

"I've never heard it put so eloquently. I am beginning to understand," said Sage.

"Here, Duolos Dayroar. Take your agapate. You don't have to believe what I am telling you, just come with us and see for yourself. There isn't much left for you here and we could certainly use your company," concluded Gad.

"Yes, Duolos, a short while with us, and you won't need much faith. We are seeing with our own eyes," explained Sage.

"Where are you going?" asked Duolos.

"Currently we are on our way to Aprioria in search of someone Reverie knows and in search of more agapate. From there we do not know where our journey will lead, I can only hope that Telle will have a vision to guide us as he has had thus far," Gad replied.

"I've never been fond of the Apriorians. They are too driven. Their ambition is paramount to all other aspects of life. They have no appreciation for the world around them. But if that is where you are headed, then you should keep to the banks of the Trankilo River. Its waters are calm and serene, in many places its banks are flat, and it runs into the very heart of the city. The Western Wood will be much slower and more dangerous, especially in this darkness," said Duolos.

She then glanced down at her little lamb and said, "I have a friend who lives on the way to Aprioria, on the water. If you will let me seek his counsel, I will come with you."

With reservations, Duolos agreed to join them. That is, after making sure that they would give time for Lum to recover, so he could go with them as well. In that time, Gad, Sage, and Reverie told Duolos of their journey up to that point. She could hardly believe the stories of the thricorn and thanatoph. And the description of the Dephilim was terrifying. All of the travelers were relieved to rest and regroup under shelter for a few days. Duolos had a dry batch of firewood and they had a fire going constantly. Though lighting a fire was risky because it gave away their location to any of the enemy's scouts, the warmth was a welcome change from the cold dampness they had recently endured all too often.

One of the discoveries they made during this time was the power that Duolos' agapate held. Duolos helped the group stage a reenactment of what happened when the flock was attacked and Duolos hid in her same hiding place, clutching her "lucky stone". Much to the surprise of the group, she disappeared completely among the tall grass. Duolos spoke to them and guided them right up to her. Once they touched her they could see her, but until that point she blended in with the grass perfectly camouflaged. The group then tried the same experiment among the trees of the nearby forest and against the wall of the shack, all of which produced the same result. As long as Duolos, or whoever was holding the agapate, didn't move, they were perfectly camouflaged.

"Duolos, you should know that it is not luck that saved you from the Archeskotos, luck does not exist. You were meant to have the agapate, meant to survive. And I believe there are great reasons for that, yet to be discovered," Gad said.

Then Sage asked the question that his companions had been wondering as well, "Duolos, how did you come to live out here. Where are you from, I mean, where is your family? Surely you haven't always been by yourself with your flock."

"That is a story for another time," Duolos replied decisively.

That evening before the companions slept, they re-supplied their packs, taking as much as they could from Duolos' small cupboard. The basic necessities were all they could carry, for the journey to Aprioria would be long, and extra weight only served to weary and slow them. Yet, Duolos did take every article from her table and put them in a small ornate bag with a long strap that she put over one shoulder and across her body. The rest of the group did not protest, but all found it the slightest bit odd, for unless she planned to sell or trade the objects, they were not very useful to their purposes.

Gad noticed another dynamic already emerging between Reverie and Duolos, with regards to Sage. Reverie seemed to be threatened by Sage's interest in this new female. And Sage was oblivious to the imminent rivalry between the two. For the time being, though, Gad simply observed and continued to be ever so skeptical of Reverie's intentions. The sleep they all had that night was the best they had gotten since any of them could remember. It was if they all knew it may be a long while before they would again have peaceful circumstances in which to sleep. The chilly wind that howled around them was offset by the warm crackling fire that was still burning. They had agreed that once they all awoke they would set out.

When all of their eyes were open, and they were preparing to leave, they saw Telle had written another message in the ground outside the shack:

UPON FINDING DUOLOS
WE SHOULD CHEER
LUM IT SEEMS
BEARS A TEAR

And Telle was correct, Lum was a tear bearer. For when I witnessed the destruction of his fellow innocent, helpless sheep, I was saddened. When Lum watched from his hiding place the destruction of his friends, when he walked among the scattered remains of his family, and his little mind couldn't comprehend the terror that had happened, when he cried out in his lamb sounds, sorrow came over Me. For My love is for all My creation, great and small, weak and strong, intelligent and simple. I vowed that I would never forget the little lamb, that he would be a symbol of victory in the end, and one of My tears fell on Lum.

"Upon finding Duolos we should cheer,
Lum it seems bears a tear."

THE CIVET

harmody did not know how to respond. So much of what Zimrawth mentioned was foreign to her. But she did not sense any deception in his voice or words. The creature that stood before her seemed truly contrite.

"He sounds sincere enough," Melony whispered.

"Do you think you can find a suitable place for our parents?" Harmody asked, resigned to the fact the twins could hardly manage the task alone.

"I told you as much," said Zimrawth with a smile. "I was hiding in a crevasse a little up river from here. It is high up on the bank and not visible from the water or land. We could take them there and then fill the hole in with rock."

"Alright," said Harmody solemnly.

"I will take your parents to the place then guide you and your sister there."

Harmody showed Zimrawth to the raft where her parents lay. One at a time, Zimrawth took the bodies in his arms and carried them up the bank and up river.

When he returned, he carried Melony in his arms and Harmody followed behind on foot. When they arrived at the makeshift tomb, Harmody took time to run her fingers through her father's hair in an effort to tidy it and made their garments as neat as she could. She refrained from removing the cloth over Hebel's head.

Tears were streaming down Harmody's face as she told her twin, "It is time to say goodbye."

Melony took Harmody's hand and was led inside the rocks to her parents, where she kissed her mothers's hand and touched her father's face. She then kissed her mother's hand again and touched the outline of her face under the blood-stained cloth. The eyes of Harmody silently dripped. Melony cried as well, but had no tears. A few steps away, Zimrawth watched as the feelings of sorrow and guilt gnashed at him, galvanizing his decision to do whatever he could to undo what had been set in motion.

The girls made their way out of the final resting place of their parents. From a distance, they waited as Zimrawth took many nearby boulders and, one on top of the other, several stones deep, he sealed the entrance. It would have been a long, strenuous task for many Reflection, but Zimrawth was happy to help the girls, and lifted the rocks with ease. The final stone was one of the largest and after he set it in place he asked Harmody, "What is your family's name?"

"Cantiq," she replied.

Then with his long, strong claws, Zimrath carved into the stone:

CANTIQ
BELOVED MOTHER AND FATHER

Zimrawth turned from the stone and looked at the girls. Melony couldn't see his handiwork, but Harmody nodded in appreciation. Then softly she started singing. Her song had no words only melancholy sounds of pain and sorrow. A few moments into her song, Melony joined in, the two of them harmonizing together in both a beautiful and tormented lamentation that grew louder as they sang. Zimrawth listened, moved by the sound he had never heard come from any being other than a native of Agapia. Then Zimrawth also joined in harmony with the girls. The rocky cliffs echoing back their mournful tune. None of them seemed concerned with whether or not they were heard by anyone.

When they finished, Melony said in a soft voice, "Zimrawth is it? Thank you. I am Melony and this is my sister Harmody. We are grateful for your kindness."

"You are special girls; that I am sure of. It is clear you have experienced much pain and have a burning desire for justice. If I can assist you any further, I will," said Zimrawth.

"You can take me to Lure. If he is responsible for this evil," said Harmody softly.

"That I cannot do. I would be sending you to your doom. I know only One who can challenge Lure by Himself. But He is for another time, another age, or so said the Archeon who were closest to Alphega. No, Harmody, there is no way you alone can defeat or even hope to challenge Lure."

"You don't understand. When I make these sounds—singing you say it is called, so far it has caused all of my enemies, those who looked like you and others, to instantly be stopped, never to move again. You are the only one it had no effect on. But I believe it would affect Lure. I could paralyze him with my voice as one paralyzes a rabbit with a lilweed spear."

"This is curious indeed. You say your voice paralyzed Archeskotos, but had no effect on me? I have not the wisdom to explain that. But I do have the wisdom to know that, whatever power you possess, it will not be enough. You must trust me. That is not to say we can't fight Lure from afar. For that is exactly what I was hoping to do. Disrupt his plans. Bring resistance against him as much as I can. Rescue as many from his clutches as possible. I had hoped you would feel the same. We can find others to join us in our defiance. Together we will still not destroy him, but we may defeat him. And even if we fail, each life we save from him is more than a small victory."

"Who do you think will help us? None of my people were even strong enough to survive against his forces. If there are those that did survive, I'm sure they only did so by pledging to join him, as we were given the chance to do."

"Yes, but take me for example. Though one may pledge to join him does not mean they won't later see their grievous mistake and turn against him. There are those who would rebel against the rebellion. Besides, I happen to know that Lure holds captive a number of Archeon who refused to join him, and are waiting to be set free to fight against him."

"Where are they being held?"

"I cannot be certain, but I suspect they are in Aprioria. I am not saying we should continue your present course to find them, for as I said, the rivers are busy with his transports. The skies are also full of thanatoph with Dephilim riders. We must find a path through dense cover to Aprioria. Our best hope of this is to cross the river and go through Feloidea Forest. The forest touches the northwest part of Aprioria and should give us ample cover while we travel."

Harmody and Melony trusted the advice of Zimrawth. So the three of them made their way down to the raft and rode it to the opposite shore. With Zimrawth leading the way, and Melony guided in-between the Archeon and her sister, they quickly made it past the rocky bank and into the dense forest.

They had walked a little way when Zimrawth asked, "Sweet Cantiq sisters, if I may ask, who gave you this gift of singing?"

"We can't be certain, but it happened the same time that my sister was changed—when the darkness came. She hasn't always been this way," said Harmody.

"Yes, she certainly is distinctively beautiful. And you don't know what caused the change? It just happened when the light was removed?"

"To be sure we drank from our water skins immediately before the change occurred and there was a fish in the skin Melony drank from, but I don't know why that would cause such a reaction," explained Harmody.

At this, Zimrawth stopped walking, "Do you mind if I examine your water skins?"

Harmody handed him one of the skins, hoping for an answer.

Even in the darkness it took Zimrawth one brief glance at the water to know it contained agapate.

"I sense home in this water," he said.

"Home?" inquired Melony.

"Yes. Agapia. Apparently, you Cantiq sisters have ingested agapate. I don't know how or why it had this effect. But I can say with confidence it occurred because you drank this water."

Zimrawth handed the water skin back, "Guard this precious liquid. It is both rare and mysterious. We must not let it slip into the hands of Lure or his forces.

"Is there a way to undo what it has done to me?" asked Melony.

"If there is a way, I don't know of it. Agapate was created by Alphega. It is the most powerful substance, and there are limitless possibilities with it. With agapate, Alphega created your world and everything in it. No being can fathom its potential. Sweet Melony, I would urge you to accept your transformation as a blessing. Clearly you have abilities that the rest of us don't. Be patient and seek Alphega's purpose in your uniqueness, and before long you will discover for yourself what a gift you are. And I will help you in any way that I can," said Zimrawth as he put his arm around the blind fish-girl.

"You mentioned noble Archeon, and that you were one of them. But the evil creatures that destroyed our village are Archeskotos, and you said they used to be Archeon? So what are you, Zimrawth, an Archeon or Archeskotos?" asked Melony innocently.

Zimrawth was ashamed, but answered, "Sadly, I do not know. I desire with all my heart to be a loyal Archeon, but

I know Alphega requires total loyalty. I never betrayed Him in my heart, but my actions were faithless. Furthermore, I do not know how to regain my place in Alphega's Kingdom. There are those in Agapia who call this the Age of Justice, and that the Age of Mercy is for a future time. But those same Archeon say that Alphega searches the heart. It was in Lure's heart that he betrayed Alphega. For our purposes, let us hope I am an Archeon."

"Archeon it is then," said Harmody, too weary for such weighty discussions. "We should keep going."

"Yes," Zimrawth said, his amber eyes glowing with warmth for his new friends.

Though close in proximity to the Whistling Wood, the Feloidea Forest was more pleasant to walk through. The damp weather brought out the natural smell of the Forest's flora, even the bark of the trees had a pleasant aroma. Harmody got the feeling they were being watched, but not by a sinister force. Rather, she felt curious, friendly eyes were gazing at them. Soon they came to a clearing Zimrawth knew to be the Great Road.

"Wait here, gentle ones, while I make sure the road is clear," cautioned Zimrawth.

He moved nimbly for a creature of his size, and Harmody watched as he disappeared into the darkness. Little evidence remained in the muddy soil of the road. Zimrawth could see Sarxan tracks heading in both directions, but they had been muddled by the persistent rains. Still, he knew the Great Road to be the main artery in and out of Aprioria, and as long as they were near it, they risked being discovered. Returning to the twins, Zimrawth urged them to quickly follow him across the road. Once they were across and far off the road, he went back and covered their tracks to ensure they would not be followed.

Distancing themselves from both the River and the Road, they hiked for hours, the twins telling stories of their youth. The respite from conflict allowed the girls to at least enjoy each other's company, though great quantities of melancholy still permeated their conversation, especially with each mention of home. Every story filled Zimrawth with gladness, and the innocence of the twins comforted Zimrawth and reminded him of his days in Agapia.

"This looks like a suitable clearing to make camp," said Zimrawth, aware of the distance the young Reflection girls had traveled.

"Make camp? Shouldn't we keep on going?" Harmody questioned.

"I understand the vengeance that is fueling you, but emotions can only carry your body so far. You should rest."

"'Mody, my legs and feet are tired," said Melony.

"Alright, lets rest. But there is no need for a camp. We should only risk an hour or so at most," said Harmody, anxious to get to Aprioria.

"So be it. I'll keep watch. You two try and sleep," said Zimrawth.

Harmody propped Melony up against a smooth boulder, "Are you comfortable sister?"

"My head isn't very comfortable," replied Melony.

Harmody then balled up the satchel with the supplies and placed it behind Melony's head. Melony nodded in affirmation,

so Harmody proceeded to rest beside her sister with her back against a tree. The water skins with the agapate water were on the ground between the girls. Perched on the rock above them, Zimrawth began to softly sing a song from Agapia. The twins couldn't understand the language, but its soothing, trance-like sound did succeed in making even Harmody fall asleep.

Little glowing orbs began to dot the darkness two by two and over time they became more numerous as they came closer to them. Zimrawth was well aware of the scores of yellow eyes watching them through the trees, but he found the eyes to be more curious than hostile so he continued to let the twins sleep for the time being.

"What brings you through the Feloidea Forest? Do you have evil intentions? Where have I seen your kind before? Do you know you are greatly outnumbered strange ones?" said many voices to Zimrawth's mind. The voices were not audible. The questions were communicated directly to Zimrawth's thoughts. Whatever these creatures were that were questioning him were obviously surrounding them in the darkness with eyes fixed.

"We mean you know harm," said Zimrawth aloud.

"So you can hear us? What are you unusual creatures that can communicate with the Civet? Do you understand how rare it is that you can hear us? Can your smaller companions hear us as well?" once again the voices communicated with no sound as the eyes inched closer.

The creatures were nearly upon the twins below when Zimrawth said aloud, "Do not come one step closer. I have told you our intentions are not malicious. But we will defend ourselves if necessary."

Zimrawth's voice was loud enough this time to wake the twins. Harmody grasped for a lilweed spear, startled, but ready for a fight. "Harmody what's happening?" questioned Melony.

Staring through the darkness Harmody could see slender creatures that were smaller than Reflections, and were covered in hair. One of the animals was standing on two legs right above Melony, and Harmody could see the bare legs were grayish in color with black spots, while the torso and arms were a lighter gray with black stripes. They wore no garments on their short bodies but were covered in hair from the tips of their black clawed hands to the tips of their black clawed feet. It was apparent from the coloring that they blended in perfectly with the darkness. Pointy ears stuck up among short black hair and yellow eyes were all that betrayed their camouflage.

"Can you hear me say that I do not want to hurt you?" a voice asked Melony in her mind.

"Yes. I can hear you and I don't want to hurt you either," she replied.

"I didn't say anything," said Harmody.

"I'm not talking to you, I'm talking to whoever is standing next to me," said Melony.

"But that thing didn't say anything," said Harmody alarmed.

"Can you not hear me?" said the Civet to Harmody's mind, but received no response.

"Can you hear us?" asked another Civet.

Harmody was oblivious.

Meanwhile, Zimrawth had leapt down from the boulder and stood beside the girls. The nearest Civet wasn't as tall as his knees.

"They are communicating through our minds. I can hear them. Apparently Melony can also hear them. But I can't say why either one of us can hear them and you can't," explained Zimrawth.

As Zimrawth was speaking to Harmody, another Civet stalked on all fours up to one of the water skins containing the agapate water. Before Harmody could react, the Civet snatched up the skin and scurried back to investigate the liquid among the other Civet.

"Give that back! That does not belong to you! That water is not safe," shouted Harmody as she leapt after the Civet.

But it was too late. A group of twenty or more Civet were sniffing and pawing at the skin.

"A new smell? What is inside? What have the strangers brought with them?" the Civet were saying in their way; heard by both Zimrawth and Melony.

Harmody raised two spears overhead to hurl them into the clump of Civet, but Zimrawth grabbed both from her hands.

"These are not evil creatures!" sternly said Zimrawth. "Listen my new friends—do not touch the liquid in that skin. Please for your sakes, give it back."

"*Let go, I warned you, let go!*" sang Harmody.

The Civet stopped in their tracks. But they were not paralyzed. They were enthralled with the sound they heard. Harmody was disheartened that, again, the sound didn't work as she wanted. A few of the Civet rushed to her and were pawing at Harmody's mouth trying to understand the sound she made. Up close, Harmody could see that the Civet had long whiskers on their furry faces and she sensed that they really were amiable in spite of their aggressive curiosity.

Many of the other Civet, though interested in Harmody's voice, were undeterred in trying to drink the agapate water. The brief distraction also caught Zimrawth's focus enough to give the Civet the time to penetrate the skin. Within moments they had opened the skin and were lapping up the potent substance, much to Zimrawth's dismay. Even the Civet around Harmody darted over to the water and drank of its hidden power. Helpless to intervene, Harmody watched in bewilderment as the skin was tossed about.

While the Civet were occupied, Harmody took the other skin and hid it in the satchel behind Melony's head. She then draped the satchel over her shoulder and made sure the other skin would not be taken.

"It won't be long now, if the water changes them as it changed us, it will happen momentarily," said Harmody, looking on intently.

Realizing that any attempt to intervene at this point would be unsuccessful, Zimrawth cautioned, "Remember, brave Harmody, agapate is mysterious. It may not act in the same way with the Civet."

The first Civet to drink the water, the one called Jesha, clutched her throat and began to writhe on the forest floor. One by one the other Civet joined her, each clutching their throats.

Melony and Zimrawth could hear the creatures in their minds saying, "What is happening to us? Is it burning us? How do we stop the pain?"

"The pain will pass quickly," Melony shouted, trying to calm them, but the pain was so great none of the Civet heard her.

The Civet's questions turned to subliminal screams. Many limbs were torn off of nearby bushes at which the creatures pulled and clutched. Some of them wallowed in the rain soaked ground. Others were stilled with the intense pain they were experiencing.

Then a sound like a squawking bird and a creaking door rose from among the flailing animals. Soon the sound was joined by other similar noises. Zimrawth and the twins soon noticed that all of the Civet made the disturbing sound. Yet, as quickly as the sound began, so quickly, it stopped. Jesha stood, perplexed at the sound she made.

"H-hello? What is this? Can I hear my own voice in my ears as well as in my head?" she asked with a voice that was fluid and slinky.

"Have you never heard your own voice before?" questioned Zimrawth.

"Are you asking if we have ever made noises from our mouths like you?" another Civet said.

"What was the elixir you brought with you that has given our thoughts sound?" a third Civet asked.

"We will explain these things as well as we can. But we still do not know that you are not hostile creatures. You wrongfully took our water. There are many who would have killed you for much less an offense. We have been more than affable with you. Now give us proof that you are friendly creatures," demanded Zimrawth.

Many of the Civet continued to question one another about the sounds they were making, but Jesha responded, "Do you question the integrity of the Civet? What will assure you of our intentions? Will you follow the Civet?"

"We don't have time to follow you, we have already wasted enough of our time here, we have to get to Aprioria," interjected Harmody.

"Patience, brave Harmody, we may have found those who would aid us in our cause. Believe me, we will need as many allies as we come across," said Zimrawth.

"Do you consider the Civet your allies? Where is Aprioria? Can the Civet help you get there? Will you please come with the Civet and let us give you guidance for your journey?" said Jesha methodically.

"Jesha, do you think it wise to show these strangers to the knowing one? Are these the ones we were looking for?" said one of the other Civet.

Jesha responded by asking Zimrawth, "What are your names strangers?"

"Greetings Jesha, I am Zimrawth, once a noble Archeon. This is Harmody and Melony Cantiq, sisters who have been through much pain and tragedy of late," answered Zimrawth.

"Do you still consider Zimrawth, Harmody, and Melony strangers? Can you sense any evil in them?" said Jesha to the Civet.

The other Civet said nothing, but began to form lines on either side of the girls and Zimrawth, not in a threatening way, but a protective way. Jesha apologetically handed Harmody

the water skin saying, "Will you pardon Jesha? Will you come with her?"

Reluctantly, Harmody nodded in affirmation. So the Civet, with Jesha leading the way, led the trio through Feloidea Forest at a very brisk pace. The Civet were so dexterous that Zimrawth carried Melony on his back just so they could keep up. They continued at this brisk pace for what seemed like several miles to Harmody, who, even in her top form, was rapidly becoming fatigued. They came to a place where the trees became taller and suddenly Jesha stopped.

Looking up, Harmody could see, high in the branches above, more eyes staring down at her. Once again Melony and Zimrawth could hear voices in their heads, but Zimrawth realized they were coming from the Civet that didn't drink from the water. Harmody's eyes shifted from looking up and immediately they were drawn to a glimmer on the ground a short distance away. Harmody pointed it out to Zimrawth. Walking over to the shimmering ground, both were astonished at what they saw written there.

FROM O'ER THE RIVER BRIO THREE VOICES SING
A VOICE TO CIVET THEIR WATERS BRING
ZIMRAWTH AND THE TWINS CANTIQ
REDEMPTION REVENGE AND REVELATION SEEK

There in front of them was a gray horse with a silver horn. Zimrawth and Harmody were still speechless at the prophecy they were reading. Harmody wondered if their voices had been loud enough when they sang to reach this far into the Forest. Then she realized the foolishness of her questioning since they were currently many days away from Nahar Kome´, where the girls first unleashed their power. Zimrawth, meanwhile, took the message seriously and watched as the horned horse continued to write.

WOUNDED AND BOUND AND FROM UPSTREAM
WILL COME ONE WHO WILL JOIN OUR TEAM
SORROW AND PAIN WILL KNOW HIM WELL
YET HIS SAD TALE HE'LL NEVER TELL

I AM TELLE AND I AM LATE
A SPRINTER WILL SOON FIND AGAPATE
REST WITH CIVET 'TIL SING DO THEY
APRIORIAN LIGHT PRECEDES BATTLE DAY

When he had finished, Telle gave a nod of his head and quickly galloped into the darkness toward the Lost Lakes. All of the Civet had gathered around the trio as they were reading. As still and reverent as they had ever been, the Civet knew they had found the ones Telle had told them, through prophecy, to find. Jesha knelt at the feet of Zimrawth and Harmody in submission, looking to them now for guidance. Four of the Civet pledged their service to Melony immediately upon confirmation of who she was. At the moment, at least, Harmody's need for immediate vengeance was replaced with a newfound purpose and hope, "This Telle said there will be a battle day—"

"Yes, brave Harmody, there will be. And we must be ready," cautioned Zimrawth.

Four of the Civet pledged their service to Melony.

COUNTERFEIT LIGHT

nimus woke to the feeling of a fierce smack across the face from a Sarxan hand. "Wake up, you! Master Krue has some questions for you," said the one who slapped him.

Animus struggled to keep his eyes from closing; the trees and Sarxans that were around him spun in an endless circle in his vision. He had chords wrapped around his arms that held them next to his sides, and the same chords bound his hands in front. Most of his armor was taken off him and he was shivering in the cold. Bound to a tree, the trunk was cold against his bare back. Azarmuth was nowhere in sight, but it did give him a spark of hope to see his daughter's whistle still around his neck.

His head was suddenly jerked up by his chin by a strong hand at least as large as Oze's paw. He looked into the face of

a most enchantingly evil creature. It was not a fleshly creature, but rather its physical body was both the color and texture of ashes. Its arm, though it too resembled an ashy, burnt branch, was nonetheless firm in gripping his neck. Orange eyes glared at him as the creature's other hand pressed into the arrow wound in Animus' arm.

Animus gritted his teeth and winced in pain as the creature spoke, "Where did you get the axe? How did you bring forth flame from it?"

"You might as well just go ahead and kill me if you think I'm going to tell you anything," said Animus, recognizing this creature as fitting the description of the invaders he had heard tell of.

"Oh, you are wise to wish for death, for what you are about to endure will be much more painful. You dare challenge Krue, the Archeskotos? Very well," said Krue, motioning to two Sarxans standing nearby.

The Sarxans each produced a small fur pouch. They opened the pouches to reveal, much to Animus' dismay, snow worms. Snow worms were, on average, the size of a Reflection's finger. They had no visible eyes, and the most defining feature of their white squishy form was the dual mouths at both ends of their bodies that were the size of the circumference of their bodies. Snow worms were used as a common form of torture, but not because of their bite. True, their bite was painful as they quickly bore into flesh, but as they ate their way through muscle tissue, their bodies did not grow in size, rather they metabolized their food instantly, but unlike all other creatures, in doing so they gave off cold instead of heat. The bodies of snow worms were ice cold, and so as they adulterated their prey they brought intense cold; as though ice were directly touching the victim's bones. If not removed, the snow worms would cause Animus unbearable, intense pain as he died from the cold within him. After they killed Animus, if left alone the snow worms would consume all of Animus; not one hair or fragment of bone would be left.

Animus knew the danger. Though they were rare, he had seen snow worms in the wild. He had once witnessed a wolf as it writhed and convulsed in the snow, biting its own hide to try to remove the snow worms, only to die shortly thereafter. Animus watched as the wolf disappeared little by little, until nothing but the worms remained, and they quickly retreated under the snow.

The Sarxans were careful as they took the worms from their pouches. The pouches were already ragged from the worms trying to eat to their freedom.

"Last chance, Reflection. Tell me what I want to hear, and I will give you a quick death and spare you needless suffering," said Krue.

Angling his head in an effort to reach the whistle, Animus ignored Krue's proposal. Animus' attempt was futile however; there was no way he could reach his daughter's whistle. A little more time out in the cold of Almachora without most of his clothes would kill him regardless. He was already numb in many places. He thought to himself that if this was indeed how he was going to meet his end, he would not give his adversaries the satisfaction of seeing him suffer. So the only solution Animus could think of in the moment, as the snow worms were being placed onto his bare skin, was to lean his head forward, and with all of his might bang the back of his head against the tree he was tied against. Animus was knocked unconscious.

Krue was furious at the cleverness of Animus, and that he had achieved a small victory. Already behind schedule, not expecting an encounter with Animus, Krue could not afford the time to wait on Animus to come around. He ordered the Sarxans to remove the snow worms, which had already plunged half of their bodies into Animus' flesh. Then Krue had the Sarxans untie Animus and rebind him on the small longboat that brought superior weapons from Aprioria to aid the Sarxans in their battles with the Almachorans. Krue had been overseeing the campaign against the northern lands, but he was handing the duties over to Dephilim captains that came with him on the boat, for Krue was needed in Aprioria. Animus was secured, and the Dephilim took the last of the weapons off the longboat. Then large pieces of marbled diamond were loaded onto the boat where the weapons had been. Shortly after this transaction, Krue and a crew of six Sarxans boarded and prepared to shove off down this particular tributary of the River Brio.

"Children, I expect you to give me victory all the way to Koref Kome´and the Ice Castle," were Krue's parting words to the two Dephilim he left in charge.

The Sarxans who were responsible for moving the unconscious Animus had been careless, as Sarxans usually were. Ergo, Animus regained consciousness as they were dragging him by his legs across the rocky shore toward the longboat, but the Sarxans didn't notice. Blood from Animus' wounds stained the pebbles underneath him and, though he was still groggy from his concussion, the pebbles gave him an idea. With his eyes closed and pretending to still be knocked unconscious, Animus cupped a few pebbles in his hand.

Animus was bound sitting upright, on a bench near the back of the boat. His feet were still tied and his hands were tied together in his lap with his legs strapped to the bench. Animus slumped over to give the impression that he was still passed out. The Sarxans tossed Animus' furs over him to make sure that he wouldn't freeze to death on the way to Aprioria. This would be to Animus' advantage. When he was sure no one was looking, he moved his hands to his wound and allowed blood from his wound to drip into the pebbles in his hand.

The boat's bow was tall in relation to the size of the six-oared longboat. Crafted to resemble a Leviathan, the bow went out from the ship, upward and then curled back toward the ship. When looking straight ahead, the Sarxans would be looking at a highly detailed, seven headed leviathan carved by Aprioria's finest craftsmen. This served as a warning to them of the serious nature of sailing, being that, in general, Sarxans had little experience on water before the Archeskotos arrived.

The boat left the shore and headed downriver. Slowly Animus opened his eyes and lifted the furs so that he could peek out and see if any of his adversaries were watching him. Fortunately for Animus, all of them, even Krue, were concerned with guiding the boat away from rocks. Noticing they were only a short distance from the shore where he had been interrogated, Animus took one of the pebbles and quickly tossed it ashore in the hopes that Oze would be able to follow his scent. Immediately, Animus resumed his position of feigned unconsciousness. Animus would successfully repeat this tactic several more times sporadically while he continued the journey downriver. Eventually, his wounds and fatigue caught up with him, and he fell asleep under his furs in his slumped-over position.

Krue awoke Animus by lifting him by his throat until he was sitting straight up saying, "You thought you were wise in trying to rob me of the enjoyment of watching you suffer. Your futile attempts to prolong your wretched life will only result in more pain for you when we reach Aprioria."

Then with his black clawed fingers Krue slashed Animus from his shoulder across his chest to his opposite hip. "Alphega has already given me victory over you, for I have fully surrendered my fate to His will —there is nothing left for you to take from me," quietly said Animus.

Furious at Animus' contempt, Krue yanked one of the oars from the side of the boat and out of a Sarxan's hand and with it struck Animus' head. "You wished to be unconscious, so be it, pathetic mortal," yelled Krue.

Then Krue handed the oar back to the Sarxan saying, "If he wakes up, hit him again."

Much time passed before Animus regained consciousness. And when he did, the Sarxan charged with watching him was rowing again. Still, Animus could barely make a cohesive thought; much less remember why he had bloody pebbles in his bound hands. He closed his eyes and drifted off to sleep again, with his head pounding.

The next time, Animus was awakened by Krue talking with Dephilim guards at a post along the banks of the River Brio as the boat drifted by. Lure's forces had a firm hold on all of the major thoroughfares, be them land or water. The temperature was still cold but had warmed considerably. Animus reasoned he had been on the boat for a long time. His stomach growled and he couldn't remember when he last ate. He was cognizant enough to remember the reason for the pebbles and he quickly tossed a couple of them ashore.

They continued to drift along and Animus had been inconspicuous enough to not draw attention to himself. Occasionally, he noticed the Sarxans would relieve each other and allow each other to rest or partake of the crude meat they had onboard. Animus' stomach turned at the possibilities of the source of the meat. Animus noticed Krue neither ate nor needed rest; it was as if he was sustained by the darkness and cold that surrounded them.

Burning and soreness intensified and spread from Animus' wounds. His entire body was in sharp pain from keeping himself in the position he was in for such a long time. His mouth was parched. With every swallow, it felt like he was swallowing sand. He could hold out no more; he had to drink. He risked leaning as far to the edge of the boat as possible in hopes the river would splash upon his face and he could drink. But it was no use; he was too restrained to reach the water. Still, the rain continued to fall, so Animus cupped his bound hands and collected what rain he could. He licked his bloody palms, which still held two pebbles, and this insignificant amount of water didn't begin to quench his thirst. Yet, he had little else to do on the long cruise downriver, so he continued to drink the rainwater.

Shortly thereafter, Animus tossed his next to last pebble ashore. This time however, Krue saw him.

"I told you to guard him!" said Krue to the Sarxan closest to Animus.

Krue yanked the Sarxan up from his seat and threw him overboard. Then he turned to Animus, "What were you doing Reflection?" He pulled apart Animus' hands and saw the pebble. "Leaving a trail? How fortunate that if your friends follow you, they can watch you suffer before they join in your fate." And he let Animus keep his pebble. "Let me know if you need more," Krue sneered before again striking Animus' face.

Much time passed. Eventually, the boat came to two large wooden signs on either shore of the river as they neared Aprioria. Written in the one language it read:

BE YE WARNED, LORD LURE HAS DECLARED ALPHEGA DEAD. PRACTICE OF THE ARCHAIC WORSHIP OF ALPHEGA IS TREASON AND PUNISHABLE BY SLOW AND PAINFUL DEATH.

Looking past the sign into the thick brush, Animus saw several pairs of tiny eyes staring at him. As he looked at the beady eyes, Animus thought he heard a voice speak to his mind that said, "If you are an enemy of Lure, are you our friend? Does it cheer you to hear us tell you not to lose hope?"

Because of the numerous blows to his head, Animus was sure he must have been hallucinating. He also thought that he was developing a fever from his untreated wounded arm. But again a voice in his head asked, "Do you have a sad tale that you will never tell?"

236

Upon hearing such a question, Animus looked around. He wondered if someone knew what had happened to his family, and all of the pain he had endured recently. His thoughts turned to his family. In his mind, he saw his daughter and how she used to smile at him when she was a newborn. He remembered the innocent purity she possessed. Then he remembered the sight of her cold body. His throat tightened. How he wanted to break down, even here among his enemies. The visions in his memory were exponentially more painful than any physical wound he had received.

The boat drifted under a bridge and eventually found its way into the busy river port in western Aprioria. There was a much larger port on the Gulf of Tanaudor that was used largely in trading, but this smaller port on the River Brio had become the primary transportation locale for the military campaign that was being waged against Almachora.

When the Sarxans on the docks noticed Krue arriving, they scurried to have the boat tied-off quickly and the marbled diamond unloaded.

Again Animus heard the voices in his head, "Do you know that many boats have we waited for you? Will you follow the Civet if they rescue you? Will you fear Zimrawth if he fights for you? Will you know that, though he resembles the one that has captured you, Zimrawth is your friend? Will you join us in our cause? Can you hear us? Are you going to be looking for us to come and rescue you, friend from upstream?"

Animus replied to these voices silently, "I don't know who you are, but if you are real, and not the result of me being hit in the head so many times, then yes, I welcome your aid, and I will consider you my friends."

"Careful with that rock, you sniveling Sarxans! Put the prisoner with the others for now. And take the last of the marbled diamond to the craftsmen. Master Lure will be most pleased to have the materials to complete his effigy," Krue ordered.

There were several prisons in Aprioria, but the prison that Animus was taken to was specifically designed by Lure to hold the captive Archeon. Three Apriorians and three Sarxans escorted Animus from the docks and through the narrow twisted streets of Aprioria. All of the streets in Aprioria were winding and narrow, designed specifically for the purpose of turning the city into a large maze. The reason for this was to protect the city from pirate invasions. The pirates that tried to ransack the city, then attempt escape, would unexpectedly get lost in the city allowing the Apriorian warriors time to respond and hunt the intruders. This series of events had transpired multiple times throughout the history of the city.

The ugly, rancid streets, the streets where the poorest Apriorians, the diseased and fish mongers dwelled, were the streets that Animus was escorted through. There were beautiful parts of the city, but Animus would never have known from his view. Dark, wet walls were on either side of the narrow street, Animus had to look straight up to even see the black sky above him. Occasionally there was a torch struggling to burn near the shelter of a cloaked figure, or a candle burning inside a barren shop, lighting his path. Multiple times Apriorians would have to press themselves against the sides of the buildings in order to let Animus and his escort pass through the tight streets.

They led him down a set of stone stairs that seemed to be newly laid compared to the street he had been walking down. The stairs continued down, a greater distance than Animus thought possible. Finally, before him was a door large enough for Krue to easily pass through. Sitting outside the door was a hooded and robed figure that seemed to be in a trance-like state, clutching a small stone statue. Beside this mysterious hooded figure was another creature that resembled Krue.

The Apriorian guards didn't take the time to bind Animus any more than he already was, saying to the creature, "Brise, this is a captive of Krue, he has special plans for this one." Brise then opened the great doors and hurled him inside the blackness. The door made a deep boom as it closed behind him. Several bolts and latches echoed off of the stone walls as the door was locked securely.

Slowly, Animus felt his way through the cold dark cell. He was surprised with how large the room seemed to be. Animus' hands were skimming the jagged stone floor when suddenly his hands touched something round and hard that had a soft exterior. A large, dim light filled the room, followed by other dim lights. It was then Animus realized he was touching the calve of some large creature that radiated light from within. Then the creature spoke in a soft, weary voice, "Hello, friend. I say 'friend' because if you are in this prison with us then you must be an enemy of Lure."

Animus thought this creature also looked very similar to Krue in the darkness, "Friend? You look like you are a friend of Krue to me. Are you all in here to torture me further?" said Animus.

"Ah, yes, that is understandable. We do resemble Krue, though one would hope we look at least a little kinder. You see, Krue was once one of us, an Archeon, one of the first beings. Now he has become an Archeskotos, one of the first beings of darkness. My name is Simin," said the silvery one bound in chains, whose calve Animus' hand was still touching.

"Your wound is festering, friend. Come let me help you. My name is Xander," said another Archeon from across the cell.

Animus slowly made his way toward Xander, all the while gazing at the other Archeon who were now glowing in the darkness. "But how did so many of you end up imprisoned? It would take an army to overpower all of you. How many others like Krue are there?" asked Animus.

"There are many others that were like Krue, and Lure is more powerful than any of us. Add to their superior numbers the power of fallen pieces of agapate, and they are a formidable adversary. The chains that bind us are held together by a peculiar force. My name is Yael. You have yet to tell us your name though, friend," said the Archeon next to Xander.

"His name is Animus, I recognize his voice as one of the most devoted followers of Alphega in all of the Wisprian World. You are from Almachora are you not, Animus?" said yet another Archeon.

"Yes. How do you know me?" asked Animus, a little spooked that he was in a dark confined space with a large creature that knew this much about him.

"I don't really know you, but I know of you, as Alphega has spoken of you in the past. I have also heard several of your pleas. My name is Bliss," said the Archeon, joyfully.

Animus paused. He was overwhelmed and humbled that not only had I heard his prayers, as he had believed, but I had mentioned him in the heavenly realms. He sat speechless.

Then Xander said, "That is a great burden for a Reflection to carry, Bliss. Maintaining humility is difficult under such circumstances. There is a reason such knowledge is rarely known in the Wisprian World. Come, Animus, Bliss would not have revealed such information to you if you were unable to bear it. Know that Alphega hears your pleas and know that He loves you. Take these glad tidings and treasure them in your heart, let it be a source of encouragement to you. Anything more will be revealed another time. Now sit beside me and let me tend your wound."

Animus sat beside Xander gladdened by this new revelation. Xander extended his chain-bound hands to Animus and touched his wounded arm. A warm light radiated from his hands, and the pain in Animus' arm immediately subsided, though the wound was still visible.

Animus lost track of time as he listened to the Archeon tell of the battle in Agapia that spread to Wispria and landed them in their current prison. He was highly intrigued about the transformation that Krue and the other Archeskotos had undergone, and he wanted to know what caused such a vast change.

"It is difficult to determine if there is one cause for the change in their outward appearance, or if it is a combination of factors," said the Archeon named Eirian. "There is a bread called chaykaf that sustains Archeon when they are away from Agapia. Chaykaf was originally created exclusively for Lure.

He was the only one of us given the privilege of travelling to Wispria. You see, Alphega gave him the most magnificent set of wings—wings powerful enough to travel back and forth from Wispria to Agapia with ease. What Lure failed to account for in his uprising was that his wings would be damaged irreparably. He has been feverishly trying to recreate them himself ever since. Nevertheless, after the Gate to Agapia was destroyed, Lure and the Archeskotos refused to partake of the bread. One of the purposes of chaykaf is the renewal of our inner light, so that could be a factor. We do not have any chaykaf ourselves, this is one reason our inner lights are dim. Another possibility is that when they fell from Agapia, the fall itself burned them and gave them a darker exterior. However, we too, were brought down by the Archeskotos and were unchanged in the fall. More likely than both of these possibilities is that they have renounced their inner light. Because of Lure's hatred of Alphega, he has become increasingly hostile toward anything having a connection to Alphega. Of course, in so doing Lure was renouncing his own purpose for being, for he was created to be the most light and most pure of any of the Archeon. Therefore, by renouncing his inner light, there was a void. The greater the light that is removed the greater the void, and every void will be filled with something. So when the fallen Archeon, now Archeskotos, renounced their inner light, darkness filled the void that was left. Understand Animus, if the light that is inside of them is now darkness, how great is that darkness. For all it takes is the smallest light to penetrate the darkness, but when there is no light, the darkness is all-consuming. But take heart, for there

is a greater light coming to the Wisprian World—a light that has existed before the beginning, the Day Star. Lure knows of the Day Star as well, and he fears it above all else. That is why, as we speak, he is constructing a great light, powered by agapate, here in Aprioria. Still, Lure is deceiving even himself to think that his false light could compare to the glory of the Day Star," explained Eirian.

Before Animus could respond or ask any further questions the heavy door to the cell was slowly cracked open, and six Sarxans entered with torches, they grabbed hold of Animus and guided him out of the cell. Animus noticed the hooded figure that was outside of the door now stood in the entrance, still clutching the small statue.

"Be brave, Animus, we will all lift up your name before Alphega," said Bliss.

"I have never seen a Reflection that proved he was worthy of eternity, but you, Animus, have almost changed that," said Xander.

"There are things about me that you probably don't know, Xander, but Alphega does, and I know I am not worthy of Agapia. But to have walked with Alphega in this life, that in itself is a most gracious reward. Thank you, Bliss, if I go to my death, I will surely be happy to know that Alphega has spoken of me," said Animus.

"Krue told us bring you to him to answer questions, but now that you mention Alphega, he surely punish you according to One Law," muttered one of the Sarxans.

The door to the underground prison was shut once more, and Animus left his new friends behind. He noticed that the hooded figure again sat on the ground outside the prison beside the door. Animus tried to think of a way to free himself, but with no weapons and being heavily outnumbered he knew it was nearly impossible. He wondered if Doronorth would hear him if he blew the whistle, but decided he was too far south for even the most adept ears to hear him in Almachora.

The Sarxans led him up the long staircase from the prison, although when he reached the street level of Aprioria, they took him a different direction than the direction in which he came to the prison. He walked through many more, dark, narrow streets. Then the surroundings became a little nobler looking. The streets were still windy, but on either side were eating establishments and Apriorians engaged in the buying and selling of expensive items.

Before long, Animus passed a large open square that seemed to be the town center of Aprioria. There he saw the large blocks of marbled diamond being hoisted onto the top of a statue made of pure cat's eye stone. The statue was made in the shape of one of the Archeon, with its arms held above its head supporting a large orb that was fashioned from the pieces of marbled diamond. The statue had wings. Animus remembered what Eirian had said, and realized, because Lure was the only winged Archeon, the statue was of him. There were craftsmen still carving details into the statue, their entire bodies all painted with a black substance. Animus was looking intently at the work of their hands when the Sarxan guards led him away down a street across the square. This street was much less populated than the others, and what inhabitants he did see seemed to be Sarxan and Apriorian warriors.

The street turned back toward the square, and Animus was led to a stone building off the square that looked to be a prison, much smaller than the prison he had just left. Animus was tossed carelessly inside the cold single cell building. There were two barred windows, one that looked on the square, and one that looked out onto the Gulf of Tanaudor. The cell smelled of blood and filth and torture. The stone floor was littered not only with years of mud and dirt, but also with the remnants of ancient prisoner food, and decaying other substances that Animus dare not imagine the source of. He had never smelled anything so putrid.

As Animus tried to devise a way to escape, days passed, and he contemplated the voices he had heard in his mind. Eventually, coming from outside his cell, he heard different voices discussing that the statue was complete. A great number of Apriorians gathered in the square. Looking out of his prison window, he saw the robed figure that had been outside the dungeon that contained the Archeon, still clinging to the small black statue.

"Aczib, Aczib, Aczib!" chanted the Apriorians.

"Fellow Apriorians," spoke Aczib, raising the small statue over his head. "Lure has not only given you victory over the empiric creatures from above," at this the Archeon were led in chains into the square by Krue and several other Archeskotos. "Lure, your lord, will also now reveal to you, that he is the source of all light."

At that, Lure appeared in the square wearing a brilliant, white robe, and grasping a large piece of agapate. This particular piece of agapate was the piece of the gate that Lure first touched when he destroyed the gate to Agapia. Hence, this piece of agapate contained Lure's property of light. Lure walked up the tall staircase that had been constructed to aid in the completion of the large idolatrous statue. From the top of the effigy Lure was more than several stories above the Apriorians below. Lure then took the piece of agapate and inserted it into a slot in the top of the statue that had been carved out for this very purpose.

Immediately, dynamic light shot forth from the deceptive beacon in every direction, dispelling the darkness that had been impenetrable for many weeks. The Apriorians reacted in many different ways, some feared, some were awed and some were overjoyed at the display, but all of them hailed Lure as their god. They greeted the light with dancing, shouting, bowing and laughter, as Lure made his way back down to the foot of the statue. Animus heard several Apriorians near his cell voice their unique reactions to what they witnessed. "Lure has given us the light!" "Lure has saved us!" "Lure is all powerful!" "Lure the light-bearer!"

"It brings me great pleasure to give you this gift, inhabitants of Aprioria. I hope now you will all see and know that light does not come from some fantastical place in the sky, rather it comes from me," said Lure as he motioned for the captured Archeon to be led out in chains. "And now that we have captured the creatures that forced me to shroud this world in darkness for a time, you will now forever have this light as a reminder that I will always take care of your needs. As I continue to rid these lands of those who would rise up against you, I will always bring the riches and treasures of our conquests back to you, my loyal Apriorians," Lure announced.

At this, Lure produced a large bag that he hurled into the crowd. Before the bag landed, Animus could see that several large precious stones were falling from it. Lure continued, "These stones were taken from the palace in Lithosis. Consider it but a token for all the many ages of robbery their king has inflicted on you with the fee for passage to the Sheol Caverns. Not even the rock or the walls of Lithosis can keep me out of even their most fortified palace. The time is coming when you will rise up against Lithosis one final time, and with my help you will overthrow its king. All I ask in return is that you remain loyal to me. Help me in my fight to rid the lands of these creatures from above, these creatures that serve that false name that will not be spoken. Give me your allegiance in cleansing the lands of all those that oppose us, and you will receive bounteous rewards. In a few moments, you will witness the execution of one such Reflection that did utter the unspeakable name, one from the northern realm--clearly a crude, barbarous thing, unwilling to abide by the one simple law of Aprioria. Is it so hard to refrain from uttering one foolish word?"

"ALPHEGA!" roared the Archeon named Ari.

All the other Archeon then joined in shouting the name. Krue clubbed Ari in the back of the head for his outburst. There were not enough Archeskotos to silence all of the Archeon, though the chains still kept them immobilized. Lure did notice, however, that the Archeon were beginning to regain some of their glow. Though the statue was crafted by Lure, the light it gave off was produced by agapate that originated in Agapia. Rapidly, the light was strengthening the Archeon.

Krue approached Lure and said quietly, "It is as I feared. The light is giving strength to our brothers. They can no longer stay here. We must act quickly to send them to the Black Bogs, where they will be kept in utter darkness. Shall I prepare the caged wagons?" Lure nodded in affirmation, then asked the Sarxans that had been put in charge of Animus to bring him forth from the prison.

Whilst all Aprioria was worshipping Lure and his counterfeit light, Zimrawth saw the opportunity he had been waiting for. Days before, when Animus arrived in Aprioria via the river, the Civet had scurried back to the Feloida Forest to inform Zimrawth. Zimrawth in turn came back with three of the Civet, crossing the River Brio before the point that the River entered the borders of Aprioria. They then circled south of the city, for Zimrawth was familiar with the layout, and knowing that the Gulf of Tanaudor backed up to the prison adjacent to the square, his plan was to free Animus by overpowering his guards and escaping into the Gulf. Fortunately, Animus had been moved from the first dungeon he was thrown in, to his current location by the square with the waters of the Gulf of Tanaudor splashing on the outer walls, for Zimrawth's entire plan relied on the fact that Animus would be located in this very cell on the water. Furthermore, it was opportune that this distraction of the statue had occurred at the precise time that it did, for now Zimrawth reasoned he could free Animus without any confrontation.

Noticing the Apriorians and Archeskotos were focused on the light, Zimrawth slipped out of the waters of the Gulf of Tanaudor and into the closest dark alley that led to the square. Nearby he saw one of the vats of black substance, called tar-niish, that all the Apriorians were applying to their skin as mandated by Lure. Although Zimrawth's coloring more closely resembled an Archeon than an Archeskotos, he decided that by smearing the black substance over his form, he would easily pass for one of the Archeskotos. Once he was fully disguised, he waited for the Sarxan guards to return to Animus' cell.

Meanwhile, Animus again heard the voices of the Civet in his head, "Did you doubt that we would come for you, friend? Will you fear Zimrawth when he rescues you? Will you mistake him for one of your captors? Can you trust him enough to follow him?"

Animus answered in his mind, "Yes, I will follow this Zimrawth if he frees me."

Having been given the order by Lure to bring forth Animus, the Sarxans now arrived at his cell and opened the door. Four of them went inside and roughly brought Animus to the front door of the prison, at which point they were greeted by Zimrawth.

"I'll take it from here you Sarxan filth. Leave him," said Zimrawth intimidating the Sarxans.

"But master Lure told us bring him," said the Sarxan in charge.

"Dare you question me, you pathetic servant? Lure asked me to follow after you to make sure you didn't fail him. I will take him to Lure. But where is the other prisoner Lure requested? Bring him forth from the cell," growled Zimrawth.

"He is the only one, there was no one else in there," said the Sarxan.

"Again you challenge me? The four of you look again to be certain, I would hate to inform Lure that you misplaced one of his captives," said Zimrawth.

Quickly the Sarxans entered the prison again, and simultaneously Zimrawth shut the door and locked them in. He then turned to Animus saying, "My name is Zimrawth. I am not going to harm you. Come with me and I will lead you out of Aprioria."

"The voices told me of you. I don't think I have any other choice at the moment but to trust you. Lead the way," replied Animus.

"Light shot forth from the deceptive beacon."

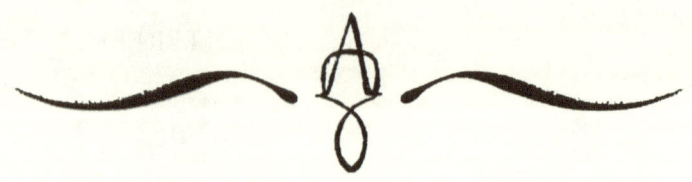

SCROLL 59

PALES VINE

fter a long hike through the tangled woods to the east of the Field of Lum, in which Duolos carried Lum on her shoulders while Sage and Reverie rode Telle, the travelers still had not reached the banks of the river. They decided to rest awhile and have some food and drink among the fern-covered ground. Lum was almost entirely healed and back to normal. Duolos gave her lamb some dried grass from his favorite field that she had packed for him.

Sage wandered a little distance away from the group, consumed with thought and longing for home. He wasn't sure exactly how long it had been since the tragic day of Odem's death, but he knew it had been too long since he had been among Sprinters. He missed his people, not only family and friends, but also his culture and way of life. He felt a connection with his newfound companions, but he had no history with them; they didn't fully understand him. He missed gazing out over the Moaning Mountains. His mouth watered when he thought of the taste of pearl port; sadly, he wasn't sure if he would ever experience the taste again.

In truth, there was another feeling welling up deep inside Sage, a feeling he had felt once before. He had been ignoring it, for the feeling both excited and burdened him. In fact, the more he thought of it, the more he forgot about his other cares. Duolos was all he could think about. He was quickly developing feelings for her. But for the time being, at least, he would fight them. He wanted to avoid being distracted and avoid the possibility of rejection. Ergo the deep feeling inside of him was pushed further down where it would nonetheless grow and mature and one day overtake him. While Sage was still lost in a wrestling match with his emotions, Gad made his way apart from the group to join him.

"You seem more melancholy than usual, Sage. Is there anything I can do to help?"

In a poor effort at deflection, Sage said, "My ankle is still bothering me. I haven't given it a proper amount of time to rest and heal."

"That may well be, and we should certainly take greater care of it and you. But I am not referring to a physical ailment. I've noticed a heaviness with you of late," said Gad with compassion.

Appreciative of the concern, Sage disclosed only part of what troubled him, "I was just thinking of home. I miss my family. I would feel better if I at least knew they were safe. The uncertainty saps the peace and focus from me. There are

moments when I want to forget this entire quest and make my way back to Eremos as quickly as possible. But the greater part of me wants to journey on and hopefully make a difference for the cause of good."

"You already are making a difference; don't lose heart. You will see the Moaning Mountains and your family again if I can help it. Now come on, rest and be at ease with the others," said Gad.

Gad placed his arm around Sage, and after a few moments the two rejoined the group. When they returned, Reverie was comparing her agapate to the piece Duolos possessed. Sage noticed and was reminded of an idea he had, while Gad also took note of Reverie's overt curiosity with every piece of agapate they encountered. Seizing an opportunity to impress Duolos, Sage took Duolos' agapate from Reverie and asked Duolos for her crooked staff.

"As I told Reverie awhile back, I find it best to fasten the stones to something, so as not to lose them," Sage said as he lodged the stone into a crevasse in the handle of the staff. The staff was made of a knotted, tangled wood. "You see, this space was made for your stone." Sage then wound a leather band around the staff where the stone was, to keep it in place.

Duolos smiled warmly in appreciation, "Thank you."

Nestled among a bed of soft ferns, Telle rested with his hoofs spread out in front of him. The ground was becoming damper and thin little streams of water were becoming more frequent as the travelers made their way to the banks of the Trankilo River. The river was wide and slow moving, yet often it would overflow its banks and run deep inland creating a swampy land close to the water, and the river had many smaller tributaries. Close by was one of these tributaries, a larger stream with many mangrove trees that stretched into the water. It appeared this was a more permanent stream and signaled that they were very close to the river. The long arched and tangled roots of the mangroves were exposed at the tops but disappeared into the water of the stream.

Duolos saw that in the water around the roots, large lung-fish were coming up for air. This was a common and welcome sight to Duolos. Taking her newly enhanced staff in hand she executed a fishing technique she had taught herself. Her staff already blended in with the roots of the mangroves and this had served her well enough in the past. But now, with the added camouflage of the stone, she was certain it would be even easier to catch her prey. She slipped her staff into the water among the roots and waited for the next lungfish to take a breath. It was only a few moments before one reared its head to the water's surface. Duolos corralled the fish in the middle of its long serpent-like body and slung it out of the water onto the bank. A few swift strokes of her staff to the fish's head and she was ready to prepare her meal.

Gad started a fire with the fire stones in his provisions. Sage was not one to cook and had learned few domestic tasks, but to do his part, he tapped his foot lightly on the ground four times. Instantly, four tiny plateaus shot up out of the ground around the fire, the perfect height for sitting on. There was even a taller mound for Gad.

"Sage, you are continually discovering new uses for your agapate. Well done! For Alphega himself put His creative

powers into the agapate; and He uses it in infinite ways. You are a good steward of your gift," said Gad.

Granted, all the while Gad was complimenting Sage, Sage continued to adjust the height of each mound, trying to achieve the perfect height down to an infinitesimal degree. Sage was all Sprinter.

Soon, Reverie, Sage and Duolos were having lungfish cooked over the open flame. Sage wanted to scowl at the foul-tasting meal, but his intense hunger and politeness bid him finish his portion. The Sprinter ate the strange-tasting meat, which only made him long even more for food he was used to. Duolos watched knowingly as her newfound friend struggled to smile as he ate.

Duolos had never seen a Sprinter before, but in Sage she saw a kindred heart. Though she hadn't known him long, she knew he was kind and regretted the way she had treated him in their first meeting. She was also confused by the way Sage communicated with Reverie. Reverie appeared to be more enamored with Sage than Sage was with Reverie, yet, frequently she caught them looking into each other's eyes. Sage would allow himself to flirt with her, though it was clear he wasn't in love with her—in fact, Duolos noticed an obvious indifference coming from Sage with regard to Reverie. Of course, Sage seemed indifferent towards many things, though she knew not why. On her own for some time, Duolos had learned contentment. However, now that such a charismatic friend was around, she was reminded of her utter loneliness and longed for Sage to at least gaze into her eyes the way he often looked at Reverie.

"I'm sorry Sage. I know lungfish is an acquired taste. I should have warned you. I hated it at first. Hopefully, that will be the first and last time you ever have to eat it," said Duolos, sheepishly.

Looking up at Duolos, and into the green eyes that were complimented by the background of ferns behind her, Sage replied, "It's not so bad. Liking the cook makes me forget about the taste."

At hearing this remark, the rest of the company was taken aback, yet not one of them spoke about it; though Duolos' heart was warmed by the compliment.

"After dinner you all should rest, I will keep watch. Hopefully we will see your friend tomorrow, Duolos," Gad said, changing the subject.

Telle, who had been munching on shrubbery, was already beginning to shut his eyes while he lay on his bed of soft ferns. The fire was becoming a small cluster of flaming embers. On one of the furs Gad took from the thanatoph, Sage cuddled up next to the warmth; followed by Reverie a few moments afterward, who draped her arm across Sage. When Duolos saw Reverie with Sage, she bid them all goodnight and chose to walk down to the stream, where she sat for some time with Lum.

She had lost track of how long she had been in thought, when from the bushes came a voice, "Duolos, is that you? Who is that yore with? You a'ight?"

Duolos was delighted to hear the familiar voice of her wise, old, friend Pales Vine. "Pales! How did you find me out here?"

"I could smell that lungfish cookin' all the way 'cross the river. I've only evah come across one individual that would go

and make a meal out of a lungfish, so I figah'd it had to be you; and I figah'd right. Whatcha doin' out here?" said the bald Reflection man.

"We were on our way to see you. And I'm with some new companions that I will introduce you to. One of them says he is an Archeon; supposedly from Agapia," replied Duolos.

"I believe it. I've seen far more sights than I wished to see, here lately. Storms a brewin' in the north, strange creatures showin' up at my doorstep, all the plants are dying—'cept my 'maters 'n figs...and lemons, olives, grapes, pumpkins—come to think of it, all of *my* plants are alive 'n well, and not just alive, they're a thrivin'. I'm telling you, you ain't never seen fruit the size I got," said Pales lighting his pipe as he sat on the bank with his two knotted bare feet dangling in the water. The dark-skinned, Fidelisine male was frequently side-tracked by his garden, whether tending or telling about it, it brought him great joy.

When their paths first crossed, two harvests prior, Duolos thought Pales' love of the earth and growing things came from a previous deprivation of it, for Pales had been a pirate. As a young boy he became a deckhand on a pirate ship from The Hidden Isles and for many decades lived on the sea, eventually commanding his own ship. Yet, Pales' nurturing and caring for his garden came not from a lack of land, but from a wisdom learned from having all that he ever wanted. For years he took whatever he needed by force and had no appreciation for it; only guilt and emptiness. Though Duolos didn't know all the details, what she did know was one day Pales left his ship and set out to become an honest man, living a secluded existence, toiling with his hands and helping things to grow. After years of sowing seeds of death and reaping desolation, Pales had spent the last few years sowing seeds of life and reaping contentment.

It had been some time since Duolos had last seen Pales' garden, but she remembered it had only one hidden entrance that was difficult to find. She was curious to see what the garden looked like now, as Pales had never seemed more enthusiastic about it, and that was saying a lot.

"Follow me. I'll introduce you to the group. I'm sure they'll be happy to know I've already found you. They are a unique group to say the least, I daresay in all of your travels you haven't met any like the ones you are about to," said Duolos, leading the way with Lum and Pales following.

When they came to the camp, a dim orange light from the dying fire flickered in shadows upon Gad's face who was keeping watch as usual. To the surprise of Duolos, Sage was also still awake; a product of his mild obsessive compulsiveness, for he had gotten the notion in his head that they weren't safe. So he wouldn't let himself sleep peacefully, jerking awake every few moments to make sure doom hadn't befallen them. The firelight cast shadows of ferns that were extra-large across Telle's stretched out body, his legs pawing at the ground as he had another vivid dream. The only one sleeping peacefully was Reverie, or so it seemed.

"I hate to rouse you so soon, but this is my friend I was searching for," whispered Duolos.

Pales' eyes widened with fear and distrust when he saw Gad, "You look like him. I've only seen one othah, a few years ago, that had your look. He was treacherously kind. Would'a smiled peacefully at me while he sent me to my death if I'd a

let him. He wanted to charter me to go on an expedition to bring back the largest piece of cat's eye stone I've ever heard tell of. I thought he was makin' up a story but apparently it did exist. He didn't realize that when he asked I had already determined to change my ways. Three days later, that's exactly what I did. I left my ship and my men without a word at the dock in Aprioria and came out here."

"No doubt you speak of Lure. For he is the only one of my kind you would have seen years ago. It is only recently that other Archeon have walked on your Earth. Rest assured, I only favor him externally, and even that I doubt, now that he has fully revealed himself. The evil inside of him no doubt has taken a toll on his outer appearance. I am Gad, one of the loyal Archeon, who may I ask are you that have beheld the Deceiver and lived?" Gad said.

"This is Pales Vine. Former explorer turned farmer," Duolos answered.

"Explorer nothin'! I was a pirate! Had my own ship. Sailed from the Hidden Isles for decades. Pales Vine wasn't my birth name, but it is who I am now. That othah fella is dead and that is the last you will hear me speak a him," Pales openly explained.

Sage whispered from his position by the fire, "A pirate!? What all did you do? Where all have you been? I'm Sage by the way, a Sprinter. Have you ever met a Sprinter, I imagine not if you've never been to the land of Eremos."

"Why yes, Sage, I have indeed met a Sprinter or two, right nice fellas, well, and lady, I should say. Got nothin' but fond recollections of 'em. Quick and jumpety, too."

Duolos interjected, "Pales is going to take us to his garden. At the very least he'll have some rations we can stock up on."

"We never agreed to go anywhere other than Aprioria," said a now awake Reverie.

"As much as I hate to admit it, I must say she is right. We don't have time to visit relaxing gardens, regardless of their worth. With every passing moment our task becomes more daunting. Lure is gaining power constantly, exponentially," said Gad.

Telle who was also awake, stuck his horn in the ground to write again:

THIS MOMENT TOO I HAVE SEEN
THIS GARDEN MORE THAN GREEN
IT IS PART OF OUR QUEST
THERE WE FIND NOT ONLY REST

"Apparently we are supposed to see this garden. Although I must say an ex-pirate turned farmer doesn't explain how you have seen Lure and are still breathing. To me that says you are either lying or you are a servant of his. How can we trust you?" said Gad.

Telle had already finished writing before Gad was through speaking:

A HORSE I WAS BUT WISDOM CHANGED ME
A PIRATE HE WAS NOW TRUTH SEE HE

Satisfied that Pales could be trusted, Gad helped ready the others to move out. Sage's rest left him more tired than he was before he lay down. He was groggy after his body realized that

it needed sleep—a sleep it didn't adequately receive. This was the consensus with the rest of the group as well. Breakfast was skipped for the purpose of leaving immediately and because they had just eaten a couple of hours prior.

Once they left the warmth of the glowing fire, the unrelenting cold once again began to take a toll on them. Pales carried a burning log from the remains of the fire as a torch and tried to keep up a brisk pace in order to stay warm. It wasn't long before they reached the bank of the main river. They looked out over the calm waters as a firm breeze blew across their faces and in the branches of the trees above them.

Pales led them across a shallow and narrow portion of the Trankilo River. Gad forded the river with ease and the others, even Telle who was carrying all of the provisions, also made it across without incident. They were, however, shaking from the frigid water when they reached the other bank. Though where they stood was not the true bank of the river. They were standing on an island that was in the middle of the Trankilo River. The island stretched for miles.

"I know what you're thinkin'," and he lit his pipe with the torch and took a long drag, "But no, this isn't the other side of the rivuh, this is an island stuck out right in the middle. The rivuh comes back together down and upstream. The part of the rivuh you jes' crossed was the narrow part, the rivuh is much deepah and widah on the othah side of the island," explained Pales nimbly making his way through the brush.

Through brambles and briars the companions trudged single file, Pales, Duolos carrying Lum, Gad, Telle, Reverie and Sage. Soon they came to a small muddy clearing and Pales halted. He produced a small shiny knife and began cutting his outer robe into strips.

Turning to each of them he said, "Don't be alarumed and please don't take offense, but I need to blindfold each of you before we go any furthuh."

Gad scoffed at the idea but went along with it in hopes Pales wouldn't blindfold Telle. His hopes didn't last long as the last large piece of robe was meant for the unicorn.

"It's so dark you don't have to worry about us remembering the way to your hidden garden," Sage reasoned.

"All the same," Pales answered handing him a blindfold.

"Unless you are on the side of evil you have nothing to fear from us," Gad made a point to say.

"Well, er, uh," Pales sighed, "I hope you know Duolos well enough to realize that no friend of hers means any ill. It's jes' my garden has never been found, and therefore adulterated, by any foul creature and I hope to keep it that way. When you see it I hope you'll undahstand."

"Don't be offended Gad, he's never even let me see the way to the garden. It's a kind of a walk of trust for him, to see if you'll trust him—it's not so much that he doesn't trust you," Duolos reassured.

Once the group was blindfolded Pales had them each hold hands, so that they would stay together, but also so they would know if any one of them let go to remove their blindfold. Then Pales led them on another hour long walk across mud and through more briars.

"These thorns and sloppy ground should be enough to keep people away from your precious garden," Reverie said petulantly.

"When you see it, you will know why he is so protective," said Duolos.

Little did the blinded ones realize Pales had purposely taken them almost in a circle in an effort to make them think the garden was far away. Actually they were only about a hundred yards from the entrance when they were blindfolded. Tall, grand oak trees with gray moss dangling from their branches dotted the island. Pales brought them to a particularly large one that from the size of it was the oldest tree on the island. Thick, abnormally tall shrubbery was on either side of the tree as far as one could see in either direction; even if there was daylight it would have been nearly impossible to see through the hedge. Pales thought it a shame that his companions couldn't see the multicolored rose vines with blossoms a meter in diameter that were intertwined throughout the hedge, another deterrent to anyone trying to trudge through them.

At the base of the old oak there was a huge pile of fallen gray moss. Pales pushed the moss aside and revealed a large wooden door in the ground.

Finally, Pales spoke, "We're gonna have to leave ya horse friend outside till I can find a way to get him through the door, in the meanwhile the rest of ya follow me."

Telle gave a snort, but stood dutifully by while the rest entered in.

Sage found that he walked down on what felt like stone steps, then through moist ground with puddles, then up more

stone steps. He didn't realize Pales was guiding them under the large tree, and therefore the floor always had water in it as it was nearly level with the river. Pales gave orders for them each to watch their head as there was one large root of the tree that proved too difficult for Pales to remove when he made the tunnel.

From the inside there was no evidence of the surrounding shrubbery, for the garden itself covered the shrubbery from the inside. The plants were so large it was difficult to spot the oak trees that were scattered throughout.

"Watch your step," Pales said too late, as Sage stepped right into an overly ripe giant fig that had fallen to the ground.

The fruit swallowed up Sage's foot all the way past his ankle and he nearly tripped.

"Oh, I guess you can take off the blindfolds now. It'll be easier to get that offaya' foot thataway," Pales said with a smile.

Sage removed his blindfold, along with the others, but instantly he forgot about the fig on his foot, for he had never beheld anything so beautiful. Even the darkness couldn't conceal the wonder. Pales helped the situation as well by lighting several torches that he had placed in a circle around the garden.

In the center of the garden was an apple tree with apples the size of Gad's head. All around the apple tree were a cluster of fig trees. On the sides of the garden, like soldiers keeping guard, were corn stalks that stretched so high into the air the tops couldn't be seen. In front of the corn, were tomato vines, in front of the tomatoes were pumpkins and squash, their vines as big around as Sages forearm and covered with long, thin thorns. The pumpkin that caught Sage's eye could have been mistaken for a small round cottage.

The garden spread out in front of them as far as they could see, every fruit and vegetable Duolos could imagine: olive, lemon, peach and pear trees, blueberry bushes, peppers, beanstalks, and eggplant. There was a cabbage patch that was more like a forest of great round trees.

"How is this possible?" inquired Reverie in disbelief.

"Even when looking down from Agapia I never saw this, this is a wonder," said Gad with awe.

Duolos was quick to tell the rest, "This is beyond anything even I expected. You don't understand, the garden has always been a cornucopia of variety, but its fruit was always of a natural size. Pales, how did you do this? This garden is supernaturally enormous. All of your plants are healthier than ever, even with no light. I behold it with my eyes, but I don't believe it."

Pales bent to the ground and grasped a handful of soil. He then walked to one of the torches that were staked into the ground so that all could see. He sifted the soil through one of his hands and into another, allowing it to fall gradually through his fingers. In front of the torchlight, the soil sparkled like a million tiny fireflies.

Astonished, Gad quickly reached down and scooped up a handful of soil as well. Examining it he remarked, "Pales, your garden is fertilized by a substance that comes not from this earth. This soil is laden with agapate!"

"Well now I don' know what the stuff is called, all I knows is on that one day while I was pluckin' some strawberries over yonder on the ground, there was the flash of light and a rain shower of these shiny little flecks a light. They were too small and too numerous to gather up, so I let them set there. Before long my plants started outgrowin' the garden. It took a lotta toil in the darkness to expand the boundaries of my garden. Prunin' here, diggin' up and plantin' there, I had to cut down some trees, not enough room, poor fellas, I hate cuttin' down trees. It was next to impossible to keep up with how fast the fruit was growin', but I managed as best I could," explained Pales.

"Do you remember me saying agapate was mysterious and the fullness of its power unknown?" Gad reminded Sage.

"What about Telle? He should see this, we can't leave him outside," Sage asked Pales, having defigged his foot.

Pales gestured back over to the tunnel in the ground that the group had walked through, under the large oak tree, "That is the only entrance to the garden, so unless you can coax your one-horned horse through there, I'm sorry, but I don't know anothah way," said Pales, genuinely apologetic.

Sage didn't have to think twice, but knew exactly what to do. "Duolos, would you mind stepping out there with Telle—"

"Uh-uh, not without your blindfold, I'll go," reminded Pales.

"Alright then, go lead Telle through the tunnel. I have a feeling it will be large enough for him when you bring him through," Sage said convincingly.

Pales was skeptical, but humored the young Sprinter.

Without lifting his foot off of the ground and while Pales was still on the way through the tunnel to get Telle, Sage's agapate enlarged the height and width of the tunnel.

From underneath the tree, a muffled voice said, "How'd he—Leviathan's breath! What on earth? Or under the earth, I should say, the tunnel got bigger!"

Gad smiled at Sage. A few moments later Pales brought Telle through the tunnel.

"The best part is, Pales, if you want the tunnel the way it was before I can do that too," bragged Sage.

"Well alright, let's see it," Pales said, brimming with anticipation of watching some great display of power.

Again keeping his foot connected with the ground Sage shrunk the tunnel to its original size.

"Wha—that's it? What didya do?" marveled Pales.

"The secret is in the stone strapped to my leg."

"Agapate," Gad interrupted, "The same substance that made your garden grow so miraculously."

Gad removed the blindfold from Telle as he continued to explain agapate to Pales. Telle slowly put one hoof in front of the other as he entered the center of the garden. There he stood glancing around marveling at what was before him. By now the others were all wandering around dwarfed by the oversized flora.

Sage called out from behind a grape vine, "Do you mind if we eat some?"

Still having an agapate lesson with Gad, Pales replied, "What else would you do with it? Of course, have as much as ya want, I don' think I'm gonna run out," as he chuckled and gave a wink toward Duolos.

With that Sage started eating, head first, into a giant grape. After that he moved to the banana tree. It took holding on with both hands to pull the peel off, but then he ate his fill of the banana log. He continued moving from fruit to fruit, until he came to several bushes, each with a different fruit on them that he didn't recognize.

"What kind of fruit is this," he yelled across the garden to Pales.

"Well I can't see from here, but you're in my rare plant section. Those are various plants from all ovah the world. I picked 'em up on my travels. Try some, they're all tasty."

Sage made his way through the odd looking plants until he saw the most wondrous sight in the entire garden. It was unmistakable. There before him was the largest, and only other, brightberry tree he had ever seen. The fruit were at least three times the size of the ones on the tree back in the Moaning Mountains. Sage wished he could show his fellow Sprinters what he had found. With a tree this size the Sprinters could export pearl port to the other lands. Then sadness struck him. Would they ever see this tree? Were the Sprinters still safe? He had to believe so. And at least this gave him some small means of comfort in his mind for destroying the only brightberry tree the Sprinters had. Gleefully he climbed the tree with great nostalgia and dangled from a limb as he buried his face in a berry.

"The soil sparkled like a million tiny fireflies."

LOSS

ehind the apple tree in the center of Pales' garden was a modest little cottage. Near the back of the garden where the okra plants towered, their towering, prickly stalks guarding the northern side, was a wooden shed used for keeping tools and a storeroom for the abundant crops. Lately the storeroom was more than full even as most of the fruits and vegetables wouldn't fit through the door.

The previously lit torches still illuminated a circle around the apple tree and cottage. In addition a fire was lit in a pit near the front door. The smoke floated up past a myriad of swollen fruit and through gargantuan leaves and limbs until it disappeared in the darkness.

Reverie removed the cloth bandage that had been around her abdomen and tossed it into the flames. Her body had

managed to put itself back together supernaturally fast, and the young, red scars covered a fourth of her abdomen, one in the front and one in the back, the entry and exit wound where the thricorn had pierced her. Duolos caught a glimpse of the scar and was shocked, but didn't want to bring embarrassment to Reverie by mentioning it. Reverie appeared to be preoccupied as she watched the edges of the cloth turn bright orange, and shrink, devoured by the fire.

It was around this fire that the group sat and discussed their next move, over bountiful meals of their own choosing, hand-selected from their garden paradise. Everyone was present except Sage who, since eating the brightberry, had been aloof, lounging in the branches of the tree native to his homeland of Eremos with his long, lanky limbs dangling over the edge.

"Though there is not a single one of us who wouldn't relish the thought of staying here in this lush haven until death or other power force us to leave, the fact remains we must continue our quest and therefore continue to Aprioria," said Gad with a reservation in his tone that suggested even he desperately wanted to stay.

"Can't we stay here for at least a fortnight?" Reverie questioned.

"It is you who determined Aprioria was where we would go. And I must say, since we started in that direction we have had ample confirmation that it was the right choice. Nevertheless, we tarried long at Duolos' home and to stay long here as well I fear would be a slothful error. We have a purpose and it is not to fill our stomachs and senses with everything good while the world around us perishes," stated Gad.

"'Tis true, a wise sayin' is that goodness is the biggest obstacle of greatness, or in your case goodness could be the greatest obstacle of your purpose," warned Pales. A breeze lifted the fu-man-chu beard and mustache out in front of Pales' face as he continued, "My eyes have frequently looked on the rivuh these days and I've seen many unsavory characters. If you are indeed determined to reach the City of Three Rivuhs, I suggest you take a different route. But again I say, stay here as long as you wish."

"My duty will not let me stay here as long as I wish. And the more I learn about you, the more I hope you will be invested in the choice we make. For I want you to join us, and therefore you will be impacted by the decision," said Gad, as Pales' curiosity was engaged.

While they were still debating, Sage had managed to climb to the top of the brightberry tree. From there he could see far out over the rest of the island and down the river in the direction of what he had been told was Aprioria. It was in that direction that he saw a bright light. Not a light like a flickering fire would give off, or even a large fire, but a bright white beam that lit the surrounding landscape around it. It was coming from inside Aprioria, for the entire city was illuminated around it. The light neither twinkled nor dimmed. It was constant. He was unsure how long it had been shining. Though none of them had seen it before, they also had not been at this particular vantage point previously. Regardless, land a great distance away from the origin of the light was also lit by it. Sage had to look quite far away to see the darkness once again maintaining its grip. To him it seemed that a two

or three day's journey down the river would bring him and his companions under the glow. Quickly, he scampered down the tree to inform the others.

"There is a light in the southwest," he said as he ran, his ankle currently feeling better, though he still wore the brace.

"I see a great city, it must be Aprioria!"

Gad was already headed toward Sage at the mention of a light. Sage pointed to the top of the brightberry tree and Gad ascended to the top.

"Sage is right, Aprioria is illuminated. We should prepare to leave," said Gad already making his way down from the tree.

A part of Sage was regretting having said anything, for now he would have to leave this tree of nostalgia.

"Pales, will you join us?" asked Gad.

"How can I leave this paradise after I've toiled so long for it?" Pales replied.

"So be it. Duolos, Reverie take what food we can carry and place it with the provisions Telle is carrying. Sage, what are you doing?" said Gad.

Sage was in the process of breaking off one of the smaller, green limbs of the brightberry tree. After he broke it he took a handful of the agapate soil and ripped off a piece of his rain-soaked pants to put the soil in. Then he wrapped the limb in the cloth surrounded by the soil and stuck it in his sack. "I destroyed the one brightberry tree in Eremos. It was a great part of life in the Moaning Mountains. The least I can do is hope this special soil will keep this branch alive until I can replant it in place of the old tree," explained Sage.

Reverie and Duolos were having difficulty loading the supplies onto Telle, for he was once again prophesying.

LURE'S PATH WAS LAID WHEN HE DESTROYED THE GATE
CONSUMED BY AMBITION THIS IS HIS FATE
TO DESTROY ALL EARTH IN REACHING HIS END
WILL OF ALL LIFE TO HIS HE'LL TRY AND BEND
ALL HIS EFFORTS HIS OWN DESTRUCTION REND'
FOR AGAPIA HE'LL NE'ER 'GAIN ASCEND
NOT EVEN BY POWER OF AGAPATE
STILL FIGHT ON WE MUST THOUGH THE HOUR IS LATE
STAND FIRM WE MUST TILL HIS POWERS ABATE

All of them stood and read the prophecy, more than once, to themselves. "What does this mean?" Sage asked.

"I don't think it changes anything; though Lure cannot, we should still try to find a way to reach Agapia. But this should at least give us all perspective. In one sense we are fighting a losing battle, but in another sense, so is Lure. Therefore, the point is not for us to win the battle. The point is to fight for the right cause," Gad replied. "Quickly now, we must make haste, with every passing moment Lure becomes more powerful."

"Well, my stubborn days are ovah. The day I see a horned hor-see writin' in rhymes is the day I start listenin' to what that hor-see is sayin'. What I mean is, I best be joinin' ya. I fought too many times for my own gain, this time I wanna fight for, as ya say, the right side," said Pales.

"Hopefully Orto will be here waitin' fer me," he continued, "But before we go, I was gonna give ya these things even before decidin' to go with ya. This-a-way."

Pales motioned for all of them to follow him over to an enormous pumpkin, still on the vine. It took all of Pales strength to roll the pumpkin to the side, but once he did, it revealed a wooden door leading underground. "Wait here," he said and moments later he returned from underground with a large chest in his hands.

"I don't go adventure'n without proper supplies. And from the looks of it, you don't have much to adventure with," Pales continued, opening the chest.

Inside were several items. There was, among other things, a wooden spyglass, a bag for carrying water, several small pieces of cane lashed together to make a sort of wind instrument, a mid-sized, hinged box with several round metal spheres, and a rusted short sword with a peculiar shaped blade. Underneath the sword was a plain blunt club made of dark wood that was chipped and nicked in many places. But there was also a bejeweled pair of thick leather gauntlets that looked as though they had never been worn. Reaching into the chest, Sage picked up a heavy metal object with a handle that led to three short tubes. It was clear it had been well used as the tubes were blackened from use, but on the outside it too was engraved and festooned with precious stones.

"What is this?" Sage asked, baffled.

"That is a powaful weapon, but most difficult to wield and control. I've only ever seen one of 'em. The one in yore hand. I took it from the dead hand of a rival captain several years ago off the coast of Averefede. We'll take it with us though, if I find anything resembling the black powder he put in it to make it work, we'll try it out," answered Pales as he descended again underground.

Pales was gone for several moments and when he returned he had completely changed his garments. He returned wearing a thick belt across his shoulder and chest, strapped in it, dangling down his back, was a most brilliantly adorned curved sword. The handle was gold and the blade a blinding silver. A black leather shirt that laced up the front led down to leather pants that were checkered with scales of metal. The black leather boots he wore were studded with nubs of metal on the bottom and dug into the soil as he walked.

"That is his pride and joy," said Duolos.

"Used to be. Used to be. Now I take joy in simplah things. But 'tis a pretty sword though, huh? Swords were a braggin' point between rival pirates in those days," said Pales.

"Well go ahead Duolos grab ya a weapon," Pales said.

"Oh, no. I don't need one. I've got my staff. And I also have my dagger," replied Duolos.

"Yore dagger? Ya brought it withya? Well that is one weapon I will concede makes my sword look down-right average," grumbled Pales.

"But I will take those gauntlets if they'll fit," said Duolos.

"Yes, that they will. In fact they were made fer a lady. Only she never got to wear 'em," Pales' voice seemed to sadden momentarily, then he continued, "but they have quite an effective grip on 'em. They are good for holding onta thangs."

The companions loaded the equipment onto Telle with the rest of the supplies and made their way out of Pales' wondrous garden.

"What, no blindfold for the leaving?" asked Gad.

"Yore my comrades now. And I don' wanna cut up any more a my clothes," smiled Pales.

Pales did not blindfold them as they had earned his trust. They crossed the Trankilo River to the western shore and, though the River bank was milder terrain, they decided to make their way south through the woods in order to avoid detection. Sage continually and obsessively checked the branch of brightberry tree in his backpack to make sure the backpack wasn't damaging it.

The companions journeyed long and rested sparingly, pressing on through more than one night's sleep in an effort to travel quickly. Sage and his Reflection companions took turns resting by riding Telle. The slope was steady but not steep, and eventually they came to a place where there was a vast rocky drop-off. They were above the tops of the trees below and could see all the way to the river on their left. Even in the darkness the river was visible because it was illuminated by a swarm of torches by the water. Gad saw a large number of warriors congregated. Thanatoph could be heard in the distant sky above the torches.

"I told ya the rivuh was swarmin' with enemies," said Pales, looking through his spyglass.

"I never doubted you, Pales. But this seems to be more than a small band; more than just a scouting or transporting army. Something significant is happening, I can hear thanatoph and I also make out several blue rhinocs. There appears to be more than one Archeskotos with both Apriorians and…are those? Yes, Sarxans, also," said Gad, "Look at those enormous barges. They are floating three wagons full of what looks like prisoners."

They continued to scout and they saw the barges come ashore and the prisoners and battle caravan cut throught the tall grasses in the direction of the Bog Path.

Gad continued, "They appear to be readying to take the path to the Black Bogs; they must be taking the prisoners to the Nwarbet. Wait. Yes I can see clearly now, those are the captured Archeon. They are taking the Archeon to the Nwarbet. We have to help them. We are indeed on the correct path! Our coming this way at this moment was more than providence. If we can release my brothers then we will have greatly aided our chances in this war. We'll need to make our way down and quickly, while they are still gathering, but quietly, and with the cover of the trees."

"How do you think Telle will be able to get down? That is almost a straight drop, much more difficult than maneuvering in the Canyons of Flame. It's not a problem for me, but that is an easy climb for a Sprinter. Should I use the agapate?" asked Sage.

Telle gave a snort and a head nod signaling he agreed with Sage.

"The agapate will draw too much attention to us. But I agree this will not be an easy decent. How do the rest of you feel about it?" asked Gad.

Pales, Reverie and Duolos acknowledged the challenge but each thought they could make the climb. Then Duolos took Lum and, using rope from the supplies, tied the lamb's legs, and then bound the lamb firmly across her neck, shoulders and under her arms.

"I'll be able to carry Lum across my shoulders to get him down, I especially feel comfortable climbing with the grip these gauntlets that Pales gave me have," Duolos said, winking at her old friend.

That gave Gad an idea. "Telle, trust me. Reverie, I need your agapate," he said.

Knowing she would lose any protest argument, she half-heartedly handed Gad the necklace. The necklace was too small to fit over Gad's head, so he wore it on his arm, as a bracelet. He then squatted and lifted the unicorn onto his large frame, mirroring Lum and Duolos. Before any of the others could comment, Gad leapt off of the cliff.

The agapate did lighten Telle for Gad, but Gad had hoped he could float down to the bottom; this didn't happen as he planned. Gad and Telle fell with typical speed from the top of the cliff. However Gad landed on his feet, and in doing so the agapate helped him once again, and the jarring Gad expected when he landed was merely a small jolt. Gad went down to his knees, but this allowed him to, somewhat gently, set Telle on all fours.

Telle shook his head in irritation and stomped his feet several times in a display of disapproval.

"I'm sorry friend, but it was the only option I could come up with," said Gad, a little amused at Telle's demonstration.

After seeing Telle and Gad make it down safely, the others followed behind.

When they reached the bottom Pales was quick to ask, "So what's the plan, big fella?"

280

"Do you really expect to succeed against so great an army?" asked Reverie in disbelief, putting her hand out to indicate she wanted the agapate back.

Gad replied, "Yes. I would be foolish to deny that we are vastly outnumbered. However, all we need do is free those Archeon and almost immediately we will surpass their force in power. We will still be outnumbered at that point, but one Archeon can stand their ground against many of these warriors. And remember, we have the power of the agapate. Sage, our success in this battle will start with you," Gad picked up a twig and began to sketch in the mud as he continued, "Make haste through the forest until you make it to the path, but don't go onto the path. You should stay on the edge of the woods until you see the path bend. When you arrive at the bend, remain there in the woods, the rest of us will stay hidden until you have carried out your task. And this is your task; when you see the front of their lines at the turn, all you need do is use your agapate to block the path and make it so the lead wagon cannot move. I, carrying Duolos' staff to avoid detection; if Duolos will allow me," Duolos nodded in affirmation as Gad continued, "will move through the guards unnoticed and find a way to get into a wagon, while their forces are moving down the path toward Sage. As soon as the path is blocked, I will release the Archeon. I think it best that Pales, Duolos, and Reverie stay back until the Archeon are released, once they are, you three focus your attacks on the Dephilim riders. If you can knock one off and take control of a rhinoc, use it to trample their own forces. Telle, you are our escape plan. If anyone is badly injured, ride in and rescue them. If anyone needs help, call on Telle," explained Gad.

"If this is the plan, then I wish to accompany Sage," said Reverie.

"Very well. It is probably wise that one of us be there to assist him since all of our plans depend on the obstruction of the road. Reverie, with your agapate of speed, be ready to act without delay. If anything goes wrong someone with your speed can set it right. Sage, be brave and swift, I know you'll come through," Gad said.

So Sage and Reverie cut through the woods at a brisk pace to head the convoy off at the front.

"I don't want Lum to get caught up in the fighting," said Duolos, apprehensive.

Gad placed his hand on the shepherdess' shoulder, "Neither do I. Telle said your lamb bears one of Alphega's tears, so his safety is paramount. If you do nothing else in this battle, you will have done your part if Lum is unharmed."

At hearing this, Duolos was pleased, for she knew in her heart that she would die before any harm came to her sweet lamb. Fortunately for Duolos, Pales felt the same way toward her, for he had grown to view her as a daughter. Whether he realized it or not, protecting Duolos was a large reason for Pales' deciding to join Gad. She walked with Lum beside Pales and Telle to the edge of the forest; where Gad told them to wait in silence. The captured Archeon caravan had not yet set out down the path.

Gad took the staff from Duolos and walked out onto the soggy path. Gad disappeared quickly in the darkness, yet while he walked with the staff he didn't completely blend in with the surroundings. He would have to be careful, for only when he was completely still did the staff conceal him. When the torches from the wagons and warriors approached he would have to be completely motionless to go undetected. He moved out into the middle of the path and, after judging a far enough distance between him and the bend where Sage would be, he brought his body low to the ground. The screeches of thanatoph could be heard high overhead, but they did not spot him. The trees that lined the narrow path formed a canopy above the path in many places. Only where the trees from either side of the path didn't meet could the thanotoph be seen. Where Gad was currently, he had plenty of cover from the trees. Yet, a little further down the path there was a clearing and Gad knew that, were he there, the thanatoph could possibly see him from above if he moved. Gad waited quite some time for his enemies to arrive.

As the convoy neared, Gad saw that two blue rhinocs were at the front. Blue rhinocs were much larger than their white and black rhinoceros descendants. Their color was not a bright blue, but a midnight blue that appeared almost black. In fact, a blue rhinoc was darker than a black rhinoceros. Their hides were also thick and difficult to pierce, and they had a short, thick mane of blue-black hair around their stout necks. With legs like tree trunks, they also had one huge horn that was as black as onyx, a sought-after luxury from Lithosis to Koref Kome´.

Behind the rhinocs were two Archeskotos. On either side of the war wagons were legions of warriors that included Sarxans and Apriorians. Seeing the distance between the two lead rhinocs, Gad thought he would be able to lie still in the middle of the path and hope they passed him on either

side. Then when the first wagon came near he would stand up against the side of it, using the wagon for cover while he looked for a way to release the Archeon.

Sage and Reverie arrived at the bend, and Sage found a tree to hide behind that was concealing, yet also allowed him to see down the path. Sage tried to not blink as he watched for the coming army. Then there was a tickle on his neck. Sage scratched his neck, but he found no bug or branch. Still his eyes were fixed on the path. Again there was a tickle. Again Sage scratched, but this time his hand found lips, Reverie's soft, full lips. She had crept up behind Sage and was blowing gently on his neck. Sage allowed his eyes to leave the path.

Looking into Reverie's eyes he whispered, "What are you doing? Reverie? We—"

"We have some time before they will be here. I've been waiting a long time to be alone with you. Follow me," said Reverie in a soft voice.

Sage was caught so off-guard by the advance that he didn't respond. He just allowed himself to gaze into her blue eyes that shone in the darkness. Though he felt a deep connection with Duolos, he had been enchanted by Reverie from the moment he laid eyes on her. Reverie lightly caressed Sage's hand then took it in her own as she quickly pulled him further away from the path and into the wilderness. Sage turned his head to look back toward the path, but Reverie's hand touched his chin and pulled his mouth to hers. Her dangling chestnut hair felt like feathers against his face and he inhaled the fragrant breath from her nose as he kissed her. The sensation warmed Sage's entire body, he had never kissed a Reflection before, and he wondered if all Reflection women were as intoxicating as Reverie. She moved his hand to her side and he slid it gently between her hips and ribs, passing over her tender scar. Reverie didn't flinch as Sage had expected, so he continued to run his hands over her smooth body, all the while their mouths never separating. Sage gave himself over fully to the seduction. In that moment he had found something he thought to be as satisfying as the chaykaf, but he was wrong. As quickly as Sage had forgotten the world around him and allowed himself to be consumed with Reverie, he was thrust back into reality by Gad's call.

While Sage and Reverie were having their tryst, Gad was compromised. The front two rhinocs had passed by him on either side as he had hoped. Then he was able to quickly grab the front of the lead wagon, it firmly hitting him in the chest. This tactic allowed him to not move and still grasp the staff. The nearby warriors dismissed the jolt of the wagon as a bump in the road. As the rolling prison continued down the path, Gad grasped the bars with his hands and the staff in his mouth and, as motionless as a giant sloth, made his way around the edge of the wagon searching for a way to let the Archeon out. Gad had successfully navigated his way around the wagon when he was dumbfounded; there was a series of chains around the bars but there was no lock. He wondered to himself what power could be holding the chains together. He was running out of time. The convoy was almost to the bend in the path, and Gad hadn't discovered a way to release his friends.

While he was frantically thinking, he caught the end of a conversation between two Apriorians, "—that's one way to

clear the fools out of the forest. Who led the attacks?" "Aven. They call him Aven."

Looking to the front he expected the imminent appearance of Sage, but nothing happened. Gad came to the conclusion that once the road was blocked perhaps Sage could use the agapate to break through the wooden floor of the wagon. Still, there was one place on the wagon he hadn't looked, the top. He climbed on top, but the urgency of his situation caused him to move too fast. Gad failed to realize that the wagon had now moved into an open area on the path where the thanatoph riders could watch the convoy. As he moved he was no longer hidden and the thanatoph rider above saw him and swooped down catching the Archeon in its jaws and slinging him to the ground at the back of the convoy.

Immediately upon seeing Gad, the Dephilim drivers of the enormous prison wagons took off at full speed down the rarely traveled Bog Path followed by most of the escort of Sarxan and Apriorian warriors. The four blue rhinocs at the back of the caravan turned to face Gad. Also, another thanatoph that circled overhead swooped down and landed between Gad and the imprisoned Archeon.

"I cannot reach you brothers," Gad cried to the captive Archeon. "Telle, take Duolos and Pales and get them to safety! Use the staff if you must. I will find my way back to you," he said as he hurled it like a spear back down the path toward the shepherdess, "Sage is late! Where is Sage?! Sage!" he continued.

Hearing Gad's cry in the distance, Sage broke away from Reverie. A torrent of guilt flooded him for many reasons. Yet looking at Reverie, he noticed not the slightest hint of guilt from her. In fact, she was smiling, even as Gad continued to call for help.

"I'll see you again soon, Sage," she said with a wink, continuing to lie on the moist earth.

After covering himself, Sage headed toward his Archeon friend, "I'm coming Gad! Hold on!" Sage's ankle wasn't fully healed, nevertheless he ran at near full speed for the first time in a long while.

The four blue rhinocs, with thick leather armored plates hanging from underneath their saddles, surrounded Gad. Great strands of drool fell from the Dephilim riders on the backs of the blue rhinocs as they prepared to charge. Gad stood broad-legged, hunkered down for the brute force that would be barreling towards him. For an instant, he looked to see if Telle was making a successful escape, then turned to face his adversaries.

The unicorn fled through the trees with Duolos, Lum, Pales, and the agapate staff, but a lanky Archeskotos named Nree led a detachment of Dephilim, Sarxan scouts and slingers, and heavy-armored Apriorians to chase them. Telle wished more than ever that he had Reverie's agapate that gave him such speed. He knew of the power in Duolos' staff, but wasn't sure if it would hide all four of them, so he continued to navigate through the bushes and trees as fast as he could. After handing the staff to her friend Pales, Duolos had one hand holding onto Telle, and the other hand had a firm grip on Lum to ensure that the lamb wasn't jostled off of Telle during the jerky ride.

"Hor-see if ya can make it to Orto, I've got a few surprises at my garden that will turn the tide in our fayva'," shouted Pales.

Telle heard the old man and headed in a direction straight for the river.

Gad decided his best chance of survival was against one rhinoc rather than four. So he picked one of them and charged directly toward it, the other three rhinocs closing in behind him. Though Gad was large, one blue rhinoc was still bigger than an Archeon. As Gad ran towards the beast his main focus was to avoid the horn. "Agapia!" he roared as he made contact with the rhinoc. Gad immediately grabbed the one huge horn of the beast and both were nearly motionless as a battle of strength ensued. The rhinoc's feet dug into the mud for leverage and wet snorts came from the nostrils that were pressed up against Gad. Both of Gad's hands slid closer to the tip of the horn and, letting out a fierce growl, he broke the horn out of the creatures head. The other three rhinocs were upon him now, their horns thrusting all around him. Gad climbed up onto the wounded rhinoc and was met by the Dephilim rider. The Dephilim jumped out of his saddle and threw Gad to the ground beside the wounded rhinoc. Several stomps from the large blue mass made contact all over Gad's body. He rolled to get out of the way, but was met by one of the other three armored giant animals. As he struggled to his feet, Gad was brought again to his knees by the Dephilim that had leapt onto his back.

Meanwhile, the three war wagons carrying the chained Archeon were continuing to move down the Bog Path toward Sage and, unknown to all, Zimrawth hidden in a treetop. As soon as Sage saw the blue rhinocs at the front of the convoy, he leapt into the air, gaining a lot of air because of the speed at which he was running. Coming down with both feet connecting the ground simultaneously, Sage sent a ripple of earth straight to the rhinocs lifting them up off of the ground and turning the front wagon on its side. The Archeon inside were tossed about and hurled on top of one another, but not seriously harmed. Unfortunately for Sage, though he stopped the progress of the caravan, this meant that a small army was now cornered, all of them focused on Sage. Sage looked up to see a hailstorm of stones from Sarxan slingers coming towards him. Immediately, Sage planted his agapate-strapped foot hard into the ground and a wall of earth rose up to protect him. It was as if he had a wave of mud that came from the ground that curved and hardened over the top of him. A chorus of erratic thumps sounded as the black stones from the slings of the Sarxans hit the soil shield. Sage was unscathed.

The same Archeskotos that had brought Animus to Aprioria, Krue, saw this display and immediately suspected it was the power of agapate. Nearly trampling bumbling Sarxans and shoving Apriorians aside, Krue brandished Azarmuth, the blazing axe he had stolen from Animus, and headed for Sage.

It was at this moment that Zimrawth, still in the treetop he had chosen to scout from, realized the ambush he was waiting to initiate was going to take place sooner rather than later, but he had no time to inform the twins and Animus. Seeing this stranger in need, Zimrawth decided he would break cover and try and free the Archeon. Zimrawth remembered the description Animus had given of his axe and the Archeskotos who had taken it, and he knew Krue was the

culprit. He reasoned that if he could take Krue by surprise and somehow get the axe, then he could use the axe to release the Archeon.

Though he was unharmed for the moment, Sage was still deeply concerned about his friends, and the guilt of allowing himself to be distracted by Reverie was gnawing at him. Fueled by his anger at himself for being so foolish, he darted from behind the earth wall and ran toward Gad. Krue was so taken aback by the sudden offensive of this small creature who was so overwhelmingly outnumbered that he allowed Sage to sprint right by him. Krue turned to pursue Sage which was just the distraction Zimrawth needed. By this time the Sarxans and Apriorians were thoroughly confused, and as Krue was about to catch Sage he was tackled from behind by Zimrawth. Azarmuth was jolted from Krue's gray hands in the fall, and Zimrawth quickly sprang up to retrieve it.

"Attack him you fools!" commanded Krue, enraged.

Immediately the Apriorians closest to Zimrawth swung their war hammers at him. But their efforts were futile, for Zimrawth had already pressed past them. Animus' words echoed in Zimrawth's head as he remembered what the warrior from the north had told him about the special axe. So when Zimrawth went to strike the thick wooden planks on the underside of the front wagon with Azarmuth, he did it with the purpose of setting the wagon ablaze. The attempt was successful and the wooden portion of the war wagon was on fire. Though the Archeon inside were still in chains, they would no longer be chained to the floor of the wagon as the wood was consumed by flame. On the inside the Archeon were careful to stay away from the blaze, but at the same time were jerking their chains from the weakened floor. In moments the Archeon in the front wagon would be free, but their feet and hands would still be chained.

Zimrawth had no sooner struck the wagon, than he himself was struck by several blows from Apriorians, and then knocked to the ground by Krue. "Traitor!" snarled Krue as he ripped Azarmuth away from him with a jealousy that came from not knowing how to bring forth fire from the axe himself. The Apriorians then proceeded to pound Zimrawth with hammers as he was on the ground. Krue raised the axe overhead to strike Zimrawth with a deadly blow, but as he did the flaming wagon floor shattered as the Archeon broke free and charged the Archeskotos.

Krue was knocked down, but maintained enough control of the axe to bury it into the leg of Zimrawth as he fell. Though in so doing, the axe remained in Zimrawth's leg, and was once again dislodged from Krue's grip. As he removed the axe from his leg, Zimrawth was disheartened to see that no light came from his wound. Badly maimed, at least Zimrawth was lost in the battle happening all around him. Continuing to fight using their shoulders and heads, the Archeon caused an adequate enough distraction that Zimrawth, unnoticed, was able to crawl off of the path and into the woods, his wounds substantial. Suddenly, the Archeon could fight no more, for they could not move. A force was holding them in place.

Ominously, an Apriorian stepped forward wearing a long robe of blackened chain mail. He too was painted dull black all over his body, but he also had symbols painted on him as well.

Beside the Apriorian walked another Archeskotos that Zimrawth recognized was Brise, an Archeskotos that was one of Lure's most trusted. Even Krue stopped fighting as this Apriorian held up a small version of the statue of Lure that gave off the light. Only this statue was black and gave off no light, but it was no less special. For it also contained a piece of agapate. Lure himself had given this piece of agapate to this mysterious figure. This particular agapate had bonded with a lodestone and had great magnetic power, which the robed Reflection was using to hold the chains around the Archeon in place.

Zimrawth watched from the safety of the trees, on the side of the path opposite his initial tree hiding spot, while all of the Sarxans and Apriorians were looking on in awe at the one he remembered to be called Aczib, the Magician. He knew he could not free the Archeon given the current circumstances, and the most he could hope for was to escape while he could. He feared the Archeon would be forever lost, for he needed the reinforcements of Animus and the others, but slowed by his injuries, he wouldn't be able to get to them in time. Except, he thought to himself, perhaps the stranger that blocked the path could, and wondered where he had gone. He went, as quickly as his battered body could take him, through the trees, in the direction of Sage.

In all of the fighting Sage was overlooked, and he ran down Bog Path until he finally reached Gad. Two of the rhinocs lay dead in the mud and their Dephilim riders were not in sight. The thanatoph were swooping down and snapping their toothy jaws at Gad who was badly wounded from the intense fight. Sage arrived just in time to watch Gad avoid an attacking thanatoph only to be stabbed simultaneously by the horns of both remaining rhinocs. Gad's inner light was streaming out of his many open wounds, but he still continued to fight. He dislodged himself from the rhinocs' horns as the next thanatoph swooped down. Gad grabbed the long head of the winged creature and, with all of the energy he had left, he impaled the thanatoph's head on the horn of one of the rhinocs. With a deep thud, the creature fell to the ground, its great wings flailing around and bucking the Dephilim from its back.

Sage grasped Odem's slingshot in his hand. Remembering his father, Sage hurled a nearby stone in the direction of the thrown Dephilim. The stone found its mark, opening a gash right above the creature's eye.

Gad stumbled away from the writhing thanatoph and shouted through the fray, "Sage, it's too late for me, get to safety! Telle and the others went back toward the garden. Go with them!"

"There is nothing you can say to make me leave you, so keep fighting!" answered Sage, picking up another stone and hurling it at the Dephilim.

Inspired by Sage's courage and determination, Gad avoided the dive of the second thanatoph and made his way over to the Dephilim that Sage had wounded. Gad grabbed the hideous creature on either side of its head and twisted. The Dephilim squirmed as its head was rotated halfway around its neck. Gad pressed the Dephilim's face into the ground while its body was still lying flat on its back, now motionless.

The rhinoc wrestled its horn out of the dead thanatoph's neck, and Sage and Gad still had two rhinocs and a thanatoph

to contend with. Sage was becoming very adept at using his earth agapate, and he had a plan. He ran away from Gad and directly toward the rhinocs.

"Sage, wait. What are you doing?" asked Gad.

Sage didn't reply but just before reaching the rhinocs he turned to the side and began to run circles around them. With every speedy step he took, earth shot up behind him, and within moments the rhinocs were surrounded on all sides by a thick earth wall.

"You are worthy of the agapate you carry, Sage! That was a most creative tactic," cheered Gad, "Now we don't have long before they smash through that trap. We should head for the forest to avoid the thanatoph."

They headed in the same direction Telle had gone and, after avoiding another dive from the thanatoph, they were safe in the trees. The two remaining rhinocs were quickly destroying the wall of rock and dirt, so Sage and Gad continued to run until the light that poured out of Gad was well hidden by the darkness and trees.

"I can't run any more, Sage," said Gad as he collapsed beside a tree. "You didn't happen to keep any of that chaykaf did you? I could sure use a piece now."

"No, I didn't. It is with Telle. Are you badly hurt?" Sage said as he went to him, concerned. How Sage wished he had kept some for himself, so that he would have it to give to Gad in this moment.

Gad's physical body was gone in many places, and in its place, there was bright light. He was unable to sit up, so he sunk against the back of the tree.

"Oh, Gad, I'm so sorry. I didn't make it in time. I was too late," said Sage, knowing in his mind that if he hadn't allowed Reverie to seduce him he would have made it in time.

"Sage, listen to me. Don't blame yourself for what happened today," Gad said as he pulled Sage closer to him.

Sage held Gad's head in one hand and placed the other on Gad's shoulder as Gad continued, "Sage, though you will not see me or hear me much longer, I will be with you. Archeon are immortal beings. The light within me will help watch over you," Gad's eyes grew brighter and he seemed to be gazing on another world as he continued, "I see Agapia. It is more beautiful than I remember. Too long have I been away. I can see, yes, it must be, the Day Star, its light terrifyingly bright. The veil is so thin between the two realms—the physical and spirit. It is as simple as looking around this tree. True, the gate was the physical entrance to Agapia, but the spirit realm, the realm of Alphega and the other spiritual beings is ever-close to you. Sage you must never give up, Sage the Determined. Find the way to Agapia. I go there now. If Telle is right, you will see me again there. Do not imprison yourself by dwelling on mistakes you have made, they are in the past. Telle has seen the future Alphega has given you—take hold of it. If you are still breathing, it is never too late." When he finished speaking, Gad reached out with his right arm toward the dark sky overhead. Tremors began surging through him and, like a bolt of lightning, his physical body was gone in a combustion of light—leaving Sage's arms empty.

The emptiness in his arms, however, was nothing compared to the emptiness he felt in his heart after being the

cause, he felt, of yet another death of someone he was close to. The rain turned to snow and was falling gently on the Sprinter. As quickly and unexpectedly as his father's death, Gad too was gone; the fact was surreal to Sage. A cooler breeze rustled the leaves of the trees in the dark sky overhead. Sage found it difficult to weep, his emotions numb from the quantity of hurt he had recently experienced. Like an itch that after so much scratching begins to sting and bleed, so Sage had grieved to the point that it was no longer a release, but a torture, like a cruel jest of fate.

However, he would press on; of that fact he was sure. If for no other reason than he wanted to live up to the name Gad had given him, Sage the Determined. He was determined. And nothing would prevent him from finding his way to Agapia. He had died to a part of himself, though, he just realized it. He was no longer concerned with appearances. Honesty and truth were more important than saving face. He would go to Telle and the others and tell them it was his fault that Gad was gone. He would tell them it was his weakness for the seductive quality of Reverie that allowed him to abandon his friends. Though selfishness was one of his negative qualities, at least, he thought, a lack of integrity would no longer be.

"Are you hurt friend?" said Zimrawth from behind him, struggling to stand.

Sage turned and thought he remembered briefly glancing back at Zimrawth in the fight, "Not me, my friend was. But now he is gone."

"I saw only one of you," replied Zimrawth.

"Gad was down the path from where I saw you. He fought them alone for so long. Then in a flash of light, he was gone," explained Sage.

"Gad, the Archeon? He was a friend of yours? And now he has become light?!" Zimrawth asked with sadness and amazement. "This is both terribly sad and joyous news."

"Did you know him?" asked Sage.

"Yes. In Agapia. I knew him quite well. And there will be a time for mourning. But for now, listen, friend. I know how saddened you must be by this. But there is a chance Gad's sacrifice will not be in vain. On the other side of the path, through the Western Wood, north of the Lost Lakes, there is a Reflection named Animus and an army standing by for the very purpose of setting the Archeon free. Unfortunately, I am in no condition to reach them in any timely manner. But I have seen the natural speed you posess. If you could find them and lead them back here, we may still win this battle. Tell Animus that Zimrawth has his axe," said Zimrawth.

"Say no more. I will go," Sage replied.

"The one he remembered to be called Aczib, the Magician."

SAGE'S RUN

fter Sage struck out through the Western Wood with speed worthy of one named Swiftsoul, Zimrawth knelt to the ground saying, "Gad, my brother from the world of light and love, forgive me. You were stronger than I, for I could not resist the evil one. I gave in to his lies. And now I am reaping the fruits of my wayward choice. I am glad that you at least will live on as light, if only I could join you. If only I too could bask in the light of Agapia. I fear I have already condemned myself to live as eternal darkness. I am to blame for these Apriorians and their abominable worship of Lure. I am at fault for not speaking the truth to them, for not telling them that there is only One worthy of worship. I did not tell them of You, Alphega. I could have told them before it was too late, but I was held captive by fear. Forgive me for all of these things Alphega, search my being. Surely you know that though I am the greatest of cowards, it was never my desire to oppose you, and in doing so become a traitor. For I know that such a course is folly. I never intended to aid in the destruction of any of my Archeon brothers or any of the helpless creatures of this world. Have mercy on me. If there is a path for me that will bring me to Agapia, if it isn't too late for me, may grace help me find it."

Zimrawth was not alone in his quest for redemption. At the same moment, Sage was darting through the woods with all speed; running in such a way as to physically punish himself for his mistake, the mistake with Reverie that took Gad from him. Snow was falling thick through the trees now and Sage's visibility was decreased not just by snowflakes, but by the tears of regret blurring his vision. Sage's belief in Me was no longer a question of faith but of forgiveness. He marveled at how I could ever forgive him when he was having such difficulty forgiving himself. His lungs burned and, though he was fit, he was feeling a nauseating feeling in his stomach. Still he pushed himself harder. Whips of self-hate and spurs of failure drove him to run faster still. His legs were passed the point of pain to a place of no feeling at all; they felt deadened. One thing he assured himself of, he would get to Animus in time to save the Archeon and Zimrawth. The possibility of another failure haunted him to the point that he could not even entertain the thought.

"This is what you were built for Sage, you are a Sprinter— now run!" he yelled out loud to himself.

He paid no attention to the branches and bushes that he bumped and banged into on his way through the woods. His legs and arms were covered in stripes of cuts and spots of bruises, though he was unaware. His ankle made a futile attempt to remind him of his injury, but his self-loathing quickly silenced the pain.

Back in Eremos, Odem had taught him to pace himself when he ran, so as not to use all of his energy at once. Sage gave no heed to his training. Finally his stomach betrayed him and he slowed just enough to keep from choking on the vomit that came forth from him. Once the momentary sick feeling subsided, Sage again ran at full speed.

"Sage Swiftsoul the Determined, the determined! Do not give up. Run!" he yelled again, "for Odem, for my family, for Gad, for Alphega, for Zimrawth and Telle, for Duolos and Pales and Lum, for the Archeon, run Sage!"

Sage lost all concept of time, but he did not lose his way. He found the others, rather, they found him. He was yelling so loudly that Animus and the twins heard him and ran to meet him unaware of who he was.

"Where is Zimrawth, stranger?" asked Animus.

Sage struggled to breathe, but managed to tell them of Zimrawth's injured leg, and he also remembered to mention the axe Zimrawth had in his possession. He explained that the caravan had been intercepted by his friends, but that the Archeon were not yet rescued.

"Can you take us to the battle?" asked Harmody impatiently.

He was beyond exhaustion, but Sage nodded in confirmation.

Harmody responded quickly, "Melony, hurry back to the Lost Lakes and rally the Civet. Tell them to follow our trail to the battle. Animus—"

"We go," Animus finished Harmody's thought.

So Sage, Harmody, and Animus ran back through the forest nearly as quickly as Sage had just run to meet them.

The four civet that were leashed to Melony guided her nimbly back through the forest to meet Jesha.

Occasionally a small branch or root would catch Melony off guard, but generally the four civet that acted as her guides were careful to look out for Melony even as they traveled quickly through the brush.

"Hurry my friends," said Melony, unaware that her guides had already made it back to Jesha.

"Where are your sister and Animus?" asked Jesha.

"The battle has already begun. They have gone to help Zimrawth. We must set out now to join them," said Melony.

"Will you listen my fellow Civet? Is this our time at hand? Have we not waited long for this moment? Will you follow me, Jesha, into battle?!" said Jesha, calling all of the Civet to her.

"Jesha, you and the other Civet use your keen senses to follow Harmody and Animus' trail. It will lead you to the Archeon," exclaimed Harmody.

Sage arrived back at the location in the forest where he had left Zimrawth, but Zimrawth was not there. Extreme fatigue caused Sage to collapse against a nearby tree trunk. He was unsure how far he had run and how much time had passed, but he was sure his body had never been put through so much adversity in any task he had ever undertaken—which for a Sprinter of the Moaning Mountains, especially a Swiftsoul, was a profound statement.

"This is where I left him," said Sage. "I cannot go any further."

Animus' instincts as a hunter had already alerted him to noise down the path that he could only assume was the enemy.

"Quickly, we will keep to the woods but move with haste to catch up to the caravan," said Animus.

Harmody followed as Sage stayed slumped against the tree. It was only moments before Harmody and Animus could see the stalled caravan. Aczib continued to hold the escaped Archeon in place with his powerful agapate that had a magnetic power over the metal chains that bound the Archeon. In addition, Krue had ordered the Sarxans to clear the path and demanded that the eight Archeon from the destroyed wagon be crammed into the remaining two wagons.

Animus and Harmody observed their adversary, waiting for the right time to attack. They hoped it would be later rather than sooner in order to give Melony and Jesha and the rest of the Civet time to arrive. They were unaware that several meters ahead of them in the forest Zimrawth was also watching and listening.

The vast numbers of Sarxans and Apriorians finished clearing the path. And the convoy was ready to move again.

Anxiously, Harmody looked back in the direction from which they came to see if Melony was anywhere to be seen. All she could see were the bushes and trees closest to her. Beyond that was darkness, with no evidence of the beady, glowing eyes of the Civet to be seen.

Animus had hoped he would be greeted by Zimrawth and his axe, and in his haste, he hadn't brought another weapon with him. So both he and Harmody were reluctant to act, and as it turned out, they didn't have to initiate contact.

For as the wagons began to roll, Zimrawth burst through the woods to make one final assault on them. He headed straight for the second wagon and struck it with Azarmuth as he had the first wagon, bursting the floor of it into flames. As he did, his wounded leg gave way and he fell into the muddy earth.

Because Zimrawth had previously rescued Animus from certain tortuous execution in Aprioria, Animus needed no other reason to rush out, unarmed, into an insurmountable foe, than to try and return the favor. Harmody hurried after Animus, lilweed spears in hand. Immediately, she hurled two spears at the waists of the first Sarxans to reach the fallen Zimrawth, their legs were quickly paralyzed. As if he were Oze, Animus barreled through several Sarxans trying to get to Zimrawth—breaking limbs and using their own weapons against them as he went.

Zimrawth's effort paid off as the second wagon crumbled like the first. The only disadvantage was that this wagon was upright, so though it couldn't move any further, the Archeon were still held captive by the bars around and above them—which they were pulling themselves up by to avoid the smoldering wagon floor.

Harmody soon emptied every remaining lilweed spear from her quiver in holding back the tide of Sarxans and Apriorians surrounding Zimrawth and Animus. But her efforts were futile against such overwhelming numbers. Harmody could no longer wait on Melony, she let her voice soar, *"In the name of Alphega!"* she sang out.

Her beautifully powerful voice pierced through the dark and was heard by many Sarxans and Apriorians alike. This gave Animus time to help Zimrawth break away from those surrounding them. All the Archeon listened in awe and thankfulness for the sound they heard.

Harmody's voice alone had paralyzed nearly a third of the enemy's forces; those who were close enough to hear the stunning sound. Sarxans and Apriorians were frozen in a bloody tableau of conflict. Yet, Aczib was not one of them. He, Brise and Krue were far enough at the front of the caravan, away from the fighting, that they were unaffected. Still, Aczib was cunning enough to realize he didn't want to meet the same fate. So he mounted a blue rhinoc and took off down the path in the direction of the Bogs yelling back at them saying, "Brise, you must alert Master Lure, make haste to Aprioria. Krue, stay and finish them off!" Aczib's plan was to head down the Bog Path. He then would double back through the forest to remain in close enough contact with the Archeon to hold their chains in place using the agapate statue, but remain at a far enough distance away to avoid the immobilizing voice that had befallen his warriors.

Brise, however, was not the only one from the caravan that went for help. The last remaining thanatoph rider that had battled Gad had already returned to Aprioria when Sage ran through the Western Wood to find Animus. Shortly after Harmody's voice had afforded Animus and Zimrawth a few moments time, that thanatoph returned with ten other thanatoph. Each not only ridden by a Dephilim, but on the underside of each thanatoph was strapped another Dephilim. When the thanatoph swooped close to the ground these Dephilim underneath would cut their straps and land on the ground providing more ground support.

Hearing their shrieks in the dark sky, Zimrawth looked upward to see their shadowy forms amidst the black expanse.

"Head for the trees," Zimrawth said to Animus.

But it was too late. Krue and the other warriors had already cut off their escape path. Animus kept fighting, but as a Reflection, he was already bleeding from many injuries. Zimrawth also had many injuries, but could weather many more blows from Apriorians and Sarxans than could Animus. Harmody had managed to avoid getting hemmed in, but several Sarxans were chasing her on the edge of the woods as she tried to lend support to Animus.

Krue reached Animus, his former captive. Picking him up by the back of the neck, he hurled him with ease several feet down the path. Zimrawth was too surrounded to aid Animus, and Krue leapt past his minions to finish off his nuisance.

Blood flowed from many open wounds on Animus' body. Krue relished the thought that he would now personally be able to dispatch Animus, the prisoner he was previously ordered to keep alive. Animus was on all fours struggling to stand, as Krue said, "Cry out to Alphega, Reflection. He will not answer you."

It was then that thunderous steps were heard cracking branches. Ferocious deliverance had come. Led across mountains and streams, and through forests, darkness and rains by the overwhelming scent of Animus' blood, Oze tore through the trees. Letting out a terrible roar, he barreled into Krue, his jaws grasping the Archeskotos by the throat. Krue had met his match in size, ferocity and mercilessness. Like divine retribution, the cave bear swiftly shredded the unsuspecting Archeskotos into many pieces.

Animus cheered, "Oze, you found me! One second later and I would have been a little disappointed."

Zimrawth saw the attack and was both glad that Oze had saved Animus, but also wary since the enormous bear had so utterly ripped apart the physical body of the Archeskotos.

"Animus, remember Krue cannot be killed! Oze has only released his dark spirit from the bonds of a physical form!" cried out Zimrawth.

Still for the moment, Krue could harm them no more. And that was fortunate, for though they were, at present, under part of the canopy of trees, the Dephilim that were strapped underneath the thanatoph had dropped through the trees and, along with the numerous remaining Sarxans and Apriorians, eleven Dephilim were now surrounding Zimrawth, Harmody, Oze and Animus.

Harmody tried to speak, but her voice was still silent from the power it had recently released.

Having faught his way over to Animus, Zimrawth handed the axe to Animus saying, "Take your axe—your valiance brings glory to Alphega."

Zimrawth then grabbed the nearest Sarxan warrior and hurled him into several others.

For the next few moments, the four ragged companions bravely held their own against the superior numbers of the enemy, but they were fading quickly.

They were so involved in dodging weapons and blows that they failed to notice that Melony, Jesha and the Civet had arrived. The army of voices completely surrounded those involved in the skirmish with their friends. Melony began the song of which

every single one of the Civet had learned a different line. Each sang one after the other until the song was complete, at which time all of the evil creatures were stilled. Even the thanatoph had swooped down, heard the song, and plummeted to the ground with great thuds. This is the song they sang:

Darkness rise up no more
Be stilled by our hopeful song
We denounce your proud war
To Alphega we belong
Lure has deceived the Earth
Yet truth will still sing from us
If all life kill, if dearth
Songs of rocks will waken dust
Path of ruin be long
Redemption's way is a turn
Turn from self, pride and wrong
To rejoice in life unearned

When the prophetic and powerful song had been sung, all of them stood motionless—the evil creatures from paralysis, the good creatures from amazement at what had transpired before them.

Finally one of the captive Archeon, the one called Matthan, shouted, "Glory to Alphega! For only His power could have given us such a victory!"

Many of the other Archeon nodded or spoke in affirmation to this statement. Animus, Harmody, and Zimrawth all collapsed to the ground out of exhaustion, too tired to realize the Archeon were still imprisoned in the wagons. Meanwhile, Oze was chewing on a paralyzed Dephilim's arm, until Animus said, "No Oze! They aren't worthy of eating. We'll get you some food. We all need to eat."

It was then that Zimrawth realized, "Where is the small, speedy creature, the one that went and found you?"

Sage had missed the entire battle. He was still in the place where they left him slumped against the tree, resting. That is, until a familiar hand touched his head. Reverie knelt down behind him to sooth his fatigued body.

"You helped win the battle Sage. Had you not run for help, the Archeon may be in the Black Bogs by now," said Reverie softly.

"Where have you been? And so what if I did help? If I had been where I was supposed to be, instead of with you, Gad would still be here!" Sage replied, brushing away her hand.

"I know, Sage. Believe me, as guilty as you feel, and rightly so, I feel even more guilty. But that will help us going forward. We just have to keep this guilt close to us to honor Gad. We must always carry this guilt with us. That is what Gad would want," said Reverie deceptively.

"Gad said not to dwell on the mistakes of my past. I don't think Gad would want me to dwell on the mistake I made with you. But I will not make it again," Sage answered.

"We'll talk about this again later. Come, let's join our friends and celebrate," said Reverie helping him to his feet.

"Did you hear me? That will not happen again," spoke Sage resolutely.

Reverie nodded and took his hand guiding him onto the path.

Aczib had been in the woods on the eastern side of the path throughout the battle maintaining the power over the metal bonds of the Archeon. But he realized that if the Archeon were still bound, they would know that he was nearby and search for him. Consequently, he released the agapate's power over them, and decided that he would surreptitiously follow them on his blue rhinoc from a distance, while he waited for Brise to return with reinforcements.

When Sage reached the others, they were on their feet as the chains that bound the Archeon around their hands and feet, had fallen off. Yet, the bars of the caged wagons were constructed specifically to keep Archeon from being able to bend them and thus free themselves. One of the three wagons was fully intact but the other was reduced to just the bars on the ground. The Archeon in the partially destroyed cage were in the process of grabbing the bottom of the bars and lifting the cage off of the ground over their heads. There were enough Archeon that they succeeded in this. At which point with a coordinated effort, they hurled the heavy piece away from all of them and ran out from underneath it. The cage knocked into several paralyzed Apriorians and a stilled thanatoph as it came to rest on the path.

Glancing around, Sage noticed that the narrow Bog Path was littered with bodies and equipment. He stood amazed at the unmoving forces of the enemy.

"What happened? How did they get like this?" Sage enquired of anyone that would answer him.

Harmody had regained her voice and answered labouredly, "We did it—my sister and I and all of the Civet that you see here. I'm Harmody."

"You did this? But how?" asked Sage.

"My friend, there is much to tell you, and I'm sure you have much to tell us, friend of Gad. But for now, we should release the last of the Archeon and leave this place. For I am certain that reinforcements for Lure's forces will return soon," said Zimrawth.

"Of course, you are right. I'm Sage by the way, in all of the fighting I forgot to introduce myself," Sage replied.

"Nice to meet you, Sage," said Animus.

"Oh, and this is Reverie, she also has been journeying with Gad and Telle," said Sage.

"Did you say Telle?" asked Zimrawth.

Realizing that Telle, Duolos, Lum and Pales were all missing, Sage didn't respond.

"Sage?" said Zimrawth. "Animus, use Azarmuth to burn the wooden bottom of the remaining wagon."

"They left when everything went wrong. I haven't seen them, they probably don't know Gad is gone," said Sage, concerned.

"I believe they went back to Pale's garden, Sage," said Reverie, touching his shoulder.

"We have to find them," said Sage.

"Do you mean Telle, the horned horse?" asked Zimrawth.

"Yes. You know him?" answered Sage.

"Yes, and we will help you find him. As soon as the Archeon are released, we will follow you to the place you believe you will find Telle," Zimrawth said.

The Archeon in the final wagon freed themselves in the same manner those of the first wagon had done. So the

twenty-four newly freed Archeon, Sage, Reverie, Animus, Oze, Harmody and Melony set out to find Telle. Jesha and the rest of the Civet assembled to return to the Feloidea Forest to keep watch over their home. But the four Civet that were Melony's guides stayed with her.

"Thank you, Jesha. Thank you," said Harmody as they parted ways.

"Will you let the Civet know the next time you need our help? Are we not forever bound in this bond of friendship with the Cantiq twins? Do you doubt that you will see us again?" answered Jesha, who could also speak again.

"No I don't doubt that, Jesha. Though I will miss you all until that time," said Melony, "To Alphega we belong!"

Animus added, "I will always be indebted to you my friends. You will always have my profound gratitude for rescuing me from the Apriorian prison and certain death."

The Civet all nodded in humble appreciation of Animus' words, before scurrying off to the Feloidea Forest.

Sage and Reverie led the others through the forest in the direction of Orto. Then, once they were far enough away from the Bog Path, they headed toward the river. Following the river would certainly be faster, and they reasoned that Lure's forces would be focused on the site of the recently concluded battle, so it would probably be safe as well.

The only problem was that, because of their exhaustion and injuries, the Sprinter and Reflection weren't able to move at a fast pace. So Sage, Reverie, and Harmody each rode on the shoulders of an Archeon. Animus rode Oze, and Zimrawth carried Melony and her four Civet as they went into the edge of the water and ran, knee deep for an Archeon, upstream. Zimrawth lagged behind with Melony, his leg still giving him significant difficulty. The water was frigid, but to the cave bear from the north and the Archeon it had no effect. Sage's feet would occasionally get splashed with water and he was glad it wasn't him who was walking in it. The light from each of the Archeon cast a glow in the dark water around them, and occasionally Sage would see that fish and other creatures were attracted to the twenty-four fast moving lights.

Sage thought about how he would give the Archeon all of the remaining chaykaf when he found Telle. But that notion was challenged in his mind when Sage realized he would then have none left for himself, and he was looking forward to having a piece.

Sage was also beginning to wonder if he could remember how to find Pale's garden. Fortunately, he didn't have to. For after some time, they reached the island in the middle of the river, and the sounds of battle guided them directly to where they were needed.

"'In the name of Alphega!' she sang out."

THE FALL OF ORTO

hile the Archeon were set free in the battle of Bog Path, Pales had managed to swiftly guide Telle back to Orto, outrunning Nree and his forces, in time to fully deploy all of the garden's hidden defenses. Unfortunately, Sage had returned the passage into the garden to its original size, so Telle could not enter through the underground tunnel with Pales, Duolos and Lum. So instead, Telle allowed his riders to dismount, taking the supplies, including the chaykaf, into Orto. Telle then circled around the edge of the garden, where he would await the enemy, hidden by the trees, and surprise them.

Once inside the garden, Pales immediately began turning a crank that pulled a rope made of vines that was fastened to the largest of the enormous pumpkins.

"The traps outside are always set, so hopefully that'll buy us 'nough time tah prepayah the othah defenses," Pales said to Duolos.

The sheer weight of the fruit nearly broke Pales' contraption, but he did manage to hoist the pumpkin off the ground, high above the inner entrance of the tunnel into Orto. In case the enemy discovered the entrance, Pales' would cut the rope and the heavy pumpkin would crush those that came up through the tunnel, simultaneously blocking the entrance.

Pales had just finished preparing the pumpkin when Nree arrived at the outer hedges with his troops. "What is this place? Search for an entrance or else find a way through these barriers!" said Nree to the Sarxans and Apriorians under his command.

The Sarxans were cutting their way through the thick, dense shrubs, when two of them were snatched up in the air in a net high above. A few moments later two others fell into a pit of stakes, and were impaled. The Apriorians much more gingerly walked around the edges of the barrier, searching for an entrance. Telle noticed as three of them were becoming precariously close to him. Deciding to use surprise to his advantage, the unicorn charged at them, trampling the first, kicking the second with his back legs and stabbing the third with his horn. He then quickly ran off into the darkness to prepare for his next attack.

"Stop this futility! Cut down some of these tress and build a ramp to mount this wall!" Nree said to the Dephilim, Sarxans and Apriorians. So they began felling trees and building a ramp.

At the same time, Duolos took Lum and placed him safely inside the underground weapons shed. She also removed from the stash two bows and several arrows.

"Pales, I found these in the weapons storage, something tells me we may need them momentarily," said Duolos.

"That's my girl! Quick thinkin'," said Pales as he removed a vast net made of vines from the entrance to a mound that was partially underground on the eastern side of Orto.

"You remembah, Rufus, don'cha?" asked Pales.

"Yes," said Duolos hesitantly.

"Well he a spent so much time eatin' bugs that had this special dirt on 'em, that I guess he just growed too, almost ovahnight," said Pales. "Rufus come on out 'ere."

The ground shook, then was still. The ground shook again, and was still once more. Then out of the mound hopped Rufus. At this point, a giant, sixteen-hundred-pound creature not unlike a frog.

Duolos gasped in fear and amazement.

"Now don' ya go worryin', he only eats things that go attackin' the plants," said Pales.

Outside the garden, as much time passed, Nree became impatient. The ramp building was taking longer than he had planned because of their limited tools. "Leave the ramp building to the Sarxans. I don't care what you have to do. Tear through the vines and shrubs and clear a path to the inside!" Nree screamed at the three Dephilim at his side.

The three beasts barreled through the rose thorns and shrubs. They gnashed, cracked, and broke the thorny branches. But they too were being sliced and stuck by the great thorns.

Pales and Duolos could hear them and saw the garden walls shaking where the Dephilim were trying to penetrate. Pales took the bow and several arrows and climbed one of the great oak trees that gave a line of sight to outside the garden. Duolos, with bow in hand, took cover behind a giant melon staring at the disturbance in the wall. Rufus didn't need to be told what to do. He sensed that something was attacking the flora and with several great bounds went to eat the intruders. Arriving at the wall, Rufus couldn't yet make out the vandals of his sanctuary, so with one great leap, the frog leapt over the wall to the other side. Rufus immediately launched his meaty, wet tongue at one on the Dephilim. Slimy, suffocating, constricting death greeted the Dephilim in the belly of the frog, the Dephilim's dark spirit released. A second Dephilim met the same fate. The third Dephilim broke through the thorny wall, but was immediately met with arrows from both Pales and Duolos. One after the other, they injected their arrows into the dark creature, until it was motionless on the ground.

Rufus' belly was already full from the unusually large meal, but now he fought, not to guard the garden, but to protect himself, for several Sarxans and Apriorians were now attacking the amphibian.

After taking down the Dephilim, Pales' attention turned to those who were attacking his frog-like friend.

Nree wasted no time in following the crude path through the garden wall that the Dephilim had made. But as he was entering, Telle sped from his cover and drove his horn into the belly of the lanky Archeskotos, sending Nree to the ground.

Telle continued his assault by raising his front legs and bringing them down repeatedly on top of Nree.

It was then that Sage and the others, with the Archeon, found their way to Orto. The Archeon made quick work of the remaining Sarxans and Apriorians. Nree managed to crawl from underneath the hooves of Telle, and he jumped onto a branch of the first tree that he came to. From there Nree saw the twenty-four Archeon, and realized that if he continued to fight, he would not survive the battle. So Nree jumped from branch to branch, staying in the trees all the way to the Trankilo River, avoiding Telle and the others. Once at the river, Nree happened upon Aczib, who had been following the Archeon on his blue rhinoc from a distance. Nree relayed all the information about the garden and its defenses, and he and Aczib set off to meet Brise and gather reinforcements.

"Well look'e here, would ya? Jest in time ta miss out on all the fightin'," hollered Pales down from the tree he was perched in.

"We had plenty of action ourselves, Pales," said Sage, walking into the garden through the breach in the wall of vines.

"Oh sure, ya'll come on in, make ya' selves at home why don' cha?" joked Pales, as he made his way down from the tree.

Duolos rushed out from the garden and embraced Sage, "We did it. We rescued the Archeon. I'm so happy to see you!"

Sage was saddened and shamed, "We did. We rescued the Archeon. All but Gad, he became light."

Duolos was stilled and sobbed upon hearing the news. Telle gently brushed her with his tail.

Zimrawth put his arm around her, "Gad is not gone forever. He is just changed. He is actually more powerful than when you saw him last."

"This is Zimrawth," said Sage. He wanted to take this moment to tell his friends that it was his fault that Gad was gone, but he couldn't yet bring himself to do it.

At that point all of the new companions exchanged introductions with Pales and Duolos, who also brought Lum out of hiding.

Pales was particularly fascinated with Melony. "My lady you are purtier than all the jewels o' the Hidden Isles. On the seas we heard tales a mermaids and such, but not a one a them tales does you justice. I hope I don' offend ya," said Pales realizing Melony was just a young girl.

"No offense taken. Nice to meet you. I'm Melony, and I wasn't always like this. I was born a Reflection just like my sister," said Melony.

"My sister lost her sight and went through quite a transformation after the light went out," said Harmody, putting her hand around her sister's shoulder and guiding her away from Pales.

"Fahgive me. I'm so sorry ta hear that," said Pales reassuringly.

At that time the Archeon named Matthan spoke, "It is most fortunate to have such friends as these in the midst of such dark times. And, Pales, we would be most thankful to be able to regroup here in such an enchanting garden. But we must also make preparations to either defend this place or else decide which direction to go from here."

"Well, why not both at the same time?" asked Pales. "Sage, can ya do that thingy with your foot an' fix that 'ere hole in my wall?"

"What about, Rufus?" asked Duolos.

"Oh, he can make it back inside the garden when'ere he wants. But that is a good idy. Rufus, get back in yer hole!" said Pales, and the still bloated, great amphibian leapt over all of them on his way back to his lair.

"I would be glad to mend the wall, Pales," answered Sage. And with one tap of his foot on the ground, a great wall of earth rose up from the ground and filled the breach in the garden's defense.

"That is really fascinating, Sage," said Zimrawth.

"Now we are at least pertected for awhile until ya make up yore mind," said Pales.

Matthan responded, "Thank you, Pales. We should also post guards around the wall, while we make our plans. Ari, Yael, Gwyn, Obed, Victor, Chidi, and Herald, spread out around the perimeter of the garden and watch for signs of the enemy. Because I assure you, Lure's forces will return sooner than we would like them to."

"Well and if'n I can show ya'll? If my defenses don' hold, I've got one more surprise. Right this'a'way," said Pales as he led them to the northeast corner of Orto, through portions of the garden that Sage and the others had not seen before.

Eventually he brought them to a towering thicket of bamboo that was vast in both its height and breadth across this side of the garden. The ground was also moister around this portion of the garden. Pales produced an axe that was stashed right at the edge of the bamboo, apparently for this particular purpose, and he began chopping down several of the chutes.

"Jes' be patient now. It'll be worth the wait, I ga'ron'tee," said Pales, breathing heavily as he continued to chop.

Further into the thicket he went and disappeared from the group for some time. Finally he re-appeared saying, "a'ight, come own now."

Sage and Duolos led the way followed by Animus and the others. The path Pales had cut was plenty wide for a Reflection, but the Archeon were breaking other stalks as they went. Once through the thicket a large overflow pool from the Trankilo River was revealed, and floating in the center of the pool was a large pirate-looking ship.

"Say hello to my girl, the Redemption," said Pales proudly. "I built every piece of her out of materials in this 'ere garden, and I mean before everythin' growed so big."

The deep pool that the ship rested in was surrounded on all sides by the bamboo, except for an opening in the bamboo across from where they now stood, where a tributary from the river fed the pool.

"I've got anotha natural barrier of thick thorny vines that cross that 'ere tributary, that I planted a whiles back. I'm'onna go chop those down now, too, 'case we need to set sail outta here," said Pales as he made his way to the other side of the pool and walked down the banks of the tributary. "'tween the vines and the bamboo, I had to make sure no snoopy Sarxan or other river wanderer ever found my baby."

Before he disappeared down the banks of the tributary, Pales continued, "Go on ahead now, follow the dock on out to her. Climb aboard and explore. I keep her stocked full o' provisions. She's got 'nough dried food and barrels of water to keep a full crew fed for a good long while. 'Course I never thought she would actually have a crew, but then you all went an' showed up, so I don' know," his voice trailing off in the distance.

Sage and Animus followed the bamboo dock out to the Redemption and climbed aboard to look around. Reverie followed after them. The Archeon that weren't keeping guard on the other side of the garden examined the ship from a distance, but were too concerned with staying alert and battle ready to allow themselves to become too distracted.

In patches around the edges of the water were very tall pliable reeds. Harmody almost didn't recognize them as lilweed because of their immense size, having grown in the soil of Pales' garden. But once she realized what the reeds were, she quickly set about the task of replenishing her spear supply with young, fresh lilweed spears. It made her happy to engage in a task that reminded her so much of home. She thought of her father and how he taught her to carve lilweed into spears. She missed her parents.

Telle, meanwhile was again prophesying in the soggy ground. Pales returned from his task in time to read the prophecy with the others. It read:

THE BATTLE WE NOW FIGHT WILL SOON BE LOST
FOES TOO MANY, FLEE, OR US THEY WILL EXHAUST
GO MUST WE INTO ALL THE WISPRIAN WORLD
ELSE REMAIN TOGETHER AND FAIL WITH TRUTH FURLED

THERE ARE THOSE WHO WOULD FOLLOW IF THEY HEAR
TO DUNGEON I GO TO FIND THE LAST TEAR
NO ONE CAN GO ON THIS JOURNEY ALONE
BUT JOURNEY NE'ER WILL BE IF WE ALL STAY HOME

When they had all finished reading Telle's latest prophecy, Matthan called all the Archeon together, and they quickly agreed that this prophecy meant they should immediately split up. They discussed between themselves how to best divide up, and where they each should go. They decided to separate themselves into six groups of four Archeon each. Each of the six groups had a higher ranking Archeon leading them. They were divided as follows: Dunamis took with him Anesis, Zaylos, and Olumide, these were the four that would be positioned on the outskirts of Aprioria, in close proximity to the bulk of Lure's forces. To Lithosis went Bliss with Yori, Gwyn, and Umut. On the long journey to the Ice Castle went Xander with Zadok, Zareen, and Herald. Simin took with him Eirian, Yael, and Obed to the mountains of Sarx. To watch over the cities of Fidelis and Emethia, Ari led Wayra, Thabo, and Chidi. And finally Matthan boarded Pales' ship with Niyr, Gennadius, and Victor.

Before the Archeon departed, Sage realized there was something he needed to do. Reaching into the packs that Telle had carried, he pulled out Gad's chaykaf. After taking a portion of it for himself, and secretly putting it in his backsack, he approached Matthan and said, "Matthan, this is the last of Gad's chaykaf. I know he would want you and the other Archeon to have it."

"Thank you, Sage," said Matthan, as his inner light, along with the other Archeon's shone brighter at the thought of chaykaf.

The Archeon split the chaykaf evenly between them, some choosing to consume it immediately, others choosing to save it for a more dire situation, but all of them were overjoyed to have it, exchanging warm smiles with Sage for his gesture.

Zimrawth, however, though he was largely responsible for their rescue, was not offered any of the nourishment from Agapia. None of the others spoke up in Zimrawth's defense, but all present noticed the rift between the Archeon and their outcast.

Animus was troubled by this and said, "Xander, before you go, could you heal Zimrawth's leg, as you healed my arm?"

"Are you asking me to do this for him?" asked Xander.

Puzzled, Animus replied, "If possible, yes."

Xander hesitantly moved to Zimrawth and touched the wound he had sustained from Azarmuth.

"Thank you, brother," said Zimrawth with relief.

"Thank Animus," stated Xander.

Pales then guided the Archeon that were venturing out across the Wisprian World past the ship to the back exit of the garden. There the Archeon brothers embraced one another and spoke blessings and prayers over one another. It was a somber moment, but also a moment that was energized with the hope that somehow perhaps their efforts would bring about the defeat of Lure. Within moments the Archeon changed shape into various creatures. Many of them took the shape of Sarxans, some Reflections and even a couple of them, in honor of Sage, changed into Sprinters. They did this in order to travel unnoticed across Wispria.

So the Archeon scattered, leaving behind only the four that were to board the Redemption. Whatever chance they had of winning the upcoming battle was now surely gone thought Pales, and he suggested everyone place their supplies on the ship and be prepared to set sail at the first sign of the battle turning against them.

Knowing that he would most likely be leaving Orto behind saddened Pales greatly. He made his way through the garden to Rufus' hole, and called Rufus out. Large and intimidating as Rufus was, Pales knew that battle was no place for a peaceful giant amphibious creature. Pales also knew that Rufus' belly would take days to digest the food that was already there, so to have Rufus take part in the battle to come would be cruel on the part of Pales. Somberly, Pales grabbed a shovel from the supplies and crudely filled in Rufus' hole. He then led Rufus to the northeast section of the garden, following the tributary that was the escape route of the ship that led to the Trankilo River. Looking up into the overgrown frog-like eyes, Pales said, "Go on, get outta here. Ya free now. 'Course ya been free ever since ya growed so big, ya jes didn't know it. Ya coulda left here any time ya wanted. And now ya have to, Rufus. For your sake. We did have some adventures you and me though, didn't we? So long, Rufus."

The frog sat there staring for quite some time. Once he had convinced himself that Rufus at least vaguely understood the situation, though comprehension was never one of Rufus' strengths, Pales followed the tributary back inside the garden.

BIG

He was an older man that wasn't a stranger to letting go, but he surprised himself at how attached to the frog he had grown. Pales mashed a single tear into his cheek.

When Pales returned he found that many of the smaller members of the party, namely all those that weren't Archeon, had allowed the exhaustion of the day's battles to get the best of them. After loading the supplies onto the ship, Sage, Animus, Duolos, Lum, Harmody, Melony with her Civet, and Reverie were all asleep on the ship's dock, with snow gently falling on them. Oze and Telle were also resting in the moist earth next to the water. All of the remaining Archeon and Zimrawth were now at the southwest portion of the garden, awaiting any sign of the enemy. Pales couldn't sleep and didn't want to, he walked through the garden. Back and forth, through every section, taking it all in—Pales loved his garden dearly.

Though she appeared to be asleep, Reverie had simply been biding her time with her eyes closed. She had been waiting for the perfect moment to carry out her plan. Gingerly, she stood and made her way over to Sage. She gently removed the agapate brace from his ankle. Sliding the staff of agapate out from under Duolos' arm was an even easier task. Animus' axe intimidated her, but Animus wasn't touching it, and she simply lifted it off of the ground from beside him. Had Reverie known the extent to which the companions were fatigued and weary, she wouldn't have even been as careful as she was. But Reverie was careful, and Reverie now possessed every piece of the group's agapate.

Having paid close attention when Pales exited the garden, Reverie now took that same path. Pales, Zimrawth and all of the Archeon were in the other portion of the garden, and so Reverie walked, unimpeded, out of the garden. Once outside, and wearing her own agapate of speed, she set off in the direction of Aprioria to find Lure's forces.

After joining Brise and returning to Aprioria, Aczib and Nree made sure that they would not make an assault on the garden unprepared. Aczib exchanged the smaller blue rhinocs that were in the Bog Path battle, for mace-tails. Mace-tails were large reptilian creatures that had a strong, bony tail shaped like a mace. Their backs were also protected by a spiked shell. The mace-tails were large enough that when harnesses were fastened to their back, as many as eight Sarxans could ride on one of them. With regards to battle, the mace-tails specialized in destruction of structures, for their tails could smash through nearly anything. Twelve mace-tails, each carrying eight Sarxans were part of the invasion force that Aczib assembled. Because of the dropping temperatures, like the thanatoph, mace-tails were draped and fastened with many layers of furs dangling from their bony exteriors. This particular detachment of mace-tails was also outfitted with fire pots attached to the creature's body armor. They brought fire for the sole purpose of destroying Orto.

In addition to the mace-tails, Aczib gathered six thanatoph, four additional Archeskotos, several Dephilim and legions of Sarxans and Apriorians; a hefty detachment, yet still a small percentage of the overall forces in Lure's service.

Reverie easily spotted the conspicuous mass of warriors as they were just leaving the confines of Aprioria and making their way north along the Trankilo River. She quickly caught Aczib's attention by, at the same time stomping her foot in the ground to raise up a mound of earth, and setting a small shrub on fire with Animus' axe.

"I bring these gifts of agapate to be used in the service of Lure!" said Reverie, as she moved to hand the pieces of Agapate to Aczib. "Lure knows me. I was once his loyal servant, Treace, of the Archeskotos. But alas, my physical body was destroyed by the Archeon remnant at Casusbelia. I then inhabited a thricorn, and after that, the body of this Reflection woman, called Reverie. I have learned much in my time with the worshipers of He Whose Name I will not speak. In addition to the Archeon, there is a unicorn, called Telle, who is particularly vexing in his organization of those who would oppose Lure, as he has great prophetic powers."

Aczib smiled as he took the items that contained the agapate saying, "If I had known, Reverie, I could have left most of this army back in Aprioria. The power that the agapate contains will be more than sufficient in giving us victory over the horse and his companions. I however, do not want you participating in the battle. You may yet be of some use to us in your current state. Continue your current path to Aprioria. Find me when I return from this battle, and I will take you to Lure to assess how you may best be utilized, and to bestow upon you a reward for your most loyal service."

So Reverie continued to Aprioria, and Aczib and his army made haste to Orto, to raze the garden that was northeast of their current position. The forces of evil moved with speed through the night while the inhabitants of Orto rested.

The first to wake up in the garden was Sage, immediately realizing his agapate was gone. He woke Animus and Duolos, who also realized they had been robbed. Shortly everyone was awake and noticed that Reverie was not among them. Sage held out hope that she didn't steal all the agapate, but within himself he realized the truth of what had happened. Duolos and Lum crossed the garden to find Pales to tell him of the news. Likewise, Telle went to the front of the garden to see if there was any new sign of their enemy.

Telle reached the few Archeon that remained. Those in the limbs above keeping watch saw Aczib's army in the distance through the trees. This set off a chain of events that happened nearly simultaneously: Aczib used the earth agapate to completely uproot a large portion of the front wall of Orto, with Azarmuth he then set fire to several of the garden's trees, and the mace-tails smashed through much of the rest of the garden's barrier. Lastly, the thanatoph dropped Dephilim behind the walls, effectively surrounding the Archeon, and cutting them off from Sage, Animus, and the ship.

"To the Redemption!" yelled Pales, already running toward the ship. "Cut the ropes that hold the ship! Shove off!" he yelled toward Sage and Animus.

The Archeon in the trees quickly leapt down and ran to help release the vessel. Zimrawth and the other Archeon on foot were also able to barrel through several Sarxans on their way to the ship. Telle, Duolos and Lum however were already surrounded by enemies.

Reaching the ship, the Archeon helped Animus and Sage unfurl the sails and prepare the vessel. Several Sarxan and Apriorian warriors had also reached the ship by now, and the Archeon fought at the same time they were trying to escape. As soon as Sage saw that Telle was surrounded, he instinctively ran to go help his friend. Sage was intercepted by Zimrawth, who was running to get on board the ship.

"Let them go, Sage. We have to try to escape to fight another day!" said Zimrawth, as he turned Sage back in the direction of the ship.

Meanwhile, on board the Redemption, a weary Animus and Oze fought bravely beside their new Archeon friends. The thanatoph above were their primary concern now, but the Archeon were working together to slay the flying creatures as they would swoop down to attack. While the garden was becoming overrun with the enemy, the ship was slowly purged of invaders. The ropes had been cut and the Redemption was slowly moving out into the waters of the Trankilo River. Telle, Duolos and Lum had already been overcome and captured by Aczib's men, but Sage and Pales continued to fight off Sarxans as they tried to help their friends.

"Sage! Pales! It is too late for the others, run to the ship!" yelled out Zimrawth.

Harmody stood onboard, protected by a wall of Archeon, ready to hurl a spear with rope attached to pull them on board if either of the two of them made it back close enough to the ship. Sage had become accustomed to fighting with his agapate, but now that it was stolen he was relying on the deeply ingrained fighting tactics that Odem had taught him. Sage dispatched his pursuers and used his speed to run alongside the Redemption which was now in swifter currents and gaining speed. Harmody was drawing back her spear to extend the rope to

Sage, when Melony, who was standing beside Harmody, was suddenly snatched up into the air by the claws of a thanatoph that swooped in behind the Archeon. The force with which Melony was grabbed separated her from her Civet guides who remained on the ship. Frantically, Harmody hurled the spear at the winged beast, lodging the spear in its breast. The thanatoph was jerked by the rope enough to release Melony from its claws, but the beast effortlessly snapped the rope that was the link between the spear and the ship, and circled in the air for another attack on the ship. Melony plummeted from a considerable height, but landed in the tall bamboo that towered over Orto. Though blind, she grasped with her hands and flailed with her feet enough in the pliable bamboo to minimize the injuries from her fall. Immediately Aczib sent a detatchment of Apriorians to apprehend her. Harmody was already at the edge of the ship in the process of jumping over board to run to her sister's aid, when Zimrawth tackled her to the deck of the ship.

"You cannot help Melony if you are captured as well. I know where they will take her. You will see your sister again," said Zimrawth sternly but with compassion.

Oze and the Archeon, Niyr and Gennadius, were battling the last of the thanatoph that had swooped back down onto the deck of the ship. When the winged beast dove down the cave bear leapt onto its back and the two Archeon grabbed the creature's wings to hold it onto the deck of the ship and keep it from flying away while Oze sank his teeth into the thanatoph's neck. At the same moment that Oze was engaged in slaying the thanatoph, Animus was thrown off of the back of the ship by two remaining Dephilim. Oze roared as he saw his master fall into the water below, and quickly rendered the responsible Dephilim from their limbs. The bear watched from the ship as Animus swam to shore. Looking back, Animus sternly gave his bear the signal to stay on board the ship and not come after him.

The Redemption was now fully caught up in the currents of the Trankilo River and was sailing downriver, away from Orto and toward the Gulf of Tanaudor.

Victor, one of the Archeon onboard said to his superior, "Matthan, we have secured the vessel. There are no remaining forces of Lure onboard to contend with. Do we continue to make for the Gulf of Tanaudor, or do we go back to help those left behind?"

Zimrawth, who was still clutching a sobbing, angry Harmody tightly in his massive arms said, "Remember Telle's prophecy, we cannot go back for them or we will all suffer the same fate. Aczib will not kill our friends on the field of battle, he will want to take them back as prizes for Lure, and I know exactly where they will take them."

"Zimrawth, you served Lure in Aprioria did you not, Archeskotos?" said Matthan, agitated. "I will make the decisions for this ship. And yes, we cannot go back for our friends. But neither can we expect to know exactly where they will take our friends, and neither can we expect to be able to set them free. We have our own path to travel."

Ashamed, Zimrawth did not respond.

At this Harmody screamed and fought wildly to free herself from Zimrawth, "Let me go! I have to help my sister!"

Gently, Matthan said, "Though we are not going back, your sister is not alone, and if we can find a way to help her we will."

The Civet that were guiding Melony had already rushed over to Harmody and were pressing themselves up against Harmody's tear-sprinkled legs.

Through blurry eyes, Harmody watched, still held by Zimrawth, as Orto was engulfed in flames. The four other Archeon and Oze also looked on in sorrow as the Redemption sailed into the cold, snowy, darkness.

Left behind in the garden of Orto, Sage, Pales, Duolos, Lum, Animus, Melony and Telle were all apprehended and bound by two Archeskotos, Huth and Glife. A battered and black-seeping Nree also guarded the captors with eyes that longed to witness their punishment. What weapons and supplies had not been loaded onboard the Redemption, were taken from them by their captors.

The traitorous Reverie was nowhere to be seen.

"Burn it all," said Aczib to a combined detachment of Apriorians and Sarxans. He was satisfied with the ease by which the battle was won, but disgusted that the ship was able to set sail with many of his quarry aboard, and that not one of the twenty-four Archeon were among those captured. Nree had not known of the ship, neither had Reverie mentioned it, and so Aczib was not prepared for such, which upset him greatly.

With many torches, and flaming arrows they set large portions of the garden ablaze at once. All watched. Sage and his companions were filled with sorrow at the sight of the towering corn stalks and soaring bamboo fully engulfed in flame. Sage was particularly saddened to see another brightberry tree destroyed, but at the same time he took a small amount of solace in knowing that his backsack with the branch was safely on board the Redemption. He hoped just maybe he would see it again. The Archeskotos watched the inferno with smiles on their faces. Aczib's arms were extended out from his sides and they held Duolos' agapate staff in one hand and Animus' axe in the other. Around his neck he wore Reverie's necklace and attatched to his leg was Sage's brace. His eyes were crazed as he considered the power he now possessed and he shouted, "Praise be to Lure!"

Pales looked on in utter despair. The work of his hands, his labor of love that was a symbol of his new life, that he had toiled over for a length of time he couldn't calculate, was destroyed before his eyes—with him helpless to intervene.

I knew the great pain he felt inside. I, more than any other, knew the pain of watching one's creation destroyed. The empathy I felt for Pales caused me to shed a sixth tear that came to rest on Pales' hand.

The moment the tear touched his hand, it was as if he was also given an idea. While the others watched the burning garden, Pales knelt down. With bound hands, he stashed the agapate soil in every pocket he had available. He even put soil in the inside of his boots.

The captive companions were swiftly and brutishly led from the fiery garden, back across the frigid Trankilo River, and toward Aprioria to await execution. Animus was resigned to the fact he would go back to the very place he had been set free from. Telle did not despair; in fact, he was quite at peace considering the circumstances. Duolos calmed her own fears by looking out for Lum, who was only spared from slaughter because Aczib sensed something unique and powerful about the lamb, and he wanted to discover and exploit that power. Melony would have used her powerful voice, but immediately upon her capture Aczib had her mouth bound with a cloth, knowledgeable as he was of her special powers. Sage felt a sickness coming over him that swiftly stole away his energy. Pales looked over his shoulder the entire journey in the direction of his ruined private paradise. I kept record of the soil in his pockets.

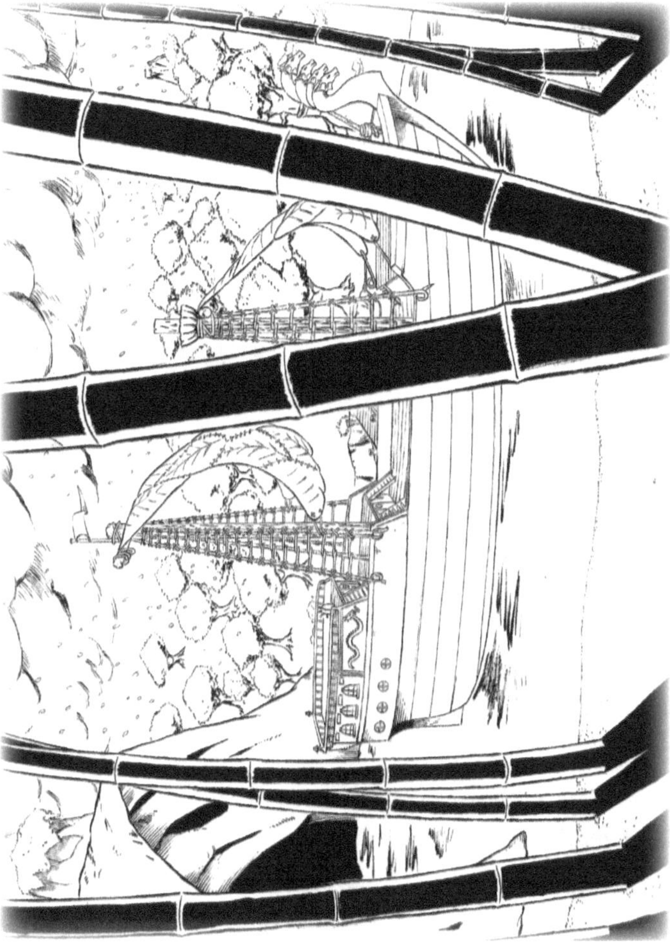

"'Say hello to my girl, the Redemption.'"

NEVER TOO LATE

Kelly and Rowand eventually made the slow, arduous journey from Treetop City to Aprioria. Their steps had been fraught with much pain and torment since all their fellow Treetop residents were connected at their lips by chains with hooks. Every time Kelly stumbled or fell he caused great hurt to his friends—and on the long trek he fell many times. Upon their arrival, they were immediately thrown into the dungeon overlooking Statue Square. They watched from the same cell that once held Animus, as one after another of their friends were executed to bloodthirsty cheers in Statue Square. The light that the statue emitted was so bright that every corner of the cell was lit. Though the light illuminated the darkness, it brought no comfort with it. For this light was not the light they were accustomed to, it was not light from Agapia. In fact, this

was the fortieth day of darkness; it had been forty days since the Gate to Agapia had been destroyed. The gruesome deaths so many of their friends endured, executed in this counterfeit light, on display for the crowd's entertainment, was all the more discomforting. Through all this, the two friends hardly spoke, out of shock and exhaustion. Furthermore the hook, now removed, had made talking quite painful for Rowand as it were.

Finally, the wounded Rowand said through the pain, "Kelly, I was going to wait and tell you and Capone together, but everything happened so fast, the opportunity never came. One of these great creatures that looked like the one that captured us, only more kind, came to me in the Forest of Fools not too long before the attack. The being said that the Treetop City would be attacked, but that right before the attack your brother would return. The being also said that you and your brother would save the Treetop City and that I should name you my successor. Apparently, this creature thought you had the means to rebuild the city after the battle. Well, if you do, time is running out," said Rowand, before laughing in disbelief.

"Well, whoever this was did say that Capone would return before the battle, you say? And that he did. And completely unexpectedly I might add," said Kelly with hope.

"Did you not hear me? He looked like one of the heartless behemoths that murdered your brother. You do know that, right? Your brother is dead. So that part of what the stranger said was clearly not true," Rowand said, suddenly realizing how unintentionally harsh he sounded towards the man whose brother had recently been slain.

At this, Kelly buried his face in his hands and said no more.

Back on board the Redemption, Harmody, Zimrawth and the Archeon had thoroughly explored all the ship's compartments, finding many helpful items for their journey. One item, in particular, was a map showing much of the Wisprian World. Presumably drawn by Pales, the map hung on the wall in the captain's chambers. There was also writing on the map that seemed to have been recently added containing points of interest, such as: "Sage's mountain", "the Nwarbet", and "the Field of Lum", among others. Zimrawth suspected that these new landmarks were probably added by Pales or Sage when the provisions were being loaded onto the ship. Zimrawth also had enough knowledge of Wispria to realize there were parts of the world that were not included on this particular map. When they looked at the map, however, they saw a large sea-serpent looking creature drawn in the Gulf of Tanaudor. This gave none of them any comfort, because, though they were currently sailing without incident down the Trankilo River, they seemed to be sailing directly into the waters of what the Archeon knew to be the Leviathan.

Though their voyage had only begun, a distinct separation had already occurred. Zimrawth spent his time with Harmody, Oze kept to himself, and Matthan, Victor, Niyr and Gennadius primarily conversed with one another. Zimrawth, was especially hurt by this development. He understood the Archeon's perspective; understood why they didn't share the chaykaf with him; understood why they viewed him as fallen, for he was. *But*, he thought to himself, *if Alphega were here, would He view me the same way? Would He say it is too late for me?* Zimrawth was distressed that there was no hope for him.

If his Archeon family seemed to be resolved to the fact that he was beyond salvageable, did that mean it was so? Moving to the back of the ship, Zimrawth sought solitude. His thoughts turned to Gad, his fellow Archeon that was now light. Staring up in the direction of Agapia, his voice floating over the dark waters of the Trankilo River, Zimrawth sang softly:

> What a great mystery is becoming light
> 'Tis a gift, not earned by virtue, favor or might
> To lose one's life in love with Him is the Way
> Seek to save one's own soul, will throw the gift away
> How sad for those who, doubting, reject the gift
> Or by selfish disobedience cause a rift
> 'tween the Creator and His beloved ones
> Surely only grace can save His daughters and sons

Kelly was suddenly startled as the door to the dungeon was opened. He was certan that his captors were coming to lead him to the same fate as the rest of his fellow Treetop City inhabitants. Rowand was the last and most recent of his friends to be executed in front of the Apriorian masses, and he could no longer bear to hear the crowd mock their deaths. He covered his ears to try to block out each one of their screams. However, to his surprise, Kelly was not being led away at this time. Instead, new prisoners were put into his cell.

Four Dephilim led Telle, Sage, Duolos, Lum, Melony, Animus and Pales into the stone dungeon. Part of Kelly was happy to have company, but at the same time, it was not the company he wanted. None of them were Capone. As much as he didn't want his brother to endure the same fate, a large part of him had not accepted his brother's death, especially given the news that Rowand had told him. Nevertheless, Kelly hoped that somehow Capone's back wasn't ever broken and that he had somehow managed to pick himself up off the road and escape. Kelly glanced at his new cellmates, before sadly turning his attention out of the window that looked upon the Gulf of Tanaudor, lit by the light from Lure's statue.

As he sat dejected, chained to the cold stone floor and walls, Sage's watery eyes were focused down. His illness was worsening; a sickness deep within that seemed more than physical. Immediately he thought of Reverie and what had transpired between them. Although he was plagued by guilt over the incident, he felt the sickness was deeper than mere guilt. *What did she do to me?* Sage thought to himself. This was a physical illness. His very bones hurt.

In the streets outside he heard the Apriorians, led by one called Dahij, who appeared to be an Apriorian military commander, chanting, "Death to Alphega and all those who oppose Lure!"

The whites of their eyes looked crazed, set off by the black substance they had put on their faces as required by Lure to honor the Archeskotos. The mob bowed face down on their knees at the foot of the marbled diamond and cat's eye stone statue of Lure, as they had done every few hours since the effigy had been completed. They were mesmerized by the manufactured light it gave off. "There is one god, Lure and Aczib is his prophet," they began chanting in unison.

That moment, Dahij saw an Apriorian in the crowd that did not have any of the black substance on his face or body.

He motioned for two Sarxans to bring this Reflection man to him, saying to the crowd, "Loyal worshipers of Lure, you all know that lord Lure will not allow anyone to wear any white garments in his presence. He is the only one pure enough to wear white."

"Lure is holy!" a voice in the crowd shouted.

Continuing, Dahij said, "You also know that no one can approach lord Lure without first covering themselves with the tar-niish, yes?"

The Sarxans arrived at the foot of the statue, throwing the struggling, pale-faced male at the feet of Dahij. "Observe," Dahij continued, "here we have one who thought himself better than all of the rest of you. Here we have one who thought himself worthy to appear before lord Lure without the tar-niish." He then addressed the offender saying, "turn and face all of those you thought yourself better than."

The male turned and was gripped with terror as he looked out over the multitude of his fellow Apriorians, staring into crazed tar-niish-covered faces. Before he had a chance to fully take in the intimidating scene, Dahij produced a sword with a wide, curved blade, not unlike Pales' sword, and swiftly separated the guilty one's head from his body.

Disgusted, Animus watched the square, all too familiar with his present surroundings, and all too familiar with the barbarism of Sarxans. The cold brutality of Dahij, however, was something he did not expect from an Apriorian male. Heavy, dark emotions invaded Animus' mind like a dense fog rolling in from the sea. Unlike his last stay in this place, he heard no voices from the Civet this time. He was certain Zimrawth was not waiting outside to rescue him and his companions. In addition, the prison was currently guarded by the three Archeskotos that apprehended them, as well as a host of Dephilim and Apriorians. The enemy was not going to allow Animus to escape as he had done before. Animus' thoughts turned to the only One Who he knew could help them, Me.

Even so, he was currently battling off a level of despair he had never dealt with before. Rarer than agapate was a day when Animus lost faith and hope and gave into despair. The weight of the death of his loved ones, and being separated from Oze, and ending up back in the same prison he had been delivered from was too great even for one of My most faithful. Profound grief for his children and wife gripped him. If the statements the Archeon had said about him were true, that he was known in Agapia for his faithfulness, then why did he have to endure so much pain and loss? The male with the broad shoulders, rock solid arms, fearless personality, and a warrior's countenance, for now, felt like the smallest and weakest one among them.

Meanwhile, Sage's thoughts were held captive by Gad's final words and he was whispering them aloud, "If you are still breathing it is never too late. If you are still breathing it is never too late. If you are still breathing it is never too late. If you are still breathing it is never too late. If you are still breathing it is never too late. If you are still breathing it is never too late. If you are still breathing it is never too late. If you are still breathing it is never too late. If you are still breathing it is never too late. If you are still breathing it is never too late. If you are still breathing it is never too late. If you are still breathing it is never too late—"

While he sat downcast and disconsolate, Sage was interrupted by a most alarming and exciting voice. Chained beside Sage, and unable to angle his horn in such a way as to write, Telle, the unicorn, spoke, "It is not too late."

"Telle?! You can talk? Why didn't you talk before?" asked Sage, astonished.

"I didn't talk before because I didn't need to. But I can't very well write chained up like this," Telle answered, in a matter of fact tone.

Sage's astonishment was soon completely overtaken by his nagging guilt. Somehow, the fact that Telle heard Sage and could speak, made Sage feel that he couldn't hide his struggle any longer.

"It is because of me that Gad is dead," said Sage, expecting to procure a drastic reaction from Telle.

Telle calmly replied, "Do not place more significance on your actions than is warranted, Sage."

"You don't understand. During the battle, I allowed Reverie to distract me. Not that I'm blaming her, because I went along with it. But when I should have been at my position waiting for Gad, I was off in the wood with Reverie engaging in—well that is best not said. The point is I failed. And Gad told me to let go of my guilt. But how, when I know what I did?" Sage explained.

"You made a bad choice. You made a mistake. That is true. But to allow the guilt of that choice to consume you would be to make another bad choice. Likewise, to assume that your actions could have such profound repercussions, while in some cases that may be true, is still to have a bloated sense of one's place in this world. Who can say whether or not Gad would have not become light, even if you had been where you were supposed to be? Gad is at peace, and he is not gone, he is just changed—for the better. If there is anything Gad would want you to take away from your mistake, it would be simply—be at peace, and allow this event to change you for the better. Furthermore, we now know that Reverie was a servant of the enemy, for surely it was she who stole the agapate. The fact that she sought to make you stumble merely confirms to me what I already knew, that you are important to our cause. But that said, again, do not view yourself with too much importance, because that is itself another evil altogether, and one much more insidious. After all, Lure's inflated self-worth is how this entire war began," explained Telle with compassion and caution.

At that moment, a great cheer arose from the crowd in the square outside their cell as Lure appeared before the illuminated statue of himself. Sage turned and looked out from the barred window that faced the square, and for the first time saw Lure.

"My children. My loves. Did I not tell you I would provide you with more than you could ever desire? Did I not tell you we would see victory after victory?" said a voice that was far more gentle and relaxing than ever Sage expected from the most evil being in the world. Though he did see a great similarity between Lure's voice and Reverie's.

"YES! Glory to Lure! The king that gives us exactly what we want! Our king!", these phrases and others like them were shouted by the Apriorians and Sarxans gathered in the square.

"Today the Treetop City, tomorrow the kingdom of Lithosis!" said Lure to another round of manic cheering.

BBG

At this, Duolos shouted, "My father, the king, will be ready for all of you! Alphega, grant him victory!"

Animus and Melony both individually turned their heads in Duolos' direction.

"You are the princess of Lithosis?" asked Melony in amazement.

"I was the princess of Lithosis. I am a shepherdess now. I may not have agreed with many of my father's policies. Yes, I wanted a life free from the deception and lies whispered in the halls of the palace. I wanted freedom from expectations and decisions that had already been made for the direction of my life. My father is a flawed man, but I still love him. I still want the best for him. And if I make it out of this situation, I will do all in my power to help him defeat these who are cheering for his death," explained Duolos.

Pales, who was sitting next to her, put his hand on her shoulder saying, "An' ya bettah believe yore fathah loves you, Duo. He must be missin' you something' awful. Whatevah I can do ta get ya back to him, I will do."

"After Lithosis, the Ice Castle, and Agapia!" shouted Lure, with great wings spread broad behind him.

"It seems conquering the lands of Almachora is also part of his plan," said Animus softly.

An Apriorian woman was so enamored with him that she brought her infant and presented it at Lure's feet, in a gesture of sacrifice. Not to be outdone, other mothers followed. Others without children cut themselves to show their crazed devotion to the alluring, charismatic leader.

Upon seeing Lure, Sage said with a new resolve, "Now that I behold my enemy, it is strange, but I am no longer intimidated. Before me is the most vile and dangerous creature my eyes have seen, yet now that I see him, I no longer fear him. For in seeing my enemy, my mind is made up. I do not side with him. And if Lure exists, so also Alphega must exist—with whom I do side. As terrible a sight as Lure is, I am convinced that Alphega must be even more terrifyingly good. Knowing this in my heart... knowing this... is why seeing Lure emboldens me. Telle, I believe. It is not too late. I am still breathing, and I believe."

Then, despite their current circumstances, a broad smile took hold of Sage's face as he said with tears of joy in his eyes, "It is never too late. I am here in this prison, held captive by the essence of evil, I have been through a lifetime of pain and suffering in the past several days, I have made deadly mistakes, and yet... I am still breathing, it isn't too late. It isn't too late to believe. Alphega, do you hear me? I believe." Sage felt a warmth in his soul from hearing himself address Me—because he knew he was heard.

Telle then continued in a deep, slightly raspy voice, "He can hear you, Sage. Now I have something to show you. Take your hands and place them on my horn."

Sage did so, and a force shot through his hands and gripped him, forcing him to close his eyes and grasp the horn tighter. White mountain tops that stretched far beyond the clouds became visible to Sage. Looking down he could see that he was standing on top of one of these peaks with the clouds below him spread out like ground. These mountains were unlike anything he had ever imagined. Sage was in awe of their vastness and perfection. Continuing to witness the vision, he saw himself leap and soar through the air from one peak to another with greater ease than breathing. Sage laughed in the vision, and laughed aloud in the cell among the others. The vision was so bright with overwhelming happiness he could not look at it any longer. Sage opened his eyes. Tears fell down his face accompanied by a toothy grin. Sage continued to smile but grit his teeth. His nostrils flared as he took in a deep breath. This was a ferocious joy he felt—a joy that could drive out darkness and sadness by force.

"You saw a glimpse of Agapia and how your life would be there," said Telle.

"I am overjoyed at the sight, but saddened as nothing in this world will ever compare to what I have just seen. I want to be there, Telle," Sage answered.

"You have seen this vision in order to show you the end destination. Do not become consumed with the destination however, stay focused on the journey. For, we are on the right path. Hope is not lost. Look around you. You are all gathered here together, the seven of you."

Sage looked at his left hand where he had grasped Telle's horn and noticed a symbol appeared in his flesh. The symbol resembled that of a foreign alphabet's letters combined with a tear. Sage then looked individually at his new friends with him in the cell. Sage's companions greeted him with smiles, as they couldn't help but overhear his talk with Telle, and each of them was glad to see Sage work through and overcome his doubt and despair. He saw Animus, Melony, Pales, Doulos, Lum, and then he noticed a Reflection male that had been in the cell with them all along. The stranger had been keeping to himself, continuing to look out the window at the peaceful waters of the Gulf of Tanaudor, until he saw Telle speak. When Sage called Telle by name, and then when Telle counted the stranger as one of the seven, Kelly was stunned with disbelief.

The stranger was about to question Telle, but Telle spoke first, "Yes Kelly, you too."

Kelly was speechless that this talking unicorn knew his name, and furthermore that the unicorn's name was Telle.

"I know Kelly. I have seen what you lost in the Forest of Fools. Take heart, it is not too late," said Telle.

"It was you then? You are the one that sent the messenger to Capone to give me these shoes. But you are a horned horse. What, or who, are you? What do you want with me?" questioned Kelly.

"These are questions that all of your other companions in this cell have also asked. Don't worry. You will be given answers. But first we must break out of this prison, and quickly. Kelly..." Telle's silvery agapate-infused eyes stared directly at Kelly's agapate-laden quill as Telle urged, "you know what to do."

Kelly thought for a moment, then slowly removed the quill and inkwell from his pocket and prepared to draw.

Telle continued, "All of you can still be victorious. For six of you have been anointed with immense power by Alphega. One of you still has great pain to endure, before the seventh tear falls, but I see clearly now. You are the seven. Each of you bears one of the Tears of Alphega."

"This was a ferocious joy he felt."

UPCOMING BOOKS IN THE WISPRIAN WORLD SERIES:

BOOK II – THE DAY STAR
BOOK III – WIND OF AGAPIA

Acknowledgements, About the Author,
Notes from the Author and more can be found at:
www.thewisprianworld.com

www.thewisprianworld.com

www.ingramcontent.com/pod-product-compliance
Lightning Source LLC
Chambersburg PA
CBHW031611100726
47898CB00006B/1744